GROUNDSKEEPING

GROUNDSKEEPING

LEE COLE

ALFRED A. KNOPF   NEW YORK   2022

THIS IS A BORZOI BOOK
PUBLISHED BY ALFRED A. KNOPF

All rights reserved. Published in the United States by Alfred A. Knopf,
a division of Penguin Random House LLC, New York, and distributed in
Canada by Penguin Random House Canada Limited, Toronto.

www.aaknopf.com

Knopf, Borzoi Books, and the colophon are registered
trademarks of Penguin Random House LLC.

Grateful acknowledgment is made to the following for
permission to reprint previously published material:
Alfred A. Knopf: Excerpt from "The Motive for Metaphor" from *The Collected
Poems of Wallace Stevens* by Wallace Stevens, copyright © 1954 by Wallace
Stevens and copyright renewed 1982 by Holly Stevens. Reprinted by permission
of Alfred A. Knopf, an imprint of the Knopf Doubleday Publishing Group,
a division of Penguin Random House LLC. All rights reserved.

Library of Congress Cataloging-in-Publication Data
Names: Cole, Lee, 1990– author.
Title: Groundskeeping / Lee Cole.
Description: First edition. | New York : Alfred A. Knopf, [2022] |
"A Borzoi book."
Identifiers: LCCN 2021022465 (print) | LCCN 2021022466 (ebook) |
ISBN 9780593320501 (hardcover) | ISBN 9780593320518 (ebook) |
ISBN 9781524712181 (open market)
Subjects: GSAFD: Love stories. | LCGFT: Romance fiction. | Novels.
Classification: LCC PS3603.O4288 G76 2022 (print) |
LCC PS3603.O4288 (ebook) | DDC 813/.6—dc23
LC record available at https://lccn.loc.gov/2021022465
LC ebook record available at https://lccn.loc.gov/2021022466

Front-of-jacket image: *Quercus obtusiloba* (Post Oak),
c. 1812 © The British Library Board/Leemage/Bridgeman Images
Jacket design by Linda Huang

Manufactured in Canada
First Edition

In Memory of Creston Shelton

PART 1

I'VE ALWAYS HAD THE SAME PREDICAMENT. When I'm home, in Kentucky, all I want is to leave. When I'm away, I'm homesick for a place that never was.

This is what I told Alma the night we met.

A grad student had thrown a party, and we'd both gone. I don't know how long we'd been talking or how the conversation started, but I'd seen her watching me. That's why I went over. She was watching me like I might try to steal something from her.

What does that mean, a place that never was? she said.

All around us, people were talking in groups of twos and threes. It was a house way out in the country, decorated in the way you'd expect of a grad student—someone with an overdeveloped sense of irony and curation, who also happened to be broke. Foreign film posters. A lamp made from antlers with a buckskin shade. Those chili pepper Christmas lights. We were standing in the pink glow of a Wurlitzer jukebox. In her right hand, she held a Solo cup and an unlit cigarette. Her long denim skirt was of the kind I associated with Pentecostals. On the other side of the Wurlitzer stood a life-sized cardboard cutout of Walt Whitman—the one where he's got his hat cocked and his fist on his hip. I kept catching sight of him in my periphery and thinking it was another person standing there, eavesdropping.

I don't know what I'm talking about, I said. I'm a little drunk.

I can tell, she said. She took a sip of her drink and slipped her bra strap back onto her shoulder. She looked around for a moment, sort of bobbing her head to the music, which was not coming from the jukebox, but from some other mysterious source. People were dancing in an attention-seeking way. She let her eyes pass over them briefly, then she turned back to me and shook her hair. It was all tangled and cut short in a kind of bob. The sort of dark hair that seemed red in a certain light—the light from the Wurlitzer, for instance.

I hail from Virginia myself, she said, putting on a phony accent.

Do you ever feel a sense of suffocation when you think about it? Like, you start to hyperventilate and sweat, and next thing you know, you're completely overcome with this fear that if you go home, you'll be trapped there and never be able to leave?

The question seemed to amuse her. No, she said.

Yeah, me neither, I said.

She laughed at this. I grew up in DC basically, she said. So, not the *real* Virginia. This is my first time in Kentucky.

Just visiting?

Something like that. It's not what I expected.

Did you expect all of us to play banjos and tie our pants with rope?

She laughed again. No, she said, I just thought it'd be—I don't know. She gnawed on her lip and looked up at the ceiling, searching for the right word.

Trashier?

That isn't the way I'd put it.

You go to the right places, you'll find that. Where I grew up is like that.

And where is that?

I grew up in Melber, I said, but it's not much more than a stop sign and a post office.

And it's . . . under-resourced?

A flicker of memory: every Halloween of my childhood, a round bale of hay was soaked in kerosene, lit on fire, and rolled downhill on Melber's main thoroughfare. People lined the street to watch as the bale jounced and tumbled, embers floating upward, bits of smoldering straw scattered in the road. I thought about this spectacle, and how no one ever explained to me why it was done, or for what purpose beyond entertainment and half-baked tradition. I remembered my dad's heavy hands on my shoulders and the heat from the flames on my cheeks, how you could see the glimmer reflected in everyone's eyes. And so, yes, in a town without a movie theater or a mall, where burning a bale of hay counted as entertainment, I thought it was safe to say that Melber was under-resourced.

I say I'm from Paducah, I told her. It's the closest major town—if you can call it that. They sell these T-shirts that say PADUCAH, KENTUCKY: HALFWAY BETWEEN POSSUM TROT AND MONKEY'S EYEBROW. Then there's a cartoon picture of a monkey and possum, hanging by their tails from separate trees, reaching out to each other, Sistine Chapel–style.

Wait, how is it between a monkey and a possum?

Geographically, I said. Those are the names of towns—Possum Trot and Monkey's Eyebrow.

No.

Yes.

That's amazing.

I could think of another word.

Well, she said, you're not there anymore. She raised her beer to me. I didn't have a drink at the moment, so I fist-bumped the Solo cup. She was closer to me than she needed to be, I thought—close enough that I could see the faint hairs on her upper lip and feel the heat from her body and her breath. I couldn't place what it was about her that attracted me. Maybe some sense of shared understanding, real or imagined—that we were of a kind. Maybe it didn't matter. I figured these sorts of things suffered from close scrutiny anyhow. She was a pretty girl at a party who seemed to enjoy talking with me, and with whom I wanted to be close. Better to leave it at that.

I'd probably feel differently about Virginia if I was born there, she said.

Where were you born?

She eyed me slyly for a moment, as if trying to discern whether I really cared. A country that no longer exists, she said.

Is this a riddle?

Her brows drew together almost imperceptibly. No, it's not a riddle, she said. She took a drink. There were teeth impressions on the lip of the Solo cup where she'd been chewing on it.

What happened to the country?

I hope you find the right place, she said, not seeming to have heard my question. Maybe you'll know it when you see it and you'll feel at home. Then she touched my arm and said, I'm going to the porch to smoke. It was nice meeting you.

I gave her my name and she gave me hers—Alma, she said. Shaking her hand was like putting a letter in a mailbox, not knowing if you'd ever get a reply. You dropped the envelope and shut the metal hatch, and then you were empty-handed. Before she walked away, she asked me what I did—if I was a graduate student or TA or what. I told her I was a writer, but maybe my speech was slurred. She looked at me like I'd meant to say I was something else.

Someone took me home. I remember it was a pickup truck with eagles airbrushed in mid-flight on the doors against a backdrop of rippling stars and stripes. The image was ethereal, and I stood there in the driveway looking at it for a long time, mesmerized. Someone was standing in the yard, very drunk, naming off the cities of the world that would be underwater in the next fifty years. Houston, Dhaka, Miami, Mumbai. He was counting on his fingers. Alexandria, Rio, Atlantic City, New Orleans.

The driver of the airbrushed truck materialized finally and told me to get in. I'd seen him at the party but hadn't spoken to him. Every time I'd gone to fetch a beer in the kitchen, he'd been leaning against the avocado fridge, talking about John Ashbery.

I'm gonna roll down the window in case you need to be sick, he said, and so I rode in the passenger seat with the wind drying my eyes, high beams unfurling the road ahead of us. He asked my permission to smoke and I said, *Of course,* as if we were old friends and I was offended he'd even asked. I'll take one too if you don't mind, I said.

This is my last one, he said. There was a long pause. We can float it though, if you want.

That's okay, I said, and though I meant that it was fine for him to smoke it alone, he went ahead and passed it to me. This guy, the driver, was wearing a PBS T-shirt and a ratty red sock hat. Whose truck is this? I said, suddenly aware that it couldn't be his.

My older brother's.

I took a drag and passed the cigarette back to him. It's nice, I said, for some reason. I didn't really have an opinion about the truck.

The woods opened out onto a big pasture, rows of mown hay in a wash of moonlight. A clapboard house stood against the tree line, with a gambrel barn beside it, and in the lighted window of the house, I saw a man and woman embracing. They seemed to be standing in a kitchen. There were plates on the table. Maybe they'd just eaten, though it was very late. Regardless, they were having a moment. They didn't know I could see them, passing by, as I was, in the dark.

I met a girl, I said.

I saw that, he said, amused. That's the visiting writer, you know. She got the big fellowship.

We had a vibe, I said, though I wasn't sure if I even believed this.

No, you didn't.

I'm telling you, man.

She's with someone, I think. Now, where am I taking you?

Home, I said.

Where's home?

Home was a cracker box house on the south edge of Louisville with kudzu branching along the walls and an elaborate, jury-rigged tangle of antennae on the roof. It was my grandfather's house, and I lived there with him and my uncle Cort, in a basement room. I'd been there since returning from Colorado a few weeks earlier, where I'd worked for a year with the city forestry division of Aurora. I'd been laid off from the forestry job, failed to make rent, and slept in my car for two months. Having no place else to go, and not wanting to live with either of my divorced parents in western Kentucky, I moved into my grandfather's house, where I could stay rent-free till I "got back on my feet." I got a job as a groundskeeper for Ashby College, a small private school of some renown in the foothills half an hour from the city. Anybody that worked for the college could attend exactly one class for free, and my motive in accepting the job was that I could take a writing workshop. This is what led me to the grad student's party in the country. It was a welcome party, for all the new and returning students. I was supposed to start work on

Monday, and my first class was Monday evening. It was Saturday then—or early Sunday morning, technically. I'd have to take an Uber back and retrieve Pop's truck sometime in the morning.

So are you TAing? the driver wanted to know.

No, I said. He had the heated seat on. I was slouched down, feeling very sleepy and comfortable in its warmth.

He cracked the window, flicked out the cigarette filter. You don't get a stipend, then? he said.

I'm just taking classes.

Nondegree?

I nodded.

I TAed for the first time last semester, he said, shaking his head wearily. Creative nonfiction. I had these grand ideas that I'd teach them about selfhood and identity and the personal essay as a process of self-disclosure and all that. But I had to spend most classes explaining the difference between past and present tense. They switch between the two willy-nilly. And all they want to write about is dead grandparents. It's the only tragedy any of them have encountered. I swear to God, if I read one more dying grandfather story, I'm gonna blow my brains out.

We slung around a curve, headlights panning the trees, and when the road straightened, a creature appeared in the middle, straddling the dashed line—a large bird. The driver stomped the brake. The car shook violently as the antilock mechanism kicked in. We came to a halt a few feet from it, and in the bluish light of the halogen beams, I saw that it was a peacock—iridescent and stately, oil-sheen feathers trailing like a bridal train. The bird looked at us with small red eyes.

Holy shit, the driver said.

For a long time, the bird stared, undaunted.

Maybe it escaped, he said.

Escaped from what?

He didn't answer. Finally, the peacock waddled to the other side, twitching its plumes, pecking casually at insects on the ground. We drove on and did not speak the rest of the way, apart from my perfunctory *Thanks for the ride.* He merely nodded, all the color blanched from his face. He looked like he'd seen his doppelgänger in a dream and now knew his death was imminent. Maybe I looked the same. My heart was still thumping as I pelted up the gravel drive to Pop's house.

In the basement, I stretched my legs on the tweed couch and opened my notebook. I wrote down what I remembered. My conversation with Alma. The truck with the airbrushed eagles. The peacock. When I'd recounted everything, I wrote a description of the present moment:

> I've got my bare legs stretched out on the tweed couch. I'm drunk. The couch is itchy. Through the casement window, I can see a birch tree. It reminds me of a Japanese painting. A string of threadbare flags is draped from the tree. The neighbor put them up. They're called prayer flags, I think. Further on there's a church steeple. Lilac sky. Birds are beginning to sing, so I guess it's dawn.
>
> It's dim in the basement and the air feels like a root cellar's—cool and damp. All of Pop's antiques and old tools are down here, too many to name, but here's what I can see on or near the workbench:
>
> Crosscut saws.
> Posthole diggers.
> A rust-speckled Pepsi sign.
> Railroad jack.
> Kerosene lamps.
> Purple Heart in a glass case.

I thought for a minute, trying to decide if I'd forgotten anything important about the night. I wrote: *Cardboard cutout of Walt Whitman at the party,* and closed the notebook.

I found it hard to fall asleep without the television playing. I'd been watching *The Man Who Shot Liberty Valance* earlier and it was still paused. Pop had a big bookshelf of VHS tapes next to the basement TV. A lot of John Ford westerns. Billy Wilder. Hitchcock. The films were taped from television and included commercials for food processors and obsolete technologies, but I didn't mind so much.

As I drifted off with the movie playing, I tried to think of one quotation of Whitman's that wasn't *I am large, I contain multitudes*—just one—but I came up with nothing. I thought about Alma, leaning against the Wurlitzer, an aura of light from the neon tubes. What *did* I mean by a place that never was? It sounded corny when I thought of it now. My eyes were closed; I could hear Jimmy Stewart talking to Vera Miles. But Whitman was gnawing at me—that I was unable to remember. I fetched my copy of *Leaves of Grass* and found the first line I'd highlighted, years earlier when I'd read it for the first time. *I help myself to material and immaterial,* it said. *No guard can shut me off, no law prevent me.* I read it two or three times, aloud. It settled me down, and I was able to sleep then, the book in my arms.

POP CAME HOME FROM CHURCH WITH A BUCKET OF FRIED chicken and a bayonet. I'd been watching TV all morning with a dull headache and met him in the kitchen, still a little hungover. He set the chicken on the table and waggled the bayonet, grinning proudly. Seventy bucks, he said. That's how much I paid Sparky. He thought it was turn of the century—the last century, I mean. But it's Civil War. Ask me how I know.

Who's Sparky?

Pop waved off the question. This old guy at church, he said. Not important. Ask me how I know.

How do you know?

He motioned me over and held the blade up to the sunlight pouring through the kitchen window. The markings near the socket, he said, running his fingernail over the steel. I bent down, squinting, and saw faint letters engraved there. Chavasse, he said. That means it was imported from England during the war, on the Enfield musket. Both sides used them.

Cool, I said, not knowing what else to say.

He held it out at arm's length, admiring, then sighed and set it on the table. He took off his bucket hat and hung it on the coatrack. He was wearing his one pair of nice slacks and a short-sleeve dress shirt with a narrow tie. His shoes were Velcro sneakers. It was hard for him to bend over and tie laces anymore. Oh, I got us some KFC, too, he said, as an afterthought.

I see that.

Uncle Cort came plodding into the kitchen, groggy-eyed. He usually slept till about that time—eleven in the morning—and was wearing his pajamas still: sweatpants and a T-shirt, only he'd put on his crocodile cowboy boots and had the sweatpants tucked into them. His hair, as always, was slicked back with gel, little rebellious curls at the nape of his neck. It always made him look like he'd just stepped out of the shower. He stared impassively at the chicken.

The colonel, he said.

That's right, Cort, Pop said. Get in here and get you some lunch.

Not a real colonel, Cort said, taking down a paper plate from the cabinet.

We know that, Cort, Pop said. Cort, my mother's brother, was fifty-two years old and had never lived on his own or held down a job for more than a few weeks. His longest stint of employment had been at Walmart, corralling carts in the parking lot. He'd been fired for accosting a customer who he claimed was shoplifting, but who turned out to be completely innocent.

Cort brought his pill organizer to the table, with its little plastic compartments for each day of the week, and shook a glossy rainbow of tablets and capsules into his palm. He'd been involved in a near-fatal car accident when he was twenty-two, and since then he'd taken a bevy of medications every day, including enough Roxicodone to kill someone without his tolerance.

We opened the bucket, selected our pieces. There's fried taters in there, too, Pop said. Cort took out the little paper box with the potato wedges and dumped most of them on his plate. The rusted bayonet just sat there in the middle of the kitchen table while we ate. I wondered if it had been used to kill someone—if some young boy's blood was still dried on the blade.

Sparky got it from a flea market, Pop said, chewing as he spoke. He sucked the grease from his thumb, blotted his lips with a napkin. Didn't know what he had. It's always the same story with these old relics. Nobody knows what they have.

Colonel Tom Parker, Elvis's manager? He wasn't a real colonel either.

All right, Cort, Pop said. We know.

I looked through the kitchen window. Outside, in the bright noon light, a man stood across the street filling a wading pool with a garden hose. He wore swim trunks with blue flames and a camo T-shirt and smoked a cigarette while he waited. I wondered if the pool was for him or his kids. All the houses on the street were like Pop's—vinyl-sided boxes or split-levels from the '70s. Chain-link fences and plastic lawn furniture. Pickups in the driveways. Above the twisted trees and the power lines like musical staves, I could just make out the steam stacks of the Mill Creek Generating Station, a coal-fired power plant not five miles away. It occurred to me, as I made a mental note of all this, that including the stacks in a description of the neighborhood, as they poured their white vapor into the azure vastness of the September sky, would seem like the unsubtle, physical instantiation of some generalized industrial oppression, looming over the town. It would seem too much like a symbol. But there it was, nonetheless. This place had a way of collapsing the concrete and the symbolic—text and subtext. Nothing was hidden. If you looked, it was all right there on the surface. But of course, not many people were looking.

Can you imagine using one of these things? Pop said, picking up the bayonet, flicking the fine point with his thumb. It's one thing to stand on a hill and shoot at somebody. It's another thing to walk right up and poke a fella in the gut. We trained with bayonets when I was in the service, but we never used them.

I could've joined the army, Cort said. I talked to a recruiter.

You have flat feet, Cort, Pop said.

The recruiter said that didn't matter. He said I'd make a grade A soldier. That was what he said.

Then why didn't you? I said.

Cort looked at me like he'd suddenly realized I was in the room. Why didn't I what?

Why didn't you join?

Cort stared for a long time, sucking his teeth, then shrugged and went back to his food. He had a habit of sniffing each bite before he put it into his mouth. He refrained from bathing for days at a time and tried to compensate by using cologne samples he found in men's magazines. He didn't like to be touched, and if you came close to him by accident he would flinch. These eccentricities had never been spoken of directly by my mother or Pop, as far as I could remember. Everyone felt guilty because of the accident and accepted that it was simply the way he was—a lonely, reclusive person, angry at the way his life had turned out.

So what, you'll be working as a landscaper, that right? Cort said. He gnawed on a drumstick, pulling off strings of meat, and watched me, waiting for an answer, though he already knew more or less what I'd be doing.

Groundskeeping, I said.

What's the difference?

I wasn't actually sure if there was a difference, but "groundskeeper" sounded more reputable, as though I'd been entrusted with something valuable—the "grounds."

I'm hoping it will be mostly forestry work.

You're good at that, Pop said, pointing at me with the bayonet. I watched you climb that cedar with the storm damage. You're like a damn monkey. That could be your calling.

I gave him an *aw shucks* grin. Thanks, Pop.

It's an honorable vocation. Requires a lot of skill. Tell you what, you need any practice, that maple out back has needed a trimming for months.

I guess you'll be working with illegals? Cort said.

I don't know, Cort, I said, sighing.

I'd be willing to bet. I'd bet good money.

Okay now, Pop said. Eat your chicken, both of you.

We stared at each other a moment, then went back to our food. Pop loosened his tie knot, leaned back in his chair. He studied the bayonet. His stomach rose and fell easefully. In the street, a kid dressed like Batman rode past on a scooter. He turned and seemed to look at me as he went by, but then it was hard to say with the mask.

A skilled vocation, Pop said, picking away a flake of rust. Something to be proud of.

I WAS RUNNING LATE. I FOUND THE PLACE—A PINK STUCCO building on campus—with two minutes to spare. The sign out front said MAINTENANCE AND LANDSCAPE SERVICES. There were garages with zero-turn mowers and weed-eaters in the lower level. A fleet of pickups sat in the equipment yard, along with backhoes and skid loaders and a few chipper trucks—dump trucks with wood chippers hitched to the back.

We were supposed to meet in the office above the storage garages. I climbed the stairs in my scuffed-up work boots, carrying a water bottle and a grocery sack with my lunch inside. On the second floor, I found twenty or so men, either sitting at a long conference table or standing with their arms crossed. Some of them, I guessed, were new hires like me, and some had been around for a long time.

A man I assumed to be the supervisor was just beginning to speak. I took a seat at the vinyl table, the surface strewn with pine needles and granola bar wrappers, marked with sticky rings from soda cans. The man introduced himself as Kelly. He looked like a high school basketball coach, his golf shirt tucked into pleated khakis, and he seemed to be flexing his muscled arms intentionally while he explained the work we'd be doing.

There are 215 acres and over twenty thousand trees on campus, and it's our job to take care of all of them, he said. He told us we'd be divided into crews. Each crew would have a specialty. We would work for just under six hours each day, which allowed them to avoid giving us a lunch break, according to Kentucky law. Instead, we got two fifteen-minute breaks, which could be combined, if we chose, into a half-hour lunch. There were some grumbles among the workers when he said this.

Now undoubtably some of you are students, he said, and undoubtably some of you view this job as a means to an end. But when you're here, I expect you to work. That clear? We all nodded as subtly as possible. All right, let's get into our crews, then we'll watch the safety videos and get a move on.

Kelly read out our names, dividing us into groups of three. He read my name, then the names of my crew members. Randy Blythe and James Mas—

He paused, squinting at the roster. How do you pronounce this? he said. Mason-do?

Masondo, someone said. I turned to the source and saw a man leaning against a filing cabinet. He was tall and sinewy, veins wriggling up his forearms. He looked to be about my age. He had a hard hat under his free arm and a dozen or so carabiners clipped to his belt.

You're the climber, correct? Kelly said.

That's right, said James Masondo.

Well, this name might give me some trouble at first.

It's really not that hard to pronounce.

What is it anyway? The origin, I mean.

James Masondo shook his head. It's South African, man, he said.

Oh, Kelly said. Well, whatever. Y'all are gonna be a forestry crew, since you've all three got experience.

Though I didn't show it, I was relieved to hear this. I'd dreaded mowing lawns all day. Trimming and cutting down trees would be a continuation of what I had been doing in Colorado.

We watched our safety videos, which mainly covered the Vermeer wood chipper we'd be using. At some point during the video, Kelly materialized behind me and whispered close to my ear, You ever see the movie *Fargo*?

Yes, I said.

Just don't be a retard and get sucked into that thing, he said. We'd be scooping up what's left of you with shovels.

After the video, we trickled out to the equipment yard. I got our chipper truck started. James came over and we shook hands. You're Owen Callahan? he said.

I nodded.

Good to know you've done this before.

Same, I said. You met the third guy?

Not yet.

The other men prepared for the day around us. They gassed up saws and sharpened pruners. They twisted chain tensioners with screwdrivers and combed their beards in fish-eye mirrors. We stood drinking scorched coffee from our Styrofoam cups, steam curling up in the morning air. James was the only Black person on any of the crews. There were a few Latino men, a guy from Laos. Otherwise, everyone was white.

You a student? I said.

He nodded. Getting my master's in history.

From around here? I tried to say this in a way that sounded friendly rather than hostile.

Louisville, he said. He explained that his mother was a social worker at a behavioral health center. She was from Louisville originally. His father lived in Johannesburg. He said he'd lived in South Africa till he was five. Since then, he'd been in Louisville.

Peace Corps, he said, anticipating my next question. How they met.

Right.

She's writing a novel about it, like everyone else who joins the Peace Corps.

The sound of wheezing reached us from across the yard—a man ambling over, hand outstretched, breathing asthmatically. You must be Randy? I said.

Rando, he said, catching his breath. Everybody calls me Rando.

Rando it is, I said.

We got acquainted while the truck idled, breathing diesel fumes, smoking our cigarettes. Rando was older—sixty at least. He sounded like he'd smoked his voice with forty years' worth of Pall Malls. He liked to talk, I could tell that much right away.

You young dudes will be doing all the aerial acrobatics, he said. I'm too old and too fat. I quit drinking ten years ago, but I got to keep the beer gut. He clapped his belly hard. I got the sense that this was something he said often, that it was always followed by the same belly clap. They had me on mowing duty, he said. I was doing that for three years, but I got these boils on my lower back from sitting—you don't wanna hear about it. Suffice to say, it's ugly. Kelly's putting me with y'all till the boils heal.

Somebody told me Kelly had fifteen confirmed kills in Iraq, James said. That true?

Seventeen, Rando said.

James whistled.

That's a lot of people, I said.

No shit, James said. There are serial killers with lower body counts.

He's a bad person, really, Rando said. You'll figure that out though.

We all turned to look at Kelly. He was standing near the entrance to one of the garages, speaking with a landscape crew who were holding weed trimmers. I tried to imagine how trivial something like weed trimming would seem if you'd killed seventeen people.

Was it all at once, or spread out over time? I asked.

Rando shrugged. You'll have to ask him.

James and I pre-tripped the chipper truck while Rando watched, puffing his Pall Mall and scratching his whiskered jowls. He had the largest coffee thermos I'd ever seen—big enough to hold a whole pot. You're doing great, he said, in between swallows of coffee. I'm just gonna stand here and offer moral support.

I rode with James in the chipper truck—he was the only one with a CDL—and Rando drove a separate pickup with all the pole saws and pruners in the back. Our work for the day was a row of Bradford pears lining a sidewalk near the history building. None of them were tall enough to climb, so we did our trimming from the ground. Rando gathered the branches as they fell, constantly smoking. We trimmed for clearance, so that the branches would be at least eight feet above the walkway. It was easy work.

At noon, we took a break and sat in the shade, eating lunch. Rando told us the half-hour thing was bullshit. Nobody checks up on us, he said. We could take a two-hour lunch if we wanted. No one would know shit.

I'd brought a banana, cherry Pop-Tarts, and beef jerky. James had a bologna sandwich. Rando had some kind of beef stew in a Tupperware container, congealed grease on the surface.

Isn't that cold? I said.

It's better cold, he said.

Several classes let out at once—a sudden, moving current of

students on the sidewalk, parting around our cone perimeter. I wondered if any of them would be in my class later. I looked out across the grassy quad at the college buildings on the other side— Georgian-style structures of red brick with dormer windows and columns. There were students over that way, too. Toting backpacks in groups of three or four. Tapping their thumbs on their phones. Ashby was a beautiful place, really. There were flower beds along all the sidewalks. Black-eyed Susans. Purple asters. Huge, gnarled oak trees shaded everything. Their lacework shadows flickered on the grass when a breeze kicked up, and you could hear the wind ruffling the leaves—a sound like ocean surf. But none of the students seemed to notice. Moreover, none of them seemed to notice us—the groundskeepers taking their lunch.

We can take our time, Rando was saying. Digest our food. We could sit here all fuckin day and no one would care.

THERE HAD BEEN NO COURSE DESCRIPTION FOR THE CREATIVE writing class, and I knew nothing about it, except that it had a "workshop component" and was the only writing class on offer that semester that admitted nondegree students. I realized as I left work that first day that I wouldn't have time to go home and shower. So, I scrubbed my hands with gritty soap and brushed the flakes of sawdust from my hair in the bathroom. I tried to dry my armpits under the hand dryer, but it didn't do much good.

Before class, I sat on a concrete ledge by the bicycle racks in front of the humanities building and smoked. A few people—a girl and two boys who looked to be about twenty—moseyed out and fiddled with their bike locks. The girl had on a peasant top and billowy pants. The boys were affecting a similar faux-bohemian look and seemed enthralled by her. They were talking about Donald Trump, the Republican nominee, and how best to address his existence.

Let his name go unsaid, the girl insisted.

That's right, one boy agreed. That's so totally right.

What if you need to refer to him? said the other boy. What do you say—the one who shall not be named?

You *don't* refer to him, she said. That's the most radical act. Don't give him the satisfaction.

What's radical about it? I said.

The girl looked at me like I'd physically attacked her. Excuse me? What's so radical about it?

She turned to the two boys and arched her eyebrows, then they went on their way. I don't know why I said anything, or why it annoyed me. I wanted to tell them it was asinine, that ignoring the absurd calamity of Trump's ascendance wouldn't make it go away. I wanted to call them back and tell them that it was the least radical thing they could do. But everyone was busy pretending not to notice his existence, as if this might make it less depressing, and I expected things to continue this way until he either won or didn't.

The class met in the chemistry building. When I sat down, there were four other students in the room, half-erased equations and molecule diagrams written in chalk on the blackboard. I kept waiting for everyone else to show up. I sat next to a guy in a Cincinnati Reds hat. He was tall and wore a mustache and light stubble, achieving that Goldilocks zone of facial hair that avoided seeming either manicured or shabby. His features made him seem constantly amused. He was handsome, in other words—one of those faces that's so symmetrical it gives off the impression of sociopathy. Yo, he said.

Is this everybody?

I guess.

I don't know what to expect from this, honestly, I said.

Me neither. I just signed up because of the "workshop component."

Me too.

The desks were arranged in a semicircle. Across from us sat a girl with buzzed hair in a houndstooth coat. Under the coat, she wore leg warmers of different colors and ankle boots that looked like they were from another century. She was reading feverishly from a book I'd never heard of, big eyes dancing over the text. Though the air in the classrooms had a chill to it, it was still very much summer outside, and I wondered how she stood it wearing all those layers.

The instructor came in panting after ten minutes. I am so sorry, he said, setting down his shoulder bag, still breathless, smoothing the unkempt curls plastered to his forehead. This building is a labyrinth.

He took an aluminum bottle from his bag and guzzled water from it, his Adam's apple jumping like a piston. He wiped his mouth, screwed on the cap, and sat finally, smiling at us, clasping his fingers on the desk. So, he said, his beard still dripping, I'm Tony Kaufman. We're all here for Jungle Narratives, yes?

We all looked at each other.

That's the course title, he said. I told them to update it in the catalogue. Did they not?

We shook our heads.

Typical.

He dabbed his hairline with the handkerchief, stuffed it back into the pocket of his jeans, and peered at the class roster. Well, it should be easy to memorize five names, he said. He sighed, tossed the page onto the desk. I guess I should begin at the beginning, he said. The germ for this class was planted ten years ago when my father died in Peru. He was an anthropologist, and one summer he went to Peru, backpacking around the country, and—well, he died, under what you'd call *mysterious circumstances,* I guess. An undiagnosed illness. Since then, I've been obsessed with what happened to him, and it's become the subject of my novel, which I've been working on for, oh, about eight years now. I've been to Peru twice, doing research, asking questions. I'm going again over winter break. I've spent the last eight years thinking about my father in the jungle, and I realized, you know, there's kind of a whole *genre* of stories about the jungle. Why not teach a class that explores it? That's the general idea, anyway. I don't know, *exactly,* what constitutes a jungle narrative, but we're going to figure it out together I hope over the course of the semester.

The girl in the houndstooth coat seemed very into this, nodding eagerly. The guy next to me in the Reds hat raised his hand. Dr. Kaufman, he said.

Please, no hand raising, he said. I want this class to be open and sort of freewheeling. We're just some people talking in a room, okay? We're just having a conversation.

Right, okay. So, Dr. Kaufman—

I'm not a doctor. Just call me Tony.

Okay. Tony, what's the "workshop component"?

I'm so glad you asked, he said. My hope is that toward the end of the semester, we'll all workshop our own jungle narratives, in the form of a story or a play or a series of poems. Or even a film—God, I hadn't thought of that actually.

He scratched a note on the class roster, and from my seat, I could just make it out. *Have them make jungle films?* it said. *Camera rentals from film dept?*

Question, said the houndstooth girl. What if we've never . . . been to the jungle?

It can be about a metaphorical jungle, Tony said.

She narrowed her eyes and nodded slowly. Right on, she said.

What if we *have* been to the jungle? said another student, a heavyset guy with long black hair that hung past his shoulders. His resting facial expression seemed to convey barely concealed rage.

Well, then you can write about that! Tony said, his tone brightening. What jungle have you been to?

Oh I haven't been, he said. I might go though, in the spring. I'm interested in ayahuasca.

Tony's smile faded. I see, he said. Well, class will be over by then, so I guess you'll have to write about the metaphorical jungle, too. Just out of curiosity, has anyone been to an actual jungle?

Question, said the houndstooth girl. Do the . . . *Florida Everglades* count as a jungle?

Tony puffed his cheeks and blew the air out slowly. You know, sure, why not?

Right on, she said.

With introductions out of the way, Tony stood and tried to write something on the blackboard. The chalk broke. He picked up another stick and tried again, but it snapped as well. Fuck, he mumbled. He tried to keep going with the tiny nubbin of chalk that was left, but finally gave up. He wiped his palms on his pant legs, leaving white handprints. I was going to write a quotation, he said. The gist of which is that literature is not a way of escaping life but of seeing it clearly. I want that to be the foundation of our class. Good literature is supposed to give us a shock of recognition. We read a passage and we think, "I've felt that!" It reconnects us to the world and other people and the felt presence of immediate experience.

The houndstooth girl was scribbling furiously on her notepad. Can you repeat that last part? she said. The felt presence . . .

Tony sighed with his shoulders. Of immediate experience, he said.

How are we supposed to have the shock of recognition if none of us have been to the jungle? said the guy in the Reds hat.

We've all been to our metaphorical jungles, Tony said. It's just a matter of discovering what that means for each of us.

After class, I swung by the English department and picked up a copy of the readings for next week from our class cubby. On my way out, I passed a cracked door in the empty hallway, a light on inside. Without stopping, I peeked into the office, and sitting at the desk was Alma, the visiting writer I'd met at the welcome party. She had her socked feet propped on a stack of folders and was reading, and as I passed the doorway, she glanced up from the page and looked at me directly. I averted my eyes and kept walking. Hey! she called out. I froze, backed up to the threshold, and nudged the door open a little.

Hey there, I said.

Do you work here? It's freezing in this building. She had her shoulders hunched and wore a cardigan pulled tight. I looked down at my work boots and pants, my MAINTENANCE AND LAND-SCAPE SERVICES T-shirt.

Not really, I said. I'm just getting out of class.

Oh, she said. I'm sorry, I thought—sorry, never mind.

It is cold in here though.

Right? Anyway. Sorry to bother.

It's fine, I said.

She had a to-go coffee on the desk. She took a drink from it, turned over her book, which she'd laid facedown on her lap, and went back to reading. When she realized I was still standing there, she glanced up again.

Do you remember me? I said.

Her eyes narrowed a bit. She looked slightly alarmed now, like I was someone who might mean to hurt her. The building was empty and silent. Only the emergency lights were burning in the hallway.

We met at that party, I said. I took off my hat and offered a congenial smile, to let her know all was well, that I was harmless.

Her eyes brightened. Yes! she said. The Kentucky boy. You had that whole fully formed theory about yourself.

Yeah, I was a little tipsy.

I'm used to it. Dudes with fully formed theories about themselves, I mean.

I nodded, drummed my fingers on the doorjamb. What else was there to say? She was looking at me, waiting, sliding the cardboard sleeve on her to-go cup up and down.

Sorry I mistook you for whatever, she said. They gave me this office and I figured I might as well use it. Problem is, it's cold as shit when the sun goes down.

Don't worry about it, I said. The office was pretty bare, save for the desk and the stack of folders beside it. The window looked out on an expanse of clipped grass, lit by streetlamps, and a few dark trees. I could see the silhouettes of the pear trees we'd trimmed that day. Well, hopefully I'll see you around, I said.

That'd be nice. It's Owen, right?

I was surprised she remembered. She seemed embarrassed to have asked, and broke eye contact. That's right, I said. And you're Alma?

She didn't answer. She turned back to her book and smiled vaguely as if she knew a secret. Nice to meet you again, she said. I went on my way, boots squeaking on the polished tile, my heart beating fast.

POP'S NIGHTLY SNACK WAS CRUMBLE-IN. THIS INVOLVED crumbling day-old cornbread into a glass of milk, sprinkling it generously with black pepper, and eating it with a spoon like cereal. He ate his crumble-in, slurping the milk-sodden chunks, while I told him about my day. *The Magnificent Seven* played on the living room TV. In a tense scene, Eli Wallach and his fellow bandits came to the village they planned to loot, only to be confronted by Yul Brynner and Steve McQueen, who pointed out all the walls and fortifications they'd built. Pop brought a spoonful to his mouth without taking his eyes from the screen, milk dribbling onto his chin.

He sat like this in the easy chair every night, shirt open, an oscillating fan blowing the wisps of white hair that encircled his bald, age-spotted pate. There was a cordless phone on the end table and a list of names and numbers on notebook paper between the glass top and the wood. Many of the contacts were crossed out—old friends and relatives who'd died. He had his atlases and almanacs stacked there, too, and the TV guide from the paper. A caddy draped over the armrest held his remote controls and his magnifying glasses. The Civil War bayonet was lying on the phone book. He'd kept it within arm's reach there on the end table since he brought it home, as if it might come to some use.

So this guy Kelly, he said, still looking at the screen. You say he's a veteran?

Yeah, I said. Apparently he killed seventeen people.

Pop looked at me. He told you that?

No, but that's the rumor.

He brags about it?

I don't know.

Pop shook his head, took another spoonful of cornbread mush into his mouth. Nobody who's actually killed a man will brag about it. Least not in my experience.

Pop had fought in World War II, been wounded at Okinawa. Maybe he was right when it came to his generation, but I wasn't so sure about Kelly, who'd fought in a very different war.

I told him about the job and the work it would entail. Then I told him about Jungle Narratives and Tony and the notions about art and life I'd been pondering since that afternoon. He seemed to be only halfway paying attention, his eyes still locked on the TV. There was a commercial break finally. I guess the movie was taped from cable sometime in the '90s. It was a commercial I remembered from childhood for a box set of CDs called *Pure Moods*. The music was synthy and sort of tribal sounding, and the announcer spoke with a fake British accent over crossfaded images of breaking waves and unicorns and women twirling in skirts.

Pop wrenched his gaze from the screen and set the glass of pep-pery milk on the table. This guy, Tony, he said. He a successful writer?

I didn't know the answer to this question. Something told me no, though I wasn't sure what it meant, precisely, to be a successful writer of fiction. He has a teaching job, I said. I think he knows what he's talking about.

Pop nodded slowly and scratched his sideburn. Well, he said, I know your mother wishes you were doing something different. But I got faith. And there's always the forestry work. That's a solid job. Always be a need for tree trimmers.

Right, I said.

We sat for a moment without speaking. The living room was dark, save for the pitching tones of blue light on the carpet. Since my grandmother's death, the house had fallen into disarray. Nei-ther Pop nor Uncle Cort put much stock in tidiness, and so there were beer cans and empty cereal boxes and grease-spotted fast-food sacks littered about. Still, all my grandmother's decorative touches remained. Her crocheted antimacassars were still draped over the recliners' headrests. Her porcelain chickens and toadstools and milk-glass bowls still filled the china cabinets. *Blue Boy* by Thomas Gainsborough and *Pinkie* by Thomas Lawrence hung side by side in gilt frames above the TV, and her sheer lace curtains still stirred in the breeze. Every piece of Tupperware in the kitchen drawers bore her initials in red Sharpie. I wondered if Pop found it comforting or spooky—or some measure of both. He could've moved if he'd wanted, after she passed, so I supposed he preferred it here in this place, where her absence was so conspicuous.

When you were young, I said, and you visited other towns, did you ever think about living in them? Or did you always know you'd come back to Kentucky?

You mean when I was hoboing?

Yeah.

He paused the movie and thought about it. Well, I did live in other towns, he said. I worked in Detroit at a bowling alley for a year, setting up pins. Before they had machines to reset the pins automatically. Then there was New Orleans for six months. Lived off bananas. Ships from South America would throw out the over-ripe bananas, and there'd be this big ol heap. I ate ten bananas a day.

He'd told me these stories from his hoboing days many times, but I didn't let on that I'd heard them before. I'd heard *all* his stories many times by then, so that they took on the resonance of myth—as if I'd inherited them from previous lives. No one believed me when I told them he'd been a hobo. Sometimes *I* barely believed it. It seemed too vaudevillian—like Red Skelton's hobo clown Freddie the Freeloader. But it was true.

I worked in Chicago at a railyard, cut timber in Texarkana, he said. Then, course, I spent a year in San Francisco and two years in the Pacific. I lived all over.

But you always came back.

Well, yeah, he said. My folks were here.

That's why?

Mainly, he said. All I could think about overseas was getting back and setting out a tobacco crop. I listened to the Kentucky Derby on the radio once, and when they sang "My Old Kentucky Home," it brought me to tears, no kidding. I really missed it.

Then why'd you keep leaving?

Pop smiled vaguely and rubbed the nape of his neck. Well, he said, I guess I just get antsy. That's why it's so hard for me to sit in this goddang chair all day. He looked at me with kindness, the crow's feet at the corners of his eyes pinching up. He was waiting to see if I had any further questions, but I didn't. The sound of chirring crickets drifted through an open window. Now and then we heard a car gunning past on the street or the far-off whine of a siren. The blipping, slide-whistle noises of Cort's video game down the hall.

I reckon all that's behind me now, Pop said sadly, as if he himself had just now realized its truth. No more hoboing.

I guess so, I said.

We sat for a few more moments, hearing the video game, hearing the crickets outside and the buzzing bass of a passing car's stereo system. Then Pop pressed PLAY and the movie continued.

RANDO LIKED TALKING ABOUT THE BEATLES. OH YEAH DUDE, he said, I got it all, every album, mint condition. Every CD, every cassette.

We were at a job site on the second day—a big ash tree by the student center, most of it dead from emerald ash borer. James and I were stepping into our harnesses, preparing to climb. Rando sat in the cab of his pickup with the door open, eating a bear claw, classic rock playing on the radio. It was "Hey Jude" that got him on the subject.

I got red vinyls, blue, green, he said, I have this shit in German dude, shit I can't even understand. I got this *Yellow Submarine* EP with a little plastic submarine in the sleeve that came with it. Oh yeah dude, I have everything, I have lunch boxes. I have like twenty fuckin lunch boxes. You get into that shit and it just goes on forever dude. I had people bringing me shit from Europe in suitcases, bootlegs on VHS and shit. I had over ten thousand dollars in Beatles memorabilia. I had to get out of it though. You can just go on forever with that stuff.

Yeah, *Magical Mystery*'s my favorite I guess, I told him. This was all I could think to say. I didn't know much about the Beatles.

Oh shit dude, that's the best one. 1967. That's when they started dropping acid. That "Blue Jay Way," that's trippy, man, that's George Harrison on the Hammond B3. He wrote it, too. On those speakers in my place, I put that vinyl on, and I swear it sounds like they're right there in your room with you, the fuckin Beatles dude, right there in your living room. The fidelity, man, I'm telling you, it's crazy. I mean, *wow.*

I guess you'll be a rich man, you ever sell any of that stuff, James said.

No poor people in America, Rando said. Only temporarily embarrassed millionaires. That's Steinbeck.

I thought it was Woody Guthrie, I said.

Rando shrugged and brushed bear claw crumbs from his whiskers. You dudes probably know better than me, being college educated and all.

James and I set our lines using throw balls. I made a good pitch, saw the line sail through the crotch I was aiming for, heard the steel ball thump down in the grass on the other side. It was only the fourth try. It made me feel good to set a line after only a few tries. Some guys stood there for half an hour. We strung up our friction savers, attached our handsaws in their plastic scabbards to our hips. They were Japanese blades, toothed and razor-sharp. With all my gear attached and jangling—hitches and carabiners and coils of rope—I felt solid and formidable, like some early mountaineer or arctic explorer. I clipped in and "humped the air"—reaching up the line with my ascender device, then dragging it toward me and thrusting my hips at the same time. Soon I reached a branch I could stand on, the muscles in my arms and abdomen aflame. I was fifteen feet high and out of breath among the cool shadows and the chattering leaves. James was humping the air on the other side. When I'd caught my breath and my heart rate slowed, I looked for the dead to cut out. The tree was a lost cause, but we were told to leave it and cut out the dead, so that's what we would do.

Rando was still jawing about the Beatles—actually shouting factoids up to us with his hands cupped around his mouth. Most people don't know that it was the Beatles' dentist that turned them on to acid, he was saying. They went to a dinner party at his house, and he dosed them without their knowledge. Things started getting squiggly, and John Lennon was like, "Hey man, how much gin is in this martini?" and the dentist tells them he put this new drug called LSD in their fuckin cocktails. He could get it then, see, cause it was legal in the early '60s for a medical professional to possess.

They were friends with their dentist? James said, extending to make his undercut on a dead limb, his voice strained.

Oh yeah dude, he said. Fuck yeah. This was 1965, back when you really *knew* your dentist. Same as the baker and the neighborhood butcher. You had a *relationship* with your neighbors, went over to their houses.

And then they dosed you with acid without your consent, James said. Sounds like a great era. Let's go back to that.

Rando went on and on, stacking brush as it fell, pausing occasionally to pull the earmuffs down from his hard hat over his ears and fire up the chipper. Whenever we sawed a heavy branch, and we heard the wood begin to creak as it bent and gave way, we shouted, Headache! This was the same as saying "heads up," but every arborist I'd worked with said "headache." I don't know why.

Rando told us about the first time the Beatles met Bob Dylan, and the first time they met the Rolling Stones, and the first time they met Eric Clapton and Elvis Presley. They actually jammed with Elvis, you believe that? he said. There are no recordings, but they got guitars out and jammed. Just think about it—Elvis and the Beatles. Can you imagine what that would be worth?

I'd forgotten my lunch, so when we took our break, I went to the student center to hunt down a candy bar. Inside, the air was cool and smelled of garlic and grease. There were students eating personal pizzas at the tables, waiting in line at the bookstore. A baby grand piano sat out in the open in the high-ceilinged lobby. A gangly, acne-splotched guy was playing the first few bars of the *Moonlight Sonata,* over and over. He played with great passion and feeling—eyes closed, brow knitted, working the sustain pedal with a lime-green flip-flop. No one was watching.

I found the vending machine and pulled off my work gloves—the kind with the palms dipped in blue rubber—and put them in my back pocket. They were already shredded and sour smelling. I'd have to replace them soon and it hadn't even been two weeks. I fed a dollar bill into the machine and a coil pushed the candy bar slowly toward the edge, but it didn't drop. I had to feed another dollar bill into the slot. The *Moonlight Sonata,* or at least the first thirty seconds of it, echoed behind me throughout this ordeal.

On my way out I glanced at a bulletin board, and among the pictures of lost dogs and the fringed tutoring flyers with tear-off tabs, I saw an advertisement for a reading by none other than the visiting writer. Her photo was right there. She sat in an Adirondack chair, holding a gray, unamused cat in her lap. Behind her was a wall of scarred brick. It was a flattering photograph, if a little self-serious. More than anything, it had the effect of making her look older than she was—or at least than I thought she was. Her full name, I learned, was Alma Hadzic. I folded the flyer and put it in my pocket.

MY FATHER AND I SPOKE EVERY TWO OR THREE MONTHS. HIS wife, Bonnie, had esophageal cancer, which had spread to her lungs. It had been a long struggle, with all the associated tortures— surgery, chemotherapy, radiation. None of it had done any good. My father was unaccustomed to helplessness, and as a result, he'd become deeply depressed. She'd been in remission while I was living in Colorado, but now that the cancer had returned, I decided I'd make an effort to talk more often. I called him one night. He caught me up on the recent news. Bonnie was undergoing radiation once more. Her most recent procedure had been to install a feeding tube in her stomach. She'd been an energetic woman in her early fifties, who curled her hair every day and bleached her teeth and attended Tae Bo classes, who smiled vivaciously at strangers that passed by on the sidewalk. Now she was stooped and wore a wig and shuffled like an elderly woman. The pockets of her robe were stuffed with blood-flecked tissues.

My father sounded exhausted. He told me how hard things had been, how he didn't know who to trust. They had been at the hospital earlier that day for a radiation treatment. These people, he said. There are all these people in the waiting room, and they all want to tell you how bad it's been for them. It's like it's some kind of contest to see who has it the worst. She gets depressed when we go because they tell her these horror stories.

They're probably just afraid, I said. They want everybody to be as scared as they are.

It's like they're proud of it or something, he said. It's nothing to be proud of though. It's a horrible thing.

I gazed out the open casement window, to the birch tree and the prayer flags. Dozens of sparrows were flitting about and chirping madly in the branches. I didn't know what to say to him, what would be comforting.

It's hard getting up, he said. I just lie there in bed and dread it.

Maybe the radiation will help.

He sighed. So, what's this new job?

I told him it was forestry work, like what I'd been doing in Colorado. He didn't know much about what I was doing there, but he'd never approved. I hadn't told him that after I'd lost the job, I'd lived out of my car in Walmart parking lots for two months, surviving on saltines and peanut butter. But he knew I had debt, that I'd gone to Colorado with no prospects, that my bank account was always empty, and he knew that it was dangerous work.

So you do this job and they pay for your tuition? he said. Do you get paid by the hour on top of that?

Minimum wage, I said.

He grunted thoughtfully. I could picture his dubious expression. And what would you study?

This and that. Some writing classes. Whatever interests me, I guess.

This and that, he said.

That's right.

Are you still on drugs?

No.

Are you sure?

Yes, I'm sure I'm not on drugs.

You'll be trimming from a cherry picker?

Climbing with a harness, I said.

Climbing trees with a chainsaw. Brilliant. Well, I'll tell you straight up, son, I wish you'd find something else to do. Have I ever told you about the job I almost took at the uranium plant?

I'd heard the story before, but I knew it didn't matter—he was going to tell me anyhow. I sighed and said, What about it?

Well, when I was about your age, I interviewed for a job out there, back when it was Union Carbide. This job involved cleaning ventilation ducts.

He went on to explain the work, which sounded almost comically ill-advised. The long and the short of it was that he would've been required to crawl around in a big metal pipe and clean it with a pressure washer. The pipes were part of the plant's ventilation system, transporting poisonous gases and other by-products of uranium enrichment. I might've found it incredible if the plant in

Paducah wasn't known for its sketchy practices. In the fifties, they'd had workers eating their lunch on tables coated with radioactive dust.

This guy giving the interview told me to think long and hard on it, my father said. It paid well, and the money was tempting, but in the end, I turned it down. Some things just aren't worth it. You catch what I mean, son?

I told him I did. What he left out of this story, which he'd told way back when I hired on to the job in Aurora, was that he'd gone on to work for twenty-five years as a firefighter—a vocation not known for its safety. But I guess that wasn't the point. The point was that he wanted something better for me.

Maybe it will only be temporary, I said.

He grunted again. I tried to imagine what he looked like, where he was sitting in the house. I thought I could hear a TV playing softly, so it was most likely the leather recliner in the living room. My father was a tree trunk of a man, with big stout arms and shoulders and a gleaming shaved head. He put baby oil on his head every day for some reason. There was always a bottle in my parents' bathroom. I could remember being a little kid and coming up behind him as he read the paper in the morning and sniffing his scalp, which I thought smelled like pizza crust. For a while, I would tell him that—your head smells like pizza crust—and he'd laugh good-naturedly.

With nothing left to talk about, he told me he'd better go. He had to feed Bonnie a bottle of Ensure. Have you considered working for Home Depot? he said, as an afterthought. Your cousin Bart works there. They have good benefits.

Who?

Bart, he said. Your cousin, Bart?

I didn't remember any cousin named Bart, but it was certainly possible that I had one. There were a lot of second and third cousins on my dad's side who I'd met only once or never, and who, nonetheless, he always expected me to know about.

No, I haven't considered Home Depot, I said. I'll give it some thought.

What about the navy? They'd let you in as an officer with your college degree. Could be something to think on.

Cool, I said. Will do.

Well, goodbye, he said.

Okay, I said. I told him I'd be keeping both of them "in my thoughts," especially Bonnie, but I think he'd already hung up.

THE DETAILS YOU CHOOSE REVEAL WHAT YOU THINK IS important, and if you choose trivial details, you'll out yourself as having a trivial intellect. This is what Tony told us. We were discussing how everything in *Heart of Darkness* was filtered through Marlow's consciousness, and therefore inflected by his biases and aversions. This was the power of point of view, Tony explained.

One student had dropped the course, which left the handsome dude in the Reds hat, the girl in the houndstooth coat, and the big guy with long black hair who was interested in ayahuasca. Their names were Casey, Joanna, and Trent, respectively.

How do you know what details are important? asked Joanna.

Tony made no attempt to disguise his exasperation. He had his fingertips spread on the desk and was looking down at his papers and his open copy of *Heart of Darkness,* bookmarked with two dozen curled sticky notes.

Let's say your life has fallen apart, he said.

My life is great, Joanna said.

Hypothetically, Tony said. Your life has fallen apart. You live in some nowhere town. You've got nothing to do, no prospects or opportunities. Maybe because of this—because of your psychological state, as it were—you notice the abandoned grain elevators on your way home from work, how they're gray and the painted letters are scaled. And you notice the run-down neighborhoods, cars on concrete blocks, a half-starved dog chained to a post. Now, someone who's just won the lottery, they wouldn't see the same things, would they? Maybe this guy that won the lottery would notice the pretty dandelions growing wild in the lawns, or the sunset behind the grain elevators. These things are important to either man because his interior life is mirrored in the exterior world. But a writer—a writer can get into the bad habit of *cataloguing,* simply naming the things that make up a particular setting without filtering them through the lens of a character's point of view. The writer, in an effort to be specific, might give us the particular species of trees growing in the yards of the run-down neighborhood, but would the particular species of trees be *important* to the man whose life has fallen apart? Or to the man who has just won the lottery? The answer's no. It would be trivial information.

What if the man whose life has fallen apart is an arborist, I wanted to know? What if it was his job to know the names of trees? But I didn't ask this. I pondered, instead, what the world would look like to me if I'd won the lottery. If the sun would be brighter. If flowers would stand out suddenly in the foreground, more than they already did. Would I still notice the abandoned grain elevators? The half-starved dog? Would I still be so obsessed with naming the world?

We're not journalists, Tony said. We don't report on the world. We remake it, according to our specifications.

I LOOKED HER UP, TWO DAYS BEFORE HER READING. HER surname appeared sometimes with the diacritical marks—Hadžić—and sometimes without, though mostly she seemed to have dropped them in her social media and recent publications. As it turned out, she'd published a book of short stories with a small press two years prior and was "at work on a novel." The collection had been short-listed for a prize I'd never heard of. These accomplishments were all the more impressive because of her age—she was only twenty-six. Ashby had awarded her a Driscoll Fellowship, which meant, essentially, that she would live and write in one of the university guesthouses for the duration of the school year, rent-free, and receive a small stipend. The only requirement was that she give two lectures on craft, one per semester, and lead two master classes. It seemed like a good gig.

I discovered an old interview, in which she gave a short account of her family history. Her parents had grown up and met in Sarajevo, when it was still part of Yugoslavia. She was born there in

1990. This is what she'd meant on the night we met, I supposed, by a country that no longer existed. Yugoslavia dissolved in the year following her birth. Her parents were Bosniak. They fled just before the eruption of the Bosnian War, settling first in Germany, then the United States—in Queens at first, then the suburbs of DC.

I did an image search and found a picture of her with a handsome movie star I recognized, at some formal-looking gala or reception. I might've thought they were together, but there was something starstruck about her expression. Her eyes looked almost crazed, and the man, the movie actor, had a calm, bemused expression. He held a flute of champagne down by his leg and looked like he'd been stopped for a picture on his way to someone else.

When I'd scrolled through all the extant pictures of her that Google had to offer, and had begun seeing the faces of other, unrelated Alma Hadzics—Alma Hadzics who were doctors and real estate agents and recently arrested drunk drivers—I closed my laptop and opened my notebook to a fresh blank page. *You're not a journalist,* I wrote. Then I tried to think of myself as a character, with a particular point of view that made me see the world in a particular way. I imagined that I'd won the lottery and glanced around the basement room, trying to notice the things that a lottery winner would notice. I decided that a lottery winner would feel repulsed by the environment, so I wrote down some of the things that made it deficient—the vague scent of mothballs, the damp air, the sticky traps in the corners with the tangled corpses of cave crickets and spiders and small, desiccated lizards who'd tried to eat the cave crickets and spiders. Then I tried to imagine what the basement would look like if my life had fallen apart. It didn't take much imagination, and I wondered if my life really *had* fallen apart—if I was only now beginning to piece it together again. I remembered the line from Richard Hugo's poem—*Say your life broke down. The last good kiss you had was years ago.* I wrote it down and considered it for a long time, sitting there on the tweed couch in Pop's basement, surrounded by his silent antiques. What did you do when you reached that point? What did you notice?

ALMA'S READING WAS IN A BAR ON BARDSTOWN ROAD CALLED
The Bard's Town. Their whole theme was Shakespeare. A cartoon
Shakespeare in tights and a frilly ruff waved his neon arm from the
sign. Inside, it was made to look like a Renaissance-era tavern and
had the bready smell of old spilt beer. By the time I arrived, she
was already onstage. People were watching from their tables, the
flicker of tealight candles reflected in their beer glasses. Alma wore
a floral print dress and hiking boots with red laces. She explained
that she would be reading a series of prose poems she called *Misconnected.* They were found poems, she explained, and were collaged
from Craigslist personal ads called "missed connections."

I read them pretty much every day, she said, partly because I
wonder if I'll show up in any of them, and partly because they're
such perfect distillations of loneliness and longing.

Her lips were touching the silver grille of the microphone. Every
time she made a *p* or *b* sound, the audio popped. She kept her eyes
lowered as she spoke, as if by not perceiving the audience, we would
cease to exist, and read the poems from her phone, scrolling slowly,
her face lit pale blue by the screen. They were hit or miss, but
when they hit, they really hit. The good ones were funny and gut-
wrenching, thanks in no small part to her delivery, which oscillated
almost imperceptibly between irony and sincerity—sometimes
walking the thin line between them. They had titles like "Blue
Hair, Taco Bell" and "Beautiful Hardee's Girl." "Beautiful Hardee's
Girl" was the best, I thought, and not just because I'd once worked
at a Hardee's. *I drove through on my Harley,* began the first stanza. *I
showed you tattoos of what I wanted, already written on my arms. You
unmatched me, but I sent the first message, I crossed the street. I saw you in
booty shorts and a yellow tank top, and I knew you'd want to take a ride.*

When it was over, I found her at the bar, settling her tab. She
turned and said, Oh, it's you!

It's me, I said.

She smiled eagerly, tucking a coil of hair behind her ear. So, she
said, do you feel at home yet?

Not yet. I liked your poems.

Thanks! She finished signing her receipt and snapped the leather
booklet shut. I don't usually write poetry, at least not poetry that

should see the light of day, but these were more like little narratives. It took a long time to write them. I had to read a lot of Craigslist ads.

You have to dig through the trash to find the good stuff, I said.

That's true.

Do you ever read the *Pennysaver*? There's good stuff in it. If I'm feeling blocked, I read the *Pennysaver*.

She cocked her head and looked at me with a sudden curiosity. Are you a writer? Did you tell me that?

I'm trying to be, I said.

Are you in the master's program?

I'm just taking classes.

Oh, she said. She drew her brows together—estimating me with her eyes, it seemed.

What are you getting into now? I said.

Her expression brightened. I'm meeting some people down the street at Akiko's, the karaoke bar. You wanna come with? I gotta get out of this Renaissance fair bullshit.

She gestured to the door with her thumbs and hopped down from the barstool. I paid for my beer and we walked out together.

The night was cool, a whiff of smoke on the breeze—someone burning leaves. We had to pass the corner gas station where a lot of heroin addicts hung out. There'd been three overdose deaths in the bathroom in the last six months. There were bikers in the lot, their motorcycles rumbling and snorting. A panhandler asked us for money. I'd like to buy a blue slushie, he explained. There were track marks and bruises along his thin arms.

That's a good enough reason, Alma said. She fished around in her purse and dropped some change into his cupped hands.

Have a blessed night, the man said.

Save for the cursive pink neon glowing in the window, Akiko's was dark. A soundboard stood in the back corner, next to a makeshift stage with fake palm trees. A man was singing Tom Petty when we came in. He was surprisingly good and sang with genuine feeling, as if the addressee of the song could hear him, wherever she was in the world.

Alma found the people she was meeting—a towering, rail-thin

white dude named Jeff who had the most prominent Adam's apple I'd ever seen, and a girl named Margaret, who was small and had lustrous black hair hanging past her waist. Jeff was waiting for his boyfriend, a PhD student in mathematics, to show up. We're gonna do "Islands in the Stream," he explained to Alma, leaning in and shouting over the music.

I don't know that one, she said.

Kenny Rogers and Dolly Parton?

She shrugged. Sorry, I don't know my country music.

Jeff shook his head. What kind of self-respecting southerner are you?

There are two people ahead of me, Margaret said. I'm doing "My Heart Will Go On."

Can't wait, Alma said.

The reading was great, said Jeff.

I need a cigarette, Alma said, rummaging in her purse. She glanced at me. Oh, this is Owen, she said. He's a writer. Owen, meet everyone.

Hi Owen, they said, more or less in unison.

She gave up on finding one and looked up at me. Could I maybe bum one from you? she said, cringing.

Sure thing, I said.

We went out to the patio. There was another bar outside, with a thatch roof and a handful of people standing around. Someone had hash oil in a vape pen, the odor strong, like burnt butter and grass clippings.

Alma struggled to light her cig, flicking the wheel over and over. She turned her back to the breeze and got it lit finally, passed the lighter back to me. Strands of hair blew across her face and she gathered them with her fingers and tucked them back. She seemed cold. Her dress had fluttery sleeves, but her arms were still mostly bare. You could see how slender-waisted she was in the dress, how lithe, and I felt a rush of attraction.

I promised myself I wouldn't do this when I was a kid, she said, holding up the cigarette. Everybody smokes here though.

Highest cancer rates in the nation.

What part of Kentucky did you say you were from? she said.

Western—close to Paducah.

Right. Between Possum Trot and Monkey's Elbow.

Eyebrow, I said.

Ah, she said. I wrote it down in my notebook as "Monkey's Elbow."

It excited me to know she'd found our conversation at the party noteworthy.

Are there horses there? she said.

Some. It's not really horse country though.

What's there?

Tobacco, I said. Corn, soybeans, cattle. Fast food, churches, plants.

Like *plant* plants?

Like factories sort of.

What kind?

There's a lot, I said. There was USEC, the uranium plant. West-vaco, the paper mill. Westlake Chemical in Calvert City. Honeywell across the river in Metropolis. BelCo, where my stepdad works. They all make poison, basically. You could say we're the poisonous chemical capital of America.

She lifted her eyebrows and nodded, took a drag. The group of people behind us were talking about who they would kidnap, if they had to kidnap someone. They all seemed to agree that Bill Gates's daughter was the obvious choice, then one of them said, Wait, he has a daughter, right?

My ex worked at a tofu factory for like three weeks, she said. It was like a summer thing, when we were in college, but he was really into telling people about his "factory job," as if he'd worked in a steel mill or something. I was like, "Okay dude, it was fucking tofu and you quit after three weeks to work at a Panera."

We both laughed. Another whiff of the vaped weed drifted by. She scrunched her face and fake-coughed. I hate that, she said, meaning the smell. Anyway, that's the only person I know who's worked in a factory.

I find that surprising.

Is it though?

An awkward lull followed. I took a few drags and eavesdropped on the huddle of would-be kidnappers, who were discussing whether it would be fair to give Bill Gates's daughter some portion of the ransom.

So what else is there in Paducah, besides poisonous chemicals? she said. Family?

Yeah, they're all still there.

Do you write about them?

Sometimes.

So do you consider yourself more of a *regional* writer?

I'm not sure I know what that means.

If you were going to be introduced, would you want to be introduced as a "Kentucky writer"? Or would you prefer "American writer"?

Kentucky is America, I said. If you write about one, you're writing about the other.

But do you want to be thought of like that?

I didn't used to, I said. When I first started writing stories, I set them all in Westchester. I didn't want anyone to know where I was from.

Westchester?

That's where John Cheever set all his stories.

But he lived there. Had you ever *been* to Westchester?

Definitely not, I said.

She laughed. That's great, she said. Westchester. She crushed the cigarette against the sole of her boot and let it drop into a metal pail, where other filters were planted in the gray sand. At some point you changed your mind though? she said. You started writing about Kentucky?

You're supposed to write what you know. That's what I knew.

Well, good for you, she said. You found your material.

We went back inside, where the crowd was now shoulder to shoulder and the air was muggy with body heat. Margaret sang her song onstage, swishing her long hair and swaying from side to side. Conversation was impossible. We stood in the vicinity of Jeff and his boyfriend, shouting unimportant things to each other over the music occasionally.

When a half hour had passed, she leaned over to my ear and said, I'm going home I think.

I'll walk out with you, I said.

Stepping onto the sidewalk from the suffocation of the bar was a great relief. We walked without urgency. It wasn't the right direction for me, and at some point, when we'd been going a few minutes in silence, she asked, Which way are you?

That way, I said, pointing back. West.

We're going east.

If you go east far enough, you'll wind up in the west.

She rolled her eyes. My car's up here, she said. You walking? Driving?

I drove, but I should probably sober up.

I can give you a lift. You could get a ride to your car in the morning.

I said no thanks. Even if she'd been willing to go as far as the South End, I didn't want her to see that I lived in my grandfather's basement. I feel like walking awhile longer, I said.

She seemed surprised by this—a little disappointed, even. All right, she said. Well, maybe I'll walk, too. Where should we walk?

I told her I hadn't planned any particular destination. We'll just see where we end up, she said, and we started walking again in the same direction we'd been going. We passed the entrance to the Cave Hill cemetery, with its Corinthian clock tower, and followed a walkway that skirted the brick wall. Shards of colored glass were set in the cement along the top of the wall, and in the overhanging branches, the purring of cicadas could be heard, quieter now that summer had ended and the nights were brisk. Now and then, we'd pass a wrought-iron gate and through it glimpse the rolling lawn and the serried ranks of obelisks and headstones.

So you grew up in DC? I said, realizing suddenly that I hadn't asked her anything about her own life, really. Where she came from.

Alexandria, she said.

I knew very little about Alexandria, except that it was a wealthy suburb. Though she'd said she was from Virginia at our first meeting, for some reason I'd imagined an immigrant enclave in the city itself.

So what was Alexandria like?

She drew a deep breath and exhaled. What do you imagine, when you imagine Alexandria, Virginia?

I thought about it. I don't know, redbrick houses? Country clubs? I'm imagining a really affable golden retriever in every driveway.

That's not far off, she said, smiling. We had a nice house. The neighborhood was shady and pleasant. It all would've been very *Leave It to Beaver* if we hadn't been European. Technically I'm European, too, but naturalized.

Really, I said, though of course I knew this from Googling her name. From where at?

Sarajevo, she said. We're Bosniak. We left at the start of the war— my mother and me and my sister. My dad left a little later.

I let this hang in the air a moment. That must've been difficult, I said.

I have no memory of it, she said. But I suspect "difficult" would not begin to describe what it was like for my parents. Or my sister. She was five, so she remembers some of it.

So your earliest memories are here, in the States?

Yeah, in Queens, she said. We all lived with my grandparents in an apartment in Astoria, for like two years when I was four or five. Packed in like sardines. I remember having to sleep on a cot next to the radiator, and the radiator would hiss and knock. My sister told me there were little monsters living inside it, and they were whispering and banging around, trying to get out. That might be my earliest memory, actually. To this day, I have that thought whenever I hear a radiator knocking. I'm like, "There are the little monsters trying to get out."

She picked at her cuticles while she walked, her brow knitted. She seemed to be weighing whether to tell me more. They've become very assimilated now, she said. My dad loves Bruce Springsteen. He's been to see him live like three times.

Who doesn't love the Boss?

I could take him or leave him.

What?!

She laughed. My dad has this big fancy grill in our backyard, she said, and last Fourth of July, they had a little get-together with neighbors and friends—something they'd never, ever done. He has this CD he burned that's just labeled "USA." It's got, like, John Cougar Mellencamp, Johnny Cash, Bob Seger, and a whole lot of Bruce. My sister and I were standing there eating our hot dogs—beef hot dogs, I should say, they still don't eat pork—listening to the USA CD while our mother intermittently lit a sparkler, and my sister was like, "Name one thing more American than this moment."

We both laughed. I felt the competing desires, as I often did when meeting someone new, to know everything at once and to save it all for later. It was like the feeling one has reading a good book, the sensation of being propelled toward the end and at the same time wishing to linger.

We walked on a little further, and after a minute, she said, The dog, however, is not an affable golden retriever. She's a fussy Pomeranian named Daphne. My mom's dog, really. My dad had an aquarium with tiger barbs and tetras and angelfish. My older sister always had hermit crabs, for some reason. She'd get them in Virginia Beach, then they'd outgrow their shell and die. She never got them a replacement shell. It always seemed less to me like she was keeping a pet and more like she was imprisoning and torturing them.

What did you have?

I had books, she said. I was a lonely kid.

The stone wall of the cemetery became a fence, through which the undulating expanse of the grounds could be seen—the bluish garden lights, a dark row of poplars. One of the nearby headstones had glow-in-the-dark toys arranged at its foot, giving it the appearance of radioactivity. Did you know Colonel Sanders is buried in here? she said. I read about it in a Kentucky travel guide. People leave buckets of chicken on his grave, isn't that sad? What if that was your legacy? You were just the chicken guy. Not to mention the waste of food.

I'm sure the possums and other critters eat it.

Did you just say *critters*?

I guess I did.

What's the difference between a critter and a varmint?

I think they're in the same ballpark, I said. Did you know Colonel Sanders wasn't a real colonel?

No! she said, spreading her fingers over her breastbone, feigning shock.

I learned this recently.

Do you know what else I read in the travel guide? The word "Kentucky" means "dark and bloody ground." That's what the Cherokee called it. Sort of ominous, right?

I've heard that, I said, though I couldn't remember where. I seemed to recall that it was a myth—this idea that the land had been a more-or-less constant theater of war among the Native Americans and the early colonists—but I didn't say as much to her.

I actually thought of you when I read it, she said.

Why?

I thought you'd find it interesting, what with your simultaneous aversion and attraction to the state.

You remembered that?

Sure I did.

I felt glad to have made an impression. As we walked, I thought of how easy it would be, in terms of distance, to put my arm around her. She was right there. Her clothes were not what I would call sexy, but she was shapely enough that they couldn't conceal her fig-ure, the way the Pentecostal skirt she'd been wearing the night we met could not conceal the slope of her hips. I'd fantasized about her leading me to a back room. I thought about it then, as we walked together, close enough to feel each other's warmth.

What other weird words do you use? she said.

Weird?

Yeah, like vernacular. Besides "critter."

I don't know.

I'm going to listen from now on and keep track. If I notice any, I'll let you know.

Okay, I said, unsure if I had a choice in the matter.

Do you say "ain't"?

No.

What about "I reckon"?

Not typically. My granddad does though.

Does he have an accent?

Oh yeah.

You don't have much of an accent, she said. It's still there, but only when you say certain words. My mother knew no English whatsoever when she came over. My father said this was very humiliating for her, trying to communicate and being treated like a dolt when you're so well educated. She's a doctor. But now they have less of an accent than you have even.

I didn't like hearing this or thinking of myself as someone who had an accent. I'd worked for a long time to eradicate any hint of it. I traced this self-consciousness back to a single moment in childhood, when my sixth-grade history teacher heard me say "Washington" like "Warshington" and asked, Where's the *r* in that word? All my classmates laughed at me, and I resolved to change the way I spoke. But maybe this was only the narrative I'd come up with. Nothing ever has only one cause. Television was also to blame. Pop told me once, when I came back from college, that I talked like the people on TV. I took it as a high compliment, though it wasn't meant that way.

Count to eleven from nine, she said.

Why?

Just try it.

Nine, ten, eleven, I said.

Ten, she said, emphasizing the *e*. Not *tin,* like the metal. *Ten.*

Right, I said. Thanks for pointing that out.

No problem, she said. I'll add that to the list. Entry number one.

We reached the corner of the wall and continued on, passing rows of dim shops and restaurants. We went beneath a highway overpass, and on the other side, entered Irish Hill. It was a lot like Germantown, with its attendant shotgun houses and steep lawns and corner bars, only the people who'd settled there were Irish Catholic.

I could eat, she said. Could you eat?

I told her I could. We walked a few blocks further, till we found ourselves in Clifton, on Frankfort Avenue. The sidewalks were once again bustling with people—most of them drunk and rosy-cheeked, speaking brashly, stumbling about. We picked one of a string of bars and went through it to a screened-in patio with wooden tables. When the waitress came, we ordered onion rings, fried oysters, and two tallboys of Lone Star beer, which I'd never seen anywhere else in Kentucky. It was not very different from other kinds of cheap, metallic-tasting pilsners, but it was from Texas, and I wanted to drink it for the sake of novelty. Alma got what I got, assuming it was a local beer. She seemed confused when I told her it wasn't.

A little TV sat on a dish cart in the corner. A wildlife show was playing—wildebeests and giraffes and flocks of egrets on the savannah. They were all drinking from these shallow, muddy pools, and now and then a crocodile would emerge and drag one of them thrashing into the murk.

I asked her questions about her life, and as we drank, the stories poured forth. She seemed happy to tell them, as if the chance didn't come up that often. I could've listened to her all night. I'd spent too much of my life with people from Kentucky, whose failures and crutches and small joys were predictable, precisely because they were mine as well. For most of my life, I'd wanted to get away from that, which is to say I'd wanted to get away from myself. Being with Alma—listening to her—I could forget, momentarily, who I was and where I was from.

She told me about her life in New York, where she'd been living before the fellowship. She'd had an apartment, a walk-up in Greenpoint that she'd subleased to an old college roommate. She didn't say where she'd gone to school, but I got the sense it was someplace fancy. The apartment was above a cell phone store that never seemed to have customers. She had her writing desk next to the largest window, which gave her two hours of midmorning light, before the westering sun, having breached the rooftops across the street, vanished once again above her. I'm like an old cat, she said. I like to just sit in the sunlight and be warm and look out the window. Drink my coffee. I'm lucky if I write fifty words during those two hours.

She said she wrote, or tried to write, till about two or three o'clock, at which point she went for a walk if the weather allowed it. Down the street was a Polish bakery with glistening doughnuts in the window. The old women who worked there spoke Polish to each other and wore matching cornflower aprons. I saw Jack White there once, she said. He was eating an éclair.

Sometimes she walked for hours, she said. Once she even walked as far as Flushing and had to ask her grandparents to come get her in their old Volvo. She visited them most weekends in their small duplex in Astoria. These were her father's parents. Her mother's parents were dead—of natural causes, she added.

It's better than the flat where we all lived in the beginning, she said, but still small. They have a few antiques from Bosnia—just little things, what they could carry in their luggage and their plastic IOM bags, which was not much. I used to sit with my grandfather when I was little and have him show me the antiques and tell me the stories behind them, over and over, she said. He had pocket watches, some old, brittle Soviet books. He had a poster from the 1984 Olympics in Sarajevo—this man in red, skiing, which I thought was so cool. He had a black-and-white photograph of soldiers on a street corner, when the city was occupied by the Nazis. My grandmother had an embroidered hijab from her wedding, which she let me put on, and these porcelain figurines, of like a peasant boy and girl in folk costumes. I remember asking if that was her and my grandfather when they were little, and she laughed and laughed.

My parents have told them for years, "Come to DC," but they refuse, Alma said. Astoria is home to them. There are other Bosnians there, people they can speak the language with. They wouldn't really have that in DC. My parents, when they got here, wanted a fresh start. But my grandparents were too old. Why learn English when there are Bosnians here in Queens who understand us perfectly? When we can buy the foods we like and go to a mosque with people who believe what we believe? Of course, there are Serbs, and *Bosnian Serbs* in Astoria, too, which is very interesting to me. They eat the same foods, speak a similar language more or less, but the hatred is still there. Just a few months ago, someone graffitied the doors of the Cultural Center with a Serbian cross—you know what I'm talking about?

I shook my head.

It's a nationalist thing. But to spray-paint it on the doors, it's like a swastika, you know?

Jesus.

Yeah, it's crazy.

Do you go to mosque regularly? I said.

Hardly ever. It's more cultural, she said. It's like—what do you call Christians who only go to church on Christmas and Easter?

Christmas-and-Easter Christians.

She laughed. Right, well it's like that. A lot of European Muslims are like that. A lot of Turks, too.

So they're Ramadan-and-Eid Muslims.

Ramadan is a whole month, at the end of which is Eid al-Fitr, she said. And not even, really. I've never fasted for Ramadan. My father does, but my mother never has. Her family were intellectuals. Sarajevo was very cosmopolitan, according to my parents. She snapped her fingers, as if she suddenly remembered something. Fair-weather Christians, she said. That's the phrase I was trying to think of. Like a fair-weather friend, only the friend in this case is God, I guess.

We finished our fried oysters and wiped the grease from our fingers on our napkins. We sat back in easeful silence. It felt good to be sitting still after walking so long, cross-breezes passing gently through the patio screens.

I was supposed to write today, she sighed. I told myself I would, but I didn't. I haven't written anything in two weeks.

It must be a lot of pressure, I said. Having this fellowship. Being given all this time.

I wondered when that would come up. People are afraid to mention it.

That you're a writer?

She nodded.

They're probably intimidated, I said.

But not you.

I didn't know when I met you. Maybe I never would've talked to you if I'd known you were such a big deal.

She rolled her eyes. You were pretty drunk, she said.

I didn't know anyone at the party. Getting drunk seemed like the thing to do.

And you thought I looked approachable?

I don't remember, honestly.

I do, she said. I remember the first thing you said to me. You said, "Howdy."

No.

Yes!

I've never said "howdy" in my life.

You did that night.

Then what did I say?

You said you didn't know anyone, that you'd just moved back from—somewhere. Colorado?

Yeah.

Then you said the thing about your predicament.

I didn't call it that, surely.

Yes, you did. You called it your "fundamental predicament."

I groaned. Why did you keep talking to me?

She twisted her mouth to keep from smiling. We each took a drink of our beers.

Well, maybe you'll get some writing done in the morning, I said.

Maybe so.

I have to work in the morning.

She clicked on her phone's display. It's almost midnight, she said.

I'll be all right.

Do you mean you have to get up and write? Or real work?

Real work, I guess.

What do you do?

Campus groundskeeping, I said. It's like work-study sort of. I work for them, and they pay my tuition.

Is that like landscaping?

More involved than that, I said. I trim trees and drag brush mostly.

That sounds not fun.

It's not particularly, but I've had worse jobs.

Like what? She leaned forward, brow furrowed, and rested her chin on her clasped hands. Some part of me relished recounting my history of shitty odd jobs. I'd painted houses, flipped burgers at a Hardee's, shelved children's books at a library. Before the forestry job in Denver, I'd washed dishes at a Thai restaurant in Boulder. Most of the money I made—especially in Colorado—went to buy beer or pills or newly legalized weed. My family's euphemism for this was "partying," as in, *When are you going to quit partying and get your act together?* I'd heard some version of this question many times. But it hadn't felt much like a party. More than anything, I'd felt pathetic and lonely, and this loneliness had reached a kind of unbearable fever pitch. The tendency was to glamorize, to try and make it all seem rugged and blue-collar, when really, it had been difficult and repetitive and often humiliating. I glamorized, then I felt guilty for glamorizing. This was always the pattern.

I've cut down trees, painted houses, cleaned toilets, I said. You name it, I've probably done it.

She smirked and pulled apart an onion ring. I bet you can't wait to put all that in your author bio, she said.

I laughed, looked down at my hands in my lap. I could feel the prickle of blood rising to my cheeks.

Hey, no reason to be embarrassed, she said. It sounds pretty good, actually. Especially the last part. "You name it, I've done it." That could be your signature line, if you were, like, in local-access commercials where you offered up your services. You'd point at the camera and say, "You name it, I've done it."

She took a drink of beer and made a face. This isn't very good beer, she said.

No, I said, not really. It's a novelty beer.

She studied the writing on the can, as if she might find some evidence there for why it tasted the way it did.

What jobs have you had? I said.

Me? She seemed a little shocked that I'd asked, as if it were in poor taste. You know, not much, really. I did a little academic consulting after college. I still do that a little bit, for a handful of clients.

So what does that mean?

It's like tutoring, sort of, but for kids who are trying to get into

Ivy League schools. I help edit their college essays, which basically just means writing their essays for them.

And they pay you?

Their parents pay me. You wouldn't believe how desperate some people are for their kids to go to a good school.

That doesn't bother you? Ethically?

No, she said. She took a gulp of beer—too much. She had to hold it in her cheeks and swallow it a little at a time. When it was down, she brought her fist to her chest and suppressed a burp. I mean, yeah, sometimes, she said. But at least I'm not working at McKinsey or Goldman Sachs or something, you know?

I guess. Do you know people who work at Goldman Sachs?

Sure, she said, as if this were usual. As if everybody knew somebody who worked at Goldman Sachs. The helicopter moms are gonna pay someone. Anyway, it's not like I do it very much anymore. It's just a side hustle now.

I don't know whether I'd consider my side hustle to be writing or groundskeeping, I said. I guess groundskeeping, since I take it less seriously. But then again, it takes up more of my time.

When you were doing all those shitty jobs, did the knowledge that you could use it for material make it worthwhile? In other words, did you think, it's okay that I'm cleaning toilets, because actually I'm an undercover writer?

I didn't feel like an undercover writer.

What did you feel like?

I felt like a failure, I said.

The lines in her face went slack, and she looked at me with sudden pity. I hated that this was what I'd elicited. I turned my eyes to the TV, where a zebra was being dismembered by hyenas.

Do you still feel that way? she said, a new shyness to her voice.

I try not to think about it. Not really.

A light rain had begun to fall, pattering on the tin roof. People from outside—smokers—huddled in the doorway, hair and shoulders damp. A lavender bush was growing outside the screen, near our table, and as the rain dappled the dried flowers, their fragrance grew heady and pleasant. I breathed deeply through my nostrils and looked at her sitting across from me—at her almond eyes and her long, graceful neck—at the pale freckles across the bridge of her nose. She looked, at times, like she'd stepped out of a Modigliani painting. We should go somewhere, I said.

What do you mean?

What I meant was that I wanted to go home with her, but I knew the timing wasn't right. We didn't know each other well enough. Still, I felt a sense of inertia now, as if we'd set something inevitable in motion, something that would continue without much effort.

Let's keep walking, I said.

It's raining.

It'll stop, I said, and sure enough, as we settled our check at the bar and drained the last of our beers, the rain ceased.

We walked east down Frankfort Avenue, faint breezes churning the rain-cooled air. Now and then we'd pass a bar with a crowd out front, murmuring in a haze of tobacco smoke, and someone would ask us for a light. When the sidewalk crowds thinned out, I took her hand in mine and she let me, and suddenly we were walking with a new, quiet closeness.

It's chilly, she said at one point, and I put my arm around her waist and tugged her close. She put her head on my shoulder and seemed to sigh, and I thought, maybe I'm wrong. Maybe she *will* take me home. Maybe whatever is pulling us together is stronger than I'd supposed. But she drew away after a minute or two and stopped in the middle of the sidewalk. She looked up at me expectantly. I might've kissed her, but this wasn't what her expression seemed to invite.

I should tell you something, she said.

We'd stopped by the entrance to an alleyway, where two men in stained aprons sat on a stoop, scrolling on their cell phones. Muffled music drifted out from a kitchen's open door behind them—accordions and Spanish singing.

I'm sort of seeing someone, she said.

Sort of?

She clenched her eyes shut, as if it were physically painful to talk about. Not sort of, definitely, she said. For a couple months now.

And it's serious?

I don't know. We're together, and I like him, I think. I do like him.

You sound really committed.

I just don't know if we should be getting all cozy like this.

But you want to?

She looked away from me to the men in the alley, chewing her lip. Yeah, she said quietly, but I'm already in this thing. We just established that it's official or whatever, and I can't just unestablish it. And it's good. It's a good relationship. I'm happy with it.

My ears and cheeks had been hot but now the blood was leaching away. All right, I said. Whatever you want.

I'm sorry. Maybe we can just hang out, you know? Without expectations. I don't really know anyone here.

That's fine, I said. I wasn't expecting anything to happen anyhow.

You weren't?

Well, I said, looking down at my shoes.

So bashful, she said.

We split an Uber back to our cars, and when the driver let us out at The Bard's Town, it seemed impossible to me that she'd been reading there that very same night. It felt like weeks ago. I thought about her poem, how the Harley rider had tattooed what he wanted on his arms, and what he wanted, I guessed, was the beautiful Hardee's girl, with her booty shorts and her yellow tank top. That the author of the Craigslist post could not have guessed where his words would end up.

Our cars were parked in opposite directions, and we stood for a minute, trying to figure how to part ways gracefully. Swift clouds passed over the moon. I could almost discern the scent of her shampoo where her head had rested against my shoulder—apricot or peach. I should go, I said. I have to be up early.

Right, she said. Keeper of the Grounds. Well, I'm this way.

Where at? I can walk you over if it's far.

That's another weird thing you say, she said. "Where at." Most people just say "where." I'll add it to the list.

What list?

The list of weird vernacular that you use.

Oh right, I said. Thanks.

No problem, she said. And no, it's just a block. I can walk it alone.

Do I hug you now? Or would that be crossing the line?

I'd meant this as a joke, but it came off as derisive. She gave me a scolding look. A hug would be fine, she said, and we hugged briefly. Maybe we can go for another walk soon? she said. In the daylight?

We exchanged numbers and she walked away, waving behind her as if she knew, without having to look, that I'd be watching her. She reached her car—an old beater Honda—and I saw the taillights blink as she pressed the key fob. I turned and began the long journey home.

I WENT FOR A DRIVE THE NEXT DAY. JUST MOVING TO BE moving. To see what I could see. What I saw mostly were knobby hills and high-tension lines, billboards for personal injury lawyers and adult video outlets. My mother called as I was on my way back. I lowered the volume on NPR and answered, though I didn't particularly want to. When I'd moved to Colorado, I'd borrowed $800 from my mother. I never repaid it. She'd never brought it up, and neither had I. But it loomed over our relationship—this debt. I told myself I'd repay her as soon as I got ahead, but there was always some unforeseen expense, some reason I could give myself for putting it off.

When are you coming home? she said, first thing.

I don't have any imminent plans, I said. I'm getting settled into this job.

Groundskeeping.

That's right.

She made a hard-to-decipher noise in her throat. Well, she said, the reason I'm calling is to tell you that Greg just found out BelCo is closing their plant.

Greg, who my mother married a year after my parents divorced, had worked at BelCo for twenty-odd years. It had always been mysterious to me, what BelCo made exactly. Whenever I asked, Greg's stock answer was, Various synthetics. Whatever the case, he was a machinist by trade, and the irony of the plant closing was that he'd spent the last five years improving automation, thereby lessening the need for human labor. They supported Trump, chiefly because of his promise to bring back American manufacturing. Any hope I may have had for them to renounce their support was now, I knew, completely gone.

There's been talk of the plant closing for a few years now, she said, but we hoped it would be the Murfreesboro plant rather than Calvert City.

I'm sorry to hear that, I said.

Yeah, well, she said. We'll be all right. Greg'll have till June of next year. It's the floor workers he's worried about, mostly. They'll be let go by Christmas.

What will you do? In June, I mean.

Hard to say, she said. Greg'll look for work around here and over the Tennessee line. We might look into selling the house and moving into something smaller. Who knows, maybe I'll go back to work.

Do you want to go back to work?

Not particularly, she sighed.

A long silence passed. I turned off the highway onto the frontage road, passing a Walmart and an RV dealership. The hills were gentler here, rising into smooth humps. Beams of light shot through the clouds.

So when am I gonna get to read what you've been writing? she said.

I haven't really written anything yet, I said. It's just bits and pieces. Journal entries.

You've gotta write a bestseller and support me in my old age.

I'll get right on that.

Or you could become a high school teacher.

So you've said.

Have you talked to your dad?

Yeah, I talked to him not long ago.

I guess you got the latest on Bonnie?

Yeah, he told me. Radiation again.

She sighed. So sad, she said. Course, you know we never got along, but I hate to see the woman suffer. They basically have to kill you to kill the cancer.

It is sad, I agreed. I didn't know what else to say.

She sighed a third time. My son is twenty-eight, she said.

What about it?

I became a mother at twenty-eight. I had you that year.

I know.

We'd already bought a house and been married five years.

Okay.

And here you are homeless.

I'm not homeless.

You would be, she said, if not for your grandfather. You'd be on the streets.

I doubt that.

Well, what do you plan to do?

I don't know.

That's your answer?

It's not an answer.

Exactly, she said. That's exactly the problem. I don't want you living off his kindness like Cort.

I have to go, I said, suddenly exhausted.

What do you have to do that's so pressing?

Maybe I have to fill out rental applications.

Don't be a smart aleck.

I have to go, I said, and hung up.

I TOLD JAMES ABOUT JUNGLE NARRATIVES ON OUR LUNCH break Monday. Sounds potentially racist, he said.

Probably, I said. Yet to be seen.

What are you reading? he said, chewing his usual bologna sandwich.

We started with *Heart of Darkness*.

That doesn't bode well.

We'd been trimming a silver maple on the lawn of a university guesthouse. The guesthouses were fieldstone cottages on campus,

divided into furnished apartments and rented out to visiting profes-
sors and lecturers. As we were working that morning, the curtains
parted intermittently in one of the upstairs windows, and a man's
face would peer out briefly. All the dead had been cut, but some of
the limbs were too large for the chipper and would have to be sawn
into segments with a chainsaw.

I tossed my apple core into the chipper bed and stowed my trash
and water bottle in the truck. Rando had eaten more of his beef
stew. Evidently it hadn't set well. He leaned his shoulder against the
chipper, clutching his belly, wincing. The gurgle and squelch of his
digestion was audible.

Jesus Christ, Rando, James said, snapping on his chaps. Bring
something else to eat, man.

I'm fine, Rando said. He spat in the grass, took the soft pack of
Pall Malls from his breast pocket, and shook loose a smoke. Beef
doesn't really go bad. If it was chicken, then I'd worry.

Beef *does* very much go bad, I said.

He lit his cig, clawed his fingers through his sweat-soaked hair.
I'm fine, he said again.

The professor's white, I assume? James said.

Yeah, I said. I let down the pickup's tailgate and took out the
sixteen-inch Husqvarna. I removed the orange plastic sheath,
checked the gas. It was a good, light saw. Anything heavier was
rarely needed for the work we were doing, though we had a larger
logging saw with a twenty-eight-inch bar. It had been four months
since I'd used a chainsaw. I turned it over in my hands, adjusting
to the heft of it, clicking the chain brake back and forth a couple
times.

James fogged his safety glasses with his breath and used his shirt
to wipe the lenses. The problem with Conrad is that he saw Africa
as a place that was acted on by history, rather than a place that created history, he said. We were always the victims. That's Achebe's
critique.

Maybe we'll read Achebe.

I would hope so, James said. Why don't you just drop it?

I'd feel too guilty. This class is like the guy's pet project. He's
been thinking about it since his father died in the Peruvian jungle

ten years ago, and if I drop, it'll leave like three other people in the class.

Maybe he should've chosen a different pet project.

Y'all ever see those old Tarzan movies with Johnny Weissmuller? Rando said. Black-and-white pictures. Now *those* were *wild,* dude. They've got that scene where he wrestles a fuckin lion. Probably a stunt double, but still, the *lion* didn't have a stunt double. It was a real lion.

What does Tarzan have to do with anything? I said.

Rando turned up his palms. Hey, I'm just saying, you're talking jungle narratives, first thing that comes to mind, for me, is Tarzan, king of the jungle.

I don't think we'll be studying Tarzan movies, I said.

Never know.

He wrestled a lion? James said.

Oh yeah dude, Rando said. How do you think he got his fur loincloth?

I started the saw and began cutting a limb balanced on the chipper bed. It never failed to give me a little rush—the vibrations running up through my arms, the smell of smoke and heated wood, sawdust spewing from the back of the blade. The lopped-off pieces thumped in the grass and rolled to a stop. When I had the branch down to a narrow stick, Rando fired the chipper and engaged the drum, and with a grinding, teeth-chattering roar, the limb was drawn, lurching, through the frayed rubber flaps and into the dark maw, till it had dematerialized completely.

When we'd shut off the drum and the chipper was running in neutral, I noticed a man standing on the porch of the guesthouse, clutching the collar of his bathrobe to his throat. His thin gray hair was mussed, and he looked as though he'd just stumbled from bed. We all stared at him. His lips were moving. I motioned for Rando to kill the chipper. James lifted his earmuffs and said, Can we help you?

I was just saying, is there any way to turn those down? the man shouted.

Turn what down? he said.

The chainsaws, is there a way to turn them down? I'm trying to work. I work at home.

James looked back at us like, *You hearing this guy?* I shrugged.

He means the volume control, James, Rando said.

The what?

The volume control knob? That's on every chainsaw?

Oh, James said, catching on. He turned back to the man. You must mean the volume modulator?

Well, yes, the man said, uncertainty in his voice. I guess that's what I mean.

You want us to turn down the *volume* of our chainsaws using the *volume modulator knob*—that's your request?

Yeah, the man said. If you could.

Of course, sir, James said. We'll make those adjustments ASAP.

The man smiled affably, gave us the thumbs-up. When he'd gone back inside, we all had a good laugh.

WHEN I GOT HOME LATER AND PULLED INTO THE GRAVEL drive, Pop was lying in the front yard, Uncle Cort crouched beside him. My heart quickened. I left the car running and jogged over.

My legs give out, Pop said.

I can't lift him with my back the way it is, said Cort, who was shirtless. His pale belly sagged over low-slung jeans and a belt with a turquoise buckle.

What were you doing, Pop? I said.

He tried to rise up on his elbows but didn't have the strength and let his head fall back against the ground. He swallowed hard and blinked, staring up at the sky. My legs just give out, he said again. The weed-grown yard was bordered on one side by a low, cinder-block wall. Along the top, in the cavities of the cement blocks, Pop had planted purple zinnias and bell peppers and cherry tomato vines. A trowel and a ripped bag of topsoil lay in the grass nearby.

I can't lift him, Cort said.

You said that already.

Well, I can't. He stood from his crouch unsteadily and looked at me, thumbs in his belt loops. He had the facial expression of a person trying to decipher a foul odor.

Pop was frail—140 pounds at most. Still, not nothing. I'd gone to the library after work, and it was twilight now. Cicadas trilled in the big bur oak overhead. On the horizon, past the rooftops of houses and the Shell station sign with the price of gas, clouds like big pink mushrooms were gathered in the afterglow.

All right, let's try this, I said. I moved behind him, sat him up, and hooked my arms under his. When I got him standing, his thin legs quivered and collapsed. I sat him back down on his butt, caught my breath. Okay, I said. Cort, could you get his feet?

I told you, I *can't* lift anything.

What did you do when he fell before I got here?

I called the neighbors, Cort said. And besides, he wasn't falling as much then.

I sighed. All right, Pop, I'm just gonna pick you up and carry you.

You sure you can? Pop said.

I think so.

I squatted, hooked my left arm under his knees and my right around his shoulders. It occurred to me that there was probably a better way to do this—a fireman's carry, or whatever they did with wounded soldiers in battle—but I didn't know the technique. So I carried him like that, the way a groom carries his bride across the threshold, taking stutter steps, breathing through clenched teeth. I eased him down into his recliner, where he adjusted his T-shirt and smoothed his hair on the sides. Thanks, pard, he said, unable to meet my eyes.

It's all right, I said. But don't go mess around in the yard and get so tired you can't stand.

His hands were trembling a little. He wedged them between his thighs and nodded. Roger that, he said.

Cort came in a moment later and said, You happy, Dad?

Happy about what?

You got your attention for the day, created your little drama.

Cort, I said. Come on.

The pepper plant on the end had wilted, Pop said. I's just trying to dig it up.

Cause that's necessary, Cort said.

I wanted to do it. Who said anything about necessary?

All right, Cort, I said. Let him be.

Cort shook his head and stalked off down the hallway to his room. I sat in the other recliner on the edge of the cushion, hands dangling between my knees. You had anything to eat yet? I asked.

He shook his head.

What sounds good?

I'd planned to reheat that Mickey D's from last night, he said.

I'll do it, you hang tight.

I heated the half burger in the microwave, and through the wall, even over the hum, I could hear Cort playing his video game. I could never remember what the game was called, but the gist was that you were a little guy in an open world. You started with nothing, then you acquired tools and supplies and you went around building things—castles and fortresses with all kinds of defense mechanisms in place. There were other little guys who kept trying to take what you had, and you had to fight them off and rebuild what they destroyed. You were always in a hurry, building or rebuilding, defending what you had, acquiring new resources. It seemed exhausting.

Why can't he just relax? I'd asked Cort once. Rest on his laurels?

Cort had sighed extravagantly. Then you lose, he'd said. What would be the point? Why even play?

I DISCOVERED THAT WE *WERE* WATCHING TARZAN MOVIES IN Jungle Narratives. Two of them, in fact. We were also watching Herzog's *Fitzcarraldo,* and *Burden of Dreams,* Les Blank's documentary about the making of *Fitzcarraldo.* Film, Tony explained, had been as important as the novel in the development and proliferation of jungle narratives.

Now, I know what you're thinking, he said. You're thinking, "Tony, is Tarzan, king of the jungle, really so vital in that lineage?" And the answer is yes, absolutely.

It was too late, at that point, for me to drop the class. I was in it for the long haul.

Casey caught up to me after class and we smoked a cigarette outside by the hedges. Campus was empty and dark, save for the cones of light that shone down from sodium lamps onto the sidewalks. A sprinkler was chittering somewhere out of sight.

What a shitshow, Casey said. He took off the Reds hat, tousled his flattened hair.

I know, I said.

Tarzan?

I know.

We stood in silence for a minute, listening to the sprinkler. A woman walked by alone on the other side of the quad, and when I coughed, she jerked her head our way, startled, and walked a little faster, her heels echoing off the high brick walls.

That girl in class is cute though, Casey said.

Joanna? I can't tell with all the layers.

She's into ventriloquism and puppet shows, he said, as if these were ordinary things to be into. My friend knows her. Friend of a friend, really. He gestured with his cigarette in hand as he spoke, drawing arcs of light.

She looks the part, I said.

I just have this feeling she makes weird noises in bed.

And that's a positive?

Hell yes.

I smiled and shook my head. I became conscious suddenly that he was younger than me, by five or six years I'd guess, if not more, and so was Joanna. This seemed to be the case with most of my peers. I was twenty-eight. Was this old for grad school? I didn't like the idea of being old. It made all sorts of things problematic.

So are you a writer? he said.

Yeah, I said, a little too eagerly. You?

Yeah, I dabble, he said. I was hoping this class would have more writing and a little less jungle. Pretty heavy on the jungle so far. You from Louisville?

Western Kentucky originally.

Sweet, sweet, he said. Well, Louisville's a good town for writers. My girlfriend's a writer. Most of my friends are either writers or musicians. The class isn't representative of the larger scene.

Maybe we'll get to the workshop component soon.

Man, I hope so.

I dropped my filter and ground it with my boot. Well, I'll see you later, I said, and for some reason, I shook his hand. I don't know why I'm shaking your hand, I said.

He shook it vigorously with an expression of faux seriousness. Yes, yes, he said. Very well my good man.

I laughed and started off toward the parking garage. When I got to the car, I texted James that Tarzan had been added to the syllabus. *LOL Rando was right!!* he texted back. The garage was empty and bright. I sat there with the engine running, phone in my lap, wishing I had something to say to Alma. I even composed a few attempts, but nothing seemed right. Why was I wasting my time? She was with someone, and even if she wasn't, she would find out eventually where I lived, that I was dead broke. You should focus on writing, I thought. You know how to be alone. You're good at it. What's so wrong with being alone?

THE SIGN IN THE WINDOW SAID MAKE AMERICA GREAT AGAIN. It was Cort's window, facing the street.

I set my safety glasses and hard hat on the kitchen counter, poured a glass of water, and drank it at the sink. My clothes smelled like gasoline. Dried blood was smeared on my knuckles from the razor bark of a honey locust. How was your day? Pop called out from his recliner.

Is Cort home?

Well, Pop said, I reckon he's back there in his room.

I went down the hallway and opened Cort's door without knocking. It was the first time I'd really been in his room since I moved in. The back wall, above his headboard, was covered with magazine clippings and sheets of paper, upon which he'd typed up and printed little motivational aphorisms. The clippings were of dapper-looking men in suits, cut from *GQ*. The printed aphorisms were all clichés or overused quotations. *A journey of a thousand miles begins with a single step. If you're going through hell, keep going—Winston Churchill.*

The righteous indignation I'd felt upon seeing the MAGA sign deflated a little, but not enough to abandon my mission. He was sitting at his computer desk, playing his game. He wore some kind of headset and didn't bother to turn around. Can I help you? he said.

I want you to take the sign down.

Don't think so.

I'm not asking.

This is my room, and by extension my window, with which I can do whatever I want.

It affects me, I said.

You don't believe in the message? He chuckled and shook his head, still facing the monitor. On the screen, his little guy had a pixelated mallet and was scurrying around a pyramid, knocking pieces off.

I walked back to the living room and stood over Pop, who was eating saltines from a sleeve and watching *Bonanza.* I want Cort to take down the sign in his window, I said.

I heard Cort say, Unfuckingbelievable. His swivel chair squeaked, followed by footsteps. Soon he was standing at the entrance of the hallway.

What sign? Pop said.

It says "Make America Great Again."

What is that supposed to mean?

It signals to the world that you're a dumbass.

I'm not taking it down, Cort said. It's my room.

You don't pay rent, I said.

Neither do you, he said.

Okay, then it should be Pop's decision. Pop, do you want a sign in the window that tells the world we're racists and dumbasses?

His eyes moved uncertainly between me and Cort. Well, he said, flicking a saltine crumb from his chest hair, it's Cort's room, so I don't see why he can't put up whatever sign he wants. He doesn't come to your room and tell *you* what you can put up.

Exactly, Cort said. Thank you.

It says something about the house. It says something about all of us, not just Cort.

What does it say? That we're patriotic?

Exactly, Dad, Cort said. That's exactly what it says.

I stood there with my jaw clenched. I wanted to storm into his room, grab the sign, and tear it to pieces. Instead, I picked up the Civil War bayonet and stabbed it into the phone book. The point was sharper than I imagined. It went all the way through and stuck in the end table. Pop flinched and looked at the upright blade, astounded. Right away, I felt like an idiot.

That was stupid, I said.

What are you doing!?

I don't know, I'm sorry.

That's my phone book!

I tried to pull it out, which took some doing. The book rose with it, sliding off the blade and tumbling to the floor. Pop shook his head.

Everybody just needs to cool their jets, y'all hear me? Cool em!

Sorry, I said.

Ruin my damn phone book, he mumbled, retrieving it from the floor. He stuck his pinkie through the hole and wiggled it. Just cool the jets, all right? he said, though Cort was already walking away.

Got it, I said. Jets cooled.

In the basement, whatever anger had been knotted in my chest fell loose, replaced by sadness. I couldn't decide whether I was really upset about the sign, or only embarrassed to be associated with it. Clearly, Cort was in some kind of pain. It was easy for me to forget this. If I could forget, I could pretend that it was solely his fault— the way he was. A puritanical impulse, inherited from my parents no doubt. Who knew what the sign even meant to him? It wasn't a thesis or an argument. It was just another crude expression of his anger. A middle finger raised to everyone whose life had gone better than his. This was no excuse, of course. But when I thought of it this way, I could almost understand it.

HERZOG'S FITZCARRALDO WAS ABOUT A MAN NAMED FITZCARRALDO who wanted to build an opera house in Iquitos. In order to secure the funds, he turned to the harvest of rubber, and in his quest, forced a tribe of natives to move a three-hundred-ton steamship over an isthmus. We watched *Burden of Dreams* the following week, which Tony called an "ouroboros." In one scene, Herzog stood awkwardly with his arms folded against a backdrop of dense foliage and addressed the camera directly, his eyes haggard and vacant. He said that the only harmony in the jungle was the harmony of collective and overwhelming murder—that it was a suffocating density of fornication and death and growth.

At home, I stretched out in the basement with an ice pack on my knee and put on *North by Northwest.* If there was ever a palate cleanser for the grotesquery of Klaus Kinski, it was Cary Grant. I dozed off early in the movie. It must have been 2 a.m. when Alma called. I answered groggily, not yet knowing who it was. I hadn't attached her name to the number.

You answered! she said.

Alma?

I'm sorry, let me start by saying that. I know it's—what time is it?

Like two.

Jesus, okay. Then I'm really sorry. You probably work in the morning.

It's fine. I sat up and blinked, my head still numb with sleep. The ice in the pack had melted to warm water on my knee. The movie had ended long ago, leaving only the low shush of static on the screen.

Fuck, she said, then hiccupped. She was drunk, that was clear, but something about it seemed a little theatrical, like she had to pretend, to me or to herself, that she was drunker than she actually was in order to justify a 2 a.m. phone call.

Where are you? I said.

I'm home. I had some people over earlier, but they just left. Where are you?

I looked around at the dim basement—the platoon of beer cans in the corner, black banana peels on paper plates, stained coffee cups. Pallid moonlight slanting down from the window. Home, I said.

Right. You were sleeping.

Bingo.

Well, I was just thinking about you. I didn't expect you to answer, honestly, but now that you have, I'm glad to hear your voice.

It's good to hear you, too.

I had an argument with someone today. I was under the mistaken impression that Kentucky was in the Confederacy, but this person said that it wasn't, that actually it was a border state or something. It wasn't really an argument, more like a brief dispute settled by Wikipedia, but it made me think of you. It seemed like something you would know.

Yeah, Kentucky was neutral. Plenty of slaveholders here though.

Right, she said. Well, sorry to bother you.

No bother.

Let's go on that walk soon, yeah? I'm serious.

Anytime.

When I'd hung up, I lay back and stared at the ceiling, unable now to sleep. I heard the whine of floorboards, back and forth above me. Someone pacing. It had to be Pop—it was his room. I listened to the creak of his footsteps for a long time, trying to ease back into sleep. Pacing from one point to another. Moving just to be moving.

JAMES TEXTED ME THAT WEEKEND AND ASKED IF I WANTED to go to a bar in Germantown called Schadenfreude. It's where everybody goes, he assured me.

I didn't have a closet in the basement, only a portable clothing rack. I stood in front of the rack for a long time after supper, scraping the metal hangers back and forth along the bar, trying to decide which of my shirts was the most "hip." Most of my nice shirts I'd had since high school. They were plaid and came from places like Dillard's or the Gap. The rest were work flannels or paint-spattered sweatshirts. I needed something vintage.

I went upstairs and found Pop watching an episode of *Gunsmoke*. He didn't have his false teeth in, so his jaw looked collapsed, his lips drawn inward over the gums. The end table was crowded with coffee mugs and glasses with the remnants of crumble-in. I'd do the dishes first thing tomorrow, I told myself.

Can I borrow one of your shirts? I said.

He peered at me, confused. One of my shirts?

Yeah.

What for? You spill something?

To wear, I said. I'm going out.

In one of my shirts?

Yeah, if you don't mind.

He gave me a troubled look, then cocked his eyebrow and said, Well, I can't see why not.

I rummaged through the shirts in his closet. They were soft from years of wear, and they all had his smell—an old person smell, though it couldn't be reduced to just that. It was complex, with hints of aftershave and sweat and medicinal ointments. I found what I was looking for—a cream-colored shirt printed with tiny crosses. Judging by the tags, it had been made sometime in the 1970s.

I put it on with my slimmest pair of jeans and drank a glass of water at the kitchen sink, waiting for James to call. Cort came out, popped open his pill organizer at the counter, and dry swallowed a gabapentin and two Roxicodone tablets. He noticed my presence and ran his bloodshot eyes over me, head to toe. What's this getup? he said.

I'm going out.

To a costume party?

To a bar in Germantown.

I used to eat in Germantown sometimes. Bunch of freaks and weirdos living there now.

Do you need something, Cort?

He pointed to the fridge. Just cheese dip, he said. He opened the refrigerator door, took out a jar of queso, and heated it in the microwave. He kept his eyes on me the whole time, then took the jar to his room.

It was nearly ten when James called. I jogged out to his car, which turned out to be a minivan. Nice ride, I said, as I closed the door and situated myself.

It was my mom's, he said.

Spacious.

He shifted into drive and goosed the accelerator, running a stop sign. On the interstate, he weaved through traffic, pushing ninety. Soon, the city glimmered ahead of us. It was not much of a skyline, but it was heartening to me nonetheless every time I saw it. Banners with the portraits of famous Louisville natives were draped over the facades of buildings—Muhammad Ali, Diane Sawyer, Jennifer Lawrence. The lights on the JFK Bridge shifted between purple and pink and green, staining the tousled surface of the Ohio River where the blurred city was reflected.

My girlfriend works there, James said, pointing to Joe's Crab Shack. It was on the riverfront, next to an old paddle-wheel steamboat that had been turned into a museum.

I didn't know you had a girlfriend, I said.

Her name's Taylor. I think she cheated on me with one of her coworkers.

You think?

It was never confirmed. It's all good now though, we worked through it.

I didn't know what to say to this. I lit a cigarette, cracked the window. How's school going? I said, wanting to change the subject.

Mostly working on my thesis.

What's it about?

Foreign policy during the Eisenhower administration. All our problems—all the shit we got into in Southeast Asia and Iraq and Afghanistan—can be traced back to the Eisenhower years. That postwar period, you know?

Totally, I said. I had no idea whether this was true, but it sounded plausible.

A minute or two of silence passed before James said, He's a crab sheller.

Who?

The guy she may have slept with, at Joe's. His only job is to sit there and de-shell crabs, all fuckin day. Name's Vincent. Guy spent a year in jail for robbing a convenience store.

Okay.

Here I am, working my ass off, getting a degree, and she wants to fuck around with this loser who's elbow deep in crab shells all day. Explain that to me.

I don't know, maybe—

It's whatever. We worked through it. I don't even care.

We took the parkway, bumping hip-hop, veering northwest at some point into Germantown. He didn't really slow down, though the pavement was rutted with potholes, and he paid little mind to stop signs. The minivan juddered along, shocks squeaking. I braced myself with the grab handle above the door. We passed weatherboard shotgun houses and corner bars with neon in the windows. We passed union halls. PLUMBING AND CONSTRUCTION SUPPLY. CUSTOM EXHAUST. Blue tarps over pickup trucks. WELDING EQUIPMENT CO. We passed brick warehouses with shattered windows. Rainbow murals. Graffitied dumpsters. Coils of razor wire on fences. Young people smoking on stoops, walking their dogs. Tattooed arms. Girls with Joan Jett hair. Freaks and weirdos, as Cort called them. I tried to pay attention to all of it as it blurred past us.

A crowd of people stood in front of Schadenfreude, talking and smoking. Music pulsed inside. It was an old building, white paint flaking from the bricks. A FALLS CITY BEER sign hung above the door, a Louisville beer that had gone extinct and recently been revived.

We squeezed through the crowd, showed our IDs to the checker. The main room was not large, but the tables had been pushed aside and people were dancing in the middle of the scuffed parquet floor. A DJ stood behind two turntables in the back, removing records from their sleeves, bobbing his head slightly. On a giant screen behind him, an episode of *The Smurfs* was projected, only in slow motion, and interspersed sporadically with clips of '80s horror movies. Papa Smurf would be talking and gesturing at a snail's pace in a forest of toadstools, then you'd see a teenage girl screaming and running barefoot in the woods. The horror clips were never overtly violent, but you knew they were from horror movies, and there was something almost more ominous about them taken out of context and juxtaposed against the Smurfs.

We went to the bar and waited a long time for two tallboys of Coors, then we leaned against the brass rail, kind of nodding our heads to the music and pouring beer down our throats so we'd be loose enough to dance eventually. James pointed out people he knew, most of whom were in the music scene or were grad students at Ashby or the University of Louisville.

That's Karen, he said. She's doing a rhetoric PhD. That's Lucy over there waiting for the bathroom. She's a trip. That guy, Micah, is a rapper. I've played drums for him in a couple live shows.

You play drums?

Drums, bass, a little guitar.

I took long pulls from my beer, till the can was almost empty and my stomach was full of effervescence. I couldn't tell if I had a buzz yet. The idea of dancing was not yet appealing, so probably not. The music was good though. In the span of twenty minutes, they'd played A Tribe Called Quest, Animal Collective, New Order, and Janet Jackson. I drained the beer, set the can on the bar. Cigarette? I said, pantomiming the act of smoking.

You read my mind, James said.

We weaved through the bodies on the dance floor and emerged from the trapped air into the night. I'm feeling that beer, James said.

Me too, I said, though I wasn't. Mostly I just felt bloated. But it was good to be outside and to make conversation without shouting.

This place is dope, right? he said.

Yeah, I said. I like the music.

It's a good mix of old and new.

We'd been outside a few minutes when someone tapped my shoulder and said, Dr. Livingstone, I presume?

I swung around to find Casey from Jungle Narratives. I thought that was you, holy shit! he said. He hugged me like we were old friends who'd been apart for decades. An old Polaroid camera hung on a strap around his neck. Let me take your picture, he said. He raised the camera before I could object, and the flash went off. He fanned the ejected print over his shoulder and showed it to me. The image was still forming, my face taking shape in a white void.

This is my buddy James, I said. Casey slipped the picture into his shirt pocket and shook James's hand. James is getting his master's in history, I said, leaving out that we knew each other through campus groundskeeping. It didn't seem relevant.

James gave me a sidelong glance. That's true, he said.

Owen and I are learning about the jungle together, Casey said.

He's told me, James said.

Are you here a lot? Casey said. I've never seen you.

First time, I said.

Vell, he said, putting on a femme German accent. Velcome to Germantown.

Thanks.

I used to live just right over there, he said, pointing to what looked like a school playground.

Where do you live now?

Old Louisville, he said. You should come over and shuck some oysters with me this week.

Oysters?

My buddy Cram gave me a whole bag of oysters. Now I have to shuck them.

That's too bad.

He shrugged. Somebody has to do it. Hey, you just missed Will Oldham.

Who?

Bonnie "Prince" Billy?

No shit?

Totally, he just got into an Uber, like, fourteen seconds ago. He's here pretty regular.

Cool beans.

James stooped to pick something up from a patch of trampled dirt near the sidewalk. It was a trucker hat. He held it up for us to see. Musical notes were stitched on the front. It said NO BLACKS, NO WHITES, JUST BLUES.

Oh my God, James said. Who thought this was a good idea?

I'm sure they thought they were being really progressive, I said.

This has to be a joke, right?

Put it on, Casey said, raising the big camera to his eye.

James put on the hat. He pointed to the stitching on the front and gave a dubious, tight-lipped smile. Casey snapped the picture and we hovered over his shoulder as it developed. Beautiful, Casey said, before we could even really see it fully. He placed the photo in his breast pocket with the others.

Another beer? James said, grinding his cig against the bricks. He'd left the hat on.

After you, I said.

We went inside. Casey saw me staring at the Smurfs video above the DJ. He leaned over and shouted, Pretty cool huh? over the music.

Yeah, I guess.

I know the girl who makes it, he said. It's her art. She's got another one where she combines clips of *Gumby* with footage of NASCAR crashes. It's wild.

Nice, I said.

She did a music video for Ty Segall. I'll introduce you, she's around here somewhere.

As we were standing at the bar, a guy with long wavy hair and forks and knives tattooed on his forearms came up to Casey. This is my buddy Cram, Casey shouted.

Cram nodded hello.

You're the oyster guy? I said.

What? He cupped his hand around his ear.

The *oyster* guy.

I don't have any more, man. That was a one-time thing.

Oh, I said. I was suddenly unsure whether the oysters were actually oysters, or whether it was a code word for something illicit.

By the time I'd gotten my second tallboy and drunk down most of it, I was ready for some halfhearted dancing. Though there were contemporary songs occasionally, most of the music was from the '80s or early '90s. When "Age of Consent" by New Order came on, there was a swell of excitement and people rushed to the dance floor, as if it had been released last week and not in 1983. Then again, it was plausible. That sound was the current fashion—analog synths and drum machines. Everything came back; everything got an afterlife. The armpits of Pop's shirt were damp, and I could smell him—the residues of his life that the fabric had collected. Could he have guessed, when he bought this Arrow shirt from Sears in 1972, that one day it would wind up here?

After, the DJ played "Basketball" by Kurtis Blow, and people seemed to know all the lyrics, including James and Casey. Then it was Prince, who had died earlier that year, and LCD Soundsystem. Mostly, I couldn't get out of my own head. I wanted to say something original and funny, but the music was too loud, and I couldn't think of anything. All I could think of was my inability to think of something to say. Dancing did not come naturally to me. James danced with a woman who looked much older—maybe in her late thirties—and they kissed at one point. I pretended not to see this. What business was it of mine if he kissed girls that weren't his Crab Shack girlfriend? Maybe they had some kind of arrangement?

Casey danced by himself. He was good enough—or good enough looking—that people stared. He undulated his shoulders, did a kind of "Jailhouse Rock" move with his legs. Like any good dancer, his movements seemed both practiced and effortless at the same time. A few women tried to dance in his vicinity, sidling close, but he moved away from them each time. He leaned over to me after a while and said, You okay? You look uncomfortable.

I'm just in my head, I said.

It's better out here, he said.

At some point, Casey disappeared. James grew more and more intoxicated, till his eyes had a peaceful, drowsy look. He took the NO BLACKS, NO WHITES, JUST BLUES hat from his head and rested it on mine, lopsided. I righted the hat and leaned in to hear what he was saying.

You like Schadenfreude?

Sure, I said.

This is where it's happening, he slurred.

Where what's happening?

He closed his eyes for a few seconds, and when he opened them, he said, Everything. Everybody's here. He clamped both hands on my shoulders and squeezed. It's the place to be, yeah?

It seemed he wanted my blessing for some reason, so I said, Yeah, certainly looks that way, and this appeared to satisfy him. He stumbled to the bar and signaled for another drink.

I grew tired of dancing and waited in line for the bathroom. Nobody came out. A bartender beat on the door, but whoever was inside made no sign of recognition, and someone yelled for another bartender who was supposed to have a key. The situation did not seem to be progressing, so I went outside to look for a secluded place to piss. I walked down the block, till the music and the babble of voices outside grew faint, replaced by the low ringing of cicadas in the treetops. The houses and the lawns were dim, but I didn't want to take a chance on someone seeing me and calling the cops, so I went as far as the alley at the end of the block and did my business behind a dumpster. Honeysuckle grew lushly on the chain-link fence along the alley, the little flowers giving off their scent like perfume. I wished I could go home with a girl—go home to a real bed that I did not have to fold back into a couch every morning. But I'd never been any good at flirtation. The women I'd slept with— not that many, really—had always found *me* somehow, rather than the other way around. They came to me and said, *Here's the deal.* Everything was decided, and I simply went along with it. But I was always more attracted to the women who were like me, who seemed sort of bashful and quietly judgmental. Though of course, I never ended up with these women, because for anything to happen, at least one party needed to overcome their shyness and make a move.

I left the alley and started back toward Schadenfreude, buckling my jeans. An old car was parked at the curb with its dome light on. It looked familiar. There were two people kissing inside—a man in the passenger seat leaning over to kiss a woman who held his cheek with her hand. I couldn't see the woman's face, but as I drew nearer, I recognized Casey's Cincinnati Reds hat and his stonewashed denim jacket. From the shadow of a hawthorn tree, its branches overhanging a wooden fence, I watched as they went on kissing for a few minutes. When they pulled apart, I saw the girl's face clearly. It was Alma.

A FEW DAYS LATER, CASEY INVITED ME OVER TO HIS PLACE after Jungle Narratives to shuck some oysters. These are oysters as in bivalves, right? I said.

What else would they be? he said.

He lived in a restored Victorian row house in Old Louisville, with big bay windows and ivy fluttering on the bricks. I expected him to say he lived in the lower level, but the whole house was his. You don't have any roommates? I asked.

Nope, he said, switching on the lights in the hallway and the kitchen. The space was stylish and modern, with philodendrons in the windows and leafy vines overflowing their pots on high shelves. Two large photographs hung over the defunct fireplace. In one, a bouquet of fake roses lay abandoned on a misty gravel road. In the other, an impassive woman with red hair and a million freckles stared directly at the camera. In her hands, she held a photo of herself holding a photo of herself holding a photo of herself, ad infinitum. It's like the Land O Lakes butter label, Casey said, standing behind me with his arms folded.

Right, I said.

Also on the mantel were several of the Polaroid photographs Casey had taken at Schadenfreude. I picked up the photo of James in the NO BLACKS, NO WHITES, JUST BLUES hat. In the stark light of the flashbulb, he looked overexposed and a little haggard. You could hardly read the hat.

I loved that guy, Casey said. What was his name?

James.

Right. Man, he was funny. But in, like, a chill way, you know?

I guess so.

This is me with David Lynch, he said. He took down a framed photo. Sure enough, there he was smiling goofily next to David Lynch, who seemed less than thrilled to be having his picture taken. Casey had what looked like a press pass on a lanyard around his neck.

How did this happen?

It was at this festival, he said, nonchalantly. I'm gonna put on a record. You wanna pick?

You pick, I said.

His record collection was prodigious. He stood before the built-in shelving and walked his fingers over the spines. He pointed out the highlights, including *Another Green World,* a Brian Eno record.

This is a first pressing, he said. Very, *very* rare. I got it for three hundred, which is actually a steal. It could fetch five hundred, easy.

Wow.

Finally, he found the one he wanted—*Fear of Music* by Talking Heads—and put it on. In the kitchen, he dumped a net of oysters into the sink. Gray, barnacled shells clattered against the stainless steel and a weird smell arose. We stood there looking at them.

How long have you had these? I said.

Just five days.

Don't they go bad?

They're alive, he said. As long as the shell is closed, they're alive and that means they're still good. I think.

Isn't that mussels?

Oysters, too, he said.

He gave me a shucking knife. We each picked a shell from the sink basin and went to work. You gotta get the knife into the hinge, he said.

Then what?

Then you pry.

I tried this for five minutes. The blade kept slipping. A couple times I nearly stabbed the webbing of my thumb, but I didn't want to admit defeat. I looked over at Casey, who was flushed and grunting softly. He seemed to be putting all his strength into it, the tendons in his neck taut. Finally, the shell opened. The funk we'd smelled a trace of earlier became overpowering. I thought they were alive, Casey said, sincerely disappointed.

We made grilled cheese sandwiches instead and ate them in the living room, listening to *Fear of Music*. I'd heard of Talking Heads, and knew a few of their songs, but I'd never really listened the way I was listening then. This is fantastic, I said after a while.

You've never heard this?

I shook my head.

Have you watched *Stop Making Sense*?

No, I said. Is it a music video?

What!? He clutched his head. It's only the greatest concert documentary ever made. We're watching it *right now*.

He fetched his laptop, opened it on the coffee table, and found the full version on YouTube. Within a few minutes, we were watching David Byrne play his solo version of "Psycho Killer." Slowly, the rest of the band joined him.

That's Tina Weymouth, Casey said, when the bass player came out. She's my dream girl.

Christ Frantz followed, then Jerry Harrison, then all the auxiliary players and backup singers. When everyone was onstage, they played "Burning Down the House." Casey was leaning forward on the couch, a string of cheese dangling from his lip. I could see the laptop screen reflected in his eyes. Isn't this amazing? he said.

When the movie was over, we smoked a bowl and talked about Jungle Narratives. He asked me what my metaphorical jungle was going to be, and I said I wasn't sure—maybe the mountains of eastern Kentucky.

I got you, he said. Like a modern-day *Deliverance* story.

Not really, I said. But maybe.

He nodded and set the glass pipe and the lighter on the coffee table. My metaphorical jungle is the aftermath of my dad's death, he said.

A silence passed. He looked at me like he was waiting for a reaction.

Sorry to hear that, I said. I didn't know your dad passed away.

Car accident, he said. He fake-coughed into his fist. It's cool though, you don't have to say anything or whatever. I was just saying because you said what your metaphorical jungle was, and I knew you'd probably ask what my metaphorical jungle was, and I wanted to tell you up front before you asked.

He picked up the pipe, packed the charred weed down into the bowl with the Bic, and took a hit. He clutched his breath for a long time, then let the smoke out slowly through his nostrils. I declined when he offered the bowl to me—I didn't smoke that often anymore and was already too stoned—and he sat there with it held limply in his lap.

I inherited some money, he said. That's how I can afford to live here. I like to be up front about it with people. I know you were probably wondering.

I wasn't, I lied.

The money went into a trust. I can access it as long as I'm taking classes. Otherwise, I wouldn't get it till I was twenty-six. Doesn't mean I have to *pass* the classes.

You don't have to explain.

No, I know, he said, sitting up straight. Should we listen to another record?

I should probably go soon, I said.

Right, he said. That's cool.

I tugged on my boots and began lacing them. I wanted to ask him about Alma, but I didn't know how to broach the subject. I couldn't very well say that I'd watched them kissing in her car from the shadows.

So you said you have a girlfriend?

Yeah, he said. He narrowed his eyes. Why do you ask?

I don't know, just curious.

I'm straight, he said. I guess I should've told you that before I invited you over for dinner.

That's not why I asked. I just—well, I saw you outside Schadenfreude with the visiting writer. I was peeing in the alley.

You saw us while you were peeing?

Not during. On my way back.

Oh, he said. Yeah, Alma.

Are you two together?

For sure. Why, you know her?

We've talked once or twice, I said, like it was no big deal. I went to her reading.

I wish I could've made it that night, he said. She's brilliant though, right? We're doing her *Misconnected* book.

Who's we?

Sestina, he said. He waited a beat, then said, The press?

Oh right, I said. Sestina was a small press in Louisville that published poetry mostly. They'd received some acclaim in the last year when one of their poets won a major prize.

I say we. It's my mom, really. She's on the board of directors over there. It's like her retirement hobby. She practiced law for thirty years, but she's always liked being plugged into the literary game.

I'm like her informal advisor. I tell her what's cool and what's pretending to be cool.

He smiled as if I would understand this burden. Sounds like they should put you on the masthead, I said.

That's what I'm saying! He took a toke from the pipe, set it down, a thin ribbon of smoke still drifting up lazily. I told her—my mom, I mean—that Alma was the real deal, he said, still holding in the hit. And not just because we're together. He released the smoke and coughed a little. For a moment he spaced out, staring at nothing in particular, then seemed to remember he'd been in the middle of saying something. She's excited, I think, he said. Alma. My mom, too. It's like, publish a little book of poems or whatever with a hip, small press, have it come out around the same time as the novel, and nobody will see you as a sellout. It's like, instant cred. You get to have your cake and eat it, too. And for Sestina, it's a no-brainer, right? Ultimately, it's a throwaway book for them—not that it's not good—just, you know, it's a side hustle. But here, they've got the opportunity—and this is what I told my mom—to publish Alma's Craigslist poems right before she comes out with this big novel at a major house. What I'm saying is that it's about credibility, on both sides. They don't publish anything because they think it's gonna make them rich. It's about prestige. That's the currency in the literary world, you feel me?

Casey seemed to realize that he'd been monologuing and blushed. He pushed up his sleeves and slid them back down again. He looked around the room, as if trying to spot something he'd misplaced. Anyway, he said casually, you have anything you want me to pass along to mi madre, let me know. I'm always on the lookout.

Will do, I said. Thanks for the offer.

He waved this off with a dismissive flourish. Of course.

So what do you like about her work?

Oh man, he said. Where to even begin. He looked up at the ceiling and moved his hands as if he were shaping a ball of clay. It's got this kind of—there's this disjunctive synthesis at work. She can do these kind of Lydia Davis–esque flash pieces, but the wordplay and the line-level stuff is pretty pyrotechnic—more like Brodkey or something. It's just so . . . formally challenging, you know? But without being affected. I mean, she's a genius. You saw her—am I right or what? She's gonna win a fuckin Pulitzer.

Yeah, the reading was impressive, I said. So you're pretty serious, then, you and her?

You mean our relationship?

Uh-huh.

Honestly? I think I'm in love with her.

Wow, I said. A heave of nausea rose up at this. I told myself it was stupid. I had no right to feel jealous, no claim to anything, really. Nothing had happened between us.

We're making plans for the future—we're even talking about moving in together. I know it's early on, but when you know, you know, right?

Totally.

My mom has this place in Charleston. We've already decided we're gonna spend Christmas there.

Like, she owns it?

Yeah, it's a little pied-à-terre. She rents it out most of the year to tourists, does the whole Airbnb thing, but we're gonna stay for two weeks, maybe go over to Hilton Head for a few days.

Sounds nice, I said. I started moving toward the door, hoping I could get out before he saw the flagrant disappointment written on my face.

He stood and touched my elbow. Listen, before you go—I wanted to ask if you'd read a story of mine and give me notes, he said. It's the one I was telling you about—my metaphorical jungle.

The one about your dad.

Right, he said. He drew the wrinkled pages from his backpack and handed them over. It's a little rough, but I'd be glad to get your thoughts on it, he said. Gotta turn it in in a few weeks.

I told him I'd read it and get back to him soon and said so long. On my way out, he gave me Talking Heads' first five records, the ones they made between '77 and '83. These are their best, he said. Everything after this is hit or miss.

In Pop's truck, I looked over the first page. It wasn't bad, but it wasn't particularly good either. The title was "My Personal Apocalypse." The first line, which I actually liked, was *No one ever tells you how the world will end.* I sat for a long time with the pages in my lap, feeling some admixture of guilt and disgust. There was a coffee stain on the story and a smudged thumbprint. The pages seemed suddenly contaminated to me. I flung them in the back seat and drove home.

THE COUCH TRANSFORMED INTO MY BED. IT WAS A HIDE-A-BED couch. I liked that turn of phrase for some reason—hide-a-bed. I lay on the bed-no-longer-hidden and looked at the things I owned. A dresser. My laptop. Three milk crates of records. My dad's old Technics turntable. My rack of shirts. Books—some in boxes still, some stacked on the ground. The floor was covered in green indoor-outdoor carpet, and looked sort of like AstroTurf. I wrote down *AstroTurf carpet* in my notebook. Then I wrote down some more of Pop's antiques, adding to what was becoming an endless list.

> *Birdhouses made of gourds.*
> *Prince Albert "crimp cut" tobacco can.*
> *Seed drills.*
> *A Hank Williams album.*
> *Coconut carved to look like a monkey's face.*

The door squealed opened, followed by footfalls on the steps. It was Pop. I could tell from the unsteady pace. It took him a long time to reach the bottom, and when he did, he squinted into the dim basement as though he couldn't see me.

I'm right here, Pop.

Oh, he said, his eyes going slack. Hey pard.

You need something?

Can't sleep.

Did you take a Valium?

No.

You could, you haven't had one today.

I know, he said. My mind's just running a mile a minute. He

twirled his finger next to his head, the way people do to suggest that someone's crazy.

Make a list of the things you need to do. That always helps me.

What things? That's the problem, I got nothing that needs doing.

What are you thinking about, then?

He picked at the glommed paint on the banister. Mostly I just wanted to tell you that I'm proud of you, for going back to school and working like this, he said. You've come a long way.

I knew what he meant—that I'd come a long way from what I'd been doing the last five years, which was mostly drinking and getting high and working a series of odd jobs that led to nothing but the continuation of those bad habits. Still, I couldn't say my present situation felt much better, or that I didn't wish, sometimes, for the comfort of those bad habits.

Yeah, things are better, I guess, I said.

How's your love life?

I laughed. My love life?

Yes, he said. You should take your love life seriously, it's serious business.

I don't know, I said. I'm playing the field.

That only takes you so far. Trust me.

I know.

Find one like your grandmother, he said.

I started to say this didn't seem likely, given that when they met, my grandmother had been a sixteen-year-old girl who lived with eight siblings on a farm without electricity, and he'd been twenty-six, freshly returned from the South Pacific with a navy pension and a newly bought parcel of land. But I knew he didn't mean the particulars. He meant the spirit of who she was, though I wasn't sure if that existed anymore. How could you divorce the spirit of a person from the particulars of her life?

What made you want to settle down? I said. When you were in your wild days?

The war, he said.

What about the war though?

He looked at me like this was a stupid question—it probably

was. He thought about it, and after a moment, he said, The things you think are dull become the things you long for.

I considered this in the subsequent silence—how it wasn't true for me yet. The things I thought were dull were still dull. The things I longed for were still romantic things, in faraway, romantic places. Then again, I hadn't been through what he'd been through, and I never would. My rite of passage into adulthood had been menial work—the thoughtless repetition of tasks that would be given to machines if only it were feasible. What kind of adult did that make? An aimless person, I figured. A person waiting to be replaced.

Pop drummed his fingers on the rail and turned to start the arduous journey back up the steps. Sorry to bother you, he said.

Write it down, I said.

What?

Whatever you're thinking about, write it down. Write it down and then it's outside you.

Why would I want that? he said, still marching upward.

IN A MOMENT OF COURAGE, OR MAYBE FOOLHARDINESS, I CALLED Alma the next day and asked if she wanted to go for a walk. I like Joe Creason Park, I said. The zoo is right next door. We can stop by if we get bored.

You wanna go to the *zoo*? she said, her voice edging on laughter.

Why not? I said. I'd gone through a big zoo phase as a kid and going to one as an adult was like mainlining nostalgia. I sometimes forgot that not everyone was as enthusiastic about zoos as I was.

Don't zoos depress you a little bit? she said. It's like animal jail.

For some, I guess. But some of those animals have got it made. The red-tailed monkeys, for instance. They've got a whole island with big oak trees to swing around in, all their meals taken care of, and they never have to worry about violent death at the hands of a leopard.

She laughed. I guess that's true, she said. I'm down, but I'm all the way out at Ashby, so it might take me a little while to get ready and get into town.

You live out there? I said, pretending I didn't already know this.

In one of the guesthouses, she said. It's part of the fellowship. Where are you? I could pick you up.

I'll pick you up, I said. An hour?

Great, she said. Can't wait.

I drove out to campus, the same route I took every morning for work. Pop's truck was a green 1995 Ford Ranger, with a camper topper and a ladder rack on the roof. I'd stashed my gloves and my hard hat in the toolbox and spritzed the upholstery with Febreze, though there was always a faint smell of gasoline and perspiration. While I was parked at the curb, waiting for her to come out, I rummaged through Pop's country music cassettes in the console, trying to find something suitable for the drive. It was hard to imagine Willie Nelson or George Jones setting the mood. I found an Emmylou Harris cassette eventually—*Quarter Moon in a Ten Cent Town*—and settled for that.

She emerged wearing her hiking boots with the red laces, a pair of dark jeans, and a gray sweatshirt that said PRINCETON in orange block letters. She jogged over and climbed into the cab. Sorry to keep you waiting, she said, a little out of breath. She clicked her seat belt and looked around at the interior of the truck. Wow, she said.

What?

Nothing, this is just a real pickup truck.

Surely you've been in a pickup truck before?

She shrugged. Maybe a couple times.

Well, it works just like a regular car.

Can I turn this down? she said. She lowered the volume till Emmylou Harris was barely audible. So much for the mood.

I asked her how she'd been since we last spoke, and she gave me the full account as we drove northward through the hills and into the run-down outskirts of the city. She said she spent her mornings writing, and in the afternoons, she rode her bicycle on campus or hiked at the arboretum nearby. She'd been to Schadenfreude the night before, which she claimed was the only good place to dance in Louisville, but the music had been mediocre—not the usual DJ, she said—and she'd left after an hour and gotten a burger at Wanda's Café, an all-night greasy spoon in Old Louisville. I have too much free time, she said. I never thought that would be a problem for me, but it is. I think I'm going a little batty.

Maybe you need structure, I said.

That's what everybody keeps telling me. But I signed up for this—the fellowship, I mean. I guess I shouldn't complain.

I wanted to ask if she'd gone to Schadenfreude with Casey, if it had been Casey beside her on a stool at Wanda's Café, sharing a milkshake, but she didn't know that I knew him, and it wasn't really my business. Nothing about her life was really my business.

I did go to a party last Friday with the guy I'm seeing, she said. That was fun, I guess. You might know him, actually—Casey Arnett? He takes some English-slash-writing classes for fun—like you.

No, I said, before I could really think through whether I wanted to lie. I mean, the name sounds vaguely familiar, but no.

Well, he knows *everyone,* so I wouldn't have been surprised.

So what's his deal? How'd you meet?

Through Sestina, she said. They were having this book launch party for another writer. I was invited, and he was there. Turns out his mom is on the board. We started hanging out and he passed my book of poems to her, which was great because they agreed to publish it. After that, we started hanging out more and more, then before I knew it, we were together.

You make it sound like an accident.

Well, she said, when I came here, I told myself I was going to be single and have fun. I wanted to put all my energy into the writing. But loneliness is a powerful motivator. I stood around at that party for an hour, drinking champagne cocktails, and he was the only person that came up to me and said hi. He introduced me to people. He was good-looking. I was like, *Why resist this?*

I weighed carefully how to respond, so that I would not sound resentful. Being well connected in Louisville isn't exactly a feat, I said. It's like being a big fish in a small pond.

The pond's not *that* small, she said. And I like being a big fish here. You can't throw a stick in Brooklyn without hitting a writer. You tell somebody in New York that you've published a book, and they're like, "Join the club." But here? People recognize it as an accomplishment.

We arrived at the park and started down one of the concrete paths. It was a crisp day in October. The leaves had just begun to change. We passed two massive oaks, the trunks of which looked like they'd been melted to a liquid and hardened suddenly in the middle of boiling. Their dry leaves shook in the breeze. Further on, the walkway was lined with shaggy spruces, their scent like menthol—sharp, clean.

Alma inhaled deeply through her nostrils and sighed. I already feel better, she said.

Me too, I said.

What did you have to feel bad about? Other than your usual woes.

I don't know, I said. Not much, really. I wanted to tell her I felt better now that she was with me, that I'd been thinking about her a lot, but I didn't want to scare her off. I kept forgetting that we didn't know each other that well, that my sense of familiarity with her had no basis in reality. What I knew for sure was that I'd never wanted to know anyone as much as I wanted to know her.

How's groundskeeping? she said.

Same old same old. Nothing too exciting.

And your writing?

I'm still taking notes, I said. I don't know what they add up to.

Notes on what?

Just things that happen. Things people say. For example, this guy I work with—Rando—he has a new conspiracy theory every day. I write them down when they're funny or especially outlandish.

His name is *Rando*?

Randy, but that's what we all call him.

We reached a plot of wilted sunflowers, some as tall as we were, heads bowed as if in prayer. Alma broke one of the stalks and brought the flower down between us, thinking it would have a pleasant smell. It stank like death. She grimaced and tossed it aside.

As we walked on, she pulled the sleeves of her sweatshirt over her fists and crossed her arms, shivering a little. Did you go to Princeton? I said.

Yep.

How was that?

She thought about the question a few moments. It was wonderful in a lot of ways, and also evil in a lot of ways. Going there as an immigrant is different than going as a legacy from some old-money family.

Was that where you always wanted to go?

I got into Dartmouth and Penn, too. I might've gone to Harvard, but they wait-listed me.

I didn't ask where you got in, I asked where you wanted to go.

It's hard to differentiate what you want from what your parents want at that age, you know?

I nodded as if I understood what she meant from experience, but I had no idea. When I was eighteen, all of my energy had been spent maintaining a clear border between what I wanted and what my parents wanted, defending its sovereignty against constant incursion.

No state schools?

She laughed. Yeah, right.

So it was Ivy League or nothing?

Not even, she said. Cornell is a joke. Stanford would've been all right. I would've been okay with Stanford.

I can't tell if you're being serious.

Why would I not be serious?

There was a finality to her response that made it seem like she'd rather talk about something else.

I always wanted to go to a highfalutin school, I said.

She smiled skeptically. Now you're just playing it up. You don't really say "highfalutin."

I just did, didn't I?

So what happened, why didn't you go to a highfalutin school?

I explained to her that I'd wanted to go to a good school when I was young, but by the time I finished high school, my grades weren't good enough, and anyhow, my parents wouldn't have been able to afford the out-of-state tuition. I ended up at the University of Kentucky, barely managing to graduate with a degree in English.

Didn't anyone tell you that you were capable of more?

My parents didn't want me to go off and become a coastal elite. If they'd had their druthers, I'd have gone to Murray State, an hour from their house.

Their *druthers?*

Yeah, you've never heard that?

No, she said, laughing. That's definitely going on the list.

When do I get to see this list?

When the time is right, she said. So what's wrong with being a coastal elite?

Nothing, as far as I'm concerned. To them, it's the worst thing you could be. I've wanted to be a coastal elite my whole life.

She looked at me as if she both pitied me and found me adorable—a look I was getting used to.

We reached the crest of a small hill, where the path forked, and from this vantage we could see the entrance to the zoo across the street. Should we go check out the animals? I said.

You're really serious about this zoo thing.

Don't I look serious?

She shook her head, trying not to smile. Okay, she said. Let's go.

The exhibits were arranged, roughly, according to biome and continent of origin. The path led us first through the African savannah. There were a lot of squalling children and harried parents pushing strollers, demanding that their kids pay attention to whatever animals were making themselves visible. Leonard, look at the warthog! shouted one of the mothers, her tone almost threatening. Look at the warthog, Leonard! Leonard! I explained to Alma that I felt like children were the worst aspect of zoos, though I knew this was hypocritical—I wouldn't have a love of zoos if my parents hadn't taken me as a kid. I was probably just like Leonard—racing from one exhibit to the next, never lingering, always in a hurry to see the *cool* animals, the stars of the zoo—the lions, tigers, and bears. As an adult, I appreciated the animals in supporting roles—the lynxes and meerkats and lemurs. Because all the kids flocked to the main attractions, you could hang out with these animals in peace and quiet. Alma listened with an amused expression while I explained my zoo theory, and when I was done, she said, So you don't like kids?

No, I like them fine, I said. It's just overwhelming when they're in big groups like this and they're all hyped up on sugar and caffeine.

But the zoo is *for* children, she said. That's the whole point.

I disagree, I said. If I won the lottery, I'd use my money to start an adults-only zoo. Instead of soft serve and funnel cakes, they'd serve beer and cocktails, and there'd be a nice farm-to-table restaurant.

Adults-only zoo sounds pretty suggestive, she said. And really, that's the *first* thing you'd do if you won the lottery?

Well, no. I'd probably buy a plane ticket to someplace exotic. Then I think I'd buy properties in different cities so I could split my time and not have to live in one place for too long. I'd spend the fall in New Orleans, winter in Los Angeles, spring in Paris, maybe the summer on a ranch in Montana or something.

I could see you on a ranch, she said—something a little flirty about her tone.

What would you do?

Hmm, she said, scratching her chin. I think I'd buy a brownstone. Like, the whole thing. Then I'd live in it.

The *very* first thing?

Maybe not, she said. I'd probably buy a plane ticket, too.

We stood for a while watching the elephants, two of which were nudging an enormous blue ball back and forth with their heads. A third, lonely-looking elephant used its snout to drink from a stagnant pool. It seemed an inefficient way to drink. Most of the water just dribbled from its mouth. We passed the ibexes and the gazelles and a flock of flamingos with dirty feathers. The whole savannah section had a barnyard smell—the smell of hay and sunbaked manure. The zebras seemed to be in high spirits, chasing each other and being generally frolicsome, but after a few minutes, one zebra mounted the other, and what had seemed like innocent fun became suddenly ominous. The zebra doing the mounting had crazed eyes and was huffing loudly, foam on his lips. We kept walking.

We entered the Jungles of Africa and saw the monkey island I'd been looking forward to. The island was surrounded by a kind of moat with jade-tinted water, and there were three huge pin oaks, in which a dozen colobus and red-tailed monkeys swung about on cables and rope nets. They had their run of the place. See, now this is what I'm talking about, I said. This isn't so bad.

I bet they have to go inside for the winter, she said. In Africa they wouldn't.

In Africa they'd have to be on high alert for danger at all times.

Maybe they're still on high alert, she said. Maybe it's in their constitution.

So you're saying you'd rather be free than play it safe if you were a monkey?

I'm saying maybe it doesn't matter. Maybe you'd be racked with anxiety anyway, for evolutionary reasons. But no, I'd choose safety over freedom any day of the week. Wouldn't you?

I don't know, I said. I thought about this question for a long time as we leaned against the rail in the shade of the oak trees. The monkeys closest to us took turns parting each other's fur, picking off insects and nibbling them. Red leaves spiraled down occasionally, lighting on the surface of the green water. It seemed to me a fundamental question, underlying the motives for all sorts of human activities—the forming of governments, raising armies, electing leaders—even mundane activities like buying a house or starting a family. You chose a place and you settled there. You put up fences. You made a stand. You did these things because you wanted safety and stability. You got tired of moving around all the time, always looking over your shoulder. I thought of my ancestors, who'd been indentured servants in Virginia, and had come through the Cumberland Gap into Kentucky where they'd all settled—some in Appalachia, some further west near Paducah. We'd been there, all my kin, ever since, for three hundred years—sharecropping, scraping by. My grandparents' generation had been the first to own land. Twenty acres to set out a crop of tobacco—that's what my grandfather bought when he returned from the war. It must have seemed like a lot to possess when everyone before you had nothing.

But then, there was that antsy feeling, when your life grew stale, when you were tired of the same repetitions. Danger became appealing after a long enough stretch of boredom, but maybe not real danger—the danger of war and genocide and actual human cruelty. Maybe that kind of danger was enough to cure you of wanderlust. But it was possible, I thought, for it to have the opposite effect. Seeing the worst could bring you to the conclusion that nothing mattered, and therefore you might as well be carefree, and live as you wanted, with total liberty.

You look like you're deep in thought, Alma said.

I gave her the short version of what I'd been thinking about. I said it was a complicated question, and I could see both sides. Why do you prefer safety? I said.

I just don't know what freedom really means anymore, she said. The word gets used to justify a lot of bad ideas. Like the free market, for instance. Or the freedom to choose your own healthcare. I'd rather have the security of knowing that when I get sick, I'll be taken care of, and profit motive and the marketplace won't have anything to do with it. I'd rather have the security of knowing that I can leave my house and not be harassed or shot at by paramilitary gangs because of my identity. People talk about freedom, but what they mean, really, is just the freedom to choose among a set of pretty limited options, most of which are just shoddy consumer products. Like, what's the difference, really, between Colgate and Crest toothpastes? They're basically the same thing. But people cherish the freedom to choose between them. People who vote Republican are voting for the freedom to choose between Colgate and Crest toothpastes. Put that on a bumper sticker.

It's a little long for a bumper sticker.

Do you disagree?

No, not at all.

She sighed. We should change the subject, she said. I start to sound like my angsty teenage self when these pass-the-bong conversations come up.

Pass-the-bong?

Yeah, it's like you're sitting in a basement or some dude's carpeted van and somebody says, "Would you rather have freedom or safety?" as they pass you the bong, and then the next thing you know, you're talking about early Homo sapiens and woolly mammoths. It's a pass-the-bong conversation.

Your teenage pass-the-bong conversations sound more interesting than mine, I said. We talked about UFOs and how the moon landing was a hoax.

You don't believe that now though, right?

What, don't you?

She smiled and shook her head. I mean it figuratively anyway, she said. I wasn't passing any bongs in high school. I was prepping for the SAT.

A chorus of sneezing sounds erupted above us. I peered up through the branches. The monkeys were forcing air through their noses. You hear that? she said. That's how they warn each other about danger.

How do you know?

I just read it, she said, pointing to a placard with cartoon monkeys and speech bubbles. I think this supports my theory. They're like us. They're just as nervous in captivity as they would be in the wild. The brain can always find something to be afraid of.

So you're saying America is Monkey Island, and we're all, like, in captivity, man.

She ignored my bad surfer-dude impression. Are you hungry? she said. Could you eat some French fries?

We went to the Jungle Outpost Restaurant, ordered a basket of curly fries, and took them to an outdoor patio. From our table, we could see a zookeeper with a parrot on her arm, surrounded by gawking children. Riotous bird sounds were being piped through the Jungle Outpost's speakers, and I thought of *Burden of Dreams* and Herzog's monologue about overwhelming murder. There had been nothing murderous about the zoo on any of my previous trips, but now, the whole thing had sinister undertones. I didn't like that I felt this way. I wished I'd never signed up for Jungle Narratives.

A bamboo grove shaded the patio. It was comfortable, just sitting there, listening to breezes rasp through the bamboo leaves. Kids squealed in the distance. The fries were not very good, but I ate them ravenously. I hadn't realized how hungry I was.

So do you really think that's your problem, staying in one place for too long? Alma said, out of the blue.

Did I say that was my problem?

You said if you won the lottery, you'd buy apartments in all these cities, so if you got bored with one place, you could just move on to the next.

It does sound appealing. You don't like the idea?

I just think it would become tiresome. And if you had a family, you'd be dragging them along, too.

I guess you'd have to decide to settle somewhere, before you had kids.

Maybe you've got it backwards though, she said. Maybe you settle down *because* you have kids, not *in order* to have them.

Maybe, I said. She shrugged and gazed thoughtfully at the bustling crowd and the thatch-roof pavilions and snow cone stands. She took a long curly fry from the basket, lowered it into her mouth, and chewed, her brows drawn together.

Desiring the exhilarations of changes, she said suddenly.

What?

This line I was trying to think of, she said. It's from a Wallace Stevens poem called "The Motive for Metaphor." The antsy feeling you were talking about—that's what made me remember it. It's a good poem.

I'll check it out, I said, and after this, there was nothing I could think of to say. I wiped the salt and grease from my fingers and we sat there quietly, listening to the bamboo rustle.

We spent the next half hour making perfunctory stops at the star exhibits—the lion enclosure, the polar bear tank. The food made me drowsy, and as the sun eased down and the air grew colder, we quickened our pace, making it back to the entrance a little after five. We pushed through the turnstiles, and on the park path, she said, Well, that was fun.

Have I turned you on to the many benefits of zoos?

Yes, she said. Consider me turned on. An awkwardness followed. That was a weird thing to say, she said, which broke the tension and allowed us to laugh, but the uneasy silence returned. Soon, we reached the parking lot and Pop's truck. I didn't want to take her home, but that seemed to be what would happen if neither of us intervened and made a suggestion.

As we got settled and buckled our seat belts, she said, Should we meet for a drink later? I have to go home and eat dinner and change, but I was thinking I'd go back to Schadenfreude tonight. The regular DJ will be there.

There was a nervousness to her voice—a failed attempt to sound casual—and this was heartening. She was nervous, too. It struck me for the first time that I was older than her, and that she was probably conscious of this.

Yeah, maybe I'll meet you there, I said.

As I drove back to Ashby, all I could think of was whether Casey would be with her at Schadenfreude. This was the proverbial elephant in the room. I thought of the lonely elephant, dipping water into his mouth from a stagnant pool in the enclosure—how conspicuous he'd been. It was impossible not to notice him, whether you were a journalist or an arborist, whether you'd won the lottery or your life had broken down. It was the fate of every elephant to be obvious.

See you later maybe? she said, when I pulled to the curb in front of the guesthouses. I'll probably go around nine or ten.

Yeah, I'll try to make it, I said, though I knew it was a foregone conclusion. I watched her go up the walk and disappear into the guesthouse, then I started home with a sigh and turned up the volume. Emmylou Harris was still singing.

POP WANTED McDONALD'S FOR SUPPER. I NEEDED TO SHOWER and pick out something halfway decent to wear, and the notion of drinking cheap beer at Schadenfreude with nothing but McDonald's and curly fries from the Jungle Outpost in my stomach sounded deeply unappealing, but I told him I'd run up and get a burger. Get something for Cort, too, Pop said.

When I got back, Cort rummaged through the sack as soon as I set it on the kitchen counter, removing his double Quarter Pounder in its cardboard clamshell. I fixed Pop's plate and set it out for him. He paused his movie, *Rio Bravo,* and shuffled into the kitchen. Smells good, he said.

I ate standing up next to the garbage, glancing at the microwave clock occasionally. The drive to Schadenfreude would take a half hour and I wanted to leave myself plenty of time. Mid-bite, Cort grimaced theatrically and spat something onto his plate.

I told you no pickles, he said.

Nobody said that.

I told Dad.

Pop scratched his head. I must've forgot, he said.

I can't eat this.

Just pick them off, I said.

They leave a residue, he said. They leave a distinct pickle residue.

I stared at him—at his crocodile boots and his tucked-in jeans, at the ketchup on his fingertips. I'd never felt so exasperated by someone. I could see the vague resemblance to my mother in his facial features—the set of his jaw, the way his nose curved. He lacked her laugh lines. I didn't know if I'd ever seen him laugh.

Eat it, don't eat it. You can do whatever you want.

Hey, Pop said.

I'm not his errand boy. From now on, if he wants dinner, he can get it himself. He's not helpless.

He appreciates your help, don't you, Cort?

Cort just looked at me, his eyes spiteful.

We both appreciate it, Pop said. It's good, you doing these little things. Especially since you're not paying rent.

What's that supposed to mean?

Pop winced a little, like he knew he'd said the wrong thing. Nothing, he said. Just that we're both glad you help out. Cort, too. Tell him how glad you are, Cort.

I'm glad, Cort said flatly.

See, he's glad.

But I don't eat pickles. I told you that.

Okay now, let's drop it, all right? Let's eat our Mickey D's in peace and maybe we can all watch *Rio Bravo* after. Y'all seen *Rio Bravo*? Dean Martin plays the town drunk.

I'm going out, I said. I ate the last bite of my burger, sucked minced onion from my fingertips.

Going out where?

Germantown.

He's going to party with the freaks and weirdos, Cort said. That's where all the dykes are now. All the college feminists.

You go out too much, Pop said. Stay in and watch *Rio Bravo,* you'd like it.

I've seen it, I said. I gotta meet someone.

Is this someone a *girl?*

Just a friend of mine, I said.

Pop grinned lasciviously. What's her name?

It's not like that, I said. I started for the basement, clapping Pop's shoulder as I walked by.

As I showered and got dressed, my mind kept circling back to what he'd said about not paying rent. It had been more than two months, and I'd put no real effort into finding an apartment. I knew it was time to look. After all, how could I bring a girl home? How could I subject someone to Cort's erratic behavior? He'd been there with Pop for two decades. They'd established their routines, grown accustomed to each other's habits and idiosyncrasies. I was a newcomer, and as much as Pop assured me I was welcome, that he was happy for my company, I was still, in some undeniable way, an interruption to the way of life they'd established. An outsider. It was a lonely realization.

On my way out, I stopped for a moment in the living room, where John Wayne and Dean Martin were in the middle of a shoot-out, firing lever-action rifles through adobe windows. One of the characters was a toothless old man named Stumpy. John Wayne let Stumpy know that he was hunkered down beside a wagon loaded with dynamite. Jumpin Jehoshaphat! cried Stumpy, and Pop laughed and laughed, pointing at the TV. Cort was sitting in the other recliner, eating tri-flavored popcorn from a giant Halloween tin. Even he smiled a little at Stumpy's antics. I said, So long, and Pop waved without turning from the screen. They hardly seemed to notice I was there.

I'D THOUGHT IT WAS A PROFOUND COINCIDENCE, SEEING everyone at Schadenfreude the way I had my first night there. I hadn't realized at the time that it was simply where everyone of a certain type in Louisville ended up—the type being artists and grad students and musicians in their twenties and early thirties. Sitting at the bar, glancing around, I saw a few who did not fit the type—a frat boy in a pink polo shirt, a young overdressed attorney or real estate agent perhaps, dancing clumsily. A vestige of Germantown's recent past sat in a shadowy corner booth—a haggard, befuddled-looking man in his middle fifties, wearing a day laborer's clothes and dirt-crusted lace-ups. You saw a man like this at a Germantown bar less and less, but now and then he cropped up. He'd be wearing more or less the same garb as the hip crowd—maybe a pinstriped mechanic's shirt with Marlboros in the pocket, trucker hat tipped back. Only these would be the clothes he'd worn for years, unironically. It might be his *actual* name stitched in cursive on the shirt pocket, and the trucker hat would bear the logo of a business that was *actually* familiar to him—maybe even his place of work. The music on the turntable would have been released when he was *actually* alive, and the beer he drank—Hamm's or Pabst or Coors Banquet—would be the beer he'd always drunk. This man would look out at the crowd around him with an expression of total bewilderment, as if his life had been commandeered, or as if perhaps he'd been dislodged from the flow of time for decades and suddenly found himself in the future. As the dance floor filled up with androgynous girls and gawky boys in skinny jeans, this man in the booth drained his beer, shook his head wearily, and walked out into the night. I doubted if he'd ever come back.

I drank steadily for an hour, watching the door for Alma. She came in around eleven, wearing a jean jacket and a corduroy skirt with green stockings. Her legs were long and slender, and she had a coltish, uncertain gait, as if she'd been drinking some before she arrived. I smiled and waved, but she didn't see me. I thought I recognized the jean jacket. I was trying to remember where I'd seen it when Casey came in behind her and rested his hands on her waist. He kissed her neck, and she reached back and patted his cheek. It was *his* stonewashed jacket, one I'd seen him wear to Jungle Narratives many times.

Alma spotted me at the bar and waved, smiling cheerily. I managed to wave back. Around that time, just as she'd begun weaving toward me, dragging Casey by the hand, Janet Jackson's "Nasty" started playing and everyone flooded the dance floor. The song had been all the rage since Donald Trump called Hillary Clinton a nasty woman in the last debate. Soon, I was alone at the bar, surrounded by empty stools, and Alma could not be seen in the jumble of bodies.

I swallowed the last of my beer, swiveled around, and signaled to the tender. Jim Beam, I said, and it struck me as something of a cliché. I'd been watching too many westerns. Cliché or not, I faced front and drank my whiskey, staring glumly at the bottles behind the bar. She'd reach me eventually, or she wouldn't. I was in no hurry to go through with the whole humiliating interaction. I could see my reflection in a mirror behind the bar. I looked comically miserable. *Don't be so melodramatic,* I told myself.

Someone nudged my shoulder after a few minutes. I turned and found Casey. Well, if it isn't Dr. Livingstone, he said.

You already made that joke, I said. I looked past him for Alma, but she'd been waylaid and dragged into a conversation.

I heard you went to the zoo, he shouted.

I shook the crushed ice in my whiskey and took a drink, buying time. Yeah, it was no big deal. Just a walk, really.

She couldn't stop talking about it. I had no idea you two knew each other so well.

James was there, too, I said impulsively.

Really? She didn't mention that.

Yeah, it was whatever. Just a group hang.

That's chill, that's chill, Casey said. Well, she went on and on, saying how great you were. I said, I know, right? I love that guy. She was like, You know him? And I was like yeah, he's great. That's why I gave him my metaphorical jungle story, cause he's so brilliant.

I didn't think I'd ever done or said anything that would indicate brilliance to Casey, but who was I to argue? That's nice of you to say, I said.

It's just the truth, he said.

I couldn't tell if all this was genuine or if he was only fucking with me. It was hard to discern tone when you were shouting over dance music. I had to say that it seemed genuine. Maybe he saw me as so unthreatening that it didn't matter.

When Alma walked over, she gave me a hug, which I wasn't expecting. Good to see you, she said, close to my ear.

You just saw me four hours ago.

Feels like longer. She leaned across the bar and ordered a beer. Casey held out a folded bill between his index and middle finger. I got it, he said.

You sure?

Don't worry about it. You need anything? he said to me.

I held up my whiskey. I'm set.

What is that?

Jim Beam.

Are you a bourbon man? I bet you know your bourbons, being a true Kentuckian.

Not really, I said. It hadn't occurred to me that Casey wasn't from Kentucky, but it made sense, what with the Cincinnati Reds hat and all. A lot of young people from Cincinnati and southern Indiana were settling in Louisville.

I was just telling Owen here that we both think he's brilliant.

Did I say that?

Not in so many words, Casey said. But that was the implication.

I just told you we had a good conversation at the zoo, Alma said.

Well, then he's a good conversationalist.

Can we go back to me being brilliant? I said. They both laughed. A lull followed, in which we all took a drink and glanced around. The DJ switched over to Solange and the energy on the dance floor shifted, becoming less jagged and frenetic.

Where's James tonight? Casey said.

I shrugged.

Thought maybe you were a package deal.

What does that mean?

Casey turned up his palms. Nothing, man.

No, what do you mean?

I mean I didn't know if you were together. Like that song—what's that duo with Paul McCartney and the Black guy? He snapped his fingers. Fuck.

We're not together.

"Ebony and Ivory," he said. Who is that, Michael Jackson and Paul McCartney, right?

Stevie Wonder, I said. Did you really think that?

Did I really think what?

You didn't really think that.

Hey, who knows? Who am I to judge?

By this point, I was eyeing the exit. The whole thing now seemed like a foolish mistake. Of course they were there together. What would any of this come to, besides disappointment?

Have you listened to this album yet? Alma said, meaning *A Seat at the Table*.

Yeah, it's great, I said.

Let's all dance. I love this song.

I might step out for a smoke.

She jutted her lower lip in a pouty frown. Casey tugged on her arm. Come on, he said.

I might come out in a minute, she said, shouting over her shoulder.

I took my whiskey outside and sat on the steps. A food truck was parked at the curb, selling tacos, and the aroma of stewed pork and pineapple made my stomach lurch. I ordered two tacos at the window and ate them over a paper plate on the steps, trying to decide whether I should just leave. Alma came out and found me before I could arrive at a decision.

There you are, she said. Are you in a mood?

Do what?

"Do what," she said, imitating me. That's another one for the list. You say that instead of "beg pardon."

I shook my head, making my annoyance obvious. Okay, I said.

What's wrong?

When you invited me out here, I thought it was to see me. Not him.

Why would you assume that?

I set my paper plate on the steps and massaged my eyes. I don't know, I said. Forget about it.

She stared for a moment, then sat beside me on the step. I'm sorry, she said, her voice softer. I don't know what I'm doing.

With what?

Seeing you, she said. Hanging out like this.

Then why are you doing it?

Because I like you.

But not enough to do anything about it.

I feel a little conflicted, okay? she said. That all right with you? I don't know why possessiveness has to come into this. I don't even know how serious Casey and I are.

He thinks you're serious.

She sighed wearily. Can I bum a cig?

I drew a Parliament from my pack and gave it to her. She lit up, blew a jet of smoke. I don't owe you anything, she said. And I should be the one who's mad at you. Imagine my surprise when Casey tells me you know each other, that you're in the jungle class.

I didn't know his last name. Didn't make the connection.

That's bullshit, she said.

Okay fine, I panicked, what do you want me to say? I don't know why I lied. Maybe I like you too and I don't wanna be all buddy-buddy with the person you're sleeping with.

But you are. You're friends.

I wouldn't say that.

Oh you wouldn't?

I have no idea what you like about him.

She rolled her eyes. I don't have to explain myself to you, she said.

Actually, never mind. I do know. He lavishes you with praise, his mom's publishing your book of poems. You get to hang out with the minor celebrities of Louisville. I guess with all that, you can look past how shallow and uninteresting he is.

She took a drag, puckering her cheeks, and looked away from me, down the dark row of shotgun houses. He's made my life easy here, she said. He's given me stability and friends and a social life, in this town where I knew no one. He's made me feel like my work is important, which is something I don't get from my Princeton friends, or even my parents. Surely you can see that?

In truth, I hadn't seen this at all and was momentarily flummoxed—that she could still need these validations.

He's rich, I said. Let's not pretend that doesn't play a role. He's rich, but he dresses like some pseudo-punk derelict, so you have that in common.

You don't know me, she said. You're talking to me like we know each other, but we don't.

I think I do know you.

She looked at me dead-on. You just want to fuck me, she said.

I couldn't read her tone, whether it was playful or mean. Her chin was twitching slightly.

I don't know, I said. Maybe you're right. But that'd be better than whatever this is—this chickenshit flirtation. Will-they-won't-they. It's boring.

You're projecting, she said quietly.

I don't think I am.

We looked at each other for a long, anxious moment. It was only when Casey came out, calling our names, that we looked away. He was with the oyster guy, Cram. We're going to my apartment, he said.

We just got here, Alma said.

It's dead in there, said Cram.

What are you talking about? There's plenty of people.

It's got no pulse. It's on ice. Rigor mortis has set in.

Cram has goodies, Casey said.

What kind of *goodies*? she asked.

You'll see, let's just go back. Owen, you're coming too.

That's all right, I said.

No, I insist. Come see what Cram's got.

If it's oysters, I'm really okay.

It's not oysters, man, Cram said.

You're coming, Casey said. Tell him he's coming, Alma.

Alma wouldn't look at me. She had her eyes lowered, watching the ember of her cigarette, burnt down nearly to her knuckles. She blew smoke from the corner of her mouth, pitched the filter into the grass, then stood and smoothed her skirt. You're coming, she said.

Cram's goodies turned out to be coke, unsurprisingly. When I arrived, he was already cutting lines on the glass coffee table. Casey ushered me inside, saying, Do a line with us. Let's do a line.

Every time I did coke, I broke into a cold, panicky sweat and ended up checking my pulse every thirty seconds to make sure I wasn't dead. I told him maybe in a few minutes.

Cool, cool, he said. No, yeah, you think about it. Pick out a record. Something good.

What are you in the mood for?

Just something *good*, man, he said, impatient. I'm delegating to you.

Alma came out of the bathroom and stood over the coffee table with her arms crossed. What is that? she said.

Booger sugar, Cram said.

Casey laughed at this. It's coke, honey, he said.

I'm not doing that.

Casey sat on the couch beside Cram and said, You don't have to.

Then why did I come home with you? I thought we were all going to talk.

Listen, babe, he said. We can talk. This will *help* us talk. He stood and kissed her, then sat back down again. Invite some people over. We'll have a party, right, Cram?

Fuck yeah, Cram said. He was using a razor blade to cut the coke. There were books scattered on the table—David Foster Wallace, *Tropic of Cancer,* Patti Smith's memoir. A wine bottle sat next to the untwisted baggie with its powdery residue. The bottle had been turned into a drip candle. Little trickles of rainbow-colored wax ran down the neck.

I went to the record shelves, cocked my head to read the spines. The fear of picking something lame paralyzed me. I'd only come because Alma told me to, because I thought there might be the promise of something in her invitation. She seemed annoyed with Casey, which boded well. Someone snorted, and when I turned around, Casey was looking up at the ceiling and blinking his eyes rapidly to keep tears from spilling out. He sniffled, pressed his thumb to the tabletop, and rubbed his gums.

Is there a genre you'd like to hear? I said.

Oh my God, he said. Will you just *pick* something, man? We're sitting here in silence. He seemed to realize that this had come off harsh and laughed, like he hadn't been serious. I mean, come on, he said. Just something upbeat, you know?

I'll help you, Alma said. She joined me at the shelves, standing close enough that her elbow touched mine. Her eyes scanned the titles, and after a few seconds, she stood on her tiptoes, reaching for the top shelf. Her shirt rode up, revealing the dimples in her lower back. She noticed me noticing this. She looked away and went to the turntable. The record she'd chosen was *Sweet England* by Shirley Collins—the antithesis of an upbeat album. She turned on the receiver, adjusted the volume. The sound, when she placed the needle, was like a match flaring up. The distortion never quieted, and soon the tinny plinking of Shirley Collins's banjo could be heard above the static, her voice ghostly and warbling. I knew of her because she sang versions of the Child Ballads—traditional folk songs that had come across the Atlantic and found their way to Appalachia. She sang a rendition of "Sweet William" that I liked. I could remember my grandmother playing her autoharp and singing "Sweet William" when I was a kid. She'd heard it from her grandmother, who'd heard it from her grandfather, who, for all I knew, heard it from one of his grandparents in England or Scotland.

Casey and Cram looked up at her with befuddled expressions. Who is this? Casey said.

It's one of your records, you should know, she said.

You know I inherited these. I haven't listened to half of them.

It's Shirley Collins.

Well, okay. This is not what I had in mind, and I think you know that.

It's what I want to listen to, Alma said.

He looked at her like he was considering whether to make a thing of it. He decided not to, and merely shook his head, turning back to the table and the line that was waiting for him. *I came from sweet England with mother and dad. We thought in America all might be had.*

This is the most boring music I've ever heard, Cram said. He was looking at his phone and scrolling, twisting a patch of beard beneath his chin.

Alma sat in a recliner with her legs drawn up under her. I brought a chair from the kitchen so I wouldn't have to sit on the couch with the boys, and nobody spoke for a long time. There was only the banjo and the ethereal singing and the popping static of the record, punctuated periodically by snorting and coughing and the click of the razor.

Well, shit, Casey said, when he'd had his fill. He leaned back against the couch cushions, his knee joggling, then stood abruptly and began to pace. I thought you were going to call some people, he said.

I don't *know* anyone, Alma said. Who am I going to call?

He scoffed. You know people.

Who did you inherit the records from? I said, trying to change the subject.

My dad, he said. I wrote all about it in my jungle narrative.

Oh.

You didn't read it. I guess I should've known—you would've mentioned it if you'd read it. Unless you didn't like it.

I skimmed it.

It's fine, he said. You don't have to read it at all if you don't want.

He went on pacing. Cram picked up a *New Yorker* on the end table and leafed through it. I found myself staring at the fork and knife tattoos on his forearms, the way they moved when his tendons flexed. What's all this shit about the jungle anyway? Cram said. You keep talking about it.

The jungle is obscenity, Casey said, in his bad German accent. It is vileness and murder and asphyxiation and choking. It is an immense fornication.

He went on in this way. His gesturing was like that of Hitler's at a rally—shaking his fist, puffing up his chest. But Herzog's manner was nothing like Hitler's. Herzog was flat and soft-spoken, and his eyes were utterly hopeless. *Joseph was an old man, an old man was he,* sang Shirley Collins, *when he wedded Virgin Mary, the Queen of Galilee.*

Nobody laughed at Casey's Herzog impression. Cram hardly noticed. He flipped idly through the magazine, set it aside. He puffed out his cheeks, drummed his fingers on his kneecaps. So, he said. What are we doing?

We could drink, Casey said. We could go out.

We *were* out, Alma said. You had us come back.

You could've said no.

The same thought occurred to me—why hadn't she said no? What was the point in coming back here? What had she hoped for?

We were at Schadenfreude last night, Casey said. We're there every weekend, and we see the same people, we dance to the same songs, drink the same beers, have the same conversations. So *forgive me* if I'm a little bored with the whole scene. I know you like it when people come up to you and say, "Oh you're that hot shit writer," and so on and so forth, but that gets a little old after a while, okay? It's not that interesting to me.

Alma stood suddenly, brushed off her corduroy skirt. She turned to me. Could you take me home, please? she said, her voice even.

Whoa, whoa, Casey said. What are you doing?

I wanna go home.

Okay, look—I'm sorry, okay?

She sighed. I'm tired, she said. I just need to go home.

Well, maybe Owen doesn't want to go home.

They both looked at me. I don't mind, I said. We can go.

You don't wanna stay either? Casey said.

It's been a long night.

Casey's eyes swiveled between us, then he breathed a bitter laugh and looked away. He stared at the framed photographs above the mantel for a long time—the abandoned roses and the woman holding a picture of herself. The polaroid of James. Whatever, he said. Go ahead.

For most of the drive, we didn't talk. Behind us, in the rearview, the moon was burning like a bare bulb. We traveled away from it, toward the indigo darkness and the black hills. Radio towers blinked their red beacons in the distance. Alma stared out the window and picked at her cuticles, her mind somewhere else. I reached over, took her hand from her lap, and held it. There was nothing around for miles it seemed, just a vast desolation, and we were two people in a little car driving into it, holding hands.

I think I have wine, she said. Would you drink some wine?

I told her I would, and this was the only exchange we had throughout the half-hour drive.

Her apartment was on the top floor of the guesthouse. I stood in the darkness a moment as she groped for a lamp in the corner and clicked it on. The guesthouses were old buildings, from the early 1800s, and it looked, inside, more or less the way I imagined it had looked two hundred years before. The floors were planked with red pine, whining underfoot, and the walls were the same exposed fieldstone from the exterior. The living room and kitchen were one large, open space. A single door led to what I assumed was a bedroom.

She offered me a chair at the kitchen table, beside the hearth. The fireplace seemed to be decorative now, though the wall around it was still stained with soot. A mahogany salt box sat at the foot of the hearth. I knew what it was only because Pop had one in the basement, though it was much smaller.

The appliances were the only modern touch. She took a bottle of white wine from the refrigerator and two fruit jars from the cabinet and set them on the table. She poured two generous glasses, then tossed the empty bottle with a clank into the recycling and sat across from me.

Your place is nice, I said.

It smells like a well, she said, and I understood immediately what she meant. It had the same drafty mineral smell—the smell of stone and rainwater.

It's very pastoral, I said.

That's one word for it. I feel like I'm living in one of those colonial reenactments. Like in the next room, there should be ladies in bonnets weaving baskets, or some guy in a leather apron pretending to be a blacksmith. But this is what I signed up for, so.

She looked to the window above the sink and the moon outside and sipped her wine. Her eyes had a lost, bewildered look, fixed on nothing in particular.

I was terrified, she said. The first night here, I was absolutely terrified.

Of what?

If I don't have people around me, telling me what I am, I start to feel like an imposter, she said. I start to feel like I don't even exist.

You mean people like Casey?

She nodded a little, drank her wine. This surprised me—that she could seem so poised on the surface, and underneath, feel that her selfhood was something tenuous and provisional. With all that she had, all that she'd accomplished. God knows, it was a familiar feeling—that the person I trotted out daily was somehow a counterfeit of the real me. But at a certain point, if the counterfeit bill got you what you wanted, what difference did it make?

I didn't want him to come with me, she said. But he called and asked what I was doing. I hadn't planned to do anything today, really. I woke up with a head cold. But once I got out, I was glad I did. I was glad you invited me.

I was glad you came along, I said.

She turned from the window and looked at me with an expression of absolute seriousness. Why do you think you know me?

I took a drink and thought about it. It seemed crucial to give the right answer, but I hadn't considered the reasons why. It was simply an intuition—that she was like me in some way. That we were of a kind.

You were watching everything, I said. I think that's why I came up to you at the party. You were watching quietly what was going on and I liked that.

And you were watching me?

I guess I was.

What did you like about it?

I liked that you were standing outside of everything.

Did you think I was judging?

Not really. Maybe.

That's the assumption people make, when you watch them quietly.

It's not true?

No, of course it is, she said. I deny it if someone asks, but of course that's what I'm doing. That's the whole point of standing on the outside.

I try to be neutral, I said. If you just let people talk, and write it down faithfully, they reveal themselves without having to make a judgment.

What did I reveal?

I don't know yet.

She nodded slightly, took another sip. The thermostat clicked and the radiators groaned to life. I thought of her first memory—monsters living in the radiators, trying to get out. A little girl on a cot in a tiny apartment, far away from home, wide awake while her family slept.

I'm so lonely, she said. Her chin began to tremble. I feel alone all the time here, and I don't know what to do about it.

After a long silence, she wiped her eyes and asked if we should listen to something. I didn't answer. She stood and went to the corner, where a suitcase turntable sat atop a stack of milk crates, and flipped through one of the crates with her back to me. She looked beautiful there in the glow of the lamp, and I was struck with such sudden affection for her that I had to hold my breath against it. Her head bowed. Lamplight golden in the wisps of her hair. All I knew then, in that moment, was that I didn't want her to be lonely. All my other motives and apprehensions collapsed into this singular desire. I watched myself stand up. I knew I would look back and say that this was when it all began. It would be over one day, and I would become once more this ghost, watching himself stand in the dark room, beginning the story without knowing the end.

I went to her, the pine planks aching underfoot. I slipped my arms around her waist, felt her body soften. When she turned, and I kissed her cracked lips, she held her eyes wide open. I stepped back, looked at her for a moment. She pulled me close again, rubbing the front of my jeans. Her sweater peeled off easily. The strong smell of Vicks VapoRub rose from her throat, made my eyes water. I kissed her chest, the flat of her stomach. Baby, she said. Baby, baby.

She shivered slightly when I laid her back on the couch. In the stark light of the floor lamp, her skin was milk-pale, a mapping of green veins in her small breasts and her shoulders. She still had on her skirt and her stockings. I peeled off the stockings, a warm humidity rising between her legs. I paused and looked at her. What do you want? I said. I wanted her to say it. I wanted to know that I hadn't been crazy, that she'd wanted me the same way I wanted her.

What?

What do you *want*?

She lowered her eyes. I want *you,* she said.

I WOKE TO THE TIMID CLACKING OF A BRANCH ON THE window and a slant of rosy light warming the bed. She was not there, but I could smell coffee. I found my jeans draped over a chair, tugged them on, and went to the kitchen shirtless. I found her peeling an orange at the counter in an oversized T-shirt and basketball shorts. Something about the baggy shorts and her thin frame in the T-shirt was reminiscent of a teenage boy at a sleepover. Do you want some orange? she said.

She handed me a wedge with strings of dangling pulp. We sat at the table and I glanced around, admiring the morning light and the little tubular, coral-like succulents on the windowsill. The coffeepot snarled, its aroma mingled with the fragrance of orange. She stared at me openly, letting her eyes pass over my arms and shoulders.

What? I said.

I can't think of a way to compliment your looks that doesn't feel embarrassing.

Why is it embarrassing?

She held an orange slice in her mouth, the way schoolchildren do to imitate a monkey, and thought about it. She took out the wedge and said, Well, I think there's something very expected about a man telling a woman she has a beautiful body. But there's something almost vapid about it when it's the other way around. Like I should be embarrassed for liking something so stereotypical.

My body is stereotypical?

You know what I mean.

You mean it feels antifeminist?

She shook her head. I wouldn't say that, she said. Forget I said anything. I've given you enough of an ego boost.

I could get used to being objectified.

You can afford to enjoy it because it's not a constant bombardment.

The coffee finished brewing and she poured us both a cup. Both mugs were state themed. Hers said VIRGINIA IS FOR LOVERS and featured the outline of the state with a heart in the middle. Mine just said NEBRASKA and had illustrations of the state bird and the state flower. The state tree was the eastern cottonwood, and I thought of the cottonwood groves in Colorado and the cotton seed-fluffs that floated down through the air like feathers in spring. The wood was soft and held so much water that when you cut into a limb with a chainsaw, it would spray out. I'd seen water gush from a sawn cottonwood limb like a faucet.

Do you think of yourself as good-looking? she said.

I don't think I'm *not* good-looking, I said. This seemed like an appropriately modest response. I thought of Maurine, my ex-girlfriend—how she always told me that one day I would leave her for someone younger and smarter. This was a constant worry of hers—she was five years older than me. The first person I'd dated long-term since high school. It had been our breakup that precipitated my move to Colorado.

You're not, she said. I mean, you're *not* not. Which is to say you are. Especially in this light.

Thanks?

Can I take your picture?

Right now?

Yeah, just the way you're sitting there with the coffee mug.

She held up her phone and touched the screen with her thumb. There, she said, smiling. That's good.

Lemme see.

She showed me the picture. My hair was sort of messy. I had my legs crossed, one hand on my bare ankle, the other around the mug. I wasn't smiling, but I looked calm and happy. That is good, I said. It's rare that I see myself in a picture and I look the way I imagine myself to look. But this is pretty close.

It's like hearing a recording of your own voice, she said. I hate that. You're like, "Is that how other people hear me?"

Right, I said. It's never the way you imagine it sounds.

Is it the way you *imagine?* Or the way you *hope?*

Maybe both.

She made a pensive noise and gazed out the window, clinking her fingernail on the ceramic mug. You know, that's how Freud described the uncanny, she said. He tells the story of sitting on a train and seeing an old, shabby-looking man in what he thought was a window. It turned out to be a mirror. He had time to think, "Who is that old man?" Then he realized that it was his own reflection.

I've had that feeling, I said. It's like seeing yourself in a dream.

Exactly! I think that about my own writing sometimes. I look back on some note I jotted down, that I've forgotten about, and I'm like, "Who was I when I wrote this? Who was that person?" Or like someone else reading your work aloud, in a workshop or something. It sounds alien coming out of their mouths, but that's how it *always* sounds, to other people. They notice things about it that we can't notice.

That requires actually showing something you've written to another human being, I said.

You never have?

Not really.

There was a long pause, in which she blew on the surface of her coffee and took a sip. This would've been her cue to say, *I'm happy to read something sometime if you want,* but something about her attitude suggested she was staving this off. Maybe till she knew I wasn't terrible. I at least had the luxury of knowing she was good, based on the reading I'd attended; there was no risk of discovering she was a hack and finding her less attractive because of it. Though there was the awkward fact that I hadn't yet read her book of stories.

Why am I dropping Freud references? she said, picking at a chip in the ceramic with her thumbnail. I'm sure I sound insufferable to you.

Not at all.

You probably think I'm cerebral.

What's wrong with cerebral?

I just wish I could think of something without thinking of a dozen other things related to it. Like, I can't just think of a tree anymore. I think about all the poems about trees that I like. The tree as cultural signifier. I think about "Birches" by Robert Frost. But you—you just think of them as what they are, I'm sure. Or you think of them in a technical sense, as something you have to work on.

Though she seemed to be paying a compliment, I wasn't sure I liked the implication—that the world was one-dimensional to me or something. It was true that I'd never thought of Robert Frost while working on a tree, but I knew the poem.

Earth's the right place for love, I said.

Right! You know it.

Why wouldn't I?

Well, I have to think of it every time I see a birch.

What's wrong with that?

I wanna be able to see it the way you see it. The thing in itself.

So ignorance is bliss.

You know that's not what I mean, she said. I'm trying to say that most of the time my brain is this storm of things referring to other things referring to other things, but when I'm with you, the storm quiets down a little bit. It's a good thing.

I told her I thought I understood, though I didn't at all. What I wanted was the storm—what I thought I wanted anyhow. That the world was still itself to me did not seem a blessing. That one day I might long to see a birch as simply a birch.

Searching for something to say, I seized on the state-themed mug. Nice Virginia cup, I said.

Thanks, she said. I sort of collect them. My goal is to have one for every state.

Do you have one for Kentucky yet?

You know, I actually don't.

We'll have to look for one.

Oh! I meant to tell you this—I was reading my travel guide the other day, and I discovered that Kentucky used to be part of Virginia. We could've both been Kentuckians, if not for the statehood petition in 1791.

You can be an honorary Kentuckian.

Oh yeah? What would I have to do?

Well, it's a complicated process, I said. But the first step is to sleep with a real Kentuckian, so you're well on your way.

She laughed. I'm glad this happened, she said.

I am too. I hope it can happen again.

I guess we should talk about that, she said.

Yeah, you should probably talk to Casey.

And say what?

That you don't want to see him anymore.

What if I talked to him about this and he was okay with it?

If he's in the picture, I'm not interested. I said this before I had a chance to weigh it, or think it through, but I realized how true it was after. I really wasn't.

Alma chewed on the inside of her cheek a moment, then said, I'm not sure I'm interested in that either. But you have to give me a little time.

Sure, I said. No pressure.

I want to see you though. Soon.

What if we went on a drive, got out of town? We could go Saturday.

That sounds nice, she said.

Good. Let's do that.

I swallowed the last of my coffee and set the mug in the sink. She walked me to the door, and when we kissed in the threshold, she pressed her hips against mine. I kissed behind her ear and along her nape. She sighed and drew away. Saturday, she said. I'll call you before then. Or text you. Or something.

We kissed again, briefly, and I went on my way, down the creaking staircase and out the front door, into the fresh autumn morning.

IN THE DAYS THAT FOLLOWED, I THOUGHT OF HER MORE OR less constantly. Driving to work, dragging brush, harnessed and aloft in the tops of trees. That was one good thing about menial work—it was basic enough that you could think about whatever you wanted. They had your body, but they couldn't have your mind.

You could daydream, rehearse conversations. You could spend all day in a fantasy, which, as it turned out, was often necessary to make it all tolerable.

Rando asked me one morning what a writing workshop was. We hadn't yet turned in our personal jungle narratives to be workshopped, but I knew the basic idea. Rando seemed confused by my answer. We were all three hoisting shovelfuls of mulch into the bed of a pickup, huffing and sweating. The dump site for the chipper trucks was an abandoned baseball field, in the center of which stood a mountain of wood chips. We were to shovel the mulch from this enormous pile into the truck, then drive the pickup back to campus and spread the mulch around saplings.

Rando cracked his back and wiped his face with a dirty handkerchief. So let me get this straight, he said. You're out here busting your ass just so you can take this class for free, wherein a bunch of blowhards trash the story you've fretted over for weeks and months? Is that about the size of it?

I blinked the sweat from my eyes and looked up at him. It sounds sort of masochistic when you put it that way, I said. And anyhow, I haven't turned in a story yet. I'm supposed to next week.

I twisted a spading fork into the pile, breaking through the sunbleached top layer to the darker, rich-smelling compost underneath. You had to loosen the mulch in order to shovel it. This was the hardest part. Most of it was pine mulch, and the humid, evergreen smell was dizzying.

I just don't get it dude, Rando said. Sounds like a dumbass thing to do. Now Hunter Thompson, there was a writer. He didn't sit in a room with a bunch of people *talking*. He went out in the world and *lived*, then he wrote about it. That's what y'all should be doing.

Duly noted, I said. I pretended it didn't matter to me much what Rando was saying, but it did. I worried about this problem every day.

It's about technique, James said. You were a musician, surely you understand that. You gotta lock yourself in a room and practice for a while. Hone your craft.

Come on now dude, you can't write a song about practicing your instrument, he said. Technique will only take you so far. Eventually, you have to go out into the world and fall in love and make mistakes, fuck up your life. I don't trust anybody who hasn't fucked up their life at one time or another.

It struck me that Rando was speaking about his life as if he hadn't fucked it up permanently, which more or less seemed to be the case. He used to play steel guitar in a regionally successful country-rock band, and by all accounts was pretty good. Then he became an alcoholic and lost everything. Somehow, in middle age, he got himself stranded here in Kentucky, working as a groundskeeper. Maybe he was happy about how things panned out, though somehow, I found this hard to fathom. I couldn't help but think about Pop, who'd gone out and lived his life the way Rando was suggesting. He hadn't stood on the outside observing, taking notes. He'd become a part of the story, assuming all of the risks that entailed. And yet, he'd rarely spoken of his time overseas, never given his account. Maybe Rando was the same way. Maybe he'd experienced many things, and because they'd never been recorded, they were all the more tenuous and valuable.

The sharp aroma rising from the mulch stung my eyes. I turned away, coughed, and gagged. I leaned against the fork. On the other side of the field, pigweed and wild carrot grew up as tall as a man through the rusted bleachers. A pair of crows preened their wings atop the old scoreboard.

Get high in the desert, Rando was saying. Swim naked in the Pacific Ocean. Meet some girl in Las Vegas and marry her in one of those Elvis chapels. Trust me. You'll look back one day and you'll say, Ol Rando was right.

I PICKED UP HER BOOK OF SHORT STORIES FROM CARMICHAEL'S on Frankfort Avenue. When I got home, I made myself some Ritz crackers and peanut butter and stretched out on the couch to read it, still in my work clothes. Pop came in before I'd finished the first paragraph. He'd been to the podiatrist to have his toenails clipped, and was wearing his #1 GRANDPA hat. He'd been weaker recently, using a tri-pointed steel cane to steady himself.

Anything good? he said, nodding at the book.

It's stories, I said, peanut butter caked to the roof of my mouth. Friend of mine wrote it.

Is this the same friend you went to visit the other night?

One and the same.

So she's a writer.

I nodded.

Interesting, he said.

Why?

Well, I don't know, he said. I don't have any *experience* in the area, but I'd have to guess that if you hitch your wagon to a writer, you're bound to be written about.

Who said anything about hitching my wagon?

You've got that look, he said. You're in the lavender haze.

I don't know about that.

All I'm saying is that it's interesting, that's all. He hobbled to the kitchen, opened the fridge. Beer bottles clinked together. He came back slowly to the living room and eased himself into the recliner with his bottle. I swallowed a drink of milk, screwed the top back on the peanut butter, and wiped my fingers on my pant leg. Something about what he'd said had gotten under my skin. I stared at him as he scanned the TV guide for the shows he'd circled that morning. He glanced up at me and smiled. What's the matter, pard?

Maybe I'm the one to worry about. Maybe I'll write about her.

Okay, okay, he said, don't get riled. Maybe nobody'll write about anybody.

He found the retro station that aired *Gunsmoke* and settled in for an episode. This is a good one, he assured me.

I stuck around and watched as Matt Dillon squared off against a group of ne'er-do-well out-of-towners. No one could agree, exactly, on the best way of handling them, but everybody agreed they should go back to where they came from.

The stories were all about young women, with oblique references to Bosnia throughout. The women were, like Alma, the graduates of celebrated schools, and were usually immigrants who had risen to their stations from difficult origins. As a result, there was always the question of how much gratitude was warranted and how much resentment was allowed. The stories were warm and generous. They were better than anything I'd written and made my own feelings of displacement seem paltry by comparison.

Only one story, the last, dealt directly with Bosnia. It was about a twelve-year-old girl named Naida returning to Sarajevo with her father. She had a basic grasp of the language, though she missed words here and there, and like Alma, had left the country when she was very young. The purpose of the trip was for her to meet her relatives who'd stayed behind—cousins and aunts and uncles. She met a second cousin named Tarik who was one year older. She'd found him standing alone in a corner of the lawn where they'd all gathered. He wore a faded T-shirt for FK Sarajevo, the city's football club, and was listening to a portable CD player. She asked him what he was listening to, and he told her it was a Bosnian punk band. Except, when he placed the headphones over her ears, it was not what she thought of as punk at all. It was synthy piano and a man singing half in Bosnian, half in English, pronouncing his *t*'s as *d*'s. When he saw that her response was not enthusiastic, he said, Hold on, and fished around in his backpack till he found a loose disc. This time it was Pink Floyd. The first track was "Time"—the one with all the chiming clocks at the beginning. Tarik looked at her expectantly.

Wow, she said. Cool.

It's called "Time," he said. That's what it's about.

Yeah, I've heard it.

Tarik took back his headphones and shrugged like, *Whatever*—like he didn't care whether she was impressed, though it was clear to Naida that he did.

While the father caught up with the rest of the family, Tarik and Naida wandered off and walked around the neighborhood. Perceiving her accent, Tarik said she wasn't really Bosnian—she was an American, clearly. Naida protested. She'd been born there, after all. Didn't that make her a Bosnian?

If you were a real Bosnian, you'd know a dead person, said Tarik.

You can't know a dead person because they're dead, Naida said.

You would've seen someone die.

Have you?

Tarik nodded. His father, he said. Then he told the story of being on a bus with his mother and father and his little sister. They were stopped in the mountains at a roadblock, waved down by men with guns. Everyone started praying on the bus. Some of the women were wailing. Tarik knew something bad was going to happen, but he didn't know what. The men with guns came on to the bus and told the women and children to get off. Tarik didn't move at first, though his mother was tugging on his coat. Tarik gripped his father's arm, not wanting to leave him behind, and the father pried his son's small fingers loose one at a time and told him to go, that all would be well. And they went out into the road and the cold air with the craggy mountains above them. Tarik kept looking back at the bus—snow swirling in the headlight beams—till it grew fainter and fainter in the fog and vanished altogether. They walked for a long time in the bitter cold, till they reached a village, the women wailing all the while.

I'm sorry, Naida said. I'm sorry that happened. A few minutes passed in silence before Naida said, But you didn't actually see anyone die—he might be alive. Even at twelve, Naida understood immediately that this was a stupid thing to say. Sorry, she said again.

But Tarik didn't seem to hear. He was kicking a can in the street as if it were a soccer ball. You're not Bosnian, he repeated, in English this time.

As twilight fell, and the forested hills lost their definition and turned black against the sky, they climbed a steep road. At the top was a break in the trees and a railing, from which one could see over the red-tiled rooftops and beyond to the mountains, where Tarik's bus had been stopped. Tarik leaned against the rail and drew a deep breath. It was autumn. The trees were yellowing, and the air was crisp with the scent of summer becoming sere and brittle. Something in Tarik seemed to soften. He asked Naida what America was like. Did she have internet? Yes, she had internet. Were there lots of big Hummers and pickup trucks? Yes, there were plenty of those. Did she eat Reese's cups? Yes, she said, laughing, she ate Reese's cups. How do you know about those?

My friend who moved to Chicago told me about them, Tarik said. He leaned against the rail, looking out over the city and the failing light, as if he were thinking about all these things and whether he would one day see them for himself.

Do you want to meet my friend Osman? Tarik asked suddenly.

Naida, relieved that he wasn't angry about what she'd said, told him she'd love to meet Osman. They walked a quarter of a mile to an apartment building. Tarik jogged up the steps and knocked on one of the doors. A woman with frosted hair answered. She looked like she'd been asleep. Tarik asked for Osman and the woman called Osman's name. Osman came out, limping slightly, and when he saw Naida, he grinned. He had the same drowsy blue eyes as his mother.

She's an American, Tarik explained. My second cousin.

I was born here, Naida said.

She's an American, Tarik said to Osman.

They went to a playground nearby. It was newly built, with freshly planted saplings, tied to stakes, surrounding it—a gesture of hope, that one day the swings and the slide might be shaded by them. Now it was nearly dark. The streetlights were coming on.

Osman had a pack of Drina cigarettes and handed them out to Naida and Tarik. He hadn't said anything yet. He just stared at Naida with a goofy grin. Osman and Tarik lit up. They blew smoke rings. They French-inhaled. They coughed and laughed. Naida just held the unsmoked cigarette down at her side. She has internet at home, Tarik said. Osman raised his eyebrows, impressed. We have to go to a café, Tarik said.

Osman said something finally—a mumbled joke that Naida could not understand. Tarik and Osman laughed, the way teenage boys laughed when they talked about sex, and Naida felt her cheeks growing hot. She turned away from them.

You don't like to smoke? Osman said, gesturing to the cigarette.

She shook her head and tried to hand it back.

No, you keep it, Osman said. Souvenir.

Tarik ground his cigarette against the metal bar of the swing set, sparks showering down. He whispered something in Osman's ear. Osman tried not to smile. Okay, he said. The sodium lamp was buzzing above them, and Naida was afraid for the first time. It was dark. She was somewhere she did not belong.

We want to show you something, Tarik said.

I think I want to go back, Naida said. She'd begun to shiver involuntarily.

But Osman was already sitting in one of the swings, bending down to unlace his sneaker.

Naida took a step back but she did not look away. Osman removed the sneaker, then rolled off the sock. She had time to think that his foot seemed strange, though it was hard to tell in the dim light. Then he rolled up his camo pant leg, and she saw that it was prosthetic—flesh-colored plastic, joined to a stump above the knee.

She grimaced without meaning to and shut her eyes. Tarik started laughing wildly. This was the reaction he'd been hoping for. She looked at her hand and saw that she'd crushed the Drina cigarette. She wiped the loose tobacco from her palm, put what was left in her pocket.

You should see your face! Tarik said. Osman was not laughing. He looked at Naida with the tranquility of someone who had revealed himself completely, who had nothing left to hide.

What happened? she said.

But Osman didn't seem interested in answering. He was fiddling with buckles on the prosthetic leg.

Please, don't, Naida said.

He twisted and the leg came off. She tried not to wince. Underneath, over the stump, he wore a kind of white sleeve. Osman peeled off the sleeve and tossed it in the mulch beside the swings. He looked at Naida, grinning his goofy grin. The skin was scarred near the stump, and there was a small, fleshy appendage, almost like a marshmallow, on the end.

Move it, Tarik said.

Osman flexed his thigh muscle, and the marshmallow wiggled.

What do you think? Tarik asked Naida.

I think—I don't know what I think.

She doesn't know what she thinks, Tarik said to Osman. Osman just grinned.

You can touch it if you want, Tarik said.

Why would I want to touch it?

Are you disgusted by it?

Naida glanced at Osman. No, she said. I just don't have any interest in touching it.

I touch it all the time, Tarik said. Everybody does. It's good luck. You touch it, and your wishes come true.

Osman was trying not to laugh. They were making this up on the spot, she could tell. She was the naïve American who would believe anything, and they didn't think she would really do it. She decided she would turn the tables.

Okay, she said.

The boys' smiles faded. What do you mean? Tarik said.

I'll touch it and make a wish.

Tarik's expression was troubled now. You don't have to, he said.

No, I want to, Naida said. I want good luck.

At this point, the retrospective narrator—an older Naida—told the reader that she often wondered now whether he'd lost his leg to a land mine or in some other fashion, but that at the time, she didn't give it much thought. She assumed, perhaps unconsciously, that it was a consequence of the war, but in the moment, he had simply been a boy without a leg.

She walked over to the swings and knelt in front of Osman. There was fear in his eyes, but at the same time, a look like he didn't want her to stop. She reached out her hand and rested her fingers on the fleshy marshmallow. It was warm and smooth with scar tissue. She closed her eyes and thought of the bus on the mountain road, snow drifting through the high beams. The tires singing. A low murmur of conversation. She thought of the roadblock and the men with guns, and she wished that they had not been there, that they had been waiting on some other road, or better yet, had all stayed home. She wished that the bus had kept going, and that Tarik and his father and his mother and his little sister had been ferried through the night to someplace safe. Maybe then, he might've been like her. He might've come to America and learned for himself that it was many things—a place of contradictions, of beauty and ugliness and unfathomable vanity. And he might've come back here one day to be called an American by someone who would know, someone who'd stayed behind and was acquainted with the dead.

When she stood and drew her hand away, Osman could not meet

her eyes. Tarik, too, bowed his head, ashamed. And Naida knew, suddenly, that she'd been foolish to waste her wish on something that had already happened.

RANDO SAID THAT WHEN HE WENT HOME EVERY NIGHT, HE made himself supper right away and then went to sleep. He'd wake up about midnight and brew coffee and start smoking Pall Malls. He'd smoke two in bed before he could even get up. He said he liked to listen to the sirens and the voices outside and watch the smoke curl up. He'd smoke whatever he had until he was out and then he'd walk to the 7-Eleven down the street and buy another pack. I never buy cartons, he said, unless there's some kind of promotion. Then he would go into his living room and he and his wife, Lynette, would smoke their cigarettes and listen to *Coast to Coast* with George Noory. I've got this little transistor job, he said. I like to turn the knobs and hear the static and the voices crackling. He'd listen to *Coast to Coast* all night, until about 4 a.m., when he'd have to brew another pot of strong coffee and start in on another pack. Between four and six thirty, when we had to be at the shop, he'd smoke that pack in its entirety, pick up another on the way to work for the day, and drink four cups of coffee, not counting the thermos he'd be sipping from all day.

He told us every morning about what he'd heard on George Noory the night before. My dad worked nights and he used to do the same thing, except he only half believed the stuff. Rando was convinced. He took it as gospel truth.

For a time, it was all about GMOs. I don't think Rando knew what GMO stood for, but he knew it was bad for you, or at least that's what George Noory said. I had to get rid of my milk dude, he said. All my bread, my cheese, my meat. It's all got it now, it's all got that GMO in it.

You sure, Rando? I said.

Oh yeah dude, it's all got that GMO now, you gotta check the labels.

Halloween was the first truly cold morning. I walked out across the lot after I'd gassed up the saws and loaded all the pole saws and pruners into the back of the pickup. The diesels were idling, making low chugging sounds. Rando stood with James and a few other guys, steam rising from their thermoses. Rando would do this thing where he'd see you coming over from far off, and as soon as you were within earshot, he'd act like he was talking about you.

That Owen, I heard Kelly say he was really slacking off, they're about to can him. Oh shit, didn't see you there, General. How you doing, buddy? He winked at me and pulled his coat a little tighter. I'd let my beard grow out some and he'd started calling me "the General," saying I looked like a Civil War general. Boy, it's coming, the cold's finally here, he said. Say, you hear about the demon children?

Demon children?

Oh yeah dude, I heard about it on *Coast to Coast* last night, they're coming out on Halloween, something about the alignment of the planets tonight.

What do they do?

They're demons dude, they possess you, take your soul. They're disguised as humans, as little kids, and they knock on your door and want candy. You go in to get it, then you come back and they take off their human costumes and that's all she wrote. I'm not kidding dude, they had a fella talking all about it.

How does this guy know about it? I asked.

How do you think? Rando said. He narrowly escaped.

I laughed and lit a smoke. I stared off at the equipment sheds and the administrative buildings beyond while the other men talked, checking my phone compulsively every few minutes.

Earth to Owen, James said.

What?

I asked if you were about ready. Clearly, you're preoccupied. He's thinking about his new lady friend.

I'd told James all about Alma and the whole complicated situation with Casey the day before. I hadn't expected him to mention it to anyone else.

You got a girl now? Rando said.

An eastern European girl, James said.

You don't say? I've known a few European girls. They're nice, but they've got a smell to them.

What does that mean?

They don't bathe the way we do, he said. They've got their own special techniques and believe in the natural oils of the body and whatnot. He took a slurp from his thermos and looked at me as if this were a completely mundane and uncontroversial statement.

I don't really want to talk about it, I said.

What's her name? said Artie, one of the other guys standing around.

Her name's Alma and she's a big-shot writer, James said. She's sort of famous.

So what's she doing with *the General*? Rando said.

That's what I'd like to know, James said. This girl grew up with a silver spoon.

I don't know if that's true, I said.

Come on, you said she went to Princeton.

Maybe she had a scholarship.

What did her parents do?

I didn't say anything.

Come on, what'd they do?

They were doctors, I think. At least her mom was.

Aha!

She's a rich girl? Rando said.

Oh yeah, said James.

Rando whistled and shook his head. I've known some rich girls, too, dude. They don't bathe like us either. They use all kinds of fancy smell-good balms and liniments.

She wants to roll around in the dirt, Artie said. I've known girls like that.

Exactly, Rando said. That's exactly right. Slumming it. I bet every rich girl has that phase.

I'm done with this whole conversation, I said. I flicked my cigarette and crouched to tighten my boot laces.

What you need is an Asian girl, Rando said. My buddy Jason was talking to this Chinese girl for a few months online. They chatted and sent pictures back and forth, and next thing you know, they're married. He says they treat their men like kings over there, that it's part of the culture. And an American man, a white man, is real exotic to them.

That's so racist, Rando, I said.

How is it racist? How is what I just said racist when it's the truth about their culture? James, did you think that was racist?

I'm not the judge of all things racist just because I'm Black, James said. But yes, it was very racist.

James hummed along to the radio as he drove. I bit off chunks from my granola bar, watching the scenery pass. Our first job site was a honey locust near the soccer practice fields. We were to remove the tree, and because of its tricky location between two outbuildings, we would not be able to flop it. We would have to limb it and lower the segments with rigging lines. It would take all day and would be difficult work, but some part of me welcomed the distraction.

I wish you hadn't told them all that, I said.

All what? About Alma? Listen man, I'm just trying to lighten things up. I'm looking at you, and I see you over here suffering, worrying about whether this girl will call you. She'll either call you or she won't. Nothing you can do about it.

It's none of Rando's business.

Rando's good for morale, James said. I think that's the only reason they keep him on. It's certainly not because of his work ethic.

Outside, leaves were drifting from the trees and swirling up from the lawns. It was a cloud-swept day, shifting between light and shadow. Some of the students were costumed. On the sidewalks, girls in skimpy nurse uniforms passed boys in hockey masks, their shirts spattered with fake blood. We went by the guesthouses, and I wondered if she was inside, if she was thinking about me as much as I was thinking about her.

What would you do if you were me? I said, turning to look at him finally.

I wouldn't be mixed up in a situation like this.

But if you were.

I don't know, man, he said. That Casey—he's a handsome dude.

He's not that handsome.

James cocked an eyebrow. I'm just saying. I'm not even one to notice these types of things, but I noticed with him. His face is, like, classically proportioned or something.

I don't wanna hear this.

Don't worry, he said, patting my knee, I think you're a handsome boy, too. Look, she's gotta make the decision on her own. All you can do is keep on being your charming self.

We pulled up to the practice fields and found the tree. James switched on the emergency blinkers. Rando pulled up soon after and set out the cones. I walked into the weblike shade of the honey locust, peering up through the branches, shielding my eyes. It was forty feet high at least, much of it dead. It had been trimmed before—you could tell that much. There were stubs and cankers—healed-over wounds from the tree's past. Someone had thought it worth saving decades ago, and now we were here to cut it down. It had taken half a century to grow. It was here, it existed, and by three o'clock that afternoon, it would be gone.

WITH LITTLE TO DO AT HOME BUT WATCH WESTERNS, AND nothing to occupy my mind, I finally wrote my jungle narrative, two days before it was due. It was about an unnamed grounds-keeper and a young woman referred to simply as "the Writer" who spend an afternoon at the zoo. They talked about their lives and how they got to where they were. It was from the perspective of the Groundskeeper, who believed himself to be in love with the Writer. After their zoo excursion, he kissed her in the car. She rebuffed him, explaining that she had a boyfriend. At the end of the story, the Groundskeeper went home, to his father's house where he was living, and his father asked him when he was going to get his life together at the supper table. There was nothing really to prompt this. They were just eating salted tomato slices from the garden. The Groundskeeper stared at the tomato slices. That was the final image of the story.

I realized only after I typed up a draft that Casey would read it and see clearly what was what. The characters weren't even thinly veiled. So, I went back and changed "the Writer" to "the Sculptor." They had their conversation not at the zoo, but at the Speed Art Museum. The narrator remained a groundskeeper, but I gave the Sculptor enough imported traits to render her unrecognizable. She became a patchwork. Inconsistent. If I'd had more time, I might've made her plausible, but the whole thing was a lost cause.

I read it through once, saved the document. It wasn't as good as I wanted it to be, but it wasn't bad either. I hadn't considered what my metaphorical jungle might be, but then I supposed that was up to my classmates' interpretation. I brushed my teeth, unfolded the hide-a-bed. I searched among my boxes of books for *The Collected Poems of Wallace Stevens*. When I'd found my worn copy, I lay in bed and read the poem Alma had quoted at the zoo—"The Motive for Metaphor." *You like it under the trees in autumn,* went the first line, *because everything is half dead.* I must've read it sometime in the past, because I'd underlined one of the stanzas. *The obscure moon lighting an obscure world / Of things that would never be quite expressed, / Where you yourself were never quite yourself / And did not want nor have to be.* It made me think of the Frank O'Hara line from "Mayakovsky"— *perhaps I am myself again.* I thought of Alma's Freud anecdote, too— seeing a stranger in the train window and realizing it was his own reflection. Everything reminded me of something else lately, and less and less of these things were in the real world. But then, books were as real as anything else, I supposed. Stories and poems were things in the world. So why did I feel so disconcerted, so much like an imposter, sitting in my basement room with this book in my lap? The moon was not obscure outside the window. It was a clear, cool stone, cratered and scarred, floating in the sky behind black branches.

ALMA CALLED ME FRIDAY AS I WAS ON MY WAY HOME FROM work. She was sniffling when I answered, as if she'd been crying, but her Hello was excessively cheery.

Are you okay? I said.

I'm great! How are you?

I'm on my way home from work.

Oh, she said. How was it?

How was my work?

Yeah.

I thought about the day. We'd trimmed two crab apple trees near one of the dormitories. The grass was littered with rotting fruit, which gave the air a sour, nauseating smell. Green, iridescent flies swarmed lazily around us as we worked, emitting a low hum, sometimes biting our ankles or careening like little kamikaze pilots for our ear canals. It was tiring, I said.

Oh, she said sadly. Well, it's the weekend now!

That's true.

Still wanna go for a drive tomorrow?

I wanted to ask her if she'd talked to Casey yet, before I agreed to this. But at the same time, I didn't want her to feel she was being rushed or that I was making unfair demands. I didn't know, really, what was fair of me to expect. It was all uncharted territory.

Yeah, that'd be good, I said. I told her I'd pick her up at nine in the morning.

Nine's a little early. Could we do ten?

Sure, I said. I'll see you then.

I got up at seven the next morning. Most days I set my alarm for half past five, so it was hard to sleep past seven, even on the weekend. When I pulled up, she was waiting on the guesthouse steps.

It was a fair morning, the sky hazy and crisscrossed with the contrails of planes. I didn't know where we were going exactly except that we were going east, the direction I usually took when I went on drives alone. Driving eastward would lead us to the Appalachian foothills. That's what I wanted her to see.

I made us a playlist, she said, waggling her phone.

All I have is a cassette player.

You don't have an adapter?

Nope.

She looked at me with dismay. That won't do, she said. I worked hard on this playlist. Where could we get an adapter?

Walmart?

Great, let's stop by Walmart.

I wasn't exactly anxious to spend the first part of my morning at a Walmart, but she seemed resolved and I was curious about the music she'd picked and why she wanted me to hear it so badly. We pulled off at the next exit and found a Walmart. I sat in the car while she ran in. Near one of the cart returns, a stray dog was tearing apart a box of Honey Buns and eating them ravenously, plastic packaging and all. The dog seemed to notice me staring and looked up as if to say, *You got a problem, buddy?*

Alma came through the automatic doors after ten minutes and jogged out to the truck. When we were pulling onto the interstate on-ramp, she said, Did you know there are guns in there?

What do you mean?

Like, in the sporting goods section. There was a counter, and behind the counter there were all these rifles in a rack. They were just out in the open.

Yeah, I said. It's a Walmart. Haven't you been to a Walmart?

I think, she said. I'm sure I went with my parents sometime when I was little. I just didn't know you were allowed to have guns *out* like that. What keeps somebody from grabbing one?

They're not loaded, I said.

But how do you know?

They don't have magazines in them.

What's a magazine?

Like the thing that holds the bullets. It clicks into a slot under the gun. You've seen people do it in action movies, I'm sure.

I don't watch a lot of action movies, she said.

She unwrapped the adapter, tossing the swaddled plastic bag and the trash in the back seat, and pushed the fake cassette into the player.

What's the theme of this playlist? I said.

It's a mixture of songs that I think you would like and songs that I've been listening to lately that make me think of you. Some fit in both categories, obviously.

I pulled onto the state highway, which would lead us southeast through the Knobs. The grade was steep, and Pop's old Ranger went from second to third gear with a grinding rumble. Outside, fields of hewn corn swept past. Mobile homes. Propane tanks. Curing barns with sheaves of brown tobacco hanging inside. A big pickup with a lift kit and chickens in wire cages thundered past us on a straight-away, white feathers fluttering from the bed. They looked like cottonwood seed-fluffs.

I'll have to take you to a flea market, I said. See if we can get you a Kentucky mug for your collection.

Well, she said, putting on a hillbilly accent, I sure would be tickled to death if you would.

I smiled in spite of myself. That's pretty good, I said.

Yeah?

Yeah, except "sure" would be more like "shore."

Got it.

I hadn't heard most of the songs on her playlist, and she seemed to relish telling me about the artists when I asked who they were. A few of the songs were by someone named Arthur Russell, and these were by far the strangest. She explained that he was a cellist and a composer of sorts, who incorporated his cello playing into dance and ambient music. His lyrics were more like half-heard murmurs, shifting in and out of intelligibility, and the cello, played into a microphone and saturated with reverb, gave an eerie, echoic texture to the beats. It was unlike anything I'd ever heard. There was something painfully intimate and naïve about the lyrics when I caught a line here or there—something very private. It was as if he were singing only to himself.

The songs I recognized were by Vashti Bunyan and Talking Heads. She played "Cities," the one where David Byrne goes on and on about finding himself a city to live in. This is like your theme song, she said. Cause you're, like, rootless or whatever.

Yeah, I got it, thanks.

The road threaded between ledges of cut limestone, the slopes above shaggy with scrub pine and cedar. Emerging from the limestone corridor onto a broad curve, we could see across a great distance—the land writhing out away from us in wooded furrows and striations. Far-off mountains hazy and blue, so faint they might've been clouds. Close up, along the rust-freckled guardrail, the trees and the electrical poles were festooned with kudzu.

So this is the backwoods, Alma said.

Shore is, I said.

We came to the outskirts of a town with a flea market. The houses were small, many of them mobile homes with white latticework along the foundations and children's toys on the lawns. A Confederate flag flew from a pole in one yard, and I saw her eyes widen at the sight of it. She followed it with her gaze, turning all the way around in the seat, till it was no longer visible. I saw Confederate flags in my hometown and on my drive to work—all over the state, really. I hadn't considered that it might be alarming to her.

I thought Kentucky was neutral, she said.

Doesn't mean there aren't sympathizers.

We parked in the grass near the flea market tents. People chatted loosely in folding chairs behind the tables. They had coolers, from which they drew soda cans in melting ice and cracked the tabs. A charcoal grill was burning somewhere. Laughter and easy talk. With the weekend crowd, it was not as quiet as I'd hoped. Families milled about, perusing the stalls—potbellied men with pocketknives and cell phone holsters clipped to their belts, old women with Pentecostal hairdos, pregnant teenagers and their camo-clad, Skoal-dipping boyfriends. Alma watched these people from the truck with skittish eyes. You ready? I said.

She turned and blinked at me, startled from a reverie. Yeah, of course, she said.

Though my jeans were skinnier than the average good-ol-boy's, my boots were the steel-toe Danners I wore to work, and my hat had HUSQVARNA stitched in orange thread on the front. For these reasons, I could usually pass as someone who belonged in these situations. It was only when I opened my mouth that people eyed me with suspicion. Alma, on the other hand, drew stares, just by looking the way she looked. For one thing, she wore no makeup, and the other women at the market had foundation and lip gloss and lilac eye shadow. Alma's clothes, too, gave her away—her faded black jeans and red-laced boots, the thin camisole that she wore braless under her open flannel. The flea market girls—at least the ones without religious skirts and netted hair—had sequined hearts stitched in the hip pockets of their jeans and Mossy Oak camo sweatshirts. And they were all preternaturally tanned. When Alma pulled off her flannel in the sunlight and tied it around her waist, her skin looked shockingly pale, and you could see the tufts of hair poking out from her armpits.

But it was more than just the way she looked. It was something less tangible also. Her bearing. Her clever, inquisitive eyes. She noticed the people noticing her, and I felt a pang of guilt for bringing her here—that it had been a foolish idea. Tony always said that there were no two-dimensional characters in the real world, that everyone had depth, and that if you were going to write about someplace rural not to make it into a minstrel show. Don't dress all your backwoods characters in camo and have them chewing tobacco, he'd said. This was easy for him to say, as someone who had not come from a rural place. But looking around, many of the people *were* wearing camo, and they *were* dipping Skoal and spitting the brown juice into Mountain Dew bottles. I'm sure they had their depths and their private sorrows, but at the moment, they were staring at us and making us uncomfortable, and I didn't much care about their depths.

I took Alma's hand in mine and squeezed it. She squeezed back—two quick pumps—and we entered the shade of the tents. After a few minutes of browsing and touching the little knickknacks, she seemed less nervous. There were antique Barbies and sock monkeys, broken radios, ashtrays of hobnail milk glass and mushroom casserole dishes. There were Styrofoam heads with wigs, dime-store romance novels, wicker baskets, and dreamcatchers. We came to a stall of old farming tools. I picked up a tomahawk knife, used for cutting burley-leaf tobacco. Though rusted, the blade's edge was still sharp against my thumb. I explained to her what it was. You could still see the ingrained tobacco gum in the scarred hickory handle. My grandfather's got a few like it, I said.

How do you use it? she said.

I'm not sure.

It's to cut the stalk, said the old man running the stall. He looked to be about the same age as Pop and wore bib overalls. He sat in a lawn chair with a bottle of Dr Pepper between his legs and a table fan blowing directly on his face. Lemme see, he said, standing unsteadily and motioning for the tomahawk. I gave it over and he demonstrated how it would be used, whacking the invisible base of a tobacco plant. You cut the stalks, spear the bundles with one a these. He pointed to a spear laid out on the table. Then they set out and dry. You probably seen em round harvest time. Rows and rows of little tobacco husk teepees.

The man smiled gently. He seemed proud to have imparted this knowledge. We thanked him and went on to the next table, where a hundred or so pocketknives were laid out. Pocketknives were a hot-ticket item apparently. There were three such stalls at the flea market. A man and his son ran the stall. The son could only be described as a smaller replica of his father. They both wore black T-shirts tucked into jeans. They both had plump bellies and fat, rosy cheeks, and they both had gel-spiked hair. They were even standing the same way, their thumbs hooked in their belt loops.

Y'all need a knife? the father said.

I don't think so, I said.

What about your friend? he said, upping his chin at Alma. Can't be too careful these days.

I think I'm all right, Alma said politely, but the man didn't seem to hear.

Tanner, fetch me them cat ears, he said, and without hesitation, the little boy jogged to an open suitcase in the back and drew out a pink metal keychain, shaped like a cat's face. Thank you, Tanner, the man said. He fitted his fingers through the cat's eyes. It's like brass knuckles, he said, only the ears are spikes. You can gouge a man's eyes out and not break a sweat.

He punched the air and we both flinched a bit. He grinned at this, amused that he'd scared us. You put it on your keys, and if some gangbanger tries to mess with you in a parking lot, you punch his eyes out.

No, thanks, Alma said, her voice a little sterner.

The man tossed the cat ears onto the table and returned his thumbs to his belt loops. Suit yourself, he said.

Yeah, suit yourself, said the son, hooking his thumbs just like his dad.

We perused for another twenty minutes, arriving finally at a stall that sold coffee mugs. There was a whole shelf of Kentucky-themed mugs. She ran her fingers over them, turning them slightly to read what they said. Most had the insignia of the University of Kentucky. One had a cartoon map of the state, with all its attractions. Another featured a portrait of a horse's head and said KENTUCKY HORSE COUNCIL. What do you think the Horse Council is? she said.

It's a council of horses, I said. They get together for a meeting once a year, with a gavel and an agenda, and they vote on important horse issues, like whether they prefer oats or barley.

She replaced the mug on the shelf, tried to keep from smiling.

Too lame?

Just such a dad joke, she said.

People talk about dad jokes, but I don't remember my dad telling that many jokes.

Why not?

I shrugged. After I was about ten, he just seemed to be perpetually in a bad mood, with me especially. I think I disappointed and bewildered him.

She gave me her pitying look. Poor tenderhearted Owen, she said. So misunderstood.

Yeah, yeah, I said. Which one of these do you want? It'll be my gift to you.

Hmm, she said, tapping her fingers on her lower lip. I think this one. She took down a mug with a cartoon hillbilly. He was reclining under a tree with his legs crossed and a jug of moonshine close by. Most of his teeth were missing, of course, and a log cabin sat in the background. MY OLD KENTUCKY HOME! read the caption.

I shook my head. It was a strange thing, how thoughtlessly people trafficked in these stereotypes. I was guilty of it, too, of course. After all, how could I complain when I, too, resented their judgmental stares and hateful flags? And yet, I resented the judgments of outsiders also, their reductive opinions and assumptions. It was another form of my perennial predicament. My desire to both honor and criticize, to be *of* a place, and to merely be *in* it, as a visitor.

———

We strolled back to the grassy parking lot, holding hands and bumping against one another. A trio of children were playing near the truck. One had a lightsaber and the others had AR-15s with orange caps on the muzzles to signify that they were toys. They ceased their warfare briefly and gawked at us.

I'm a Jedi of the Old Republic, said the one with the lightsaber.

Cool beans, I said, which was my stock response whenever a child engaged me. We need to get into this truck.

All three turned around, as if noticing for the first time that the truck was there. They walked away bashfully, and when they believed they were out of earshot, they continued playing. Your bullets will be vaporized, said the Jedi.

No, they won't, said one of the others. They're hollow-points and they'll explode in your body and shred your internal organs.

When we were situated in the truck and the engine was idling, I asked, Where to?

Should we go to your place?

My place is out of the way, I said. And it's a sty right now anyhow.

I don't care, she said. That doesn't bother me. I wanna see where you live.

Maybe next time, I said.

She frowned and looked as though she might press the issue, but she didn't. Well, let's go to the guesthouse, I suppose, she said.

I drove us back the way we came. She rummaged in the back seat, looking for a bottle of water, and found the NO BLACKS, NO WHITES, JUST BLUES hat in the floorboard. After James had given it to me that night at Schadenfreude, I'd worn it to work a couple times. What is this? Alma said, looking at the front. Is it a joke?

I found it outside Schadenfreude.

She studied it a moment, then put it on and looked at herself in the visor mirror. How do I look?

Like a real trucker.

You don't think it has head lice in it, do you?

I don't think so.

Our conversation turned to politics as we drove on. She was still pretty sure Trump would lose. I had less confidence.

He takes up so much real estate in my mind, she said. It makes sense. He's a real estate developer. His biggest deal of all was to buy space in all of our minds. Even if you hate him, he's in there— maybe especially if you hate him.

The sky had darkened. Wind scattered leaves in the road and gusted against the truck on the highway, and soon it was raining— a true downpour. I clicked the wipers to full speed, but the windshield was a blur. Jesus, she said, gripping the armrest. I tried to project a sense of cool command, but my heart was beating fast, as if I were on the verge of being caught for something. In the half second of clarity that each beat of the wipers afforded, I could see the furious plinking of rain in the road and the hillsides grown rank with kudzu, still green somehow, though the deciduous trees were red and golden. Looking at the kudzu, I knew what Herzog meant by overwhelming fornication and asphyxiation. I imagined hydroplaning, waking upside down to the drip of gasoline and coolant, this girl beside me who would seem, for a moment, like a stranger. I imagined the kind of person who would find us there in the lush tangle of greenery. Our relationship, or whatever we had, would not survive a car accident. It was too early. If we lived through it, she'd never have anything else to do with me. I focused on the road, on the dashed line appearing and vanishing in the rain-blurred world.

Mercifully, the rain let up, and we arrived at the guesthouse in one piece—or two pieces, I guess. She invited me inside. In the living room, I took the NO BLACKS, NO WHITES, JUST BLUES hat from her head and tossed it. It landed between the couch and the wall. She led me back to her dim bedroom, where we dried off with the same towel. The sound of the rain rose and fell like applause, rinsing the window. We helped each other undress. Her room was messy, even more so than the night I first saw it, with clothes strewn all over the floor and draped on the open drawers of her dresser. It looked like it'd been ransacked, like someone had been desperately looking for something and may or may not have found it.

Come over here, she said, and she led me by the hand to a full-length mirror, where we continued undressing and kissing. Soon she was topless, her jeans pushed down around her ankles. I stood behind her in front of the mirror. She pressed her palms to the wall, in the position of someone being frisked, and nuzzled her backside against me. What do you want to do to me? she said. Her expression was grave—as if my answer were a matter of life and death.

I don't know. I kissed the nape of her neck and her shoulder. My heart was really throbbing now, faster than it had on the road. What do you want? I said.

I want you to tell *me.*

I wasn't any good at this sort of thing. I thought of what I could say—something bold enough to excite, but not so bold or bizarre as to be off-putting. I want to put my fingers in you, I said. This struck me as stupid immediately.

Mm, she said, nodding her head.

I rolled down her underwear. Her ass was pale and smooth, pressed against the front of my jeans. I cupped my hand between her legs from behind, feeling the patch of coarse hair. She was wet, and my fingers slipped in easily. She inhaled—sharply, quickly. I could hardly hear her over the waves of rain on the roof.

I glanced at the mirror. She was looking at me with an almost dazed expression, at what I was doing to her with my hand. I looked overly serious. My cheeks were flushed. I didn't like seeing myself this way, but I liked seeing her watching me, and I focused on that. What was she imagining? Who did she think I was?

After, when we were lying in her bed, our hearts hammering, I told her the truth. I live in my grandfather's basement, I said. She propped herself up on her elbow and looked at me, strands of hair plastered to her forehead.

What?

I don't have an apartment, I said. I live in a basement in a house with my grandfather. My uncle lives there, too. He has a lot of anger issues and is a little eccentric. I've been living there a few months.

She stared at me for a long time, her brow wrinkled, then she sat up in half lotus and looked to the dimly glowing window. The rain had all but quit. Now only the dripping of leaves and the pouring of water through the gutters could be heard. Why didn't you tell me? she said.

I think it should be obvious. I was embarrassed.

Where did you live before that?

In my Buick, I said. In Denver.

She looked at me with great concern, though it wasn't clear if the concern was for me. You were *homeless*?

Not really, I said, trying to sound flippant. I could've come back and lived with my mother, but I didn't want to admit defeat. I thought I could find another job and a place to stay. Didn't pan out though. So, I came here, moved into my granddad's. Sold the Buick, started taking classes.

She swallowed audibly.

I don't like this look, I said.

It's just . . . worrying. That you let yourself get to that point.

That I *let* myself?

Yeah, I don't know. I mean, were you mentally ill?

I laughed at this and sat up. No, I said. Although I guess it depends on what you mean by mentally ill. I was very depressed, but who wouldn't be? I'd been laid off. I couldn't afford rent. I had a semi-serious drug problem.

What do you mean "a problem"?

Look, it's the past, I said. I'm okay now, really. I just wanted to tell you where I lived because I thought it had to come up sooner or later.

She held my gaze for a long moment, then nodded slowly and said, Okay.

Okay what?

Just, okay. That's fine. You'll have to show me sometime. Your place, I mean, or whatever.

Definitely, I said. I have a hide-a-bed couch. Have you ever had sex on a hide-a-bed couch?

No.

Well, let me tell you, it's pretty luxe. The springs sound like asthmatic wheezing.

She huffed a nervous laugh and shook her head. Next time we can go there, she said.

You sound really stoked.

I'm just processing, she said. I'm fine.

She turned away from me again, to the window and the black branches outside. I watched her profile for a moment, then I stood and stretched and stepped into my jeans. Did you happen to talk to Casey? I said. I tried to pose this question as casually as I could, as if it had not been hovering over everything since the moment I picked her up.

Not yet, she said flatly. I'm getting around to it. Something had shifted in our rapport. Her eyes were suddenly mournful, and I wondered if it had been stupid to tell her where I lived. But then, what choice did I have? I had to tell her at some point. Indefinite subterfuge was never an option.

No rush, I said. I buttoned my shirt and slipped on my boots without tying them. I clomped over to the bed, bent down to kiss her. So we'll go to my place next time, then?

Next time, she said. She gave me a peck, then stood and walked into the bathroom, shutting the door behind her. There was nothing left to do but leave.

THE MORNING AFTER THE ELECTION, A BRONZE CAST OF *The Thinker* on the University of Louisville's campus was spray-painted with swastikas. The statue was the first large-scale casting of the original, supervised by Rodin himself in 1903. It was displayed at the 1904 World's Fair, and eventually bought by a wealthy lawyer who donated it to the University of Louisville, where sometime in the wee hours of November 9, 2016, it was painted with red swastikas.

When I read the news, I wrote it down in my notebook. I imagined using it one day as a detail in a piece of fiction. But it was too on-the-nose, I decided—this universal symbol of contemplation and the life of the mind, defaced with the universal symbol of hatred and ignorance. Who would believe it? But then, maybe this was simply the time we were entering. Maybe everything would be on-the-nose from here on out. We would be crass and ugly, and nothing would be hidden.

AT WORK THAT MORNING, YOU COULD TELL RIGHT AWAY who'd voted for who. The losing side, of which James and I were a part, sat at the conference table looking grim. Those on the winning side were theatrically cheery. They whistled as they poured their coffee. They smiled and said, Good morning! And, of course, they were all white and male and over the age of forty.

Kelly addressed the group. He was one of the cheery ones. Let's remember today to remain polite, he said. No politics. I understand that may be difficult, as there are undoubtably some sore losers among us, but let's try and create an atmosphere of good ol fashioned civility.

As we trimmed a pine at the first job site, James monologued about Shirer's *The Rise and Fall of the Third Reich.* Hitler was inevitable, he said. He was using a pole pruner, yanking the rope and clipping small branches quickly as Rando and I bent and gathered them. Hitler wasn't some fluke. These things don't happen by accident.

Rando seemed troubled. He'd been unusually quiet all morning and paid no mind to James as we stooped for the branches and laid them in the chipper bed.

In the same way, James said, you can trace back from the situation we're in now to particular antecedents in the culture. It's all right there.

You're probably right, I said. I'm not sure if it's more comforting to think of it that way or as a random disaster.

What about you, Rando? James said. You haven't said a word all day. Why aren't you debating with me?

Rando shrugged. I don't know dude, he said. What would be the point?

What would be the point in *debating*? Rando, I'm shocked.

Rando shrugged again. A long silence passed, in which the only noise was the snipping of the pruner. After a few minutes, James tossed the pole in the grass and went over to the orange water cooler bungee-corded to the back of the truck. He pressed the tab and water trickled into his Nalgene. He drank it, watching Rando steadily. Rando averted his face and reached for his cigarettes.

Wow, James said. Okay.

What? Rando said.

You voted for him.

Rando kept his eyes fixed on his shoes and said nothing. He shook out a cig, placed it between his lips.

Of course, James said. Fuckin great, Rando.

You didn't, did you, Rando? I said, my voice hopeful.

Rando got his Pall Mall lit. He took a puff, blew a stream of smoke. What do you want me to say? he said. He glanced at me briefly. I guess he saw the disappointment in my face. He looked away, ashamed.

You can't take it personally, Rando said. And how was I supposed to vote for *her*? She's like a fuckin robot. It's like she's been programmed to say all the right things. I don't want somebody like that on my television every day.

You'd rather have a bigot, I guess? James said. How can I not take it personally? It *is* personal. It affects me personally if I have to put my name on a registry, or if I go visit my dad overseas and I can't come back because of a travel ban. That affects me on a very personal and non-abstract level, Rando.

People vote the way they vote, Rando said. It's none of your business. I've always voted for the anti-establishment candidate. I voted for Ross Perot. I voted for Nader. Anybody who's gonna shake the system up. Usually it's a third-party candidate, but in this case, Trump seemed the most likely. And look, it doesn't matter anyway. The whole thing is an illusion. A collective hallucination. They had a guy on *Coast to Coast* just a couple days ago, an ex-CIA spook. He said it's all decided behind closed doors by the big banks and the one-percenters. They don't even *count* the votes.

Will you shut up, Rando? I said. He and James both looked at me, surprised. My voice shook uncontrollably, though I'd strained to keep it steady. Will you just shut up for once in your life?

I could see it hurt him. I don't know where it came from, really. I just blurted it out. Maybe I was thinking of my mother and father, who'd almost certainly voted the same as Rando, and who'd surely done so with the same feckless lack of concern. Maybe I imagined, or wanted to imagine, that in order to vote for him, you'd have to be like Cort—an angry person, in other words. Someone with profound disadvantages. But Rando I liked. I felt that he'd betrayed me, and like anyone who's been betrayed, I was embarrassed for allowing myself to grow fond of him.

Rando walked away from us and sat in the truck with the windows cracked, smoking and listening to the radio. James and I turned back to our work. We pruned in silence. Clouds broke apart and re-formed above us. The light dimmed and brightened, and nobody said anything till it was time to call off.

WE WORKSHOPPED MY STORY ABOUT THE GROUNDSKEEPER and the Sculptor at the art museum. Maybe it was the general mood of despair following the election, but everyone seemed glum and uninterested throughout. They admitted, begrudgingly, that some of the passages were good. They liked the dialogue, generally. It was funny sometimes, I guess, said Joanna, during the "positive remarks" round.

When it came time to critique, people were standoffish. What's the metaphorical jungle here? Tony said.

I think it's his family, said Casey.

The family stuff is enigmatic, Tony said. We don't really see them. I'm thinking maybe it's Kentucky, or what it represents.

And of course, he was right. It was and always would be. I wrote it down in my notes—*Kentucky is my jungle*—and almost laughed aloud.

What does the Sculptor like about him? Joanna said. I kept wondering that.

Maybe she likes his potential, said Trent.

What is his potential? Tony said. What motivates him?

Everyone was silent. Tony was right to ask. I hadn't given the character my own desire to become a writer. He was merely a tree trimmer. I'd given him all my other qualities except the one that was most important to me, and for that reason, he never quite came into focus.

I dropped by Tony's office hours later, as was the custom for each student after their workshop. It was on the third floor of the humanities building, which, unlike the Georgian-style administrative offices and the sleek, glass-paneled science buildings, resembled a Soviet bunker. There was one thin window in the office, in which he'd perched a spider plant that appeared to be on death's doorstep. Otherwise, it was just a desk, a computer, two chairs, and stacks of books. A few cutout *New Yorker* cartoons were taped to the wall, but I couldn't read the text.

Tony smiled politely when I sat. He had my story on the desk with all his penciled marginalia. It was clear he'd given it a lot of thought—probably much more than it deserved, or than even I had given it.

Well, he said, I'll start by saying I was really impressed. I started reading and I was like, "This guy knows how to write a sentence."

My cheeks grew hot. I made a conscious effort to keep from grinning like an idiot. He'd given no intimation of his opinion in class and kept his comments reserved—never once tipping his hand.

Thanks, I said. That's good to hear.

Good stuff, he said, leafing through the pages. Lot of interesting class stuff going on here.

Thanks.

So, he said. He put on his glasses and squinted at the computer screen. You're not in the master's program, is that correct?

That's right.

Why not?

I shuffled through various explanations, weighing each. In the end, I went with the truth. I don't really know, I said.

Well, you're good enough, he said. In fact, you should really think about applying to MFA programs. It's a little late for this cycle but maybe next year.

Okay, I said. I knew only vaguely what an MFA program was, and the only one I could say anything about was Iowa. I knew it was the best, and that Carver and Cheever taught there at the same time in the '70s.

Here's what I would do, if I were you, Tony said. Apply to the master's program in English here at Ashby, for the spring. I'll write your letter and talk to the director. You'll get in, no problem. Apply for fellowships and residencies at the same time—the good ones that give you funding. If you don't get into one, you'll at least be enrolled here and working towards a graduate degree instead of just, you know, futzing around. Then next year you can do the whole MFA thing. Sound good?

He had his hands open, palms up, on the desk, and his eyebrows arched expectantly—waiting, I guess, for me to agree with his plan for the rest of my life. My mind swarmed with objections and questions, but he'd presented it with such conviction. It was as if my future were already written. I had only to let it play out.

What if I get into both? I said.

Depends on the fellowship and how badly you want to leave. You can always discontinue the master's here. You have to do what's best for your career.

My *career*? Who knew I could call what I was doing a career? My grades are pretty underwhelming, I said. I kind of fucked up my undergrad GPA.

He waved this off. Me too, he said. Doesn't matter. Nobody cares what your grades are if you can write.

Well, I said. I noticed my palms were clammy and wiped them on my pant legs. I'll have to think about it.

Sure you will, he said. You'll have to revise this story, too, if you want to use it in your sample.

Okay, I said. I took out my notebook and a pen.

First of all, give the characters names. They're too vague. For instance—he rotated the story and pointed to a sentence he'd underlined—the narrator's talking about the Sculptor's big exhibition, and he says, "She'd gotten everything she ever wanted in life, and this was just one more thing that she'd gotten that she wanted." But nobody's gotten *everything* they ever wanted. Even kids who go to—where'd you have her going to school?

Harvard.

Right, he said. Even kids who go to an Ivy—maybe even *especially* those kids—have immense pressure put on them. It might seem like they've lived a charmed life, but nobody *really* has. Whatever you think about a person, they're always more complicated than that. It's a good rule of thumb to follow, in fiction or in life.

I scrawled furiously, trying to keep up, nodding to show I'd understood him.

And there's that mention earlier, he said, flipping back through the pages, eyes scanning. Right here, he said. "She was born in a war-torn country." Which country?

I don't know.

You should probably know. I mean, Jesus, that's pretty good counterevidence of the narrator's "charmed life" theory, wouldn't you say?

Of all Tony's critiques, this stung the most. I felt like such a fool. Her family's struggle had been so much more perilous, the stakes so much graver, than anything I could imagine. This was obvious, and I'd somehow forgotten it in the writing. I was too busy whining about being misunderstood. So what if she'd never been inside a Walmart? So what if she went to a good school? What difference did any of that make?

We need to know more about her background, Tony said. What does she want? Every character should want something. Anyway, it's all in my notes, he said, handing over the story. This was my cue to leave, apparently. He smiled politely once more and laced his fingers on the desk.

So should I stop by if I decide to apply to the fellowships?

No, no, he said. Just email me about the letters. You'll get in.

You think so?

Who knows? But yes.

Okay.

You'll get into something.

Cool, I said. I rose and started for the door.

Oh, one more thing, Tony said. This guy, your narrator—he's got this whole woe-is-me, I'm-so-lonesome-I-could-cry attitude. Get rid of that. Don't ask for the reader's pity.

Right, I said.

And his family. Isn't family important in the South? What's the situation there? We should see more of them.

I'll work on that.

Good stuff. He gave me a thumbs-up and I walked away, my story in hand.

WHEN A WEEK HAD PASSED, I TEXTED ALMA. *UP FOR A DRIVE tomorrow?* Days went by. I passed the time reading *The Jungle Book,* our last reading assignment in Jungle Narratives, and various poetry collections. Every time I looked at fiction my eyes glazed over. I reread Emily Dickinson, and noticed, in her photograph, more than a passing resemblance to Alma, but maybe I was seeing her everywhere. *The soul unto itself is an imperial friend—or the most agonizing Spy an Enemy could send.*

Still alive? I texted, four nights after the first. I permitted myself two question marks an hour later, with the unswerving resolve that this would be my final attempt at communication, no matter how badly I wanted to try in the days to come.

Still nothing.

At work, James and Rando spoke only when necessary. Days passed in virtual silence. We worked in the sickly quiet, coffee taste in our mouths, fingers stinking of nicotine, beer from the night before rising up with each belch. We chewed mealy breakfast bars and watched our breath fog the windows on breaks. The dry branches rattled overhead, and with the leaves gone, it took great skill to discern the living from the dead. You had to score the bark, look for the green pith underneath. I wondered how summer could ever turn into something like this.

I watched westerns with Pop. I jogged in the November drizzle on the neighborhood streets, sneakers tramping the pavement on quiet evenings. I rose in the predawn dark, pulling on my boots and Carhartt, stopping for coffee and a sausage biscuit at the McDonalds. The good thing was that there was nobody on the streets and you could just cruise in with your coffee and listen to the radio and take her easy. No traffic to contend with. I took highway 44 east, right into the rising sun. I saw some incredible sunrises. The dark would turn to blue and the stars would recede, and the sun would hang for a while like a halved persimmon over the hills while the diesels idled and we sharpened our saws.

TONY HAD TO BE GONE FOR THE LAST THREE WEEKS OF Jungle Narratives—a family emergency, he said—and on what would be our last day, we watched a Tarzan movie and ate pizza. I'd taken to arriving a minute or two late and sitting between Joanna and Trent, away from Casey. He didn't seem to take the hint, or else was being deliberately obtuse.

After Tony's farewell remarks, during which he teared up a little and told us we'd "made his dream of a Jungle Narratives course a reality," Casey stood and said he had an announcement. My girlfriend and I are having a party tonight. Not a rager or anything, just a few friends, a few drinks. A distraction from these post-election blues. You're all invited. You too, Tony.

Oh swell, he said. He still had tears glistening in his eyelashes.

I shouldered my bag and started for the door, hollowed by the knowledge that they were back together, but Casey called after me. Owen, you're coming, too, he said. No excuses.

I'm supposed to meet James tonight, I said. This was true. We'd made plans to play Ping-Pong at a bar in the Highlands that allegedly had a table.

He can come, too, Casey said.

I'm not sure he'll want to.

Bring him. I'm not taking no for an answer.

I could have refused. But then, there was the prospect of seeing Alma once more, of talking with her after two weeks of radio silence. This seemed worth the irritation of having to spend an evening with Casey. I told him sure, okay.

Great, he said. We're doing it at Alma's place. The guesthouse. You know how to get there?

I pretended I didn't and listened as he gave me directions.

I picked up James that night, who seemed ambivalent about the idea of a party but went along with it anyhow. I'm curious about this girl, he said, searching the radio for something worth listening to.

That's all over, I said. She stopped texting me. I think the kids nowadays call it "ghosting."

Ah, he said. That's why you've looked so miserable. I thought it was just the election.

That too.

Well, look, man, he said, did you really think that was gonna work out?

I hoped it would.

I'm talking about the rational part of your brain.

I'm not very good at listening to that part.

Yeah, well, he said. Who is? He stared out the window for a while, one foot propped on the dash, tapping his fingers on his kneecap in time to the drums on the radio. You know what, fuck it, man, he said. Let's get drunk. Right? Just, fuck all that.

I smiled for what felt like the first time in days. I remembered what Tony had said—about the groundskeeper's I'm-so-lonesome-I-could-cry attitude. I didn't want to be that person. That person was boring.

I'm down, I said. Let's get drunk.

We stopped at a liquor store, and after a minor scuffle over whether to buy Jim Beam or Maker's Mark—I preferred Jim, he preferred Maker's—we settled on personal pints of each, which had to be the most irresponsible decision, both in monetary terms and in terms of consumption.

The tape adapter was still in the truck. James plugged in his phone and played "Redbone" by Childish Gambino, which had dropped a few days earlier. Have you heard this yet? he said.

No, I said. It's funky. Doesn't even really sound like him.

The album's gonna be a whole new direction. Honestly, he's just doing whatever the fuck he wants and it's fire every time.

When we pulled up to the guesthouses, the curb was lined with cars. I had to circle the block to find a spot. I lit a cigarette on the walk, gave one to James. He was wearing pale jeans and an Adidas jacket with the bottle of Maker's sagging in the pocket. He put the cig behind his ear for later, cracked the seal on the whiskey, took a swig.

How are things with your girlfriend? The Crab Shack girl.

He coughed and returned the bottle. Taylor? he said, his voice husky. We broke up, man.

Shit. I'm sorry—I realized I never asked you any more about her, after that night.

You don't ask me a lot of questions period.

Really?

He nodded.

This was disconcerting. Before I could follow up, we reached the door, which had been wedged open, and went through the lobby and up the narrow staircase, toward the muffled throb of music.

Casey greeted us, as usual, like we were old friends, reunited after years apart. James went to shake his hand and laughed warily as Casey pulled him into a bro hug. How you been, dude? Casey said.

I'm all right, James said.

And you! Casey said, turning to me. You been giving me the cold shoulder.

What do you mean? I said. I tried to sound lighthearted and amused.

Don't hand me that, he said, wagging a finger in my face. You know you've been a bad boy. Come on in, I'll get your coats.

There were maybe fifteen other people in the apartment, chatting in small groups. A woman was performing a tarot reading on the coffee table and people sat cross-legged on the floor around it, captivated by whatever was happening with the cards. Television, the band, played over the speakers—"Marquee Moon"—and it sounded so angular and stilted after "Redbone" with its slap bass and falsetto. Alma emerged from the hallway with a hyperbolic expression of surprise.

Well, hello! she said. She hugged me, her body pressed warmly against mine for a moment. I forgot I was supposed to speak.

This must be James, she said.

That's me, he said. They shook hands.

I thought you knew each other, Casey said.

James and Alma frowned and shook their heads.

Huh, said Casey, confusion passing briefly over his features.

Well, I'm glad you both made it, Alma said to us. Can I get you something? A banana daiquiri perhaps? I'm attempting to make banana daiquiris.

James and I looked at each other and shrugged.

Why not? I said.

Great! Two banana daiquiris, coming up.

Casey went to hang up our coats. Alma went to the kitchen. Her demeanor—the whole party hostess thing—was transparently phony, I decided. I caught her eye for a moment, before she left us, and I could've sworn I detected a micro-expression of embarrassment. I said this to James, while we stood waiting for the daiquiris.

A *micro-expression*? What even is that?

You know, I said. Like, it happens so quick that if you blink, you miss it.

He shook his head. You need alcohol in your body ASAP.

Taking his advice, I sipped from the pint of Jim Beam, setting my throat aflame. A blender roared in the kitchen, drowning out the music. I wanted to get her alone. As long as there were other people around, she could keep up the party hostess act and avoid having to acknowledge her radio silence. I considered different possibilities. A cigarette in the backyard? Waiting in line for the bathroom?

She brought out two glasses of banana slush, a pink squiggly straw in each. The flavor of rum was strong. Good, I said, though really the banana tasted overripe.

Tropical, James said, his cheeks puckered.

Okay, I know, so maybe I bought too many bananas from Trader Joe's and I needed to get rid of them, she said. And maybe some of them were a tiny bit too ripe. But is it such a crime to make daiquiris and put them to good use?

Hey, no complaints here, James said.

A hand kneaded my shoulder and Casey appeared behind me. Uh-oh, he said. Did you give our bad boy a daiquiri?

They taste okay, Alma said.

You don't have to drink those, Casey said. Don't feel obligated.

It's good, I said. Best banana daiquiri I've had since the one other banana daiquiri I've had.

I gotta make a couple more, she said. BRB.

Casey introduced us to a few people. There was Dan the lit PhD, a gawky-looking dude in a dad sweater who had to push up his glasses with his thumb roughly every fifteen seconds. Angela was in the translation program and had a mane of woolen red hair and flushed cheeks. She was breaking off squares of some Norwegian candy that looked and tasted like a Kit Kat. When I said as much, her eyes grew stormy. It's not a Kit Kat! she said. It's called Kvikk Lunsj and it's better!

Priya was a poet with a book forthcoming at Sestina. Marci was another lit PhD and played bass in a punk band called The Coathangers, which had apparently opened for Chastity Belt a couple times. Jess was a bartender at Kaiju, a Godzilla-themed bar in Smoketown, but also a writer and, incidentally, a furniture restorer, if I was interested (I wasn't). I filed away all the names, hoping I would not forget them in the next thirty seconds.

Joanna from Jungle Narratives stood in a corner wearing her usual getup of legwarmers and a houndstooth coat. She held a LaCroix and watched the proceedings with the shifting, exaggerated facial expressions of a silent movie star. I felt a great relief seeing her and abandoned James to chat.

Hi Joanna, I said.

Oh hi! she said. She looked at me like my appearance was a total shock, though I was pretty certain she'd already clocked my presence.

Not drinking tonight? I said, nodding at the LaCroix.

Oh I don't drink. There's enough going on in my head without throwing gasoline on the fire.

I feel you. You know anyone here?

No, she said. Well, I know *you*. And Casey, I guess. And I know myself, or at least I'd like to think I do.

Right. You glad Jungle Narratives is over?

You know, it would be easy to make fun of that class. But I think it helped Tony work through some stuff, stuff with his dead father and all. I think maybe he got some closure. So in that sense, I'm glad I took it.

That's a really charitable way of thinking about it.

But who knows? she said after a few seconds. Maybe we were enabling him to avoid a direct confrontation with his grief.

Maybe he couldn't handle a direct confrontation.

A direct confrontation is always better, she said.

Yeah, I guess.

Most of our problems arise from the avoidance of discomfort.

Who said that?

I did. Just now.

I thought about this, sipping my daiquiri. It seemed true—that we came up with compulsions and delusions and elaborate, tortuous strategies, all to avoid little discomforts. In a way, writing was like this. You can't deal with life, so you stand outside of it, above the fray, and you let the little marks you make on a page stand in for the real thing—a prosthesis that, though all your limbs are intact, you use anyway, compelled by the fear that you'll be damaged otherwise.

I excused myself and searched the house for Alma, but she was nowhere to be seen. I parted the curtains and saw her at street level below. James stood beside her. They were talking and laughing, passing the pint bottle of Maker's.

What do you think's going on there? said Casey. He'd come up behind me and was peering over my shoulder, looking uncharacteristically perturbed.

With what?

With *them.*

They're just talking, it looks like.

They've been down there fifteen minutes.

I turned to face him and saw that he was holding something down by his leg. A trucker hat. He looked shell-shocked, his face fearfully pale. You all right? I said.

He wrenched his eyes from the window and looked at me. No, he said. I just—I just realized something. He held up the hat. NO BLACKS, NO WHITES, JUST BLUES. The same hat I'd tossed behind the couch and never retrieved. The same hat James found that night at Schadenfreude and wore. I could not grasp the implications at first, my mind sluggish with rum.

She pretended they'd never met, just now, Casey said. But you said he was with you at the zoo. I remember you saying that.

I don't know what you mean.

He laughed bitterly. Of course, he said. You'd cover for him. He's your buddy, after all.

I began to see the outline of Casey's wrongful assumption. I'm going out, I said. He didn't seem to hear me. He turned his eyes to the window once more and gazed downward.

I hurried downstairs, banana daiquiri sloshing. When I reached them at the curb, I was out of breath. We have to go, I said to James.

What? he said. They'd been laughing about something and he turned to me, still smiling. We've only been here an hour.

Just trust me.

Are you sick? Alma said, real concern in her voice. If my daiquiri made you sick, I'm gonna feel really guilty.

It's not the daiquiri.

Before I could go on, the door clapped shut behind us. We all three turned and there was Casey on the stoop, hands on his hips, eyes baleful. He threw the hat onto the sidewalk.

James cocked his head, squinting. When he saw what it was, he broke into laughter. Shit! I forgot about that thing. You still have that picture you took?

I guess you think this is funny? Casey said.

The hat? Yeah, it's hilarious.

Babe, what's wrong? Alma said.

Casey sucked his teeth and looked away, down the street. I can't believe this, he said. I feel sick. I feel like I'm gonna throw up.

Did you drink too much?

No! he snapped. Alma flinched, took a step back. I didn't fucking drink too much.

Okay, she said—quietly, carefully. What's wrong, then?

He stepped down from the stoop clumsily—he seemed pretty drunk—and came to within a few feet of her. I must be a real idiot, he said. I suspected you were seeing someone, but this? You put on your little act, this prissy Ivy League bullshit. "Oh, I've never done this before, Casey. I'm practically a virgin, Casey."

Whoa, whoa, I said. I stepped forward and put my arm between Casey and Alma.

What the fuck is wrong with you? Alma said.

By now, James's smile had faded. His eyes darted to me, in search of an explanation. I was ready to admit everything, with my next breath. Before I could speak, James put his hand on Casey's shoulder and said, What do you think is going on here, man?

Don't you fucking touch me, Casey said, smacking his hand away. You're nobody. You think you can fuck with my life? Fuck you.

Then he spat in James's face.

What happened next took place in thirty seconds, though time ceased to be something liquid and moving, and became instead a series of overexposed flashes, in which the figures were comingled. For my part, I remember shouts and locked arms. I remember Casey throwing a punch, and James punching back, striking Casey's nose. A fine spray of blood. I remember Alma and how it looked like someone shook a wet paintbrush at her, flecking her face and shirt with red droplets. I remember Casey with both hands gripping James's throat, choking him. At one point, they had each other in a mutual headlock, bent over, panting and cursing each other, blood drooling from their lips. I remember trying to break this hold, and that when I did, I was met with the sharp, snapping pain of an elbow in my face.

Then I was on my back in the grass, James hovering over me. His lips were moving, but I couldn't hear him. All I heard was blank ringing, like what follows a gunshot. I blinked and tried to sit up, the coppery taste of blood filling my mouth. My shirt was soaked with it, and when I touched my face and drew my hand away, it was there, too. A lot of it.

I don't think it's broken, James said. This was the first thing I understood.

Where's Alma?

She's inside. Listen, we need to go before the cops show up. Somebody upstairs called them.

Fuck, I said. I swallowed the thick blood in my mouth and tried to stand. It was more difficult than I'd anticipated.

Get up, he said.

Are you all right?

He barely touched me, James said. His lip was split, but other than this, he looked fine. I knew I'd been hit hard. My brain felt loose, as though it'd been jostled around in my skull.

That piece of shit, I said, when I finally got to my feet. He hit me.

That was me, actually, James said. Friendly fire. Don't worry though, it's not broken. *His* nose is broken. Yours is just busted.

What's the difference?

Big difference, James said. Come on.

As we walked, I steadied myself with my arm across his shoulders. It became easier as the dizziness passed, and soon I could do it on my own—one foot, then the other. After a stretch of time that could've been five minutes or thirty, I looked up and saw Pop's Ranger.

Give me your keys, James said.

I dropped them in his palm.

We climbed into the cab, shut the doors. Do you have any napkins or anything? he said.

Glovebox.

He swung open the hatch and drew out a wad of brown McDonald's napkins. Here, he said. Stick a couple of these in your nose.

I realized my pants were wet. I think I pissed myself, I said.

It's banana daquiri. You're fine.

As we drove away, I let my head fall back against the seat and closed my eyes. The first waves of pain were pulsing outward from the center of my face. My throat was clogged with blood and snot. No matter how much I swallowed, I couldn't clear it.

What the fuck, man, James said.

I know. I'm sorry.

What the actual fuck.

He thought—

I know what he thought. You sure didn't go out of your way to correct him.

Didn't have time.

James scoffed. Right. You realize what kind of situation that puts me in, right? To whip a white kid's ass in the middle of the fuckin street? What if the cops had pulled up and seen me covered in blood?

I know.

No, you don't. You *think* you do, but you don't.

I said nothing, kept my eyes squeezed shut against the throb of pain. *You probably deserve this,* I thought, but then, wasn't that line of thinking just another way of making the whole ordeal about me? Putting myself at the center? I couldn't think straight. I couldn't swallow or breathe.

I need water, I said.

We're stopping, James said. Hang tight.

The next time I opened my eyes, we were parked at a gas pump beneath the blinding fluorescents. I'm going in to get some paper towels, James said.

I'll go with you.

No. You look like shit. I'll go.

I watched him speed-walk to the entrance and open the door. The other pumps were vacant. Muffled country music played through the gas station speakers—Shania Twain's "Man! I Feel Like a Woman!" I folded down the visor to get a look at myself.

He was right—I looked like shit. Blood, staining my teeth, streaked down my chin and the front of my shirt. Two twisted napkins shoved into my nostrils. Eyes puffy and weeping. I flipped up the visor. The one thought that kept returning was that I wished I'd gotten to punch Casey in the face. I regretted the missed opportunity. Some part of me was embarrassed by this impulse, but the impulse was present, whether I liked it or not.

James returned with a liter bottle of water and a roll of paper towels from the gas station bathroom. I drank the water first, then stepped out and splashed my face and neck. Pink-tinted water dribbled onto the pavement. James helped me, handing over lengths of paper towel, and when my face was clean, he examined the damage—tilting my face this way and that. It's not broken, he said.

You're sure?

Ninety percent.

He drove us back to his apartment and told me I could crash on the sofa. I didn't argue. He gave me basketball shorts and a fleece blanket, and I left my bloody clothes in a pile in the bathroom.

You need anything, let me know, he said, when I'd situated myself on the couch.

I'm really sorry about this.

He was standing in the threshold of his bedroom. I couldn't quite read his expression. We'll debrief later, he said.

He shut the door, and after a few minutes, the thin bar of light beneath it went out. I lay on the couch in total darkness, hearing the sounds of other units in the building—water flushed through pipes, the chatter of televisions. I wondered where Alma was, if she was alone in the guesthouse in the aftermath of the party, if she'd helped tend to Casey or left him to his own devices. I wondered what she was thinking—if she wished she'd never met me. I wouldn't have blamed her.

MY NOSE WAS BROKEN. A DOCTOR—OR RATHER, A PHYSICIAN'S assistant—realigned it the next day at an urgent care clinic. This involved spectacular, dizzying pain. On the bright side, I was given a bottle of twenty 5 mg hydrocodone tablets. I'd been pretty strung out on painkillers for several months in Colorado and had made a soft vow never to use them again, but this seemed like an appropriate exception.

So, I used vacation time and spent the next five days submerged in opiated bliss, watching John Wayne movies with Pop. It was so good, really—this reprieve, this fluttering warmth in my chest, that I mostly forgot about Alma. Or rather, she was still present, but I couldn't bring myself to care.

Pop seemed happy to have me around, instead of "galivanting about town" as he called it. We watched *True Grit* one night. I'd forgotten, somehow, that Glen Campbell was in it, and smiled drowsily when he came onscreen in his fringed, buckskin jacket. We watched *The Shootist,* a movie that was not great, but better than I remembered. Wayne at least had the good sense to play with the tropes he'd established throughout his career in his final movie, and then, of course, there was the meta aspect, that Wayne's J.B. Books was battling cancer as the real Wayne was also battling it.

But nothing, really, could match *The Searchers,* a movie that seemed to contain all of America's strife and ugliness and rugged beauty in miniature. Watching it then, I found it hard to believe that Wayne could not have understood that the film was a critique of manifest destiny and the genocide of Native Americans, or that if he did understand, he would have participated, being the racist that he was. But maybe that's why Ford knew he was perfect for the role. In the film's final moments, when Ethan Edwards carries Debbie to the doorway, delivering her to her mother, and we see him framed there alone against the mesas and the big sky, all that vast, lonesome rangeland ahead of him, we don't merely see the character. We see Wayne himself—the strongman, the bigot, the make-believe hero. Wayne who was not even Wayne, but rather Marion Robert Morrison, born in Winterset, Iowa. The fantasy cowboy at the edge of a Technicolor frontier—that was America in a nutshell.

It's just a movie, Pop said, when I tried to explain my theory, so drugged I could barely speak.

I spent Thanksgiving with Pop and Uncle Cort, eating honey baked ham, mashed potatoes and, at Cort's insistence, a bucket of fried chicken from KFC. He informed us, once again, that Sanders was not a real colonel. We *know*, we *know*, Pop said. Eat your chicken.

Alma never called or texted, and when the painkillers ran out and the brittle, raw edge of sobriety returned, I felt not quite sad, but wistful. I wanted to see her. The whole thing felt unresolved. Maybe I'd read too many open-ended short stories, but I was suspicious of resolutions—at least in art. Then again, it was only when a story ended that you could begin to see its shape, however irregular, and when I looked back on Alma and me, there was only the suggestion of a shape—a constellation. Points of contact that may or may not have added up to anything.

I applied to the master's program in English at Ashby, with a focus in creative writing. The director told me that with Tony's endorsement, it would be no problem. We can't give you funding, unfortunately, he said. At least not for the spring. We figure out all the funding at the beginning of the academic year, and since you'd be getting in in the middle, it wouldn't be possible.

That's fine, I said. I have a job.

He told me that everyone in the program had to take a critical theory course, and that I might just want to get it over with in the spring. So, I signed up for it, plus a course on the Victorian Gothic.

Maintenance and Landscape Services would only cover one class per semester, so I'd have to pay for the second out of pocket. I told myself I had little choice. I couldn't very well spend five years getting a two-year degree by taking only one class per semester.

What Tony failed to mention about writing fellowships was how expensive it was to apply to them. I spent basically all my savings on application fees. I'd filled out the first dozen while stoned on hydrocodone, and as a result, the whole process was pretty haphazard. I lost track of where I'd applied and where I hadn't, and accidentally submitted two applications for MacDowell.

As the semester came to a close, I decided to send Alma one last email. What was the worst that could happen? Continued radio silence? I spent an hour drafting it, writing a much longer email at first and then deleting most of it. I closed my eyes and willed myself to press SEND. Then it was gone. Out of my hands.

> *Dear Alma,*
>   *I don't know how things ended up this way. Maybe you wish I'd just disappear, and I will if that's what you want. You won't hear from me again.*
>   *But . . . if there's some tiny part of you that wants to talk sometime, I'm here. No expectations. Just a conversation.*
>
>   *Yours,*
>   *Owen*

She replied the following day. *Let's talk,* she said.

I WAITED FOR A HALF HOUR OUTSIDE THE BAR, SMOKING. IT was called Linda's Beeritaville. According to Alma, they had good tacos and a decent happy hour. She'd called it a "hole-in-the-wall." It struck me that by the time a place got that designation, it was never really a hole-in-the-wall anymore.

Next door, at a gas station, a woman wearing a velvet halter top vacuumed an old Pontiac, her platinum hair shining even in the dull winter light. The car had a film of dust and there were small handprints on the doors and the tinted windows, as if a crowd of children had surrounded the car and pressed on it all at once. A sign in the gas station window advertised Misty brand cigarettes. I imagined that the woman's name was Misty, that if she were a character in a work of fiction, I would call her Misty. I watched her while she ran the nozzle over the carpets, murmuring to herself. The bumper sticker on the back of Misty's Pontiac said FORGIVEN.

Alma pulled up in her Honda finally and stepped out. She wore a moth-eaten sweater and denim overalls with the pant legs rolled up over her signature hiking boots. I could tell she was going to cry even before we embraced. She sniffled quietly against my shoulder and said she was sorry. I told her I was sorry, too. The wind blustered against us, blew her hair into my face. We went back and forth like this, saying how sorry we were, hugging each other. Jimmy Buffett was playing, unsurprisingly, on the Beeritaville patio speakers.

Inside, we ordered happy hour PBRs for a dollar apiece. The booth where we sat had splits in the fake leather and smelled like vomit and Clorox. Nautical bric-a-brac adorned the walls. Oars and bamboo fish traps. Alligator heads. I don't think I want tacos anymore, I said.

Me neither, she said.

We drank our metallic PBRs and looked at each other apprehensively. I thought we'd gotten past this part by having sex, this shyness with each other.

I haven't talked to Casey since that night, she said. He's been trying to reach me, but I think that's finally over.

I would hope so, I said. I was trying to sulk, but I couldn't quite make it convincing. I was just too happy to see her.

Sestina's not doing my poetry book anymore, she said. No surprise there.

That's gotta be disappointing.

She nodded. There were carved initials and penises on the table. She picked at them, peeling away the varnish, a dirty Band-Aid wrapped around the knuckle of her thumb. I know you're upset with me, and I don't really have a good explanation for not calling, she said. I just got scared.

Of what?

That I don't really know you, she said. And you don't know me. Maybe you think I'm some kind of free spirit, but I'm not really. I didn't have sex till I was twenty-two. I thought I could do the whole casual sex thing. I thought that's what I wanted, that I should be the kind of person that wanted that, but I'm not.

She drank from her can, aluminum clinking under the pressure of her thumb. Her eyes flitted from one thing to another, looking at anything but me.

You could've told me all that, I said. It wouldn't have mattered to me.

It freaked me out though, she said. You talking about drugs and living in your car.

Casey doing lines of coke didn't freak you out?

It did, she said. I *hated* that. I told him I hated it. I didn't even like him smoking weed. I've only smoked like twice, and I didn't even get high. I don't think I was doing it right. But you know, Casey didn't have a *problem.* And he certainly never lived in his car. His parents were lawyers in Cincinnati. I mean, his dad's dead, but he *was* a lawyer.

So that makes it all right to dabble?

I don't know, she said, pressing her eyes with her thumb and forefinger. I just know it freaked me out when you said what you said. I don't like to think of myself as a judgmental person, but maybe I am.

This is what I'd hoped she wouldn't say. It disappointed me immensely. I hadn't figured her for the sort of person who would think like this—like my parents, honestly. Like a puritan. She stared at her hands in her lap with an anguished expression, probably picking her cuticles, as was her habit, though I couldn't see. I took a gulp of beer, buying time to come up with the right response. Two men at the bar were singing along to Toby Keith—"Courtesy of the Red, White and Blue"—and this made it really difficult to think about anything other than how much I hated the song.

I can't help what my life used to be, I said finally. But you know, most ordinary people have had some kind of issue. It's normal to have a little dirt under your fingernails.

That's just it though, she said, meeting my eyes. I've spent my whole life trying to be not-normal. I wanted to go to a great school, and I did. I wanted to publish a book in my twenties, and I did. I wanted to live a comfortable life as a writer, and I am. None of those things are normal. My parents wanted me to be exceptional. My dad always said, "We went through hell so you wouldn't have to," which is corny, I know, but it's also true, and I had to live up to that. Normal wasn't in the cards. And I don't want to get mixed up in something now that will fuck up my life.

So you think I'll fuck up your life?

No, she said. I don't know. I'm just explaining.

One of the drunken men singing Toby Keith at the bar tipped back in his stool and fell hard on his ass, letting out a bark of pain. A few patrons gathered around to help him up. I was beginning to believe that this place really was a hole-in-the-wall, an exception to the rule. Can we get out of here? I said.

Yes, please.

It was mild for a winter's evening, in the low fifties, but she had her arms folded tightly and her shoulders hunched as we walked. I put my arm around her, and she let her head rest against me. It was nearly Christmas, and there were inflatable snowmen in the yellowed lawns and icicle lights dangling from the gutters of houses.

We came to a small park with a colorful playground and a plastic stegosaurus to climb on. A man and his young daughter were the only people there. While the girl swung on the monkey bars, he read a hardback novel, keeping his left hand cupped around a thermos of tea. The tea-bag string and the little paper tag were dangling out from the lid. We sat on a bench nearby.

How's the novel going? I asked her.

She gestured *so-so.* There are good days and bad, she said. Sometimes I wish I'd chosen a vocation where my mood didn't depend so much on how well the work was going.

Did you always want to be a writer?

Pretty much.

And your parents were cool with it?

Why wouldn't they be?

I thought most immigrants want their kids to be doctors or lawyers.

That's the stereotype, she said, her eyes fixed on some distant point across the park. On the other side, past the mottled white trunks of sycamores, I could see a laundromat with a burgundy awning and a corner grocery. Two squirrels on the far edge leapt through the wet leaves and scrabbled up the bark of a hickory tree. Otherwise, not much was happening over there.

My mother is a pediatrician, she said. My father is a dentist. But I think in another life, they may have been artists. My father has two novels in a drawer somewhere at home.

Are they any good?

She shrugged weakly. Who knows, she said. He won't let anyone read them. They're about Bosnia.

She raked her fingers through her hair, sort of tossing it back against the part so that it would fall slowly, strand by strand, to its natural state. It was something she did often to maintain its staged messiness. I'd known her long enough that I'd begun to notice these things—what she did with her hair, the way she picked at her cuticles when she was anxious, or moved her lips almost imperceptibly when she read an email on her phone. I felt the urge to write these things down and told myself I'd have to remember to do so when I got home. I wanted, also, to write down the woman vacuuming her Pontiac, the bumper sticker that said FORGIVEN. I wanted to write about Beeritaville and Toby Keith. Would I have noticed this world of signs if she weren't in it? All these things pointed to something more, surely. They would form the story of how we got together again. They would figure in the telling and prove themselves useful, and therefore worth my attention.

Does it make you happy to be around me? I said.

She nodded absently.

Then what does any of the other stuff matter?

She drew her bootheels up onto the edge of the bench and hugged her knees. It seems like a bad idea on multiple levels, she said. I mean, what are the long-term prospects, really? You said your parents are evangelical Christians—what happens when they find out you're dating a Muslim girl? Why would I want to be around people who are hostile to me? Who see me as an alien?

You don't know they'd be *hostile.* And for what it's worth, they see me as an alien sometimes, too.

Not in the same way, and you know that.

Well, what do you want me to tell you? That's a concern for *way* down the line. And how important is that, really?

Family is important, she said. Maybe not to you, but to me.

That kinda stuff works itself out. You can't control for it.

And what about the fact that I'm just a visitor?

What about it?

I don't live here, she said. I'm just passing through, remember? What happens in May when I go back to New York?

That will work itself out, too, I said. And I don't live here either. It's a temporary situation.

She gave me her pitying look. After a moment, she reached over and clasped her hand with mine. A breeze kicked up, flinging her hair back, wafting the musty smell of leaves from the park. I don't know, she said. I just can't see the future.

We could give it a trial run, I said. See what happens.

Across the park, a woman in jogging attire, towed by a leashed Great Pyrenees, shouted for the dog to heel. Alma broke her gaze and glanced at the woman and the shaggy, trotting animal. The little girl, having abandoned the monkey bars, was lifting piles of leaves and watching them flee from her arms on the wind. Look, she demanded of her father. I see, he said, without taking his eyes from the book.

Alma inhaled and started to speak but the breath seemed to clutch in her throat. She sighed finally. It was as if she was giving something up after a long struggle. Okay, she said.

PART 2

WHEN I GOT THE CALL, I WAS AT ALMA'S, making supper. The windows in the kitchen were steamed, my eyes still watering from the onion I'd cut a few minutes earlier. Pop fell, Cort said when I answered.

I stepped over to the stereo and dialed back the volume. Alma opened the oven to check on the brussels sprouts, poking them gently with a fork. How are we, little ones?

You need to come home and help me, he said.

Fell where?

Backyard. He was burning the trash and some old limbs.

Why weren't you doing it?

You know about my back.

Could you call the neighbor?

Neighbor's not home.

Well, how bad is it? Is he hurt? What about the fire department?

He's all right. I didn't think it was hardly worth it to call the fire department.

But you thought it was worth it to call me? I'm thirty minutes away.

He'll be fine till then.

It's twenty degrees outside, Cort.

I got him piled up with quilts.

A smoke detector went off—the keening of the alarm accompanied by an automated voice. *Fire—emergency—fire—emergency.* I plugged my free ear with my finger. Cringing, Alma raced to the sofa, stood on the arm, and pulled down the detector. She fiddled with it, unsuccessfully, finally just removing the batteries. Sorry! she mouthed.

I waved my hand to show that it was fine, but I guess she got a look at my face and knew that everything was not fine. I looked worried. I *was* worried. She stood there, dish towel draped over her shoulder, waiting to hear what had happened.

Sorry, Cort, I said.

What the hell was that?

Smoke detector.

Well, I'm real sorry to interrupt. I know you're out there playing house and all, but if you could stop by we sure would appreciate it.

I'll be there, I told him, and hung up before I said something irrevocable.

I sat on the edge of the couch with a sigh and dragged my boots over. Alma was still waiting with her arms folded. I hate to do this, I said, but I gotta go. My granddad fell.

Oh my God, she said. Something about her response seemed slightly perfunctory, but what did I expect? She still hadn't met him. It'd been about a month since we got together in earnest, without Casey in the picture, and she hadn't yet seen Pop's house or the basement where I lived. I'd been spending three or four nights out of the week with her, in the guesthouse apartment, and this arrangement had worked well enough.

He's fine, I think, I said. But it's cold, and Cort can't lift him, so I need to do it. Go ahead and eat without me.

She took the dish towel from her shoulder and twisted it nervously. Are you sure?

Unless you wanna come with me.

Do you *want* me to come with you?

I want you to come with me if *you* want to.

Do you think you'll need help?

Possibly, I said. But don't feel obligated, I can manage alone. Stay and eat if you want.

She gnawed on her lip, thinking. No, I'll go, she said. Do I have time to change? Her hair was piled in a messy knot, and she was wearing jeans and a baggy cardigan over one of my T-shirts—ASHBY MAINTENANCE AND LANDSCAPE SERVICES. Our insignia, on the breast pocket, was a spade and a rake, crossed over the silhouette of a pine tree.

Not really, I said. Just put on a coat.

She donned her parka with the fur hood, stepped into her unlaced hiking boots. I threw on my Carhartt and we were out the door and down the steps, into the clear, breathtaking cold. The sun was gone, leaving only a salmon-pink stain in the west. The trees were bare. The grass, stiff underfoot, sparkled with frost.

When we arrived, Cort was standing out front in coveralls and a neon orange hunting cap. He lifted the cuff of his glove and glanced at his watch as we reached him in the yard. Forty minutes, he said.

Cort, this my girlfriend, Alma.

I realized that this was the first time I'd called her my girlfriend, but she didn't miss a beat. She shook his hand. Great to meet you, she said. I've heard a lot.

Cort eyed her warily. This is a private family matter, he said to me. You didn't say you were bringing someone.

Don't start, Cort, I said.

I can wait in the car, Alma said.

No, you're fine. Ignore him.

You should've told me, Cort said. I don't like being surprised.

Let's just go, okay? It's not important. Show me where he is.

We followed Cort around the house to the backyard, our breath rising in silvery plumes. Out back, the yard sloped down gently to a little stand of cedar trees and a big maple. Pop burned the trash there in a metal barrel. I saw him lying beside it as we drew nearer, beneath a mound of blankets. A couple cedar limbs lay with their splintered butts near his feet, as if he'd been dragging them when he collapsed.

Hey Pop, I said, crouching beside him. Even in the growing dark, I could tell he was in bad shape. He was pale, his lips the color of a bruise. Even under the patchwork quilts and comforters, he was shivering violently, and when he spoke, he sounded like he'd been given Novocain at the dentist. I figured the temperature for eighteen, maybe seventeen above. Cold even for me, and I was moving around.

If I could get out from under this, I'll stand, Pop slurred.

We're going to help you, I said. Just hang tight.

Don't need help, he said, eyelids fluttering.

Jesus, Cort, I whispered, turning to face him. You should've called an ambulance.

He'll be fine once we get him in.

I wanted to yell at him, but it would only have wasted time, and anyhow I didn't wish to make a scene in front of Alma. She stood ten feet behind us with her arms folded tightly and her teeth chattering. I hadn't thought things would be this serious. I didn't want to alarm her.

Help me get these off, I said, and we stripped the blankets from him, till he was lying there in his pair of ragged coveralls. No coat.

Can you get his feet? I said to Alma.

What? she said, roused from a trance. She stepped forward and cupped her hand around her ear.

His feet, I said, a little more sharply than I intended. I adjusted my tone, tried to sound calm. I'll get under his shoulders and you get his feet, if you think you can.

Yeah, I think I can do that, she said.

He doesn't weigh much.

She stood over Pop and waved at him. Hi sir, she said. I'm Alma. I'm going to touch your feet if that's okay.

Pop smiled vaguely.

All right, Pop, I said, crouching behind his head. Here we go.

I held him under the arms and lifted as Alma lifted his feet. We moved uphill quickly, Alma struggling, her breath quick and shallow. Pop was completely limp, his head lolling against my shoulder. As we reached the back door, Alma said, Hang on. She lowered his legs inelegantly, practically dropping them. She stood upright, inhaling by the lungful.

We need to go, I said.

I can't breathe, she said.

I used my elbow to shove open the back door and dragged him the rest of the way, through the kitchen, into the living room, all the way to his recliner. When I was sure he wouldn't just slide to the floor, I ran to the hallway closet and pulled down crocheted blankets and bath towels and quilts and piled them onto his body. Feeling light-headed, I permitted myself a moment to catch my breath, then bounded down the steps to the basement and grabbed my electric space heater. I plugged it in beside the recliner, got it running. The heater ticked and creaked. The coils glowed. I bent over with my hands on my knees, panting. When I looked up, Alma and Cort were standing in the kitchen doorway.

Is he okay? she said.

I think he's all right, I said, though I had no idea. He looked pitiful, with his flaking lips and his half-lidded eyes. He couldn't even hold up his head. I googled "hypothermia signs" on my phone and read the Mayo Clinic article. His breathing was steady—a good sign. He was conscious. He didn't seem confused, though his speech was certainly slurred. In the few minutes it took to scroll through the article and deliberate, Pop perked up a little. His eyes, blue as pool water, grew brighter, as if lit from within. He stared at Alma across the room.

Who's this? he said.

I smiled in spite of myself. Even in this state, he couldn't help but notice a pretty girl.

She strode over, hand extended. Hello, sir, she said. Hi.

Pop, this is Alma, I said. I told you about her, remember?

I remember, he said. I'd shake your hand, but I can't seem to get my arm free.

Of course, Alma said. You're weighted down with blankets.

That would seem to be the situation, Pop said. He looked at me slyly. She's pretty, he said. When he said the word "pretty," his pronunciation was more like "perty."

I know she is, I said. She helped carry you in.

Well, I thank you, he said.

No problem at all, sir, she said, nearly shouting, as though he were going deaf.

What were you doing outside without a coat? I said.

His grin faltered. Well, I can't rightly recall, he said. I think I just planned to step out for a minute and got sidetracked with those limbs. They need to be burned.

Tonight? They needed to be burned tonight?

Well, sometime.

He was lying to me, and he wasn't very good at it. It's twenty degrees out there, Pop, I said. If that. You could've got yourself killed.

I wondered suddenly, as I said this, if killing himself may have been his intent.

He looked up at me with his placid blue eyes. You're right, he said. I'll have to be more careful.

When it became clear that Pop wasn't dying of hypothermia, Cort retired to his room. Alma and I sat with him awhile longer. Y'all wanna watch a movie? he said.

I don't think we'll have time for that, Pop, I said.

I see you have a lot of John Wayne movies, Alma shouted.

Pop winced and adjusted his hearing aid. Yeah, I suppose, he said. Always liked the Duke.

There's this essay I really love about him. By Joan Didion?

I don't know who that is.

Well, it's great, Alma said. Didion quotes this line where John Wayne tells a woman he'll build her house at the bend in the river where the cottonwoods grow. She says she's been waiting her whole life for a man like John Wayne to come along and say that to her.

War of the Wildcats, Pop said.

Beg pardon?

The movie. It's a pretty good one.

Oh, yeah, I haven't seen the movie. What's it about?

Pop considered this. He had his hands freed from the blankets now, cupped around a mug of Swiss Miss I'd made for him. Oh, you know, he said. Cowboys and Indians. There's some kind of dispute. The woman's caught between two men. One of em's a cowboy— that's the Duke—and the other's kindly like an oilman, I guess. She ends up with the Duke.

So it's a happy ending? Alma said.

I reckon you could say that.

Well, maybe next time I come over, we can watch it, how does that sound?

All right with me, Pop said. He slurped his hot chocolate, eyeing her apprehensively.

I'm gonna show Alma my room in the basement, I said. Pop nodded and reached for his remote control. We trudged downstairs. At the bottom, I flipped on the fluorescent tubes. They flickered and settled into a hum, revealing where I'd lived for five months. I had a sudden, sharp awareness of the basement through her eyes. The workbench in the back littered with tools. The half-finished sheetrock panels and the exposed pink insulation. All my boxes of books. My sad clothing rack. Whatever she was thinking, she offered a strained smile and said, So this is your subterranean lair?

I know, it's not much.

It's not so bad. You even have a window. She pointed to the casement window, the glass feathered with ice.

I gave her a minute to look around while I stood there awkwardly, hands in pockets. She admired the massive shelf of VHS tapes. So much John Wayne, she said. Should I have not mentioned Joan Didion? Was that stupid?

No, I think it was fine.

I thought that was better than saying John Wayne was a racist.

Probably so.

She flipped through a few of my records in a milk crate. Lot of Gram Parsons, she said. I didn't know what to say to this except, Yeah, he's cool. The books on the end table, next to the hide-a-bed, were all poetry. Creeley, Bishop, Lorde. She ran her finger over the spines, as if touching them would imbue her with something.

Welp, she said, clapping her palms on her thighs. Shall we go back up?

I exhaled, unsure whether I should feel relieved, but glad nonetheless that it was over. After you, I said, letting her go ahead of me so I could flip off the lights.

Upstairs, we said our goodbyes to Pop. He had *The Far Country* playing, a Jimmy Stewart western. You sure you're all right? I said.

Oh sure, he said. See, look at my toes. He pointed to his feet, sticking out from the blanket, and wiggled his toes.

What about them?

They're wiggling.

I see that.

That means they won't fall off.

I'm not sure that's what it means, but okay. I patted his shoulder and started for the door. No more shenanigans outside, I said.

Alma waved to him shyly. It was nice meeting you, she shouted.

You too, honey, he said. I'm serious about watching a movie. Y'all come out anytime. We'll watch that one you were talking about.

Sounds good, Alma said.

On the road, we drove without speaking for a while. I turned up the radio, tuned to the classical station. Something dignified was being played on a harpsichord. Alma kept leaning forward and massaging her lower back. She sighed melodramatically, waiting for me to ask.

What's wrong? I said finally.

I think I hurt my back.

You didn't hurt your back.

I think I did. There's like a twinge right here. She pushed tenderly on the spot, just above her waist and to the left of her spine.

Maybe you just tweaked it.

What does that mean?

I don't know, like a strain.

It hurts.

Okay, well, sleep on it and if it's still bothering you in the morning, go to a doctor.

What if I damaged something?

You didn't damage anything.

What if I did?

I think you'd be in more pain. Did you lift with your legs?

Yeah, I think. She nibbled at her thumb, brow furrowed. I'm not sure, she said. My mom hurt her back when she was my age and it still bothers her.

Well, I don't know what to tell you, Alma, I said. I thought you were fine coming along and helping me.

I'm smaller than you. And you have to lift things every day. You're used to it. When do I ever have to lift something heavy?

That's my point.

What point? Jesus, there is no *point,* I'm just trying to tell you that my back hurts, okay? That's it. Obviously getting your grandfather inside was the most important thing. I know it had to be done.

I turned up the harpsichord and tried not to think about Pop—about what he might've hoped for, dragging limbs to the point of exhaustion on a deathly cold night. There was no one on the road. We weaved through tunnels of trees, their branches like tangled nerve endings. A fuzzy halo encircled the moon.

When we got home, Alma took an ice pack from the freezer and went to lie down. I told her I might stay up to read, but what I did instead was write down everything I could remember about the whole ordeal that evening. What was said, the way I felt, my worries about Pop and whether he might be trying to hurt himself intentionally. I'd begun typing my handwritten, scatterbrained notes, keeping them all in a folder in my documents called "Kentucky/ Alma." I didn't yet know to what end, or what they might become. But there was something illicit—and therefore exciting—about it, as though I were building a case for my own innocence. That, or I was writing a love story, something with a happy ending. Either way, it was beginning to feel like a story. I wanted it to be a love story, more than anything, not just because it would make for better art, but because I wanted us to be happy. Perhaps there was little difference between the two. I wrote down Alma's dialogue, as close as I could remember, though in the end, it wasn't so important that I got it right. I wasn't a journalist, after all.

WHEN CLASSES RESUMED IN LATE JANUARY, I COULD FINALLY say I was in the master's program. I'm not sure if it's pride I felt, knowing this, but there was an unmistakable sense of purpose—that I wasn't just *futzing around* as Tony put it.

Victorian Gothic was taught by a woman named Dr. Theresa Unger, whose demeanor and severe, flinty-eyed beauty was itself somewhat gothic. She suffered no fools and seemed uninterested in our opinions about anything, which I liked. We were to read

Wuthering Heights and *Dracula* and *Great Expectations,* books I'd read in the past but was happy to revisit.

Critical Theory met once a week for three hours, and I could tell right away that it would be a slog. The professor was named Dr. Greta Person. I hadn't known "Person" was a name someone could have, but she had it. We called her Dr. Person. She was white, wore chunky wooden bracelets and necklaces with vague African motifs, and liked to use the word "wack." Example: *What is it that's so* wack *about Make America Great Again?*

The other students were mostly either literature PhDs or rhetoric PhDs. They were all very good at speaking in the academic register. Most of what they said I couldn't make heads or tails of, and though I was tempted at first to think the fault was mine, I realized after a while that they didn't know what they were talking about either.

The broad theme was "New Materialism and the Rhetoric of Images," and as Dr. Person went on about network theory and heteroglossia those first few weeks, I nodded as though I knew exactly what she meant, though I had no idea whatsoever.

THE EMERALD ASH BORER IS A BEETLE THE PRECISE COLOR of green glitter paint, no longer than a pinkie nail. A native of Asia, the borer is an invasive species in North America, where it has devastated American ash trees, particularly green and black ash. In Asia, ash trees have tannins that repel the bugs, but this is not the case here.

At the arboretum, on campus, there were about seventy ash trees. Of those seventy, forty-five were dead or dying from the borer. Kelly called our crew into his office in late January and told us it would be our job to remove them.

Now, I know we're working with limited resources, he said. We don't have grappling trucks or bucket trucks, and our chippers are worn out. Undoubtably, you're gonna face some difficulties. But the good news is that for the most part, you'll be able to flop them. Won't have to fool with rigging lines and all that.

Even though it was winter, and seven o'clock in the morning, he had some sort of brownie hot fudge sundae on his desk. He took a bite of melting ice cream from a red plastic spoon and looked at us. Questions?

So you want the three of us to cut down forty trees? James said.

Forty-five, Kelly said.

That'll take months.

Undoubtably, Kelly said. But I figure it's better than being out of work for the off-season, wouldn't you say?

None of us responded. We knew he was right—a few of the non-work-study employees *had* been laid off. Tree trimming, for the most part, was seasonal work. You made all your money in the spring through the fall. The exception was removals. You could fell a tree any time of the year.

When am I going back on landscaping duty? Rando said. My boils are all healed up. I put in the request weeks ago.

Don't need people on landscaping duty, I need you on this, Kelly said, fudge at the corners of his lips. You should count yourself lucky.

Rando scoffed and slouched back in his chair. This is bullshit, he said.

No, Rando. It's work. I know that might be a foreign concept to you, but try to make the best of it. You can take your time out there. I'm doing you a favor, really.

Kelly stood, wiped his fingertips with a napkin, and gestured to the door. There was nothing else to say.

We reached the arboretum and found the first tree on the list. Thirty feet high. Dead, by the look of it. A pea-gravel path lay underneath, part of a network that ran throughout the arboretum. Near the parking lot, which sat atop a hill in view of our job site, there were beds of lilies and roses, covered now with tarps. A Japanese-style garden lay to the west, with bonsai and weeping willows and an arched wooden bridge over a koi pond. I knew Alma walked here sometimes. I made a mental note that we'd have to go together in the spring.

The chipper truck beeped obnoxiously as James reversed, backing the Vermeer off the gravel and into the yellow grass. He killed the engine and stepped down. We stood there, the three of us, looking at the tree. It was a dreary morning, mist beading our hard hats.

Rando coughed and spat. So is this how's it's gonna be dudes? he said. From here on out?

How what's gonna be? James said.

These cooling relations. We need to reestablish lines of communication if this is gonna be our next few months.

We seem to be getting by, James said.

That what you want? Getting by? I know you can't still be mad at me.

James took off his safety glasses and wiped the rain from the lenses with his shirt. I'm not mad at you, he said. I don't even think about you.

Oh come on dude, Rando said. Owen, you know I'm right. Tell him.

Things probably would be more pleasant for all of us, I said.

So what, we apologize to each other? He can apologize for the way he voted, but that won't change the situation.

I won't apologize for the way I voted—are you kidding?

Then how are we supposed to be all buddy-buddy? James said. Tell me that.

People have their private reasons for whatever they do, Rando said. Emphasis on the word *private*.

You mean racism. That's always the *private* reason.

Everything's always racism with your generation. You're so quick to jump to it.

It's a safe bet, James said.

Okay, I said. Let's take a breath.

James shook his head, tugged on his gloves, and strode to the pickup. He drew the big twenty-eight-inch Husky from the back, the one we never used, and set it on the tailgate.

We probably have more in common than you think, Rando said. For instance, I support the legalization of all drugs.

Good for you, James said. He unscrewed the cap to check the oil, ran his gloved fingers over the chain, examining the teeth.

What would it take to bury the hatchet? I said. I'm ready to move on and let bygones be bygones if y'all are.

That's just it, though, James said. Nothing is actually bygone. It's an ongoing shitstorm.

Well, okay, I said. But we gotta work out here, man. We gotta be on the same page.

Listen to the General, Rando said. He's right.

James sighed and hauled the big saw over to where we were standing. He looked at us, fingers hooked through the chain brake. It was heavy, the tendons standing up on his forearms. Okay, look, he said. We don't need to hug it out or whatever. I'll refrain from verbal abuse. Mostly, I'm just bored with this whole dynamic. So, whatever. Agree to disagree, I guess.

A cease-fire, Rando said. I'll take it. He stuck out his hand and James shook it halfheartedly.

Now, if you'll excuse me, I'm gonna cut down this fuckin tree. He set the saw on the ground, yanked the pull cord once, twice. The Husky growled and dropped into a phlegmatic rumble. When it had idled a moment, he revved the motor, went to the tree, and started his top cut, without bothering to put on chaps.

WE WENT ON DRIVES SOMETIMES, JUST FOR THE SENSE OF going somewhere. It helped to stave off winter restlessness—seeing the countryside slip past and looking back on what you'd left behind. You tricked yourself into thinking you were leaving. *Desiring the exhilarations of changes.* What it came down to was boredom. We had little to do and no one to see but each other.

We started south on I-65 one evening, no destination in mind. Soon it was dusk, grazing deer emerging from the woods. We listened to a bluegrass station, the merry plinking of mandolins and banjos fading in and out of static. The sun had slipped behind the worn-down knobs to the west and there were cirrus clouds hanging like pink mist above them. A religious station came in waves of shushing static—a man and woman reciting "Hail Mary, full of grace." They went on for a long time. When they'd gone through ten cycles, Alma said, What is this? I told her I didn't know. They showed no sign of stopping. I went on listening out of morbid curiosity.

We hadn't eaten supper, and when I saw a sign for a Cracker Barrel, I suggested we stop. She told me she'd never been to one.

No way, I said.

Yes way.

I can't believe that in twenty-six years of life, you've never been to a Cracker Barrel.

We. Were. Muslim. Immigrants, she said, punctuating each word. Why would we go to a Cracker Barrel?

I wheeled into the lot, which was mostly vacant. I knew this would be the case, since most of Cracker Barrel's patrons were over the age of sixty, and therefore took their supper around 5 p.m., or thereabouts—if not earlier. It was nearly 7 p.m.

As we crossed the parking lot to the entrance, past the hedges and the wilted mums and the rocking chairs looped together with bicycle chain locks, I told her I'd been to Cracker Barrel more times than I could count, that it was the only restaurant my parents went to when I was growing up. Very rarely, on birthdays or special occasions, we went to Olive Garden. Otherwise, it was Cracker Barrel.

So you liked this place when you were kid? she said, when we'd been seated.

No, I hated it, I said. I still kind of hate it, though the hatred is mixed with nostalgia. I drew over the little peg game from where it was nestled between the flickering oil lamp and the bottle of peppers in vinegar. Alma cast her eyes about curiously. The dining floor was sparsely seated. A table of boisterous bikers sat in the back in their leather chaps and flame-printed do-rags. Three or four elderly couples were seated in our section, waiting for their food. A fire crackled in the fieldstone hearth, and the woodsmoked air was mingled with the aromas of coffee and bacon and maple syrup. All was warm and quiet. Even the hiss and clatter of the kitchen was hardly audible.

What did your parents like about it? she asked.

After mulling over the question, I explained that Cracker Barrel was cheap, and they were working-class people without a lot of money who nonetheless wanted the experience of a family outing. They loved the food and the décor not because they had bad taste, but because it was familiar to them. They'd grown up on actual farms, milking actual cows, and pulling the suckers from actual tobacco. They'd eaten stewed apples and turnip greens and ham hock, and the tools on the walls had been the tools their fathers used, in a time that was not, at least in Kentucky, some distant yesteryear. It was recent and vivid, and the ache of its passing away therefore still present, like a phantom limb. So, even though it was commodified nostalgia, used to sell gimmicky bullshit to octogenarians, I could understand why they liked it.

Apparently, some of the locations were segregating customers by race, she said, scrolling through an article on her phone.

Really?

Really. There was a big lawsuit.

It didn't surprise me. There had always been undertones of racial animus, implied by the old-timey, those-were-the-days décor—scythes and harrows and pickaxes, fastened haphazardly to the latticework walls as if ready to be taken up by a mob. It was suddenly depressing to be there, as it had been when I was a teenager. Nostalgia was always a lie, I decided. It always covered something up.

This place is pretty wild, Alma admitted, studying the black-and-white portrait of an unsmiling couple that hung above our table. Where do they get all this shit?

Believe it or not, they're all real antiques, I said. There's a big warehouse where they store and organize them all in Lebanon, Tennessee. It's like two hours from my hometown.

Maybe we could go one day, she said. It'd be good material for an essay.

For you or for me?

Our waitress walked up before she could answer, a woman just shy of too skinny with fake eyelashes and a neck tattoo of a rose peeking from her collar. Cracker Barrel waitresses tended to be either matronly older women with their netted gray hair in a bun or youngish women like this, whose heavy makeup made it impossible to tell if they were twenty-two or thirty-six and who smelled faintly of smoke from their last cigarette break. *Trailer-park pretty,* as Rando would say. *The kind of woman that belongs on the "before" side of a "Before and After Meth" poster.* It was mean-spirited, but I knew what he meant. This waitress, whose name, LUCIDA, was stitched on the front of her brown apron below two gold stars, fit Rando's description to a T. She had the look of someone on the precipice of ruin.

Y'all wanna get some drinks started or are you ready to order? she said.

Ummm, Alma said, blinking dazedly at the menu. Honestly, I haven't even had a chance to look yet. I was still taking in the ambience.

Oh—okay, hon, said Lucida, a hint of worry in her voice, as if she realized we would not be easy customers. Well, take it all in, she said. I'll be back in a few minutes with waters.

Lucida walked away and I watched Alma's eyes scan the menu. She looked distraught. What should I get? she said.

What kind of country food do you like?

I don't really like country food.

I laughed. Well, you've come to the wrong place.

You brought me here! she whispered, eyes popping with faux anger. I didn't ask for this!

The stakes are low.

I don't want to disappoint Lucida, she said, and almost immediately after, Lucida reappeared and set down our waters.

We ready? she said.

You go first, Alma said.

I ordered catfish. When the waitress turned to Alma, she panicked and ordered "chicken tenderloins"—a mistake, to be sure. "Chicken tenderloins" was just a fancy way of saying "fried chicken tenders." For her sides, she chose steamed broccoli, a kale side salad, and steamed baby carrots—sensible, healthy, and bland.

When Lucida had gathered our stained paper menus and ambled off to the kitchen, Alma looked at me and cringed. Did I make the right choice?

No, I said, laughing.

But I got fried chicken!

You got chicken tenders.

Shit, really?

I'll give you some bites of catfish.

I'm not sure if catfish is halal.

So? You eat pork.

Yeah, but pork doesn't gross me out.

So you only go by the halal rules when the animal in question coincidentally grosses you out?

I don't know, she said. It gives me a rational reason for an irrational aversion.

I fiddled with the little peg game and got to the end, setting the little colored golf tees in a pile to the side. Somehow, I'd left four. This was a poor showing. The rules on the wooden triangle said, *Leave four or more'n you're just plain "eg-no-ra-moose."*

So, she said. She steepled her fingers and rested her chin on her thumbs. What are you working on now?

I eased back, my chair creaking, and considered this question carefully. I'm polishing a few old stories, I said. Mostly I'm just taking these notes.

Like journaling?

I was about to say no, and then considered—maybe what I was doing was what normal people called journaling? I'd never considered the relationship between the noun "journalist" and the verb "to journal." The short answer was that I didn't know what I was doing.

I guess you could call it journaling, I said. I'm hoping it might turn into a longer project. I explained to her the general idea—that it would be about living with Pop and Cort, trimming trees at Ashby, meeting her. She listened while I explained, now and then taking a sip of water or tucking a strand of hair behind her ear. Gradually, her face took on a look that suggested concern for my well-being, as though I were explaining my decision to invest in an obvious pyramid scheme or to marry a woman after knowing her only a week.

I don't know what I'm doing, really, I concluded by saying. How do you know whether you're writing a journal entry or autobiographical fiction? What's the difference?

Sometimes the difference is arrogance, I think. Believing that people should care about the minutiae of your life.

Is that what it is?

She shrugged. How much have you written? Is this at a point where you could actually call it something?

I don't know, I said, though I knew exactly. Ten? Fifteen thousand words?

Wow.

Is that bad?

No, it's just—I don't know.

Then there's the separate question of whether to call it fiction or nonfiction, I said. What if I were grappling with these issues in the text itself? With the worthiness of the project? Or the ethics?

The ethics?

Like, whether it's ethically dubious to more or less transcribe a conversation I have with my mother without her permission.

Oh I think that's fine, she said. I've done that.

But what if the conversation I'm transcribing is about her unease at being written about? What if I'm telling her in the conversation that I won't write about her, and then I do?

Alma grew silent at this. She rattled the ice in her glass and took a drink. After a few moments, she said, Are you transcribing our conversations?

I tried to laugh this off, but she didn't seem to think it was funny. I'm just writing things down as they happen, I said.

I see, she said. She gazed at the photograph of the solemn couple on the wall, her expression hard to read. After a moment, she turned to face me and smiled blandly. I think you should keep writing, she said.

Yeah?

She nodded. Just keep going and see what happens. There are a lot of great novels that just meander along and plot arises because the events are framed together. I mean, plot can just be time passing, you know?

Totally.

So I wouldn't worry about shaping the material so much. You're still excavating. You know, I wrote the first draft of my novel very quickly, and of course, the second half didn't quite work and now I'm going back through it, but shaping it all is something you can worry about down the line. It's been two years since I finished that first draft and I'm still reworking. It's a long process.

The undercurrent of gentle condescension in this response was not lost on me. It was meant to cut me down to size, to let me know I had a long journey ahead and I was only a beginner. And I probably deserved that. At the same time, I was older than her, and still felt sometimes—fairly or not—that I'd "paid my dues" and she hadn't. That maybe I'd even overpaid them and was owed the difference. But this, of course, I did not say.

Lucida brought our food and we ate, mostly without talking. Alma complained that her chicken was cold and her steamed veggies flavorless. Driving home, we listened to *This American Life.* Alma let her head loll against the window, and I could tell her thoughts were far away. I was about to ask her what she was thinking when a string of red taillights brightened ahead of us. We slowed to a crawl on the interstate. In the distance, the lights of police cruisers were sweeping over the grassy median. When we reached them, I saw that a car—a little Hyundai—had careened through the guardrail. It had been raining lightly for an hour or more. The police were wearing ponchos and neon orange vests, waving the traffic onward with their flashlights. The wrecked car was shriveled and smoking, big clumps of grass and mud caught in the wheel wells. Broken glass glittered like rock salt on the shoulder and the metal railing was mangled. Lying across the rumble strip was a human body covered with rain-beaded plastic—a woman, tawny hair protruding from the cover, lifted by the damp wind. She was dead. No one attending to her. Alma leaned across the front seat to get a better look. What is it? she said, but I switched lanes and drove on before she could see.

It was an animal, I told her.

Freed from the clot of rubberneckers, I brought us back up to the speed limit. Ira Glass was still speaking on the radio, but I couldn't focus on anything he was saying. My heart was beating strangely. All the way back, and even at Alma's apartment, as I showered and brushed my teeth and lay on my back in bed, I thought about the strand of hair against the plastic, and the idea of writing anything seemed suddenly useless. I was afraid that in the morning it would still seem useless, and would never again appeal to me. I would have to find another vocation. There was always law school, I told myself, and as I drifted off, I tried to imagine my future life as a lawyer.

But by morning, the feeling had passed. Writing no longer felt useless. Do you think I'd make a good lawyer? I said, while we were eating our oatmeal.

Absolutely not, she said, without looking up. She had a big glob of peanut butter and honey in her bowl that she was trying to mix in. You're not very good at lying. And you have to be to make a good lawyer.

Isn't that what fiction is, though? Sanctioned lying?

She didn't answer. After breakfast, she stretched her bare feet on the couch with her coffee close by and read Alice Munro. I sat at the kitchen table, a slant of sunlight warming the back of my neck. The leafless branches of the maple outside the kitchen window were cast as intricate shadows on the wood grain. When the wind jostled the branches, they clawed like fingernails on the glass and the shadows danced and blurred. The image of the woman on the side of the road came to mind, and I found, thankfully, that it was easy to dispel. I sipped my coffee. I opened my laptop and set to work.

WHAT'S GOING ON WITH YOUR GRANDFATHER? MY MOTHER asked.

I'd just returned to Pop's from Critical Theory when she called. I sat in the Ranger at the curb, watching steam billow from the coal plant stacks, wholly visible now that the trees were bare.

He was up to his usual tricks, I said. Dragging limbs. Only this time he nearly froze to death.

The line was quiet. She cleared her throat and said, Where were you?

I got the sense that she already knew where I'd been, from Pop or Cort. Like any good prosecutor, she never asked a question she didn't already know the answer to.

With a friend, I said.

So I've heard. Who is this girl, anyhow?

Her name's Alma.

I see. And where's she from?

She grew up in Virginia.

Virginia, my mother said, her tone lightening. Now she was interested. Well, well, so she's a southern girl?

Yes and no. I gave her the thirty-second version of Alma's biography. When I finished, a long silence passed, followed by a sound like, Hm. Then another silence, long enough that I said, Hello?

I'm here, she said. Bosnia. Are they Orthodox in Bosnia?

Some of them, I said. Alma's Muslim.

Why?

Why is she *Muslim*? That's what you're asking me?

I mean, is she practicing?

Sort of. It's more cultural than anything.

Huh, my mother said. I was enjoying her blatant discomfort a little more than I should have. My mother had been close with the last girl I dated, Maurine. Maurine had talked on the phone with her more often than I did, and when we'd broken up, it had been clear where my mother's allegiances lay. I'd always been a little unnerved that she and Maurine had gotten along so well.

Do they have accents in Bosnia?

It's like an eastern European accent, I said. Think Dracula.

Dracula? She sounded horrified.

Yeah, you know. *I vant to suck your blod.*

Well, my mother said. Okay.

You sound really excited to meet her.

Well, it's just a little—I'm surprised. That's all. Of course, she's welcome anytime. Does she *want* to come home with you?

Yeah, I think so. Eventually. She's curious about how closely it corresponds to my fiction.

Ah, she said. So we're like case studies.

Why would you say that?

Sorry, she said. I'm joking. Well, you tell her she's welcome whenever.

I'll tell her.

I stared through the window at the yard across the street, where a squat woman wearing a ski jacket and a surgical mask was pouring bleach into a bucket. She began picking bagworms from the boughs of a spruce and dropping them into the bleach. The spruce was rust colored and wilted—probably not salvageable, but she was trying.

Greg will be leaving BelCo in March, my mother said suddenly.

I thought he had till June?

That's what we thought, too. But they're stepping up the whole timetable.

What will you do?

Don't know, she said. He's looking for work all over. Nashville, Auburn, Savannah.

That doesn't sound like all over. That just sounds like the South.

You know what I mean.

Do you want to leave?

What do you think? I've never lived anywhere else.

It could be an adventure.

That's what people keep telling me, she sighed. Listen, I need to start supper. You keep an eye on your grandfather. Let me know if things get worse and I need to come up there.

I told her I would. When we'd hung up, I sat for a while, trying to make myself go inside. I pictured the scene. Pop sitting in his chair, western on the television. Cort playing his game, locked away from the world. The same unchanging routine, night after night. The thought of going in made my stomach twist and churn in revolt.

I started the truck, geared into drive. I called Alma on the way to let her know I was coming.

INTERESTINGLY ENOUGH, AN EARLY ASSIGNMENT IN VICTORIAN Gothic was to read Freud's essay on the uncanny. The word "uncanny" translated to *unheimlich* in German, which meant, roughly, *unhomelike*. Freud gave several examples of the phenomenon, including Alma's example—seeing his own reflection on a train and mistaking himself for a stranger. Doppelgängers were uncanny. So were dolls and corpses. He recounted the experience of wandering, lost, in a strange Italian city, and finding himself suddenly in a neighborhood of "painted women." Three times, he tried to find his way out of the neighborhood, and three times he found himself precisely where he'd started. Naturally, I could relate to this—trying to get out of a place, and all your efforts merely bringing you back to it.

At one point, Freud reported, predictably, that many of his male patients found female genitalia uncanny. *Love is home-sickness,* he wrote. *Whenever a man dreams of a place or a country and says to himself, still in the dream, "this place is familiar to me, I have been there before," we may interpret the place as being his mother's genitals or her body. In this case, too, the unheimlich is what was once heimisch, homelike, familiar; the prefix "un" is the token of repression.*

I wrote down *Love is home-sickness* in my notebook and underlined it twice. I had my legs stretched out on the couch. Alma was in the shower, and I could hear her singing in there over the drumming of water on the tub floor. The smell of sage and butter still lingered from the gnocchi we'd cooked. My ears were hot from wine. Where I was—in her apartment, in the guesthouse, surrounded by pleasant things—it was very far away from Pop's basement, and further still from where I grew up. I felt tranquil and lucky. When I thought of Alma, I felt a great affection for her, and the desire to be near her and keep her from harm or trouble. But did all this add up to a sense of belonging? Some part of me still felt out of place. I lay there and pondered the line for a long time, listening to Alma's singing.

WE'D BEEN WORKING IN THE ARBORETUM FOR ABOUT A WEEK when Kelly announced that he'd taken an administrative job with the university and would be leaving Maintenance and Landscape Services by the end of April. There were only ten of us now at the morning meetings, the rest having been laid off. We all knew that Kelly had been gunning for an administrative position. He wanted an office with his name on the door, where he'd never again get chain grease smeared on his khakis.

Congratulations, Rando said, with more than a hint of sarcasm.

Thank you, Randy. As I hope y'all know, it's been a great honor serving as your fearless leader. They want to hire a replacement in-house, someone who knows what they're doing. Undoubtably, some of you will want to apply.

We'd all been drowsily eating our Pop Tarts and granola bars, waiting for our coffee to cool, but this caught our attention.

Anybody's welcome, but they *strongly prefer* someone who has a college degree, he said, putting "strongly prefer" in air quotes. That means you two, I guess. He pointed to James and me. Though I'd never thought about it before, we *were* the only grad students. Everybody else was either contract, like Rando, or in the middle of their undergraduate degree.

A degree in what? Rando said.

Anything, said Kelly. Don't matter.

I been here ten years longer than *these* motherfuckers, Rando said. No offense.

None taken, I said.

What difference does a degree make?

Kelly held up his palms. I'm just the messenger, he said.

You don't have a degree, Rando said.

I have military experience.

So what?

So that matters to some people. Look, like I said, any of y'all can apply, and I encourage you to. But I wanted to be up front and let James and Owen here know they'd have a pretty good shot.

I questioned the wisdom of announcing this in front of the other men, who were giving us hateful looks. But maybe that was Kelly's intention.

I thought we'd never hear the end of it from Rando. All morning, as we limbed and bucked a twenty-foot ash, Rando leaned against the chipper and gave us the what-for. I bust my ass for ten years, he said. I do what I'm told, I work hard, in sickness and in health. I work with *boils* on my back—fuckin boils! That's how dedicated I am. I've worked through biblical-plague shit. Then you two come along, fiddle-fart around for a few months, and suddenly every-body's lining up to suck your dicks.

No one's sucking anyone's dick, James said.

Oh, but they are! I'm out here dealing with boils like some Egyptian slave and y'all are getting your dicks sucked.

The Israelites were the slaves, I said. And who knows if what Kelly said is true. They probably won't even hire in-house.

This place, Rando said, shaking his head. This fuckin place. There's no justice here. It's all figured out behind closed doors.

Later, when James and I were alone, eating our lunch in the cab of the chipper truck, he asked me if I planned to apply. I can't really see myself doing Kelly's job, I said.

Me neither, James said, chewing his sandwich. But I can see myself enjoying the money.

How much could it possibly be?

Forty thousand, he said. Plus benefits.

How do you know?

I looked it up on my phone this morning. It's public record.

This number was more than appealing. I'd never made half as much in a year.

Are you applying? I said.

James took another big bite and nodded. I think so, he said.

What about your history degree?

I can put that on hold for a while. What I need right now is money. I'm barely making it since Taylor moved out.

It occurred to me that James had to pay rent, and probably had a car payment, too, all on the same minimum wage as me. I found it almost impossible to save money even without those extra expenses. I had student loans, two maxed-out credit cards. This second class, for which I now had to pay tuition. That was where most of my paycheck went. I'd ended the last two months with less than a hundred dollars in my bank account.

You should apply, too, man, he said. I mean, why not?

It's not what I want to do.

So you do it for a little while, then you do something else.

What if you get stuck?

James shrugged. There are worse things, he said. We both looked out at Rando, who sat smoking a Pall Mall with his back against the freshly sawn stump. It was hard to tell from that distance, but I could've sworn I saw his hand trembling as he brought the cigarette to his lips.

When we got back later and I'd scrubbed my arms with gritty soap and stored away my hard hat and my neon vest in the lockers, I filled out an application and handed it to Kelly.

THE MOONBOW. I DON'T KNOW HOW ALMA HEARD ABOUT IT, but once she had, she was determined to see it. Cumberland Falls, in the Daniel Boone National Forest, was apparently the only place in the Western Hemisphere where it could be seen reliably, and it was only a three-hour drive. I wasn't sold on the idea.

It's a rainbow, but at night, Alma said.

No, I get that, I said. But how amazing could it possibly be?

Her eyes widened comically. Gee, I don't know, she said. It's only the most miraculous natural phenomenon, made even more miraculous by the fact that it's *at night.*

I laughed and told her fine, okay—we'd go see the moonbow.

Saturday was clear and mild, and the moon that night would be just shy of full. These, Alma said, were ideal conditions to see the moonbow. She'd done all the planning, looking up the weather reports, reading online testimonials about the best vantages. We'd hoped to get to the visitor center before dusk, but we'd gotten a late start, and already the tint and slant of the light had begun to change. Gradually, the pastureland became dense forest.

I sure am awful glad you agreed to this, Alma said, in her fake-backwoods accent, which she'd been using a lot lately, especially when we were driving out in the country. It wasn't as funny as she thought it was, but it made me smile every time, if only because it was so bad.

Isn't there a Cat Stevens song called "Moonbow"? she said.

You're thinking of "Moonshadow," I said.

Oh right, she said. Can we listen to it, DJ?

I played the song on my phone, which we'd connected using the cassette adapter that Alma bought at Walmart, months earlier. The song consisted of Cat Stevens saying the word "moonshadow" about a million times, and had the childlike, nursery-rhyme vibe that most of his songs had. Still, I couldn't help but feel a little swept away by it.

This song is corny as hell, I said, but I kind of love it.

Isn't that every Cat Stevens song?

The shuffle algorithm took over and played the rest of Cat's hits over the next hour. We talked about the parade of disappointments in the news, the books we were reading, the shows we were watching. Soon the land rose into craggy bluffs and tall pines. The sky turned purple ahead of us, the late sun flashing in our mirrors. It sank down completely and left a stain of bronze light in the clouds.

Alma was the first to spot the moon, as we gathered our coats in the parking lot. Look! she said, pointing to the horizon line. And there it was, still faint, rising in the twilight. These are perfect conditions, she said. One in a million.

We could hear the rushing of the falls as soon as we stepped out, growing louder as we approached the railing. A few people had cameras set up on tripods. There were kids racing back and forth between their parents' RVs and the observation deck, screeching and cackling wildly.

Alma and I leaned with our elbows against the rail, watching the water plunge over the lip of limestone. We'd brought a thermos that was half coffee, half Irish cream and bourbon, and we traded sips, gentle warmth spreading from our stomachs to our limbs. I associated Irish cream with the holidays, when I drank enough to fall into a near-comatose stupor. I explained this to Alma, how the Christmas before last I'd been so drunk I dropped the turkey.

Is that like an old-timey, country saying? Like you "dropped the ball"?

No, I literally dropped the turkey.

I explained that my mom always insisted on roasting a turkey, but she never had the right equipment. She didn't have a turkey baster or a good carving knife. She didn't have the right pan. So we always had to improvise, and the whole thing became a slapstick ordeal. I'd been drinking Baileys since 8 a.m., plus a surreptitious swig or two of bourbon in the bathroom from my flask, which I only used on Christmas, and it was in this state of mind, with the room whirling slightly and Irish cream curdling in my stomach, that I was asked to help stuff lemon slices into the turkey's body cavity.

The thing was slippery, I explained, and it weighed as much as a toddler.

By this point, Alma was a little drunk herself and laughing breathlessly. So what happened? she said. You just dropped it?

Yeah, it went sliding across the floor, like something from the Three Stooges, and my aunt's dogs—she has three miniature Yorkies—started licking it immediately. They descended like vultures.

She banged the flat of her palm on the rail and snorted. I felt like I would do almost anything—betray my values, sell my soul, dress up in overalls and do a barefoot jig whilst playing the banjo— to make her laugh like that.

There was a good breeze that night. Jets of mist plumed upward from the basin, and when they could rise no further, they caught the wind and drifted toward us, beading in our hair and on the sleeves of our jackets. The air smelled of mist—of clean rain and wet stone.

I don't see it, Alma said, her head nuzzled against my arm.

Just wait, I said. I'd been to the falls as a kid, only during the day. My parents had stopped there on the way back from Gatlinburg, Tennessee, but all I remembered was feeling underwhelmed. I'd hoped it would be taller and more magnificent than it was. The brochures had called it "the Niagara of the South." But when I saw it, it confirmed what I already suspected at nine years old—that all the good things were elsewhere. I didn't want the Niagara of the South. I wanted the Niagara of the Niagara.

What are you gonna do when you run out of sights to see in Kentucky? I asked her.

Oh I don't think I'll run out.

But you could check off all the Greatest Hits, I said. It's not like the state will be producing new geological features anytime soon.

Then I would look for hidden things, she said. The things people don't know about yet.

There are too many other places though, I said. Too many other sights to see and so little time.

She looked at me a little sadly and patted my arm. You'll get to see all the things, she said. Don't worry.

A few minutes later, a man with a camera pointed to the falls. Other arms jutted out along the rail. The moon had breached a high bluff, and the wind pushed an upwelling of vapor from the basin into the sky, where it caught the light and produced the moonbow. It was vague—you had to squint to see it—and it was not, as I'd imagined, the full arch of a rainbow. It was more like that trick of light children created with a garden hose, pressing their thumbs over the stream to create a fine spray, and then pointing, delighted, to the ephemeral blur of color they'd conjured. I found myself smiling. It was hardly a miracle of nature, but everyone around us was whispering excitedly, dozens of cameras clicking like insects. I turned to Alma, thinking I'd say something to the effect of, *That's it?* But she was just as transfixed as the others, her lips parted, droplets of mist in her eyelashes.

Wow, she said.

I was so in love with her in this moment that I forgot about the moonbow completely. I forgot about the tourists, about work and writing and the circumstances of my life. There was no doubting it. She smiled at me expectantly, and with a little mischief, as if this moment had been the real goal all along, and the moonbow itself had been only a means to an end.

Yes? she said.

I'm just happy to be here with you, I said.

Me too, Owen, she said, and this last word—my name, which sounded so oddly formal—broke the spell. I could see ahead to a future in which we'd moved on, when I would think of this moment and the nostalgia would make my chest ache. It made my chest ache then. Preemptive nostalgia for a past that wasn't even past yet.

We looked at each other for what seemed a long time. I collected the damp strands of hair plastered to her cheeks and tucked them back behind her ears, and she began to sing "Moonshadow." We laughed and kissed.

We started back for the car, Alma walking a little ahead of me. I decided to turn back for another glimpse, to give it one last chance to move me the way it had moved her. But it was already gone. Just black pines and the cold glow of the sky. It was like nothing had been there at all.

I LEARNED THAT ONE OF MY STORIES I'D SENT OUT WAS TO be published. It was a small literary journal that only other writers had heard of, and I would be paid nothing for it, but I was happy, nonetheless. Alma insisted we celebrate. We went to a new restaurant I'd heard about in Butchertown—this chic, farm-to-table place with candles in mason jars and diagrams of pigs and cows on the walls, labeling the different cuts of meat. We each ordered the ten-course tasting menu at seventy bucks a pop—money I didn't really have, but what the hell. My work would be in print for the first time, and this only happened once.

I summarized the story while we waited for our wine. It was called "A Place That Never Was," and was about this guy who lived with his grandfather in an apartment above an antique shop. During the day, they ran the antique shop together in this small Kentucky town. The grandson was addicted to OxyContin. One day he overdosed in the shop and the grandfather had to save him with Narcan.

That's it? Alma said.

Yeah, pretty much.

That sounds interesting, she said, picking a hair from the sleeve of her sweater. Can't wait to read it.

I can send you the doc.

Maybe I want to wait and read it in print.

Yeah? Could be a couple months still.

She held the hair at arm's length and let it drop. I'll wait with bated breath, she said.

The waitress brought over a bottle of wine and began to uncork it. Shit, I said. We just wanted glasses I think. The tasting menu was one thing, but I was pretty sure that adding an eighty-dollar bottle of wine on top would overdraw my account.

Oh, said the waitress. She already had the screw in the cork. I just thought—that's my fault, I assumed you wanted the whole bottle.

We can get the whole bottle, Alma said. This is my treat.

It's too much, I said. I can't let you do that.

No, it's fine. Let's do the bottle.

You sure?

She nodded. We both turned to the waitress.

Soooo, yes on the bottle?

Yes, said Alma.

She poured our glasses, and when she'd gone, we toasted. To first-time publication, Alma said.

A rich, almost leathery smell rose from the wine. As I swallowed, I tried to calculate, roughly, the monetary value of each sip. The restaurant was loud and hectic, though the mood they seemed to be going for with the lighting and the décor was more subdued. A globe-shaped pendant lamp hung above our table, emitting a soft, flattering glow. The clientele was better dressed than we were. All the men seemed to have well-coiffed beards and wristwatches. I wondered if I should have a well-coiffed beard and a wristwatch, if that would make people take me more seriously. Beside us, a man in a suit ate alone, watching a soccer game on his cell phone, which he'd propped against the mason jar candle. The swordfish entrée he'd ordered cost forty-five dollars—I'd seen it on the menu—and he ate it in about seven minutes, not once taking his eyes off the game.

I have some news as well, Alma said. The director of the English Department contacted me yesterday. Have you met him?

Yeah, briefly, I said.

He contacted me and said that a position was opening up. A tenure-track position. Basically, he told me that if I wanted it, it was mine.

This would be teaching what—English lit? Rhetoric?

Creative writing, she said.

Holy shit.

I know.

You're not going to take it though, I'm assuming.

Well, that's the thing—I'm not sure.

The waitress brought over a platter of oysters on crushed ice and explained where they were from—Massachusetts mostly. When she'd gone, we resumed eye contact over the platter. You were saying? I said.

That I don't know, she said. My plan had been to go back to New York after this, but now—I'm not sure.

I let this new information settle and pinched a lemon wedge over the oysters. Though they were fresh, I caught a phantom scent of Casey's spoiled oysters, the ones we'd tried to shuck. My stomach tensed in apprehension. I picked out a narrow shell and slurped the bivalve. It tasted like cold, briny seawater. The phantom funk disappeared.

So you told him what, then? I said.

Who?

The director.

Oh, she said. I told him I'd have to think about it.

What's to think about? I mean, I guess it's a vote of confidence on their part, which is nice, but surely you don't want to live here long-term?

It's just not a decision I can make lightly, she said. She forked an oyster, dragged the labial-looking meat onto a saltine, and added a healthy dollop of horseradish. She took a bite and swallowed quickly, chasing it with a swig of wine.

Do you not like oysters? I said.

I love oysters.

You're missing out on the liquor, I said. All the juice in the shell. That's the best part.

Are you mansplaining oysters to me right now?

I sighed melodramatically. I'm explaining something, and I'm a man, so I guess it counts?

I like to eat them the way I eat them.

Okay, don't let me stop you.

The next course was a little glass jar of duck confit and smoked pork that we were to spread on slices of grilled bread. It was delicious, but I realized as I was finishing my first slice that I'd brought her to possibly the most pork-centric restaurant in Louisville.

It sounds like you're conflicted, I said. About the job, I mean.

What makes you say that?

I just don't know why you'd want to live in Kentucky. If it's tenure-track, you'd be building a life here.

Building a life doesn't sound so bad, she said. You have to start sometime. I have this advance now for the novel. I didn't get shit for the stories, but for the novel, I got a nice chunk of change, and it would go a long way here, as opposed to New York, where I'd burn through it on rent. And you know, I *love* my apartment in New York, I really do, but it wears on you after a while, living there. I get tired of having to haul my laundry four blocks in a shopping cart. I get tired of the little German roaches and the shitty water pressure and the probable-but-unconfirmed domestic abuse in the apartment above me. I feel like I can breathe here. I don't have to have my hackles raised all the time, and that's nice, you know?

You'd get tired of that, too, I said.

Of what?

Constantly lowered hackles. And do you *really* have your hackles lowered? This place is full of people who don't think very highly of Muslims.

Different hackles, she said. And Louisville's fine. Nobody cares here. The only times I've felt hostile energy are when *you've* taken me places, out in the boondocks or whatever. She set her toast on the plate and chewed thoughtfully. I don't think I can eat more of this. It's so rich it's making me queasy. Do you want mine?

You've only had a little bit, I said. We still have eight courses, you know.

I just can't do these fatty meats.

Fine, I said. I'll take it. She slid over the plate. I ate eagerly, smearing big chunks of meat onto the bread. It *was* rich—especially for one person to eat all of it alone. But I persisted, licking the grease from my lips. She watched me with her eyebrow cocked.

Well, I have till March to decide, she said.

Right, I said. I guess that's plenty of time.

The courses kept arriving—monkfish, seared pork belly, rare beef with sour persimmon slaw. She picked at them desultorily, took a bite or two, and slid the plates to me. By the time we left, I was gorged and sweating. A stink wafted on the breeze some nights in Butchertown—

the smell of singed hair and flesh from the slaughterhouses—and this was the case that night. Butchertown was not one of those meat-packing districts that no longer packed meat.

When we got home—meaning back to the guesthouse—I settled in to read on her sofa, the same sofa where we'd had sex for the first time. Alma pried open a beer in the kitchen and sat with me, stretching her legs across my lap and wiggling her toes. I was half-way through *Wuthering Heights,* which I'd read sometime in high school and was reading now for Victorian Gothic.

I just don't get why Heathcliff's such a heartthrob, I said after a while, closing the book and gesturing for a sip of her beer. She handed over the bottle.

Oh I had a big crush on Heathcliff, she said. What's not to like? He's dark and broody and a little dangerous.

A little? He's a sadist.

Alma shrugged. You can understand why he turns out that way though, she said. He was treated as an outsider his whole life—like a contaminant, almost. They don't even consider him human.

The things he does are pretty repulsive though.

Repulsion and attraction are two sides of the same coin.

Who says?

I say.

I smiled and took a swig of beer, considering this. I peeled at a damp corner of the bottle's label.

What are you thinking about? she said.

I was thinking that I hoped she wouldn't take the job at Ashby, but I couldn't very well say this. Just that I wish I could see the future, I said.

Like *our* future? You and me?

I guess.

It's a little early for that conversation, isn't it?

You haven't thought about it?

No, I have, she said. She motioned for the beer. I handed it back and she brought the spout to her lips. I wished I still had it so I could hold some object in my hands.

I'm staying over here practically every night, I said. We basically live together.

We could stay at your grandfather's place sometime, if you wanted.

I didn't think you were very comfortable there.

What gave you that idea?

Just the way you were. I don't know. Body language.

He seemed like a sweetheart, she said. Somehow I doubt the couch-bed is as comfortable as mine, but I wouldn't mind staying there. Do you think I'm judging you? Or your family?

I shrugged.

Well, I'm not, she said. I'm sure they're good people.

They are, I said. But how would you know? You haven't met my parents.

Maybe I should.

I laughed. Right.

What's so funny about that?

You might not think they're so good.

She tried to roll her eyes at this but didn't quite commit, so that it looked instead like she briefly glimpsed some ghost flitting in the upper corner of the room. That's an awfully big assumption, she said. Why would I think that? Because they're Republicans? I've encountered Republicans in my life, you know.

"Republican" seemed like such an inadequate word. I could've said they were Trump supporters. I could've said they were evangelical Christians, implying all the baggage that went along with that warped worldview. I could've said they were working-class, that they'd never gone to college or seen much of the world, that they'd lived in a trailer court for the first five years of their marriage, before I was born. That they loved me and were good people fundamentally, underneath all the bullshit—people who did their best, raising me as well as they knew how. All of these things would've been true, but none would've expressed who they were, really—or who they were to me.

It's complicated, I said.

Well, I want to meet them.

I thought you were worried they'd be hostile.

I am, truthfully, she said. But I've got to meet them sooner or later. And the more I've thought about it, the less worried I am. I mean, how different am I, really? It's not like I'll be wearing a hijab and blessing my food in Arabic. I'm sure they'll like me once they get to know me. I'm very charming.

She winked adorably. I couldn't help but smile. Okay, I said. If that's what you want. I was planning to go home later this month. You can come with me.

Great, she said. She leaned forward to kiss me. Her mouth tasted like beer and expensive wine and all the smoky food we'd eaten. I can't wait, she said.

THREE INCHES OF SNOW FELL ONE NIGHT IN EARLY FEBRUARY. The roads and sidewalks on campus were cleared by midmorning, and feeling restless, we tugged on our boots and heavy coats and struck out into the cold. We'd both been slightly sick and had spent the previous day under a rainbow-patterned crochet blanket, eating slices of processed cheese and watching eight hours of a not-great-but-addictive television show on her laptop. It felt good to be outside, the chilled air clearing my head. The sun cooked steam from frosted sycamores along her street, filling the sky with fog, but after a while it began to clear, disclosing splotches of blue sky. Alma hooked her arm through mine and we tramped on through the slush, content.

At the gas station on the corner, a man was huddled down by the Reddy Ice cooler, smoking crack. I'd seen him panhandling around campus, and once, weirdly, trying to sell an empty aquarium for ten dollars. Alma stopped and squinted. Is he smoking something? she said.

Yeah, I said. Crack.

What?

He's smoking a crack rock.

How do you know that?

I pointed out that he was using a glass stem and waving a torch lighter under the tip. I guess it's possible that it's crystal, I said.

But how do you know what that looks like? she said. Have you seen someone smoke crack?

When I finally turned to look at her, her pupils were dilated. She was trying not to look concerned. Yes, I said.

Who?

This guy I worked with at a restaurant, I said.

He just smoked crack at the restaurant?

Yep.

What kind of restaurant lets their employees just smoke crack?

I laughed at this, but she kept her mouth taut. It was the Kountry Kitchen in Melber, I said. They didn't know about it, or at least they pretended not to. He was a dishwasher. He got fired after his third DUI landed him in county lockup.

Why were you working there? she wanted to know.

Why have I worked anywhere? I needed money.

I didn't elaborate further. She took my arm and we walked onward, though her carriage had a new rigidity, as if she were holding her breath and tensing all her muscles at once.

You all right? I said, after a few minutes of silence.

She nodded curtly.

When the sun broke through finally, we turned around, the blinding glare from the snow leaving green afterimages in my vision.

The subject came up a few days later, of course. I'd put on a Townes Van Zandt record as we made dinner and heard Alma sigh as soon as his voice came through. Can we listen to something else? she said.

What's wrong with Townes?

It's just a little much, the whole sad-boy country thing.

Any requests?

Maybe just silence, she said. This is almost ready.

We brought our bowls of rice and vegetables to her floral sofa and ate. We didn't talk. Through the window, I could see snow whirling like wheat chaff in the street. A couple went by, hugging their coats tight.

Sad-boy country thing, huh? I said after a while.

She chewed and nodded.

What does that mean?

She waited till she'd swallowed a mouthful of rice and said, *You know. It's like, I get it, Townes. You're a white boy who's done a lot of drugs and you think that counts as a harrowing experience.*

I thought about this for a minute, watching her shovel these big heaps of rice into her mouth. She was eating like she was trying to prove something. Well, he did die from it, I said.

Self-fulfilling prophecy, she said.

Still, suffering and eventually dying from something counts as harrowing, I'd say.

They bring it on themselves.

Wow, okay. I thought addiction was an illness. Isn't that the Good Liberal stance nowadays?

Well, maybe I'm not a good liberal, she said. She scraped a last chunk of onion from the bowl and set it on the coffee table. She wouldn't look at me.

Is something wrong?

It's just, you know, hard to have sympathy when their whole shtick is to romanticize their self-caused pain.

Maybe there's a deeper pain.

She scoffed. Yeah, right.

Is that so far-fetched?

I just don't buy it.

What's this really about?

She looked at me now, her lips pursed. A long, fragile silence passed before she said, What drugs have you done?

I set my bowl on the table and turned on the sofa to face her squarely. What difference does it make? I said. I'm not doing any now—except for weed, rarely.

That's not what I asked.

What, you want me to name every drug I've used?

Is that such a difficult task? How long is the list?

There was that fear in her eyes again, the one I'd seen the night we met—that I wanted something from her, that I would take something away.

It would be easier to say what I haven't done, I said. This was true, though I'd never thought about it in those terms. I'd never been some kind of hard-core junkie, but I'd dabbled and experimented and made dumb mistakes. My own drug use had been relatively tame and not all that interesting compared to some of the people I grew up with, who still had problems with opioids and Xanax. But somehow, I didn't think this distinction would matter to Alma.

She sat there with her jaw clenched and her eyes blazing. Did you smoke crack with that dishwasher you were talking about? she said. Her voice was lower and huskier than I'd ever heard it.

Yes, I said. Once. I left out that I'd spent most of the afternoon hyperventilating in the walk-in cooler, my heart thumping like a dryer with boots inside.

Have you done meth?

No.

She forced breath through her nostrils, balled up her fists. She seemed ready to strike me. How could you smoke crack? she said. Like, *why*?

How different is it really than Casey doing lines of coke?

She blinked rapidly, shook her head. I don't know, she said. It's just different. And I never did that with Casey. I told you, I *hated* that he did that.

Well, I didn't like it much, if it's any consolation. The crack, I mean.

What about heroin? she said.

What about it?

Have you *used* it?

This was a difficult question to answer. When I was twenty-one, I'd gone home for the summer and met this guy through friends named Caven. He was an Iraq veteran—this muscled, razor-bald dude who was training to participate in Strongman competitions. He'd already won Mr. West Kentucky Strongman, and hoped to win Mr. Kentucky, but he'd blown out his knee carrying a four-hundred-pound tractor tire and become addicted to OxyContin after several unsuccessful surgeries. I smoked weed with him sometimes, took pills. He was really good at chess, and we played sometimes on his little magnetic travel board that he'd taken on two tours. One day I showed up and he claimed to have scored some raw opium—this black gunk wrapped up in aluminum. For about a week, we smoked it out of an elaborate piece he'd made from a Gatorade bottle. It was only later, when Caven the Strongman died of an overdose, that I considered the possibility that the "opium" was probably just black tar heroin. The intense nausea and chills I'd had after discontinuing its use only reinforced this theory.

All this is to say that *maybe* I had used heroin. I recounted the long story of Caven the Strongman and his opium, some part of me believing, foolishly, that she might actually find it funny. *It was all a big mix-up! As it turned out, maybe it wasn't opium after all! I'll never know! I can't ask the Strongman because he's dead! Isn't that hilarious!*

Have you injected it? she said, her voice shaking.

No, Alma.

Do you swear?

I swear.

She turned away from me, wiped her eyes with the back of her wrist. I just don't understand, she said.

It's in the past, I said. Just dumbass behavior. I'm not doing it anymore.

Did you do it for something to write about?

What? No, I did it because it felt good.

It's not interesting, she said. People think it makes them interesting, but it's predictable and boring.

I didn't say it was interesting.

Good, because it's not.

She simmered quietly for a while on the couch while I attempted to comfort her. I was of two minds. On the one hand, I could empathize with her dismay. How many people had she met at Princeton who'd smoked crack with a dishwasher by the grease traps behind the Kountry Kitchen? How many of her hallmates in her neo-Gothic dormitory had used opium/heroin with a washed-up Strongman/Iraq veteran who then later died of an overdose?

On the other hand, there was this self-protective instinct in her, this fear of contamination. And a fear of contamination always held the assumption of purity—that the fearful person believed themselves so special that they could be contaminated. In other words, she thought she was better than me.

I'm okay, she said finally. I'm just processing.

You're judging, and honestly it's a little ridiculous.

I'm trying really hard not to.

She collected herself finally, and with red eyes and clogged sinuses, she attempted a smile and said, I know it was the past. It's just scary to me. You have to understand that. I told her that I did. She brushed the hair from my forehead fondly, touched my cheek with her cold knuckles. Let's forget it, she said. I'm sorry. I didn't mean to interrogate you.

Okay, I said. It's fine.

And that was it. We went on with our evening. We read our books, watched our one hour of Netflix, and went to sleep, as though the conversation had never happened. But all the while, I was thinking of the things I'd done in the past, and how I couldn't help them now. I wished I could. I wished I could go back, movement by movement, like retracing footsteps in the snow, till I reached the point where I began. I would take a different path, across a fresh, unbroken surface, and she would see me then, perhaps, the way she wanted to see me. But who would this man be—this man without mistakes? What would she want from him?

IT WAS A THREE-HOUR DRIVE TO MY MOTHER'S HOUSE FROM Louisville. We left early on a low-skied morning, taking I-65 through the Knobs till we reached the Western Kentucky Parkway. There, the land smoothed out to corn stubble and fields of winter grass. We passed signs for Paradise, the subject of John Prine's song, and Alma scrolled hurriedly on her phone so we could listen while we were still in the vicinity. Weak sunlight had begun to sift down, and when we crossed the Green River, which really was green, its banks choked with brambles and frail trees, we could just make out the stacks of the coal-burning Paradise Fossil Plant in the distance. We only got a glimpse. It disappeared behind the hills and John Prine sang on nasally about Mr. Peabody and the town called Paradise he'd hauled away in a coal train.

About twenty minutes later, the squealing, chugging noise that was more or less constant in the Honda's engine intensified. Then the power steering died, and steam spilled out from under the hood. I cranked the wheel with all my strength, and we pulled to the shoulder in a frantic chorus of *shit, shit, shit, shit*. I knew what it was without having to look. She'd been told the last time she had her oil changed that the fan belt needed replacing, but I'd told her—as if I had any idea what I was talking about—that she could probably hold off, that the Jiffy Lube guys were just trying to sell her something.

I popped the hood and stared down into the labyrinthine workings of the engine with an approximation of masculine confidence. Sure enough, the belt was shredded. Steam was still drifting up, and the motor smelled like scorched metal. There was nothing around, just walls of forest on either side of the highway. A semitruck rumbled past without slowing, blasting a warm breath of exhaust.

I called my mom, who put me on the phone with Greg. I told him what had happened, that the fan belt had broken. Those usually don't break unless you really let them go, he said.

We really let it go, I said.

Well, hang tight, he said. We're on our way.

Before I could say anything, or offer to have it towed, he'd hung up. We waited with our coats on, traffic flying by, rocking the car. We played would-you-rather to pass the time. At one point, a possum emerged from the edge of the woods and regarded us timidly. Alma's arm shot out.

Possum! she said.

The possum looked at the busy highway, shook its head a little, as if to say, *Hell naw,* and wiggled back into the underbrush.

It's a sign, Alma said. Your spirit animal has come to visit us in our time of need.

Greg and my mom arrived in record time. Well, hello! Mom shouted, high-stepping through the dry weeds to reach us. Introductions were made, hugs exchanged. My mother had her shoulder-length black hair pulled back with bobby pins and was wearing a Patagonia sherpa fleece, which I guessed she had found thrifting. One of her main hobbies in retirement was going to thrift stores and rooting around for expensive brands. Even at fifty-six, her face was free of wrinkles, and the only sign of age and worry were the bags under her eyes, the color of fading bruises. Greg was tall and sandy-haired, with small, twinkling eyes and a paunch that he minimized with untucked flannels. He was just about the nicest guy I'd ever met, always grinning, always eager to help me with anything. My mother was the same—sweet-natured through and through— though she'd seemed worried lately that I was becoming someone she didn't recognize.

Kind of a weird place to meet, she said.

Y'all didn't have to come out here, I said.

And leave you stranded? she said.

Greg had on one of those camping headlamps, even though it was broad daylight. He put on this headlamp whenever he had to fix something, regardless of whether he actually needed the light. Let's see what we got here, Greg said. He clicked on the headlamp and squinted into the engine compartment with the kind of masculine confidence that couldn't be faked. I recounted what had happened while he fiddled and prodded. He had the distracted, concerned look of a doctor who is only half listening to your symptoms as he examines you. He sighed, clicked off the headlamp, and wiped his hands on the back of his blue jeans. Not much we can do without a new belt, he said.

I can pay to have it towed, Alma said. That's no problem.

Greg shooed away the suggestion. Absolutely not, he said. I'll get the part today, come back in the morning, and replace it.

I can't let you do that, she said.

You'd have to tow it all the way to Eddyville, which would cost you a few hundred bucks. Then you'd have to pay for the new belt, plus labor on top of all that.

That's okay, really, Alma said, but my mother was already ushering us back to Greg's truck.

We've got snacks laid out at the house, she said. We'll worry about all this tomorrow.

Mom insisted that Alma ride in the passenger seat while she and I sat in the back. It was a newish truck, with all the bells and whistles, and Greg kept punching buttons to showcase its features. It's got the best heated seats of any car I've bought, Greg said. You feel it?

Oh I feel it, Alma said. It's a little intense.

That's only the middle setting, he said, pressing a button. Here, this is high.

Wow, Alma said, squirming in her seat.

Put on the massager, Greg, Mom said. Let her try that out.

Maybe she doesn't want to be massaged by Greg's truck, I said.

I kinda think I do? Alma said.

Greg turned on the massager and the seat began to vibrate. What does it feel like? I said.

It's, like, rolling up my spine, she said.

Imagine that after a long day at work, Greg said.

I would want this except for my head, she said. Like, in the form of a helmet.

Throughout the rest of the drive back, Greg talked about all the other cars he'd owned or encountered or heard of that had required repairing. Then he got on to the subject of Honda's power train and its reliability, how the Japanese had been investing all their energy into four-cylinder motors since the 1950s, and that America had been all about the V8. He called the Japanese cars "rice cookers," which was a term I'd heard before but was a little embarrassed for Alma to hear.

When we got back, Greg and my mom went on ahead of us while we lingered behind. I think I have second-degree burns on my ass, Alma whispered, which got me laughing.

My mom whirled around, grinning slyly. What's so funny? she said.

Nothing, I said.

They're laughing about us, Greg.

Uh-oh, he said.

Not at all, Alma said. Totally unrelated.

They went inside and Alma stood there in the gravel driveway, her eyes ranging over the house and the yard. It was a modest, vinyl-sided house on a broad hill of grass. The nearest neighbor lived in a red trailer, with an electrical fence enclosing three Herefords. Otherwise, there was not much else around, at least that you could see. Their lawn eased down to a tract of woods, at the edge of which sat a hay bale with a paper target, which Greg sometimes shot with his compound bow. My mother's minivan was parked in the driveway, next to a propane tank concealed by rose bushes. This is it? she said.

Yep.

It's nice.

Yeah, I said. What were you expecting?

I don't know, she said. It looks . . . normal though.

Greg makes okay money. Or, he *made* okay money, I guess I should say.

Oh right, he's laid off. Should I not mention that?

It'll come up on its own, I bet.

So is this Melber or Paducah?

Neither. It's Gilbertsville.

I thought you said you were from Melber?

I said I grew up there. My dad still lives there but my mom lives in Gilbertsville.

Are we close to Monkey's Eyebrow or the Possum Town?

Possum Trot, I said. And no, not really.

This is very confusing. You know, most people just say they're from one place.

Oh, really? Aren't you from Yugoslavia slash Bosnia slash DC slash New York?

All right, all right.

You'll see Melber, don't worry, I said.

She made a sound like, Hm, and fixed her eyes on the house once more, as if it were an abstract painting she was trying to decipher.

Ready?

She smiled at me absently and nodded. We hoisted our duffel bags and walked up the slight incline of the driveway, through the garage and the back door that led into the kitchen.

Welcome, welcome! my mother called. There's pumpkin bread in the oven. Until then, y'all can snack. I'm sure you're hungry.

An array of finger foods was laid out on the kitchen island. There were crackers and chips, tubs of hummus, homemade salsa, a slab of cream cheese with pepper jelly dumped on top. I'd told Alma to be prepared for the cream cheese and pepper jelly—they served it every time I came home, a perfect rectangle of Philadelphia cream cheese and a glob of jalapeño-blackberry jam—so when we saw it among the other foods, I had to stifle a smile and avoid eye contact with her. I joked about it, but it was actually kind of delicious. To top it all off, there were, inexplicably, chocolate-covered strawberries. Cocktails were offered, which we declined. They seemed disappointed, but this didn't keep them from making mimosas for themselves. We never drink, Alma, my mother said.

Oh that's okay, she said. I mean, you go right ahead. I glanced back at her, and though she was smiling, her eyes kept darting between the overwhelming spread of foods and the digital clock above the microwave, as if she had somewhere to be.

We left our bags on the kitchen floor and listened quietly while they told us about their recent trip to Cuba. Most of my vacations growing up had been to the Florida Panhandle (the Redneck Riviera) or Gatlinburg, Tennessee (Redneck Aspen). It wasn't until I'd left home and my parents remarried that they began to venture elsewhere. Suddenly, with the money Greg made at the BelCo plant, my mom could afford to visit exotic, tropical climes—or at least the ports of call for Carnival and Royal Caribbean. Their most recent foray had been to Cuba, and it was all they could talk about. Cuba was wonderful. The people were beautiful. They lived a simpler life. On and on and on. It amazed me, frankly, that my parents—dyed-in-the-wool conservatives—could so readily fetishize a communist country. My mother even showed me a picture wherein they were both standing in a town square before an enormous mural of Che Guevara.

Now, who is this, Owen? my mother said, tapping Che's face in the photo. I told Greg you would know.

It's Che Guevara, I said, and I was about to give the two-minute version of his biography, but they'd already moved on to another story about acquiring black-market cigars. My mother said the people made so little there with their meager stipends, and she and Greg had made sure to tip generously. The people were so thankful, my mother said. I wished I could've taken our little tour guide home with us, she was just such a sweet thing.

The people there do the best they can with the government the way it is, Greg said. They're good people. The problems they got come back to the government. Doesn't matter how hard you work if the government takes everything from you.

Their problems might have something to do with the way they've been isolated economically, you know, I said. The American embargo.

They get around that, Greg said. His tone held the authority of a scholar's. They get help from Venezuela.

Their healthcare system is better than ours, I said. Internally, I was cringing at myself. *Why are you taking the bait? Why engage like this?*

I doubt that.

You don't have to take my word for it. Look it up.

Greg took a sip of mimosa from his champagne flute and shook his head. I don't have to look it up, he said. I was there.

Alma held her mouth in a rictus grin and said nothing throughout this exchange. They went on talking. I found myself tuning out, and pretty soon, the old familiar panic began to germinate in my chest. In its early stages, it was only a slight pressure—a spring-loaded feeling. But like the aura that precedes a migraine, it was a reliable sign of what would follow.

Alma said she was going upstairs to lie down and rest for a bit. We've got you in the guestroom, Alma, my mother said. Owen, you're on the futon in Greg's office.

Why are you on the futon? Alma said. Is it a twin bed?

We've got you in separate rooms, my mother said.

Ohhh, said Alma. Of course.

When I was left alone with my mother, she asked if I had any news. I told her about my story that was going to be published. She clapped her hands together, laced her fingers. How amazing! she said. In print?

Yeah, in a little journal.

She called Greg back into the room and made me repeat the news. Wow, he said, his tone sincere, that's big-time. Big-time congrats. We'll have to get some champagne at dinner.

Now, I want a copy, my mother said. You be sure to get me one.

Some part of me had wanted them to be underwhelmed, so that I could feel like a martyr. Then I felt idiotic and ashamed for having this impulse. Was I really so snobbish, so eager for a grievance, that I couldn't simply accept my parents' heartfelt congratulations?

So what's my character's name in this story? she said.

What do you mean?

What did you change my name to in the story? Or will it be obvious?

You're not in the story, I said.

I know how your kind of *fiction* works, she said, putting "fiction" in air quotes. You call it fiction, but really you just change the names.

That isn't what I do, I said. I might take certain biographical details and put them in, but the characters aren't real people.

Uh-huh, she said. She flashed a knowing smile.

We had a couple hours before dinner. Greg went straight out to AutoZone and bought the belt while Mom cleaned up the snack carnage. Alma and I debriefed in the guest bedroom, where she would be sleeping. Look, she said, and she motioned me over to the nightstand. Laid out there were two books—Carrie Fisher's memoir *Wishful Drinking* and *Big Little Lies* by Liane Moriarty. A sticky note beside them said, *Please borrow or take these if you want.*

What does it mean? Alma said.

I'm sure she just picked two books from her collection she thought you would like.

Does she think I'm an alcoholic manic-depressive? she said, holding up *Wishful Drinking.*

No, I said. I'm sure the criteria were just that these are irreverent and sort of left-leaning.

She frowned and studied the back of the memoir. It's really thoughtful, actually, she said. And can we talk about the cream cheese and blackberry jam combo? Forget the restaurant, I could just eat a bowl of that.

We laughed and hugged, Alma nuzzling her head against my chest. I wondered what preconceived notions she might've had, whether they'd been subverted or confirmed. But mostly, I was remembering Tony's words of advice from Jungle Narratives—that whatever you think about a person, they're always more complicated than that.

We had supper at a new restaurant in downtown Paducah. It was housed in an old railroad freight house, with high, bright windows and riveted steel beams. They served fancy versions of "poor-people food," which was hardly a new phenomenon among hip restaurants, but it was new to Paducah. It allowed middle-aged patrons to chuckle and shake their heads at the menu and say, I remember when we used to eat beans and cornbread as a necessity. I wish somebody'd told me back then that one day it'd be a delicacy! All around us, at every table, people with bemused expressions were saying similar things. Why, you could get the same thing at Cracker Barrel for half the price, Greg said. Hell, a *quarter* of the price.

They make it special, my mother said.

How special can cornbread be?

Well, you'll just have to get it and see.

When the waitress came for our drinks, they encouraged us to get whatever our hearts desired and tried mightily to push the idea of celebratory champagne.

Our son is having a story published in a magazine, Greg said.

Oh wow, said the waitress. Which magazine?

Bear Creek Review, I said meekly.

Huh, she said, her face scrunched. I don't think I've heard of that one.

It's a very big deal, my mom said. They don't just publish anybody.

Where could I get a copy? said the waitress. I couldn't decide whether she was sincerely asking or just trying to torture me.

You'd probably have to special order it, I said.

Wow, okay, she said. Maybe I'll look into it.

We ultimately decided against the champagne, Alma and I ordering cheap beers. We *never* drink, Alma, my mother said, after they'd ordered their cocktails.

Alma's eyes flitted to me briefly, as if I might respond for her. The truth was that they drank as often as anyone else, but like a lot of

Southern Baptists, they pretended it was a rare indulgence. There was an old joke—*How do you tell the difference between a Methodist and a Baptist? Answer: A Methodist will say hello to you in the liquor store.* I made a mental note to tell Alma the joke later, then realized the differences between Protestant denominations meant nothing to her, whereas in western Kentucky, they meant a lot. Southern Baptists were leery of Episcopalians, much less Catholics and Jews. Muslims might as well have been from a different planet.

I'm not judging, Alma said finally.

We really only drink when we're in Paducah, said Greg.

A lot of the counties around here are dry, my mother added.

That's a bummer, Alma said. My dad doesn't really drink. Every now and then he'll have some brandy, but that's it.

Oh? my mother said.

Yeah, he's more devout than my mother. At least, since they immigrated.

Mom perked up at this and set aside her menu. So your family is from Bosnia?

That's right, Alma said.

I looked at pictures of it online—the Dinaric Alps? Is that how you say it?

Yeah, Alma said.

Very beautiful.

Yeah, it's a beautiful country.

Do people go hiking there?

Well, Alma said, you could. You have to be careful about land mines though.

My mother's bright expression curdled. Of course, she said. And you and your family are Muslim? She said the word "Muslim" at a slightly lower volume.

That's right, Alma said. But we're not, like, devout or anything. It's more about the rituals and traditions.

Mom nodded slowly with a look of intense concentration. So have you gone on your hajj?

No, Alma said, laughing. Neither of my parents have either.

I thought you had to?

I pictured my mom staying up late the night before, reading the Wikipedia entry on Islam, memorizing its key features.

Maybe I'll go one day, Alma said. It's not something I'm prioritizing.

Alma said little else throughout dinner. Something about her silence seemed to unnerve them. They were preemptively defensive and kept correcting their own grammar. They'd say something like, *Them kids were running all over the place,* and then repeat the sentence in the next breath with the correct usage, as if they were catching themselves—*Those kids.*

After supper, we walked along the floodwall, segments of which were painted with murals depicting moments in Paducah's history. Civil War battles and strawberry pickings. Railroads and steamboats. Native Americans emerging from teepees to shake hands with the white man. We reached a mural of the uranium plant, one I'd written about and seen many times before. WELCOME TO THE ATOMIC CITY, it said. It was a view from above, and you could see the electrical towers and the stacks emitting little wisps of friendly white smoke. Beyond the facility lay a patchwork of green and khaki farms and the Ohio itself. They made postcards with the same image, sold them at the antebellum mansion off the interstate they'd turned into a rest area.

We paused at a gap in the wall and gazed at the Ohio and the wooded shores of Illinois on the other side. The wind was cold, smelling of river water and the carcasses of fish. It tossed our hair and skimmed across the green surface. Coal barges were docked on the Kentucky side, creaking as they rocked in the current.

We walked on behind my mother and Greg, exchanging faint smiles. Now and then, I'd rest my hand on the small of Alma's back or squeeze her arm reassuringly. They talked about the town and western Kentucky, how things had changed. How they'd grown up poor, which was true. It occurred to me that they were now solidly middle-class. Their rags-to-riches narrative wasn't a fiction: they really had come from nothing, and now they'd done well for themselves. They seemed to be touting this as we walked along the river, as if they wanted Alma to know they'd worked hard and that's how they had what they had. We nodded and made small sounds of recognition, to show that we'd heard them.

The next morning, Alma's Honda was sitting in the driveway. Greg and my mom had gotten up at five in the morning, replaced the belt, and Mom had driven it back with Greg following in the truck. Alma had been prepared to go and have it towed that morning, but it wasn't a total surprise to me that they'd taken care of it. I took it for granted, growing up around people who could fix things, who knew what to do when something went wrong.

I went downstairs first and let Alma sleep in. Mom fried bacon, scrambled six eggs, and baked a tray of biscuits. She refused to let me help and would not really acknowledge my thanks for retrieving the Honda, as if it were such a trivial thing it was hardly worth mentioning. She played Carly Simon and Bonnie Raitt on her Bluetooth speaker, shimmying her shoulders a little in time to the music. While we were waiting for the biscuits to brown, she perked up suddenly, spatula in one hand, and said, Oh, I almost forgot to mention—Maurine wanted me to tell you hi.

I froze with the coffee mug at my lips. When did you talk to her? I said.

Well, my mother said, her tone still chipper, though she could see, clearly, that I was upset. We talk now and then, just to catch up. She was doing real good.

I said nothing. My mother turned and switched on the oven light to check the biscuits, as though nothing at all was strange about this. These are *almost* done, she said.

Surely you can see how that makes me uncomfortable. Or how it would make Alma uncomfortable?

My mother turned to face me and leaned with her elbows on the kitchen island, still smiling. And why would that be?

You really can't see how it would make my current girlfriend uncomfortable to know that my parents were still chummy with my ex? Especially when your response to her has been so lukewarm?

Now her smile wavered. In what way has our welcome been *lukewarm*?

It's just obvious, I said, realizing almost immediately that there was no hard evidence of this, that they'd gone out of their way to make her feel welcome and that I sounded like a brat.

Well, my mother said. I just don't know anything about her. I don't know what makes her tick. She's hardly talked to us. At least with Maurine, she had a belief system. She had values.

Namely?

She was a Catholic.

She was a lapsed Catholic, I said. She didn't believe in God.

Yes, she did. Why would you say that? Of *course* she did. She huffed and glanced around her kitchen as if it suddenly disgusted her. Well, she whispered, I tell you what, it doesn't impress me a *hair's breadth* that she went to Princeton.

I had to laugh at this. I'm sure she wouldn't expect it to, I said. What it comes down to is that you can't stand that she's a so-called coastal elite, and that she's culturally Muslim.

Culturally Muslim? See, I don't even know what that means. You either believe in something or you don't. You millennials have nothing you believe in. You have no values.

I wasn't even sure I knew what it meant, precisely, beyond Alma's analogy to Christmas-and-Easter Christians. I could say that it was like cultural Judaism, but I wasn't sure that would mean anything to her.

That's condescending, I said.

Right, she said. We're so condescending. Next thing you'll be saying I'm racist, too.

Greg came in about this time, groaning theatrically, hair damp from the shower. *Shoo-wee,* that bacon smells *good,* he said. He seemed to recognize that he'd walked in on a tense moment. My mother broke eye contact with me and went to the oven. These are done, she said curtly.

Alma came down in her drawstring pajama pants and a tank top a few minutes later. She saw her car outside, and when Greg explained what they'd done, she was somewhat flabbergasted. She thanked him profusely.

What do I owe you? she said.

Don't worry about it, he said.

That's crazy, she said. I insist on at least paying for the part.

He poured himself some coffee and pretended not to have heard her.

I'm serious, she said.

It's a cheap part, took five minutes to replace. I was happy to do it.

My mother's gaze lingered on the dark hair poking from Alma's armpits as she set out the blackberry jam and the sorghum. What is sorghum? Alma said. She held up the jar and squinted at the label.

Molasses, I said. It's made from a type of grass.

Kentucky makes the best, Greg said. It's an old southern thing.

It's native to Africa, actually, I said. Slaves brought it over. Like the banjo.

We cut open our biscuits and buttered them. Alma didn't much like bacon, but she took a few nibbles to be polite. When I'd finished my eggs, I dipped out a glob of sorghum and watched the amber syrup run from the spoon onto my biscuit, the flow thinning finally to a string. Alma agreed to try some but let only the smallest trickle fall onto her biscuit. It tastes like rum, she said, chewing.

I could see that, I said. Sorghum was a delicacy I'd only ever had in Kentucky. I looked forward to it every time I came home. That and hickory-cured country ham at the holidays, with redeye gravy made from drippings and black coffee.

As we were finishing up, my mother asked when we were leaving.

Sunday, I said.

Will you be staying for church? she said. She sipped her coffee casually.

Why would we do that?

She rose with her plate, went to the sink, and ran the faucet. She squeezed detergent over the dishes piled there. I just thought you might want to, she said. Keith is doing a sermon on evolution.

Unless Southern Baptists have suddenly changed their position on evolution—and everything else, really—I think I'll pass, I said.

My mother raised her eyebrows and scrubbed at the biscuit pan. You haven't been to Relevant Church, she said. Relevant Church is a lot different from any other Baptist church I've been to, by a far sight.

Relevant Church—its actual name—was a megachurch off the interstate that looked, from a distance, much like a regional airport. They had a huge sanctuary, a gymnasium, a separate chapel for weddings. They even had a coffee bar in the lobby, where baristas fixed cappuccinos for sleepy-eyed churchgoers. Though they didn't advertise it, they were Southern Baptists. But they'd traded their fire-and-brimstone tirades for a softer, coded rhetoric. "Hell" became "separation from God," in the same way that Black people became "thugs in the inner city" and Mexicans became "illegal immigrants taking our jobs." The older generation would tell you outright that Chicago was unsafe because of "Blacks on the South Side," or that non-Christians would "burn in hell," but the baby boomers were craftier than that. The church's name was almost too good to be true. It had been called Central Baptist before all the renovation, and one could almost imagine the new young preacher, Keith, sitting around brainstorming with the deacons, trying to rebrand. *Church just isn't relevant for young people anymore—how do we make it relevant?*

So it's like a series on evolution? Alma said, clearly perplexed.

It's really about healthy skepticism, Greg said. Evolution's just a theory, but at the colleges, they don't represent it that way. They represent it as *fact.*

Alma cut her eyes at me, then back to Greg, unsure if he was joking. It is a fact, though, she said.

Greg stared at her. My mother scrubbed the cast iron violently at the sink. I could've intervened, but there was something both paralyzing and exhilarating about the whole scene—like watching a car careen toward you at an intersection in slow motion.

It's one of several theories, Greg said. Keith's point is that they ought to give equal time to the others, like creationism and intelligent design.

Aren't those the same thing? Alma said.

Not really, my mother said.

This area has an interesting history when it comes to evolution,

I said. I told her about John Scopes of the Scopes Monkey Trial, who was born and buried in Paducah. She'd never heard of him and couldn't understand what the trial was about.

I mean, what was the jury deciding? she said.

Whether Scopes broke the law by teaching evolution.

It was against the law?

At the time.

Why?

I shrugged.

Because it's indoctrination, Greg said.

But why would you teach a Christian theory at a public school? she said. I mean, with separation of church and state, it seems pretty cut and dry.

Greg let his fork clank down on the plate. His cheeks were flushed. Well, that's not how I see it, he said. My mother, meanwhile, tried to look pleasant as she scraped the pans with steel wool, a little muscle pumping rapidly at the hinge of her jaw.

WE DROVE OUT TO MY FATHER'S HOUSE IN MELBER LATER— the house where I grew up, where he now lived with his sick wife. It was our first real chance to debrief and talk privately. I told her what my mother had said about speaking with Maurine.

I can't believe that, she said. Why would she think that's okay? Why would *Maurine* think that's okay?

Who knows. Maurine's fear was always that I'd decide I was too smart for her and move on. She ingratiated herself to my family as a defense against that.

That's psychologically interesting, Alma said. That's your mother's fear, too, right? That you'll decide you're too smart for them and move on. I mean, if there was ever a way to win your mother's sympathy . . .

I'd never considered this, but it was true. She liked Maurine because Maurine gave her hope for keeping me close. Alma, by contrast, was like the living embodiment of my mother's fear, representing all that was hostile to her worldview.

It's just crazy, Alma said. She was turned away from me, looking out the window at the passing businesses—the Taco Bell, the Jiffy Lube, the Dollar General with a Mennonite buggy in the lot. Like, why would an intelligent designer make a universe that resulted in all this? In genocide and capitalism and Taco Bell?

Welcome to the Bible Belt, I said.

The road to Melber carried us past trailer courts and subdivisions, reaching, finally, the bottomlands at the Graves County line. I wished she could've seen it in the late summer, when the fields were lush with burley tobacco—velvet-green rosettes, their long leaves curled and yellowed at the edges, sprawling out in rows. Now the same fields were bare, or sown with ryegrass, waist-high and the color of straw. The creeks we crossed on ramshackle bridges were only muddy trickles, and the woods were parched and grayish brown, save only the sycamores, whose stark white branches flashed like ghosts in the passing countryside.

I narrated the scene, partly as a way of distracting myself from the nausea and anxiety I was feeling, and partly because I wanted, on some level, for her to see it the way I saw it—as a terrain imbued with significance and narrative. Here was Dan Foley's house, where I used to set off bottle rockets. Here was the abandoned Citgo station, where, as I was climbing through a window at age thirteen, a blade of glass sliced my calf. Here was Josh Briggs's house, where I used to shoot clay pigeons. Here was the trailer where Molly Miller, the first girl I kissed, used to live. I left out, of course, that Dan Foley's father had committed suicide when we were fifteen by hanging himself from the metal track of their garage door, or that Dan had gone on to join the marines and was now stationed in Texas, where he'd become an alcoholic. I left out that I'd climbed through the window of the abandoned Citgo station in order to smoke a blunt dipped in cough syrup with Josh Briggs, and that Josh Briggs had never left Melber, that he'd been fired from a good job with the river barge industry and had since done some time in jail. I didn't mention that post–high school, Molly Miller had spent about five years journeying further and further into opioid addiction, the apotheosis of which was her death by fentanyl overdose in the bathroom of Paducah's public library. Maybe because I left out these things, Alma did not seem as interested as I'd hoped. Was she thinking of how the place could've produced me? I hoped that it did not remain two-dimensional for her—a painted backdrop, seen through a passenger window. What would one see who'd never seen it? Empty fields. Churches with graffitied plywood windows. Shoddy houses and single-wides where people she'd never met once lived. To anyone from the outside, it looked like a country town, so close to vanishing that it was hardly there at all. But I could see its inexpressible privacies.

We reached, finally, the four-way stop and the green sign reading MELBER. It was the town's sole marker, the only thing that let you know you were somewhere instead of on the way to somewhere else. It was here, every Halloween, that the burning hay bale came to rest. Across the street was the post office and the hairdresser's shop with a barber pole out front and a rusted, antique Pepsi machine that no longer functioned. Next door was the town's only restaurant—the Kountry Kitchen. A letterboard sign in the lot advertised catfish and hush puppies.

Here we are, I said.

Alma looked around, her expression vaguely troubled. You weren't kidding, she said. It's not much.

My dad's place could be seen from the four-way. I turned right and pointed it out to her. It had been a batten-board house, built in the '50s, but five years prior, he'd installed this plastic siding that was supposed to make a house look like a log cabin. It looked more like Lincoln Logs to me.

When we'd parked, Alma touched my arm and said, So how sick is your stepmom?

I don't really think of her as my stepmom, I said. She's just my dad's wife.

You know what I mean.

I told her I didn't know, and this was the truth. The last time I'd seen her, she was wan and frail, but she still had all her hair and could carry on a conversation. My father never really gave me particulars on the phone. I knew that she'd only grown worse. I knew that she was now bald. I knew that her treatments had mostly failed, and that she was undergoing radiation currently, as well as an experimental drug trial. Beyond this, I knew nothing of what to expect.

I knocked, rattling the screen door, and we stood for a long time on the porch while wooden chimes clinked hollowly in the breeze. The yard, front and back, was overgrown with weeds—browning grasses and thistles and the dry seedpods of milkweed, revealing their little tufts of cotton. A sunflower patch at the corner of the house was the only evidence that anyone had made an effort at beautification, but even these were wilted—their crowns ragged, their leaves shriveled and brown, like roosting bats.

I don't think anyone's home, Alma said, just before the door swung open and my father greeted us. Well, he said. Hello, son.

He looked about the same as always—bearish and lumbering, his scalp freshly razored. He wore a shirt of red-and-black plaid and a nice fleece vest. I caught a waft of his alcohol-heavy aftershave when we hugged. This meant we would not be staying in for dinner. My guess was the Kountry Kitchen down the road.

We entered the living room, which was more or less the way it had always been. The paintings on the wood-paneled walls were the ones I remembered from childhood—a paddlewheel steamboat, a crane in flight, a beach-scene watercolor. It had the same smell—that of a cedar closet. But the bookshelf that had once held my mother's Nora Ephron and John Grisham books was now basically empty. The only two objects on the shelf were *Gone with the Wind* and *Gulliver's Travels,* neither of which were real books. They were decorative, hollow. Purchased at the furniture store.

He offered us the overstuffed leather couch and sat in his over-stuffed leather recliner, which had a built-in cupholder in the armrest. At the moment, it held a half-drunk bottle of beer. College basketball played on the TV, muted. Bonnie was nowhere to be seen, but the bedroom door was cracked. There seemed to be movement in there.

I wasn't really watching this, my father said. He flipped the channel at random and landed on one of the *Alien* movies.

The three of us settled into our cushioned seats and waited for someone to say something. I'd only told my father about Alma's existence three days earlier. So, he said. Where are you from, Alma?

Virginia, she said. She hadn't taken off her parka, zipped to her chin, and was sitting with her legs crossed and her fingers clasped around her knee. I was born in Bosnia though, when it was still Yugoslavia. We moved to Germany, then Queens, then Virginia.

My father took all this in and made a hoarse grunting sound in his throat. Well, how bout that, he said. Bosnia.

That's right.

Is that close to Russia?

You could say that. Relatively speaking.

This is your first time in Kentucky?

Yeah, but I've been here awhile now. I have a fellowship at Ashby.

It was clear from my father's expression that he wasn't sure what a writing fellowship entailed, but he nodded. Well, I thought we'd go get barbecue from the Rebel Smokehouse, he said. This new place off 45 in Leeder Bottoms. How does that sound?

Is Bonnie up for it? I said.

It was her idea. She should be out any minute.

With this, the conversation came to a dead end, and we all turned our attention to the television, where people in space were shooting guns and running from grotesque alien organisms. They were screaming at each other, but with the volume muted, I could only guess at what they were saying.

Bonnie emerged from the bedroom after about five minutes. If someone had written a description of what she looked like in a story for workshop, I would've found it a little too pat. She wore a pink fleece pullover and jeans, though she'd lost so much weight that they were ill fitting. A pink bandanna covered her bald head. Her eyebrows were gone, and had been badly penciled in. Her lipstick was imprecise. She moved unsteadily into the room, shuffling her feet, and hugged us both. She sat on the sofa beside Alma and caught her breath from the effort of moving from one room into the other. Are you hungry? she said to Alma.

Yes, Alma said, loudly. I'm excited to try the Rebel Smokehouse.

Bonnie smiled sedately. You like pulled pork? She said this less like a question and more like a hypnotist's suggestion.

I do, Alma said.

That's good. I love it, personally. You could tell it took immense effort for her to speak, but she smiled as though the conversation were easy and casual.

How have you been feeling? I said.

I'm okay, she said. I waited for her to elaborate, but she only stared at me, mucous rattling in her lungs with each inhalation. Her hands twitched like limp birds in her lap. Alma winced at whatever was happening on the TV. When I looked, I saw an alien bursting out from a man's rib cage while he writhed on the floor and kicked his heels. Dad killed the picture with the remote control.

Well, shall we go eat? he said.

The Rebel Smokehouse was such a perfect distillation of the rural South's grotesquery that it was almost unfair. It was nestled between a Harley-Davidson dealership and an indoor gun range called Range America. A sun-faded Confederate flag had been raised high on a pole in a nearby yard, so that the restaurant was literally in the shadow of it. Even if I took faithful notes, if I wrote it all down exactly as it was, who would believe me?

We crossed the parking lot, moving slowly so as not to leave Bonnie behind. Alma kept her eyes on the flag, as if it were an animal she couldn't trust. I hated that I was putting her in this situation, that my dad had brought us here. But then, I supposed he had other things on his mind.

Inside, a band was warming up. We were seated a few feet from the stage, where we could feel the thud of the bass drum in our chests and conversation would be impossible. There were about a dozen flat-screen televisions mounted on the walls, so that one could watch at least three from any angle. Most were playing college basketball. Two or three were playing an episode of *Friends,* though there were no closed captions. With the TVs flashing and the din of conversation and the shrill feedback whistle of the amplifiers two feet away, I felt the urge to cover my ears and squeeze my eyes shut like an overwhelmed child in a department store.

My father ordered something called the "Pineapple Fiesta," which turned out to be a fishbowl-sized margarita with chunks of pineapple and an upside-down bottle of Corona for garnish. He took a sip through the straw, beer bubbles rising to the undersurface inside the Corona bottle. Not bad, he said, frowning.

The band's lead vocalist tapped on his microphone. All right, he said. We're gonna play some country music. Y'all like country music? A few patrons cheered halfheartedly and called back that they did, indeed, like country music. The vocalist counted off and they launched into an up-tempo version of John Denver's "Take Me Home, Country Roads." Alma looked a little shell-shocked. I squeezed her hand under the table and she squeezed back.

Though Bonnie could not eat solid food anymore, she could still taste it. So, throughout dinner, she would place chunks of pork in her mouth, hold them there until there was nothing left to savor, and then secrete them into pieces of paper towel, which she tore from the roll on our table. By meal's end, there were fifteen or so wads of brown paper and pork in front of her on the table. Nobody really said anything important over dinner. Alma shouted perfunctory questions to Bonnie and my father—how long have you been retired? Any upcoming vacations? Bonnie didn't have the breath to shout, so my father responded with equally perfunctory answers. We can't really travel, he said. We have to be here for her treatments.

Oh, Alma said. Of course.

The band took a break between sets, allowing a window of relative quiet in which we all shuffled and fidgeted with our napkins and sipped from our ice waters. Sorry we haven't been able to talk much, my father said. Course, maybe that's good. Realizing how this sounded, he added, For your sake, I mean.

No, it's been great meeting you, Alma said. The band is good. And this pork sandwich? She formed her thumb and finger into the sign for A-OK.

How do you feel about family? Bonnie said from across the table.

Like, as a concept or my actual family?

Your family.

Her medicine's probably kicking in, Dad said.

No, I'm all right, she said. I'm talking.

Okay, Dad said gently. You're talking. Talk away.

Bonnie turned back to Alma and waited for a response, her eyelids sagging.

Well, Alma said, they're, you know—regular. My mom is very energetic. My dad less so. He likes to play chess—he's in all these online leagues. He's really good. I've never beaten him actually, though my mom claims to have beaten him once, right after they started dating. My dad disputes this. Um, what else . . . my mom is into ikebana recently? Apparently there's a class in DC. It's Japanese flower arrangement. Don't ask me why. Before ikebana, she was taking these Mexican folk dance classes, but she twisted her ankle, so. Then there was the bird-watching phase, which, to me, made no sense, seeing as how she's always disliked outdoorsy stuff, but one of her friends got into it, and honestly, I just think she likes the camaraderie and collecting all the equipment that comes with a new hobby. Once she gets all the little gadgets and field guides and special clothing, she loses interest.

Bonnie and my father were nodding, brows drawn together. Anyway, not sure I answered your question, she said. I just told you their hobbies, and obviously they're more than just their hobbies. Not that you wouldn't know that, that people are—whatever. Comprehensive. She cringed a little, picking at the webbing between her fingers.

Family is everything to me, Bonnie said.

My father looked nervous, twisting the straw in his Pineapple Fiesta—like whatever she might say next was completely out of his hands.

Oh, said Alma. Yeah, it's important, no doubt.

You want to know somebody will be there, Bonnie said.

Beg pardon? Alma leaned over the table.

You want somebody to be there for you at the last.

Bonnie, Dad said.

What?

He looked at her sadly, rested his hand on her bone-thin forearm. She's tired, he said to us. They've got her on a new thing.

I'm wide awake, Bonnie said. She slid her arm from his grip. We're talking about family.

I hear that, Dad said. I just think maybe you're tired, is all.

Bonnie looked at him for several seconds, slowly processing what he'd said. She turned back to us, coughed once, wiped her mouth shakily. He says I'm tired.

I'm sure it's been a long day, I said. I can go get the check.

I'm paying, Dad said. Obviously.

I can pay.

He looked at me like I was crazy. That's ridiculous.

I don't know if it's *ridiculous.*

What do you feel like doing, baby? he said to Bonnie. You wanna go?

She shook her head vaguely. We're talking, she said.

Okay, we're talking. Great. Well, you talk, I'm going to the rest-room. He tossed his napkin onto the table, glanced at us, then bent and kissed her on the forehead. Don't go tellin on me, now, he said. I smiled at this. It was just something he said, something he'd always said—Don't go tellin on me, now. As if he were living a double life, one half filled with misdeeds.

When he was gone, Alma and I took sips of water, moved bits of pork around on our plates. Bonnie stared at us, unflinching. The band members were drifting back to the stage slowly, two bottles of beer in each hand.

I love you, Bonnie said.

I looked up from my plate. It wasn't clear who she was speaking to—both of us maybe, her eyes unfocused.

I'm sorry? I said, though I'd heard her clear as a bell.

I love you, she said. I know we haven't said that to each other, but I wanted to say it.

Oh, I said. Okay. I could feel Alma staring at me. Both of them were looking and waiting. I was cornered. I love you, too, Bonnie, I said. When I spoke, the knot in my chest loosened, if only a little. I didn't really know her. I'd never made an effort to know her, and—to be fair—she hadn't made much of an effort to know me. But what did any of that really matter now?

Love is simple, she said. That's my advice to both of you, not that you're asking for it.

Okay, I said. I felt the powerful urge to stand and leave the table, to run away—both my legs joggling.

People try to make it complicated, but it's very simple, she said. You'll realize that when you're dying.

I have to go, I said. I stood abruptly and tipped over my water glass, scattering half-melted ice over the table. Shit, I said. I'm sorry.

Alma was already blotting the spilt water with napkins. It's fine, she said.

I have to use the bathroom.

Go, she said. I got it.

In the bathroom, I leaned against the vanity and turned on the tap. A man and his young son were finishing up at the other sink. Use lots of soap, the man said.

I am, said the boy.

Scrub em good.

When they'd gone, I looked at myself in the mirror, tried to catch my breath. Someone was sniffling in one of the stalls. I'd forgotten completely about my father. In the mirror, I saw his tasseled loafers underneath the door. Dad? I said.

He cleared his throat. Just need a minute, he said.

I approached the stall door, brought my ear close to the stainless steel. He was sobbing quietly inside. It sounded almost like stifled laughter. Are you all right, Dad?

No, I'm not, son, he said.

The sound of the band tuning up reached us through the walls, the thudding of the bass drum like an enormous heart. I touched my fingertips to the door. I'm just going to stand here, I said.

He said nothing. I couldn't be sure if he was crying still with the racket outside. Dad?

It's all right, he said, his voice steadier now. Go on, I'll be out in a minute.

Are you sure?

Yes, go on. Ask for the check. I'll be right behind you.

I returned to the table and sat. Alma looked at me like, *Are you okay?* I'm good, I said. Everything's good. She put her hand on my knee under the table.

Dad came back a few minutes later and found that the tab had already been paid and the check signed by Bonnie. What'd you do that for? he said.

She shrugged and gathered her coat and purse. I have money, she said.

Well, shit, he said. I mean, dang. It was supposed to be on me.

Hey, when it comes to free food, we'll take what we can get, Alma said.

Everybody smiled, including my father. You couldn't tell he'd been weeping. He looked so right as rain now, I wondered if I'd hallucinated the whole thing.

In the parking lot, before we split off to Alma's car, we all hugged. Bonnie said she hoped we'd stay longer next time. As we embraced, I wondered if I would ever see her again, and felt a sudden suffocating guilt. It was always like this at home—this emotional whiplash. Oscillating between guilt and repulsion, empathy and cynicism. She's very pretty and sweet, Bonnie whispered.

Thanks, I said, as we drew apart.

I said you're very pretty and sweet, she repeated to Alma.

Oh, thank you, Alma said.

When we hugged, my father told me he loved me and clapped my back hard. Then they walked away, and we walked away, and that was it. Some part of me had wanted an argument—some eruption of drama, something noteworthy. But all I felt was a hollow sadness driving away. I didn't feel like writing about any of it.

WHEN WE GOT BACK, MY MOTHER HAD HER LAPTOP OPEN ON the kitchen counter, playing Bob Dylan. A pecan pie was cooling on the stove. Welcome back! she cried, heels thumping down the hallway and into the kitchen. She held a set of dominoes in a box. I baked a pecan pie, she said.

I see that.

Your favorite.

Yeah, I know, thanks.

We bought these in Cuba. She shook the box so that the dominoes rattled inside. I thought we could play a few games.

Sounds fun, Alma said, before I could say I was too tired.

Greg came in, bleary-eyed. The commentators for a basketball game were speaking in the living room, where he'd been sitting—or more likely, napping—on the sofa. He smelled faintly of cigar smoke. Hey, hey, he said. We gonna play some dominoes?

Looks like it, I said.

We got some Dylan on for you.

Yeah, I heard.

Nobel Prize winner.

I laughed. True, true.

They knew that in high school, I'd had a borderline-unhealthy and wholly unoriginal obsession with Bob Dylan. I'd listen to the same songs over and over, the same shrill harmonica solos, till the lyrics and chord progressions were thoroughly ingrained. I knew that by playing him on my mother's tinny laptop speakers, they were trying, however tenuously, to make a connection with me. The pecan pie was also part of that effort, an extended olive branch for the pseudo-argument we'd had earlier. Ironically, I'd been allowed to listen to Dylan as a kid partly because he was a "born-again Christian." They hadn't considered, or realized, that for most of his career up to the born-again phase, he'd been a Jew singing left-ist protest songs and weird stream-of-consciousness diatribes, all of which helped inform my worldview as I grew up. But the person they were trying to connect with was my eighteen-year-old self, the last version of me that they really knew, before I moved out. And it was this person, this sulking teenager, that I reverted to somehow in their presence. But they *were* making an effort. I had to admit that.

My mother poured out the clattering dominoes on the kitchen table. I opened a beer and situated myself beside Alma. My mother and Greg sat on the other side. So, my mother said, flipping the white dominoes facedown. The game is called Mexican Train.

Really, I said.

She paused and looked at me. What?

Should I ask why it's called that, or is the answer racist?

Well, I don't rightly know, she said. Basically, everybody makes their own train, then the *Mexican* train is the one that anybody can hop on.

So the answer's yes, probably racist.

She rolled her eyes. Now, why is that racist?

Never mind. Go on.

She explained the rules, which were simple enough, and we played a couple games. The goal was to get rid of all the dominoes you drew from the pile. Whoever had the lowest score after several rounds was the winner. Though there didn't seem to be much strategy involved, Greg won game after game somehow. You gotta be kidding me! Alma shouted, when he won his fourth in a row.

Me and lady luck are like *this,* he said, crossing his fingers, and we all laughed. We took a break for pie, which my mother served on intricately flowered plates—Polish pottery, she called them. Your mom's all about this Polish pottery, Owen, Greg said. Every time we go antiquing, she buys some.

I just think they're pretty is all, she said, cutting a small sliver—serving herself last, of course.

The pie—with its homemade crust and extra layer of whole, glazed pecans on top—was wonderful, the kind of pie you ate without speaking, capable only of reverent sighs and groans of appreciation. This is so, so good, Alma said, her cheeks full. When she'd taken her last bite, she pressed the tines of her fork to the flaky crumbs on the plate and ate them, too. She scraped till the plate was clean, revealing the daisies patterned underneath.

It's my grandmother's recipe, my mom said. Real simple. I'll write it down for you.

It is great, I said. Bravo.

She tried to pretend these compliments didn't delight her. She brought us cups of decaf coffee while we put away the Cuban dominoes. Spotify seemed to be shuffling through four or five Dylan songs—"All Along the Watchtower," "Like a Rolling Stone," and "The Times They Are A-Changin'," punctuated occasionally by an advertisement for Smartwater. Every time "All Along the Watchtower" came on, Greg would hum along and half-murmur the lyrics. When "Knockin' on Heaven's Door" played, Greg said, Tell you what, this version's good, but it's hard to beat the Guns N' Roses cover.

I like the original better, I said.

Hey, he said, turning up his palm, to each his own.

Finally something you can agree to disagree on, my mother said, sitting back down with her coffee. The mug said GOD IS WITH HER, SHE WILL NOT FAIL. PSALM 46:5.

Hey, you know people used to have friendly debates about politics, Greg said. Things didn't used to be so polarized.

Whose fault is that? I said.

The media, for one, he said. And you know, the radicals have become mainstream now. It would've been unheard-of when I was a kid to promote socialism. But hey man, young people are all about it. They're gung ho. Rah-rah socialism. Never thought I'd see that.

The Republicans haven't become radical?

Let's not get back into this, my mother said.

I'm just saying, Greg said.

I think it's pretty radical to demonize immigrants, Alma said.

It's a bad situation at the border, Greg said.

Alma stared at him for a long time with her mouth pursed, considering carefully how to respond.

My mother looked on, dismayed that the fragile peace we'd established over dominoes was dissolving again before her eyes. Trump doesn't use the right language, that's for sure, she said. He has no filter.

So you agree with the substance, just not the delivery? Alma said. There was a shaky edge to her voice, as if she were holding back the urge to scream.

I don't know if I'd say *that.*

The name-calling is on both sides, Greg said. Democrats do it, too. What he's doing for this country though? The things he's accomplished? He's up there with Lincoln, in my opinion. Say whatever you want about him, but you can't say he's not a patriot. Just look at what he's done with manufacturing.

What about BelCo? I said.

The crow's feet at the corners of Greg's eyes slackened. What about it?

I'd think the plant closing is pretty good evidence that the kind of economy he's promising is a thing of the past.

Doesn't have anything to do with him.

What *does* it have to do with?

Greg leaned forward now and pushed up his mug. A little coffee sloshed onto the woven place mat. You're talking about something you don't know about, he said.

BelCo's been in trouble for a long time, my mother said. Layoffs, pay cuts. A lot of it is automation.

That's how things are gonna be from now on though, I said. Trump won't save you from that.

There's a lot of factors, Greg said. Things are tough around here, in general.

So move, I said. Maybe this is a blessing in disguise. Maybe this is an opportunity. You could go anywhere. I don't know why you don't get out.

We are, my mother said. Everyone looked at her. She clinked her fingernail on her mug and stared at me, unblinking. We're moving to Jackson, Tennessee.

Do what now? I said.

We're moving to Jackson, she said. Selling the house here. Greg is taking a job with a plant there.

It's plastics, like BelCo, he said. They make dashboards.

Oh, I said. I was too stunned to form a meaningful response. My mind raced through the different ramifications—that they'd no longer live in Kentucky, that everything I had in storage at their house would have to be moved. That I'd have no place to stay when I came home, unless it was with my dad, which didn't seem like a real possibility. Congratulations, I said at last.

Greg nodded.

When is this happening?

Next month, my mother said. She was looking at me with such cool intensity that I couldn't hold eye contact for very long. House is already on the market.

When were you going to tell me?

Tonight, she said. I'm telling you now.

I drained my decaf in the silence that followed. Outside, in the darkness, the chimes were ringing. I knew there were questions I should ask, but I couldn't bring myself to ask them, and I wasn't particularly interested in the answers. Congratulations on the job, Alma said, and after that, nobody had anything else to talk about.

We swept up the Cuban dominoes and returned them to their box. Alma went upstairs first. I found her throwing clothes into her bag, not bothering to fold them. I leaned in the doorway and watched her for a minute. I guess I'll go to the futon, I said.

No, you won't, she said. That's ridiculous. We're sleeping in the same bed.

We brushed our teeth wordlessly. Downstairs, I could still hear Bob Dylan's voice wheezing from the computer speaker, echoing off the kitchen tile, asking how it felt to be on your own, with no direction home, over and over, till someone turned him off and the house went silent.

I lay in bed for a long time, feeling guilty and confused. Was I ungrateful? Was I a snob? It was true I'd had my disagreements with Greg, but I knew he loved me, that I could depend on him. He called me his son—when he introduced me, when he asked for a favor on my behalf—a job I needed. It's for my son, he would say. He was a good person. So was my mother. They'd helped me, given me money and a place to stay without hesitation. It was clear how much my mother worried about me, how much she worried about everything. But our conversations were stilted. I didn't ask her much, and she didn't ask me the questions I wanted her to ask, the questions that would prove she knew something of my life and what I did. But what would it really prove, if she asked what I thought of the most recent story in *The New Yorker*? Would it mean she understood me any better? Her son? Her own blood? And my father—what did I expect from him? Who was I to expect anything, when he clearly had so much else to worry about?

Selfishness—maybe that's all it is, I thought. I'm selfish. It was easy to be angry, but to hold this anger and this love at the same time—this fission in my heart—that was the unending task, the difficult work. Anger alone was easy. It was cheap and lazy. And yet, wasn't this part of me valid also?

I tossed and turned, kicked at the heavy blankets. It was always like this. Always these two selves, these repellant points of view. Who I was and who I wanted to be. The future contained in the present. Always.

We rose before the day dawned and gathered our things in the dark. The half-eaten pecan pie, covered with plastic wrap, was sitting out on the counter with a sticky note—*Please take, Love Mom.* With my duffel in one hand and the pie in the other, we let ourselves out into the cold morning, latching the door softly behind us.

The interstate was empty. The heat was slow to warm up, and we could see our breath in the car, the windshield sparkling with ice crystals. The rolling countryside was pooled in the low places with fog, and as the sun rose ahead of us and lighted the fields, we saw geese grazing in the corn stubble, flapping their white wings.

We'd nearly made it to Paradise when I noticed that Alma was crying. She had her face turned away from me to the window, sniffling quietly. What's wrong? I said.

Nothing, she said. She blotted her eyes with the sleeve of her sweater. I'm fine.

Obviously not, I said. What's going on?

She wouldn't look at me, but I could see the vague reflection of her face in the glass, her pupils ticking from side to side, watching the land scroll past—farmyards and pro-life billboards and fast food. It's just sad, she said.

I wanted to say something, to offer some words of comfort, but everything I thought of seemed hollow. It was sad. This, really, was the last word you could say about it.

I GOT A CALL A WEEK LATER FROM A NUMBER IN FLORIDA. Alma had gone to the library. I was scarfing a kale salad, late for Victorian Gothic, and answered with my mouth full and one arm in my coat. I figured it for a telemarketer or something political. But the man knew my name. He asked if I was myself, and when I told him I was, he told me his name was Brad Lithgow, and that I'd been accepted for the Harry Crews Writer in Residence Program in Tallahassee, Florida. I'd never heard of anyone with the last name Lithgow other than the actor John Lithgow, and though this man did not sound like John Lithgow, I was imagining John Lithgow on the other end of the line, nonetheless. This distracted me at first from what the man was trying to explain, namely that he and the people he worked for were giving me an opportunity to write in Tallahassee for four months.

The stipend is very generous, said Brad Lithgow. The fellowship supporting the residency is $1,200 a month, made possible in large part by contributions from FSU's English Department. That's in addition to room and board at the Harry Crews Cottage, he said, which is provided at no cost to you.

Wow, I said, still trying to chew the kale in my mouth. I had only a vague memory of applying and was not at all sure how I should react. Was it a big deal? Brad Lithgow certainly seemed to think so. It seemed more like a medium-sized deal to me. Remind me, I said, what is the Harry Crews Cottage?

It's where you'll be staying, he said. It's where Harry Crews wrote portions of *The Knockout Artist.*

Oh, I said. Cool.

We have his actual typewriter on display, his old desk. He used to care for injured hawks in the garage. You'll love it. There's a banana tree in the backyard.

I didn't particularly like Harry Crews, at least what little I'd read of him, but I assumed that my past self had applied because of the stipend. Beyond the money, I'd paid very little attention to the particulars of the residencies and fellowships I'd applied to, and of course, I'd been high on a mild narcotic at the time.

Well, thanks, I said.

You're certainly welcome, said Brad Lithgow.

Do I have to say yes or no right now?

Well, he said, most years people tell us right off the bat whether they're going to take it. But you have till May, technically, to let us know. That's the absolute latest. Ideally, we'd want to know before then so we could give notice to the runner-up.

I said all right and thanked him again. He seemed perturbed at my response—that I wasn't jumping for joy. It's a real honor, I said, unconvincingly, and he said, Yes, congratulations, and that was it.

We talked about *Dracula* in Victorian Gothic, how it was presented as diary entries, newspaper articles, and letters, all of which, it's eventually revealed, have been collated by Mina into a single text—the very text, in fact, that one is reading. Her collation, in other words, is identical with the text of the novel. This was interesting to me, but mostly I found it hard to pay attention, and daydreamed instead about the Harry Crews Cottage and what my life might look like in Tallahassee. What did they have in Tallahassee? Was it close to the beach? Was it nearer to the Gulf coast or the Atlantic? Whatever vague, half-remembered factoids I knew about Tallahassee were just as likely to be vague, half-remembered factoids about Tampa, which might as well have been the same city in my mind.

When I got back to Alma's, she was eating Ben & Jerry's from the carton and watching a movie on her laptop. She blushed when I came in, as if I'd caught her in the middle of something sexual. This isn't what it looks like, she said, her mouth full of cookie dough ice cream.

I set my tote bag on the floor, collapsed onto the couch. What do you know about Harry Crews?

Harry Crews, Harry Crews. The name sounds familiar.

He was a writer from Florida.

Any good?

He's okay. But there's this fellowship in his name, this residency thing in Tallahassee. I got a call today and they told me I got it.

She set the carton on the end table and licked melted ice cream from the webbing of her thumb. What do you mean, you "got it"?

I mean I got it. They're giving it to me. I applied a couple months ago. I'd get to live in his cottage.

What cottage?

The Harry Crews Cottage. It's where he wrote *The Knockout Artist.*

What's that?

A novel. It's about boxing I think. Point is, they're giving it to me.

Do you have to pay to go?

No, they pay me.

Whoa, she said, her tone uncertain. I mean, congratulations. I didn't know you'd applied for anything like that.

I applied for a bunch before Christmas.

So I guess you'll wait to see if you get into the other ones?

I guess so, I said.

Well, that's great. That can be your safety net.

I take it you're not very impressed.

No! she said. She scooted closer to me and took my hand. It's great! I just wouldn't be thrilled, personally, about living in *Tallahassee.*

But you were thrilled about moving to Ashby?

The Ashby Fellowship is prestigious. And it pays well.

Maybe *I* should've applied to it.

Well, you couldn't, she said. You have to have a published book to apply. But I'm sure the Terry Crews Cottage is great.

Harry Crews.

Right, Harry. I'm sure it'd be a good opportunity.

It was true that when I'd applied in December, I'd fantasized about fellowships in New York and San Francisco and Europe. I'd even applied to a fellowship in Slovakia. I knew about as much of Slovakia as I did of Tallahassee, but at least Slovakia held the promise of adventure, of foreign tongues and exotic cuisines. Tallahassee held the promise of—what? A banana tree? I'd hoped that Alma would convince me, against my better judgment, that I should feel lucky and excited.

After supper, Alma read *Sense and Sensibility* with her bare feet stretched out in my lap. She snickered occasionally when she came to a clever passage. I grew bored with the collection I was reading and pushed her feet aside so that I could open my laptop and look at Tallahassee on Street View. It took me a long time to find something beautiful, dropping the little pin at random. My first attempt revealed an auto repair shop and a chain-link fence topped with coils of razor wire. My second attempt revealed a suburban lawn, indistinguishable from other suburban lawns in the country except maybe for the potted palmettos at the end of the driveway. Eventually, I landed on a street shaded by live oaks, their long, low branches bearded with Spanish moss. Look, I said, Spanish moss.

She glanced over her book at the screen. Oh cool, she said. Then she went back to reading.

I stewed for a few minutes, trying to decide whether I was really angry, and if I was, whether it was worth articulating. Sure, the Harry Crews Cottage was not the Stegner, or even the vaunted Ashby Fellowship, but it was something. Did she think it was pathetic? Possibly. Did she think I was a lightweight? A hobbyist?

I want you to read what I'm working on, I said.

She looked up at me and closed her laptop. Oh, she said. I didn't know you were at that point.

I will be soon, I said. Maybe in a month.

I don't know where I got this timeline—there was no way I'd have a finished project in a month. But I couldn't very well retract what I'd said.

Okay, she said. I mean, yeah, let's plan to do that. I'll put it on my calendar. One month hence.

You don't have to if you don't want to.

Well, you're kind of forcing the issue at this point.

Hey, I've read *your* stuff.

My stuff's published. It's a finished thing I've let out into the world.

Maybe I want your valuable feedback during the process.

She set her laptop on the cushion and folded her arms. She looked at me like I'd suggested a threesome with someone she didn't care for—like the arrangement had been agreed to tacitly at some point but not the particulars. What if I don't like it? she said. What if I can't see you the same way after I've read it?

Jesus, you're really so sure I'll be bad? Give me a little credit. You're talking to the winner of the Harry Crews Fellowship, after all. Maybe I'm good, has that crossed your mind?

Of course it has, she said. That would almost be worse. Then I'd have to think of you as competition.

Wow, I said, surprised.

I'm sorry, she said. I'm just telling you the truth.

Why would I be a threat to you? You're the big-shot writer, you've got all the power.

She laughed aloud at this.

What's funny about that?

Sorry, just—funny to hear you say it.

Because it's not true?

I don't know, she sighed. Look, I'll read it. Whatever you want me to read, I will. We're adults, right? Surely we can exchange work and talk about it like grown-ups without making it personal.

All right, I said. Fine. Give me a month.

Fine.

She went back to *Sense and Sensibility*. I considered what I had in my "Alma/Kentucky" folder—a bunch of disparate fragments with little to no cohesion. One measly month to turn them into something presentable, at which point I'd either be humiliated or seen as something threatening, or somewhere in between. I went back to Street View, trying not to think of the double bind in which I now seemed to be caught—though maybe I'd been caught in it the whole time and simply hadn't noticed. I spent the next two hours distracting myself, searching Tallahassee for evidence of beauty.

ALMA INSISTED WE SPEND A NIGHT AT POP'S, IN THE BASEMENT. It was like she wanted to prove something, like if all went well at Pop's, it would erase the tension of my mother's house and the bitter taste it left behind. I was against it, for obvious reasons, but she went on asking and eventually I relented. It wasn't even clear whether Pop would be okay with it, but we simply showed up one afternoon. He was sitting on the front porch in a folding chair, eating canned peaches with a spoon, letting the sun warm his bare feet. He shaded his eyes when we pulled up. Alma stepped out, sunlight in her hair, smiling and waving cheerfully, as if they knew each other better than they did. It had rained the night before, and though it was bright and windy, the air still smelled of mud and earthworms. Hello, sir! Alma shouted. She slowed briefly, eyes catching on the MAGA sign in Cort's window. She'd dressed up a little, wore her Pentecostal skirt and a persimmon sweater, her big tortoiseshell sunglasses. An expensive overnight bag slung over her shoulder— Coach, patterned with the letter *C*. A gift from her mother, who had no appreciation for the kind of thrown-together Salvation Army look that Alma tried to cultivate, and for which a Coach bag sort of ruined the effect.

Pop set down the can and wiped the peach syrup from his lips. Well, now, he said, who's this pretty girl comin up my driveway?

She shook his hand and bent down for a half hug. So good to see you again, she said.

Hey Pop, I said.

Pard.

We're here to visit.

Well, I'll be, he said. I thought you lived here.

I ignored this and let Alma inside. We dropped our things in the basement, and when we got back upstairs, we found Pop scooting his walker into the kitchen. How bout some cheese and crackers? he called out.

Here, I'll do it, I said.

I can do it, he said. I been doin it just fine lately. He opened the fridge door, reached inside. His right arm shook, fingers clamped to the walker handle.

I know you can, but I don't mind.

He turned and looked at me over his shoulder, breathless just from reaching into the fridge. Fine, he said. He shuffled over to the kitchen table, took a seat with difficulty. He spread his palms flat on the place mat and caught his breath. Alma sat beside him. They talked about the recent mild weather while I unwrapped the cheddar block and found the clubhouse crackers.

I figure we'll get one more freeze, Pop said. Maybe one night this week, then I'll be able to set out my peppers and tomatoes.

It's great you can still do that, Alma said. Set out a garden.

What's great about it?

Just, that you're able.

Pop snorted. I couldn't see his expression, but I could imagine it. He mentioned the maple out back that needed to be trimmed, said he was considering doing it himself. Maybe I'll get to it tomorrow, I said.

Always tomorrow, he said.

I trim trees for a living, Pop. It's the last thing I wanna do in my off time.

I set out the plate of sliced cheese and the sleeve of crackers. Alma took a whole cracker in one bite, cupping her hand under her chin. Her sweater was damp at the armpits. She'd read somewhere on the internet recently that a cotton ball and rubbing alcohol was as good as deodorant.

Pop watched her and chuckled. She knows how to eat, at least, he said to me, pointing at her.

Sorry, she said, cheeks full, crumbs falling from her mouth.

No, it's good, he said.

We thought we might stay over here tonight, I said.

He looked at me, brow tensed with uncertainty.

Did you hear me? I said, a little louder.

No, I heard you, he said. Both of you?

Yeah, just in the basement, if that's okay.

He nodded a little, looked down at his folded hands on the table. My ears were burning. Why did I care? I had nothing to feel guilty about. So what if we wanted to stay?

Sure, pard, he said. You know my home is your home.

After eating, we went downstairs and read for a while as the sun eased down. We could hear Cort above us, playing his game, muttering curses to himself now and then. There was no insulation in the ceiling, and the sound carried clearly—every cough, every dribbling of urine, every flush of a toilet. I'd hardly noticed it alone, but with Alma, it embarrassed me. I couldn't wait to wake up in the morning and leave. We could say we'd stayed a night then, and it would prove whatever Alma was trying to prove. She pretended not to notice these sounds above us. She read my copy of *Lost in the City* and I read Annie Dillard. At one point, she poked me with her toe on the couch. When I looked over, she frowned at me. Why the long face there, pard? she said.

I feel anxious.

Anxious about what? This is fine. Everything's good.

I sighed and turned a page. I was just staring at the text, not really reading.

What's Annie have to say over there?

Just that things are complex, I said. Life is irreducibly complex.

Alma rolled her eyes. Oh my goodness, she said. Don't be so glum! What's so bad about this?

I just don't know why we're here.

Like, existentially? Or here in this basement?

Basement, I think. But maybe both.

Because we spend every night at my house. And I think you resent on some level that I never come over here.

No, I said. I actually totally prefer your place, and I've said that.

Well, we're here now. I'm feeling totally relaxed and nonjudgmental.

Who said anything about judgmental?

That's your assumption.

No, you're assuming that's my assumption, which makes me think it's the correct assumption.

She crossed her eyes on purpose. Which assumption?

I smiled, shook my head. Never mind, I said.

When the sun was gone, Pop called us from upstairs and said he'd made popcorn, that he was about to start a movie. It was *Butch Cassidy and the Sundance Kid,* which Alma had somehow never seen. It's got Paul Newman and Robert Redford? I said. Outlaws in Bolivia?

Nope, she said. She sat in the recliner next to Pop's; I dragged over the rocking chair. Robert Redford—he's supposed to be handsome, right?

Are you kidding?

Sorry! she said. I didn't grow up watching a lot of movies.

What were you doing?

Reading! Maintaining my GPA!

Yeah, yeah, I said. I felt more at ease now. Pop had a space heater purring next to his ghostly white feet, a Navajo blanket over his lap. The lamplight was glowing softly, and the room smelled like buttered popcorn. A bottle of Parkay spray butter sat on the end table, so that in addition to the butter that was already in the microwave bag, he could add his own. It's butter that you can spray, he explained to me. He shook the metal bowl and spritzed the popcorn, demonstrating. See?

I see, I said. Wow.

You can spray it, he said. Alma was trying to keep from laughing, covering her mouth. This got me laughing, too.

No, I understand, I said. I've seen it before.

What's so funny?

Nothing, Pop.

You can *spray* the butter directly onto the popcorn—or corn on the cob, for that matter. Or even just corn off the cob. Or a baked potato. Heck, you could spray it on just about anything.

I got it, Pop, I said. Alma was laughing soundlessly, eyes squeezed shut.

I think it's pretty dang nifty.

I agree.

We watched the movie—the famous opening scene that shifted from sepia-toned black-and-white to color, the bicycle scene with "Raindrops Keep Fallin' on My Head." This is funnier than I expected it would be, Alma said at one point. They really have chemistry.

No kidding, I said. That's why people love it. That's why it's a classic American film.

She rolled her eyes. Okay, okay.

We were nearing the end when Cort's bedroom door whined open. We all turned around. A slice of light had fallen on the carpet. Cort shuffled to the end of the hall and looked at us.

Hey Cort, Pop said. Still a little popcorn here if you want some.

It's mostly kernels, honestly, Alma said. Hi Cort.

Cort just stood there silently, hands dangling at his sides. He looked like he was trying to piece something together, some intractable mystery. Pop paused the movie.

Come sit with us, Cort. We're watching Butch and Sundance.

She's in my chair, he said.

Almost before he'd finished his sentence, Alma brushed the popcorn crumbs from her lap and stood. I'm sorry, she said, here, I can sit on the floor.

No, I said, you're fine.

She looked at me, then at Cort, still at the edge of the light—staring, implacable. His hand shook near his hip pocket, as if with a tremor—as if he couldn't bear to stand still.

Bring a chair in from the kitchen, Pop said.

They hurt my back.

You sit in them just fine when we're eating, I said.

Not for movies.

Okay, well, take the rocking chair then. I stood and gestured to my chair but Cort didn't move.

That's my regular seat and she's in it.

Alma sidled closer to me. I put my hand on the small of her back. Not anymore, she isn't, I said.

I'm really sorry, Alma said.

Don't apologize, I said. It's not a big deal. Cort, either come sit or don't.

This is typical, Cort said.

I bowed my head, pinched the bridge of my nose. Now the floodgates were open.

Don't start something, okay, Cort? Please? Just go back to your room.

We can watch a different movie, Cort, Pop said. You can pick.

No, we're finishing this movie, I said. Cort's going back to his room and we're watching the rest.

You think everything's about you, Cort said.

All right, said Pop. Settle down.

You think you're the center of gravity.

What does that even mean?

You bring your little girlfriend over to play house, without asking me. Well, I'm not supportive of that, and this is where I live, with my things, and this is my chair, and you're violating—

Cort, enough, I said.

You're violating the norms that have been established, because you think you're entitled to just show up and do what you want. You don't live here. This isn't your house.

Pop tried to stand now, his cheeks flushed pink with embarrassment. Just let it go, Cort, Pop said. Maybe do your breathing exercises? Okay? Let it go.

Cort didn't seem to hear. He took his cell phone from the pocket of his sweatpants, swiped at the screen, and held it up to us, as if he were about to take a photo.

I'm recording this, he said.

By now, I was shivering with anger, my throat constricted. Alma had positioned herself behind me, hands drawn up to her chest. She looked frightened, though she was trying mightily not to. In my mind, I ran through scenarios in which I was forced to hit or restrain him, if I would even be able to. He was heavy. Taller than me.

This is ridiculous, Cort, I said. What are you even doing?

He stepped closer and panned the room with his phone. All of this is being recorded, he said. You're on tape.

Come on, I said. I took Alma's hand and pulled her to the front door, where our shoes were piled. Cort followed us with his phone.

This is going online, he said. Just wait.

You're a real asshole, you know that?

Owen, Pop said.

That's why no one likes to be around you.

Alma pulled on my sleeve. Let's just go, she said, her voice tremulous.

That's on tape, too, Cort said. You're just proving my point.

What point? You have no fucking point.

Pop said nothing, his face lowered to the floor. He looked ashamed—a feeling I'm sure he was accustomed to, living with Cort all these years. It was nothing new. He'd learned to accept it, sadly, and could explain the alien logic behind Cort's outbursts no better now than he ever could.

We pulled on our coats, slipped on our shoes without tying the laces, and went out. Cort followed onto the porch. This is all going online, he shouted. He recorded us as we climbed into the truck and drove away.

On the road, I could hardly breathe or think, much less talk. My stomach was seized up. My hands were jittery. It's all right, Alma said. She looked a little stunned, but she was calmer than me. It wasn't as bad as you probably think it was.

I know your bag is still there. I'll get it tomorrow and bring it to you.

I'm not worried about the bag, she said. She touched my shoulder. I'm fine.

I drew a deep breath, blew it out slowly as we took the interstate on-ramp. Little by little, the adrenaline subsided. The world came back into focus, and as it did, I felt stupid for losing my cool, for allowing him to goad me. I felt bad for what I'd said. One night— that's all she'd wanted. One night to prove where I'd been living was normal. That it wouldn't devolve into an episode of *Jerry Springer*. Even this was too much to ask.

When we arrived at the guesthouse and started down the walk for the front door, I paused and gazed up at the darkened window of her apartment, where soon we would be warm and asleep, and I saw as clearly as I'd ever seen anything that Cort had been right. I didn't live in Pop's house. I didn't live here either. They were only temporary shelters and they always had been. I wondered when, in my life, I'd be entitled to call a place my own.

Come on, babe, Alma said. She was pale, her voice still shaky. She'd opened the door and was beckoning to me, dressed in that denim skirt she'd been wearing the night we met.

Lying in bed later, I felt worse and worse about what I'd said to Cort. I went to the kitchen and paced there with my phone, a fluorescent moon outside. Cold air seeped in and lingered near the cracked window above the sink. I knew he'd be up—he was always up. I was half surprised that he answered though.

It's the middle of the night, he said.

I wanted to apologize, Cort. For what I said earlier.

Which is what exactly?

You want me to repeat it?

Yes. I do.

That you're an asshole, I said. And that no one likes you. I shouldn't have said that.

Because I'm not, or because you shouldn't have said it?

I don't think you're an asshole.

He grunted softly. But you don't like me, he said. You think you're better than me.

That's not true.

Oh, really? You don't think I'm ignorant? You don't think you're smarter than me?

Of course not, I said, though there was not much confidence in my voice.

Do you expect me to apologize?

I wouldn't expect that, no, I said. I just wanted to tell you that I felt bad.

He laughed at this. It was the first time in my life I'd heard him laugh—a low, gruff noise from deep in the chest. You don't wanna feel bad, he said.

Well, no.

Do you think I wanted to live this life?

I don't know, I said uncertainly.

Do you think that this is the life I would've chosen, if somebody'd come to me in the beginning and said, "Here are your options"?

No?

You're my nephew. I'm supposed to be the one who mentors you, who tells you what's what. But you've never respected me. His voice was breaking now—with rage or sorrow I couldn't tell. But you're too good for that.

I told him I respected him, though it wasn't really true. He mumbled something like, Whatever you say, and hung up.

I crept back to bed, where Alma was spread out facedown like a starfish. I pushed her leg over enough to lie down and went back to staring at the wooden slat ceiling, which is what I'd been doing before I decided to get up. What life would I have chosen if someone had presented me with options early on? I wouldn't have picked this—a groundskeeper trying desperately, and without much luck, to become a writer.

There was a picture of Cort as a young man in Pop's house. In it, Cort leaned against a metal walker in the front yard, wearing a Santa hat. Pop and my grandmother had their arms slung over his shoulders, grinning, though Cort's face was pinched with the same bitterness he possessed as a man in middle age. He'd been forced to use a walker for nearly two years after his car accident, bright yellow tennis balls sliced open and placed over the back legs. I had no idea why he was wearing a Santa hat. Judging by the dead grass in the yard, it was winter, and therefore maybe Christmastime. Regardless, Cort's expression projected the opposite of whatever the Santa hat was supposed to convey. Jolliness, I guess, and Cort's expression was decidedly anti-jolly. His legs were kind of twisted under him, withered-looking. He was only a few years younger than I was now. Could he have guessed, in the beginning, what would be in store? Could anyone?

RANDO RARELY TALKED ABOUT HIS ALCOHOLISM EXCEPT TO say that things had been bad for many years. I'm lucky to be alive, he said, more than once. But he never got into particulars. He could be around it now, go to a restaurant or a bar and see it. It didn't tempt him.

One day at the arboretum, felling an ash at the edge of the dense woods, we found a broken champagne bottle. Rando put his cig between his lips and stooped to pick up the largest shard of green glass. He touched the sun-faded label. This was my brand, he said, cigarette bobbing as he spoke. He held it up for us to see. Plain old Korbel.

Wouldn't have taken you for a champagne drinker, Rando, James said. He had on his chaps and was crunching down the brambles with his boot, making an escape path from the ash. There was already something of a game trail leading away from the tree, fluffs of rabbit fur caught on twigs, and James and I worked on it, tramping down what we could while Rando studied the bottle. There were flattened beer cans, too, someone's abandoned jacket. They were scattered near a placard with a map of the park, an arrow with the words YOU ARE HERE indicating the location relative to everything else. Working in the arboretum like this, some part of me always worried about finding the evidence of a crime. It was always people like us who found bodies—groundskeepers, park rangers—people who had good reason to be tromping around in ditches and remote wooded areas. Early morning joggers, too, I supposed. But the bottle and the beer cans seemed only to be the remains of someone's good time. Teenagers, maybe. Someone who had to drink in secret.

Aw dude, I had a big champagne phase, Rando said. Fuckin loved champagne. I had this buddy who was a flight attendant, got me these cases of airplane bottles. Don't ask me how. Probably not aboveboard. I was growing weed at the time and would trade him for these cases of mini Korbel bottles. We had so many little bottles of champagne, we didn't know what to do with them. Me and my wife came up with this game where we'd hide them around the house, and if you found one, you had to drink it right then on the spot, which was all right with us. We were bad off, me and Lynette, but our rationale was, "Hey, if we're drinking champagne, how bad can things be? If you're drinking champagne, life is a celebration." We hid them everywhere dude. In the cabinets, under the couch cushions, in the fuckin toilet tank. I had three bottles of champagne floating in my fuckin toilet tank at any given time. Talk about being in denial. Holy shit. I still find champagne bottles in my place. I went to put on a pair of dress shoes a few months ago and felt something in the toe. Lo and behold, I turn the shoe upside down, and out falls a fuckin champagne bottle. I was out of my fuckin gourd, man. Just looney tunes. But at the time, I thought it was normal.

He hadn't ashed his cigarette all the while he'd been speaking. It had gone out and was just a gray husk, curling out from the filter. He ran his thumb over the Korbel label for a moment, lost in thought, then flung the glass into the woods.

Why were you putting on dress shoes? I said. Going to church or something?

Rando gave me a half smile, picked at a scab on his knuckle. In a manner of speaking, he said. I had to go to a funeral.

Oh, I said. Sorry. Someone close?

My brother.

James and I both stopped our tramping and looked at him. Shit, Rando, I said. That's terrible.

Why didn't you tell us? James said.

Oh I don't know, Rando said. It was a long time coming.

Still, James said. That's a big deal. Did you even take a day off?

It was on a Saturday.

Damn, James said. I'm sorry, man.

Rando shrugged, took a fresh pack from his coat pocket, and tore off the cellophane. He smacked it against his palm. He had emphysema and a lot of other problems, Rando said. He was sick for a few years.

All was quiet for a few seconds as Rando lit up. A woodpecker hammered his beak into bark, the sound echoing from far off.

Older or younger? I said.

Younger, Rando said. He lived pretty hard. Harder than me even, if you can believe that. He was an alcoholic, too. So was my aunt, my grandmother. My father was a Bible thumper, but if he hadn't been so drunk on Jesus, he'd have been the same. Something about our genes. We all get carried away.

What was his name? I said. I don't know why I asked this. It just seemed like the thing to ask.

Tommy, Rando said. He was a carpenter. Made me a beautiful desk. Not that I've done anything with it. There's probably some fuckin champagne bottles hidden in it. He chuckled to himself and glanced at us to see if we would laugh. When we didn't, he said, Look, it's fine. We don't have to sing "Amazing Grace" or whatever. Didn't mean to get into a whole thing. Let's just get back to work.

James looked at him sadly. All right, man, he said. Let's get to work, then.

Later, when the ash was lying splintered on the ground and we'd taken a break for water, I wandered off into the woods. I didn't know where I was going. The arboretum abutted private land, and I knew the property line was somewhere in the woods. Men hunted deer on the other side. We'd heard the rifle reports some mornings, the calling out of unintelligible voices. I walked till I could no longer see the yellow paint of the Vermeer or make out the conversation between James and Rando. I reached a dry creek bed, waded through fallen leaves up the bank. I stood at the top, my chest burning, and looked out over a stand of scrub pine laden with snow. It was forty degrees in the light, but colder in the shadowy places, where these stunted pines grew. Something moved between them, jostling the branches—a squirrel. Snow fell from the boughs like sifted flour.

I walked on between the trees, through the clutter of pinecones, the air clean, and on the other side, where the woods thinned, I found an abandoned brick well. There were rotted boards over the opening, switchgrass dried to straw, grown over the sides. I went up to it, looked around. Surely this was no longer Ashby's property. I had the sense I was being watched, told myself this was ridiculous. I took the softened boards from the lid and looked down into the well. I could see nothing. James called out from the chipper.

Maybe I'd been gone awhile. Where are you? he shouted. I was suddenly dumbstruck. I didn't know how to answer. It was the strangest thing—almost like panic or delight, but not quite either. It took my breath. The YOU ARE HERE on the map had disappeared completely, if only for a few seconds, and I was no place. I wasn't in the arboretum or the woods. I certainly wasn't in Kentucky. I was somewhere outside of time—before my kin, before blood watered the trees, before there were human beings at all. It was simply what it was—unnamed—the absence of noticing, of anyone speaking or writing down what they saw.

The feeling passed, and I was once again myself, standing in the woods. I leaned over the well, straining to see, a draft of sulfurous air wafting up. But there was nothing there. No body. No bones. I called out hello and my own voice came back to me.

ALMA ANNOUNCED THAT SHE WAS GOING TO VISIT HER parents in DC. I just need to get out of here, for a few days at least, she said. I'm driving myself crazy with the novel.

We were walking on campus after supper. Warm for early March. Here and there, yellow daffodils were pushing timidly through the wet, decaying leaves.

When would this be?

A week from now. I want you to come with me and meet them. Just for a weekend.

That's a long way to go for a weekend.

I don't care, she said. I'm going stir-crazy and this is the most convenient time for me to go. She had her hand resting in the crook of my arm and was towing me forward briskly, as if we were in a hurry to get somewhere. She was wearing a green windbreaker and high-waisted jeans and her eyes were hidden behind the big Joan Didion–style sunglasses that made her expression illegible.

How much are tickets?

Not cheap, she said. It'd be like three hundred round-trip.

Jesus. I tried to remember how much money was in my bank account—about $130, if I remembered right.

I can cover you, she said. She stopped on the sidewalk and looked up at me. We were near a dormitory. On the lawn, there were kids thumping a soccer ball and shouting, the late sun burning behind spindly trees. The light made the red hues in her hair stand out, especially the stray wisps across her forehead. You can pay me back, she said. Or not. Whatever. I have the money.

What if we drove?

It's like ten hours. Our cars are decrepit. Just let me cover you.

I can't let you do that, I said.

Of course you can. She pushed her sunglasses up with her thumb. I could see myself reflected in the lenses—cheeks whiskered, brow tensed. Dark hair tousled by the breeze. I'd shorn off my Civil War beard the week before, and now when I saw myself, I thought my face looked gaunt. I looked away, through the trees and across the lawn to the brick dorm. Though it could not be seen, we'd trimmed a linden for clearance on the other side. The residents could now walk down the sidewalk to their classes without ducking slightly under a branch, which is to say they could move from one point to another without having to consider obstacles or the people charged with removing them.

I could probably come up with the money, I said. As I said this, I thought about my various options. I couldn't ask my mother, what with the money I already owed her. I could sell something, I supposed, but I didn't have much to sell—records and books mainly. Then there was my father, a long shot to be sure. But possible.

I don't want you to have to "come up" with it, she said. I'm offering to loan it to you. You can pay me back whenever or accept it as a gift. I have plenty from the advance, more than I could spend.

You could spend it, I said. I'm sure it's less than you think. And that's beside the point. It's not your responsibility.

You're overthinking this.

Just give me a couple days to move some funds around, see what I can come up with.

The prices will only go up, she said. I was hoping to take care of it tonight.

One day, then.

She chewed the inside of her cheek a moment, then nodded,

tucked her hands in the pockets of her windbreaker, and walked on, as if she didn't care whether I followed her.

We came to a small plaza in front of the pillared law library and sat on a concrete ledge. The fountain had been shut off for the winter and draped with a blue plastic tarp. An old man sat on a bench on the opposite side, reading a book. He wore a tweed hat with a mallard's feather, a coat and scarf. Cigar clamped in the corner of his lips.

The cool damp of winter returned as the sun sank, and Alma pressed close to me, shivering slightly. What's got you so stir-crazy? I said.

It's mostly the novel, she said. I feel like I'm just spinning my wheels. There's nothing to invigorate me. I'm stuck in that house and I never see anyone or do anything. Nothing *happens*.

You see me, I said.

You know what I mean, she said. She took off her sunglasses and I could see her eyes finally—glassy and haggard. It was a look I recognized, the look of burnout—someone who'd toiled away at something to a point beyond which it was actually productive.

Where are you stuck? I thought you were almost finished.

I was, she said. I had a second draft practically done when they gave me the advance. But it's like now there's this expectation that I finish it by a certain deadline, and that takes the joy out of it, you know? I feel like I have to come up with an ending even if it's not the right ending. And when I go back and read the stuff about my parents and grandparents, I feel like I'm not really being fair to them or doing them justice. It's not generous.

You can't avoid bias, I said. You can't avoid it with anyone, really, but especially your parents.

That's true for you, maybe. But you don't get along as well with your parents.

It's not that I *don't* get along with them. We're just different.

You satirize and exaggerate. I don't want to do that with my parents.

There were plenty of things I wanted to say in response to this— primarily that it was easy to defend them when you hadn't been privy to their opinions your whole life. But I resisted the urge and stared instead at the old man. He worked his tongue, rolling the wet stogie to the other corner of his mouth, and chuckled a bit at whatever he was reading. I wanted to see the cover, but he never inclined the book.

I sometimes feel like I can't be with someone and also write, she said. Like, I only have a finite amount of energy, and I expend it all on my relationship.

That's disconcerting.

She sighed deeply, scraped at the cuticle of one thumbnail with the other. It's just something I have to navigate, she said. Plenty of people do it. It's not like isolation and celibacy are viable long-term options.

Viable long-term options? You sound like you're talking about a retirement plan.

This earned a meager smile. She seemed to be looking now at the horizon, the wind mussing her hair. A corner of the blue tarp on the fountain flapped, its metal grommet tinkling against stone. You know I love you, right? she said. When she turned to look at me, her chin was quivering. This wouldn't be so hard for me if I didn't.

I was too surprised to say anything at first, and we just looked at each other. I told her I loved her, too. I kissed her eyelids, where tears had begun to well.

I want you to come with me, she said, as I kissed her neck and the ridge of her jaw. Just come with me.

I told her I would. My voice seemed to come from some place inside that was not subject to the laws of nature or economics, that had no patience for logistics. Whatever you want, I said.

LATER THAT NIGHT, I LEFT ALMA READING ON THE SOFA AND stepped outside to call my father. His phone rang for a long time. I could see my breath rising in silver curls where I stood within the light of a streetlamp. I'd given up on him answering when he finally picked up. Hey, sorry, he said. Caught me at a bad time.

I can call back.

No, no, he said. It's fine now. I was helping Bonnie in the bath.

Let me let you go, then.

She's out now, he said. I can talk.

Okay, I said. I cleared my throat, scuffed my unlaced boot on the sidewalk. How are you?

Well, he said, after a long pause, not great. But all right considering.

I waited for him to ask me how I was. When I saw that he wouldn't, I said, How's Bonnie?

She's very sick. As you saw when you were here.

What are the doctors saying?

Something different every time. One's still pushing this experimental thing. The rest are saying that what we do now should be *palliative,* which is their word for letting someone die comfortably, as if that were possible. She was on a lot of hydrocodone but they've put her on Opana now, which is stronger. She's trying to hold out on morphine.

I see, I said. I'm sorry.

Well, yeah. It is what it is.

How much time are they saying?

He sighed. Is there something you need?

I'm just asking, Dad.

That's why you called?

I looked up at the guesthouse, at Alma's lighted window on the second floor. The glass was steamed, her blurred form visible through the leaves of her peace lily. Head bowed, book in her lap, a mug of mint tea in arm's reach. I wanted to get back there as quickly as I could.

No, I said. To be honest, I called because I need your help with some money. I wanted to ask you for a loan.

A loan?

Yeah, just till I get my next paycheck.

Several seconds passed. I don't know, he said. He cleared his throat softly and let another period of silence go by, as if he were giving me a chance to retract my request. I just don't know if I can keep enabling you to fail, he said finally. This tree-trimming business, this aimlessness—how can I keep supporting that?

It hurt me physically to hear him say this. I assumed he thought I was a failure, but assuming it and hearing it were two different things. I tried to come up with some response, but the muscles in my throat tightened, and all I could think of were angry, vicious things, so I said, Never mind, and hung up.

THE BAYONET WAS BALANCED ON TWO NAILS ABOVE THE workbench. Close by lay a razor strap, a clawhammer, a fruit jar filled with bolts and washers. An assortment of old shaving brushes was balanced on the tool rack, their badger fur bristles still crusted with lather. A plywood shelf to the left held half a dozen cigar boxes, containing newspaper clippings and western belt buckles and Confederate money. For a long time, I stared at the bayonet, fluorescent tubes zinging above me. The dampened sounds of gunfire could be heard from Pop's TV upstairs, John Wayne shouting orders. Water flushed through the pipes. Cort's heavy footsteps thumping the bathroom floor.

It had remained for months on the phone book beside his recliner, and now, here it was, in its final resting place among the other old things. There was very little in the basement that had not fallen into disuse, and this, I supposed, was what made an antique an antique. Though it was true that you could use the bayonet to kill someone, as perhaps it had during the Civil War, there were now better ways, ways that cost less effort and risk. The same could be said for the harrows or the railroad jacks or the two-man crosscut saws, all mounted on the walls and collecting dust. And then, of course, some of the old things were altogether useless—which is not to say they were worthless. The Confederate money could not be used as currency, but there were rednecks who would pay ten times the printed denomination to buy it off you.

Pop had collected all the old things over the course of a lifetime. Some of them—the farming tools—had seen everyday use at one time. Others he'd acquired from flea markets and pawnshops and estate sales. He had no catalogue, no way of accounting, and so many of the artifacts were simply forgotten about once they'd been stored. This would be the bayonet's fate, I was sure. It would remain here, balanced on two nails, till Pop died, at which time it would be sold by my mother or Cort to someone else—a collector, maybe, who would keep it in his own museum of useless things.

I took it down from the wall. I used a Christmas sweater I never wore to swaddle the blade and pushed it down into my backpack.

The next morning, I drove to Frankfort Avenue where a string of antique dealers and pawnshops could be found. I parked near a railroad crossing. It was a bright, cool day, the sun glinting off windshields. The pawnshops were near a school for the blind, and a few men and women passed by my car with Seeing Eye dogs, clacking the sidewalk tentatively with retractable canes. I had to wait with a blind woman for a train to pass, the cushioned bayonet wedged in my armpit. She turned her head this way and that, smiling pleasantly. Her golden retriever was all business, his attention fixed wholly on the deafening clatter of the passing train. The boxcars were marked with vibrant graffiti.

Long one, said the blind woman.

Do what?

Long train.

Oh, I said. Yes, it is.

When the train was gone, the tolling bells ceased and the boom gate lifted. The golden retriever, seeming more at ease now, its shaggy fur lustrous in the sunlight, tugged the woman forward.

By the time I reached the first pawnshop, my throat was parched. I couldn't seem to get enough air in my lungs. I paused under the awning to collect myself and prevent it from escalating to full-blown hyperventilation. There were old campaign posters in the shop window—Kennedy and Nixon and Jimmy Carter. A painted rocking horse and a mannequin dressed like a 1920s flapper stood in the opposite window.

A cowbell clanged above me when I entered, and inside it smelled like maple syrup and sausage. Morning, came a man's voice from the back. Be right with you.

I browsed the front of the shop desultorily while I waited, lifting little knickknacks and baubles as though I might be interested in making a purchase. Through the padding of the sweater, I could feel the blade's rigidity in my armpit. I hadn't realized I was clenching it so tightly and loosened up a little.

A sign on one of the shelves said CLOWN BABYS! Sure enough, there were about a dozen tiny ceramic children made up like clowns. They had frilly collars and white-painted faces with red cheeks and diamond eyes, just like your average clown, only they were toddlers. I was studying the clown babies, distracting myself, trying to imagine who would collect such a thing and whether Freud would count them as an example of the uncanny, when the owner emerged from a back room with a coil of speaker wire around his shoulder. Help you? he said. He was a Black man in middle age with a white-flecked goatee and a cap pushed back on his bald head. The hat said GUILD SOLUTIONS, which I misread at first as GUILT SOLUTIONS. I was bewildered for a moment before I thought to say something.

Yeah, I was hoping to—well, I'm considering selling something.

The man smiled. Well, the sign out front still says pawnshop, I hope, so I guess you come to the right place. He lifted a partition and went behind the desk, tossing the speaker wire into a pile of other cables and phone jacks and computer keyboards. A paper plate, with mostly eaten pancakes and sausage patties, sat on the desk next to an electric griddle—hence the smell. He pumped a giant Purell dispenser by the register, slathered his hands. All right now, he said, pressing his palms to the scratched surface of the counter, let's see what you got.

I unrolled the sweater. The man's eyebrows arched when he saw the bayonet. Okay, he said. Okay, now. Not your everyday item.

I guess not.

What can you tell me about it?

It's Civil War, I think.

Looks like it.

Other than that, I don't really know much.

May I examine it?

Please.

The man lifted the bayonet gingerly and studied the socket,

where the word "Chavasse" was engraved. Damn, he said. It sure is Civil War. This is a rare piece.

Oh?

You bet. Have you had this appraised?

I shook my head. Not really, I said. I looked it up online.

Where'd you come across this, if you don't mind me asking?

Inherited it, I said. From my granddad.

He a big Civil War guy?

Not really, I said. Not in particular.

The man clicked his tongue, turned over the blade. Lot a those around here, he said.

Bayonets?

Civil War guys.

Yeah, I guess there would be.

You don't have any documentation with this, do you?

I sure don't, I said. Is that necessary?

He frowned. No, he said. Just better to have it. He laid the blade carefully on the snowflake-patterned sweater and leaned his elbow on the register. His eyes remained on the bayonet. He looked like he was doing long division in his head.

Well, sir, he said, after a while. What were you hoping to get for it?

Five hundred, I blurted.

That may be what it sells for *online,* but I can't go that high, he said. Condition's not good enough anyway. He sucked his teeth a moment, grazed the etchings with his forefinger. I could go two hundred.

I pretended to consider this sternly, though I had no idea what I was doing. I'd never haggled or negotiated for anything, and I was afraid that if I pressed my luck, he'd be able to intuit somehow that I'd stolen the bayonet—that it wasn't mine to sell. Could you do three hundred? I said, sounding timid in spite of my best efforts not to.

The man took off his cap and rubbed his bare scalp. About that time, the cowbell dinged. When I turned, I saw Casey standing there, holding a turntable. I hadn't seen him since the party at

Alma's, months earlier. He glanced around idly at the shop and didn't notice me at first. He was wearing sweatpants, his Reds hat and denim jacket. The turntable in his arms was the one from his apartment. He looked about the same, just as sociopathically handsome as ever, only the bridge of his nose had a bump where James had broken it. We both had that in common—James had broken our noses within the same five-minute span. If I hadn't disliked him so much, it might've been something to laugh about.

When his gaze finally settled on me, he squinted faintly, then his eyes went slack with recognition. Dr. Livingstone, he said.

Hey.

He took a step forward, adjusted his grip on the turntable, and actually reached out to shake my hand. For some reason—reflex, I guess—I took it. His hand was soft and damp. I felt the immediate desire to squirt some of the pawnshop owner's Purell into my palm. Selling something? he said.

I gestured to the bayonet.

Shit. Where'd you get that thing?

My granddad. I'm inheriting it.

The granddad you lived with?

I nodded.

He died?

Well, I said. Yeah, I'm inheriting it.

Sorry to hear that. And you're *selling* it?

I cast a furtive glance at the pawnshop owner, who was staring at us impassively. Could he tell somehow? Or was he only impatient to get on with the haggling? I don't have any use for it, I said.

Casey lifted his eyebrows and nodded, as if to say, *Fair enough.* He used his knee to hoist the turntable a little higher and eyed the portable griddle, which took up prime real estate on the counter. Hey man, you mind if I set this down? he said, nodding at the space where he'd like to put it. The pawnshop owner looked at him for a beat, then moved the griddle to the floor wordlessly and took up his paper plate and fork. Casey set the turntable on the surface without thanking the man and exhaled with relief. I never thought I'd get rid of this thing, he said. He looked at me expectantly, waiting for me to ask why. When I didn't, he said, It was my dad's. I'm selling it and all his records, too. I got to the point where I was like, *Do I really need these?* I listen to Spotify 90 percent of the time anyway, so it's like at this point, what am I doing, you know? Is it just for aesthetic reasons? Or sentimental?

Makes sense, I said.

Anyway, I'm moving to Chicago. I'm trying this Marie Kondo shit so I don't have to rent the jumbo U-Haul.

It was clear that he expected me to laugh at this. He seemed disappointed when I didn't. The pawnshop owner had gone back to eating his pancakes and sausage, and glanced up at us from his plate occasionally, chewing, looking a little annoyed and a little bored, as if we were nothing special, as if he witnessed these sorts of conversations between people like us all the time. What's in Chicago? I said.

He shrugged and scratched his ear. I just feel like Louisville's played out, he said. It's like, what else is this place going to show me that it hasn't shown me already?

A few seconds of silence passed. Well, good luck, I said. He seemed hurt, frankly, that I didn't want to talk. It was like nothing had ever happened between us, like we were standing around after Jungle Narratives last semester, smoking and shooting the shit. Like he'd never bared his ugliness. I turned my back on him. The man finished chewing, wiped his mouth with the back of his hand, and said, I could do 250. But that's the absolute highest. You won't get a better deal than that.

With no idea how to counter this and wishing more than anything to be away from Casey, I took the deal. He gave me two hundreds, two twenties, and two fives, and with this, I pushed my way out into the sunlight and the brisk air, without so much as a final glance at the bayonet and without saying goodbye to Casey. I walked quickly, crossing the tracks, along which towering stands of bamboo threw their tropical shadows on the sidewalk. The blind were numerous, scuffling their feet, tapping the ground to make sure it was still there. I weaved between them. I wanted to open up the distance between myself and what I was leaving behind. The further I got, the freer I felt—the more unburdened. There was money in my pocket. I would make it to the bank before noon. That evening, we would buy our tickets. She would ask me one last time to let her cover me, and I would roll my eyes and pretend to be insulted. I told you I'd figure it out, I would say, and at this, she would let it go.

THE NIGHT BEFORE OUR FLIGHT, WE GOT DRUNK ON TRADER JOE'S wine and fooled around. When we'd finished, we took turns chugging a glass of water at the sink, then sat in our underwear on the couch. The room was sweltering from the radiator. I propped open the window with a cereal bowl and we sprawled out with only our ankles touching. A cold breath of air drifted in and cooled the sweat on our skin to a salt film. She told me about her parents and what to expect in Alexandria the next day. Her mother's name was Ajla. She'd mentioned this before, but I'd forgotten. It's confusing, I know, but all the women on my mom's side have names that start with A, she said. My grandmother was Aida, and *her* mother was Amina.

Got it.

My dad is named Eldin. He's sort of shy. Just sprinkle some Springsteen references into conversation and he'll like you.

As Alma told me about her parents' lives, how hardworking they'd been, how much they'd struggled to make it here, I couldn't help but think of my extended family, all my aunts and uncles and cousins who'd never left the state or gone to college. Several of my cousins had substance problems. Some had criminal records or had done time in jail. The last time I'd spoken to my mother, she told me my cousin Tabitha had recently overdosed on pain pills and had to be taken to the hospital. Alma asked me what I was thinking about, and I explained all this to her. Her face took on its familiar expression of consternation.

How did you turn out differently? she said.

I started to answer, then thought for a moment, unsure how to respond. I could say that my grandparents helped, that they read to me and bought me books. I could say that I was curious as a kid, that I *wanted* to learn about the world. I could say that I was lucky. But in the end, I wasn't sure that any of these variables could account for how I turned out. And although I'd read a lot of books and managed to get a college degree, how different, materially, was my life from my cousins' lives? I worked manual labor for miserable wages. I had no home or apartment of my own. I had no car. I ate McDonald's for breakfast *every day*. How much better, really, were my circumstances?

I'm not sure, I said finally. A lot of people there—they don't see any reason to try. It's like, why even make an attempt when what's waiting for you is either a service industry job at a chain restaurant or one of the chemical plants? You know? Even if they did try, the best they could hope for would be to leave. And some people do.

Like you, she said.

Well, yeah, I did leave. But here I am again.

Hm, she said, and looked to the window, where an ambulance was passing. She had a throw pillow hugged to her belly and was petting the fringe. Her hair was mussed. Her scent, still strong, rose up from my fingers. When the noise from the siren faded, she said, What if it's ingrained though? This despair you're talking about. Like, if it's environmental, which is what you're saying, then how do you know it's not ingrained in *you*?

Despair?

She nodded.

I don't feel despair. I feel hopeful.

But what if that fades? What will you be left with?

I looked into her eyes, scrutinizing. Her chest and throat were still splotched pink from sex. The desire I'd felt, which had been so sharp and quick, left me just as suddenly. I don't know, Alma, I said. How am I supposed to answer that?

It's just a question. She stared down at the couch cushion and wound a loose thread from its stitching around her finger.

Are you asking me if I have despair in my blood somehow? Is that the implication?

She started to speak but stopped herself and shook her head. The thread was so tight around her finger that the tip had turned purple. She unwound it slowly. The blood fled, her finger whitening. Forget it, she said. I just think it's interesting what people get from their families and their upbringing.

I'm not sure I like what you're insinuating.

I'm not insinuating anything, she said. Let's just drop it, okay?

And we did, at least conversationally. I browsed Street View images of Tallahassee for a while as she read. This had become a kind of virtual escape hatch for me, a salve for feelings of suffocation and helplessness. It was a sorry state of affairs, I thought, when images of Tallahassee could offer comfort.

Eventually, we opened her MacBook and watched a TV show, though I fumed throughout the episode. Even by the time we went to bed, I could only lie there, stiff, breathing shallowly, rehearsing what I would say if the topic came up again. I closed my eyes. I tried to let it go, to think about other things. It was late, after all, and we had a flight to catch in the morning.

THE NEIGHBORHOOD IN ALEXANDRIA WHERE HER PARENTS lived corresponded more or less with what I'd imagined. The houses were Tudor, the lawns planted with hedges and holly bushes. The huge oaks and maples had only just begun to bud, while the smaller dogwoods and Bradford pears were clustered already with white blossoms. It was the kind of place I'd longed to grow up in, where the neighbor kids rode scooters and bicycles, shaggy dogs chasing after them. Where there were trampolines with nets and in-ground pools in the backyards, and a whiff of clipped grass and charcoal seemed always to carry on the breeze, no matter the time of year.

We'd arrived late afternoon, gliding over the remote hills and coal towns of eastern Kentucky and West Virginia, onward across the Blue Ridge Mountains. From the window of our jet, they looked so much like the seams and furrows of a human body. The hills rippled outward and faded finally into a kind of floodplain, and soon there were houses and parking lots and the glinting threads of highway, all of it seeming to gather into a kind of accretion, and this accretion became Washington, DC.

An Uber took us from the airport. The house was larger and statelier than either of my parents', but not so much so that I found the discrepancy gratifying. It was simply a nice brick house, with exposed timber and stucco and a big, potted elephant's ear plant on the front porch. Beyond the plant, the yard and the porch lacked any distinguishing features. The same could be said for all the houses on the block. Unlike the unkempt lawns of Melber, there were no broken washing machines, no rust-eaten cars on cinder blocks or satellite dishes or plastic trikes grown over with horseweed. The windows were not blocked out with aluminum foil and there were no plastic bucks or turkeys, punctured by bullets, in the backyards. The houses projected a kind of cleanliness that bordered on sterility. A brief wave of panic came over me as Alma started merrily for the door, backpack slung over her shoulder.

Alma's mother, Ajla, greeted us in the foyer. She reached up to hug Alma and kiss her cheek. My daughter, she said.

Hey Mama. This is Owen.

She looked me over head to toe. Her hair was darker than Alma's, and much longer. She wore a flowered skirt, a sweater, and a chunky turquoise necklace. I figured her for fifty, give or take, though because I could see the shadow of Alma's features in her face so clearly, it was hard to say.

I'm going to hug you, too, she said. Okay?

Okay, I said.

She put her arms around my neck and pulled me down. Happy to finally meet you, she said.

Likewise.

We drew apart and the three of us stood for a beat, looking around. A hallway lay ahead of us. The smell of garlic and tomato sauce was riding on a current of warm air from that direction, and I could hear the stove fan going. To the right was the dining room, to the left, the living room. It seemed, at first glance, to be one of those embalmed living rooms where nobody ever sat or congregated.

Ajla clapped her hands and twined her fingers together. So— I've got dinner on, she said. You like Italian food?

Sure, I said.

Good. Alma, you show him your room and take the bags up, then we'll eat, okay?

We stepped over a pet gate and trudged up the creaking stairs to the second floor. Up there, away from the cooking, the house had a pleasant, lived-in smell, like that of an old library or church. I followed Alma to the end of the corridor, where she let us into her bedroom. Though it had been converted to a guestroom, it still retained some of its childhood touches. There were dozens of glow-in-the-dark stars stuck to the ceiling, and a pink boombox sat on the dresser, next to stacks of CDs. Outkast, Amy Winehouse, early Kanye, Death Cab for Cutie—standard issue for anyone coming of age in the mid-aughts. Alma let her bag drop to the floor and sat on the edge of her bed.

Where am I sleeping? I said.

In here.

That's okay?

Of course, she said. They don't care.

I sat beside her. The room was quiet and dim, and though the sun was still hidden by clouds, the window glowed with pale light. I spread my fingers on the cool cotton of the quilt, wishing I could lie down. It had been a long day.

It will be baked ziti, Alma said.

What will?

Dinner. She thinks her baked ziti is really good.

It's not?

Alma shrugged one shoulder and tucked a coil of hair behind her ear. It's okay, she said. She looked at me then with an expression somewhere between a smile and a cringe. Are you okay? Is this overwhelming?

We just got here, I said. Nothing's happened yet, and your mom seems very chill.

I just don't want you to get overwhelmed, she said. We should come up with a sign—like a safe word or something that you can say if you start to feel anxious, and I'll know what it means.

Okay. What's the safe word?

She twisted her mouth and looked up at the ceiling. Hmm, she said. What about . . . Possum Trot?

Don't you think your parents would find it a little strange if I just said "Possum Trot" out of the clear blue?

Shit, no, you're right.

What if I just told you I was tired?

She laughed and stood up, smoothing the wrinkles in her black jeans. Yeah, that probably makes the most sense.

It occurred to me that she was probably checking in because *she* had felt overwhelmed at my parents' house and didn't want me to feel the same way. She was more attentive than I was to the emotional states of others.

Downstairs, Ajla was busy at the stove, Paul Simon playing through a little Bluetooth speaker on the counter. Would you like wine? she called over her shoulder. Beer? Tea? A cappuccino?

Alma and I looked at each other with a *what-do-you-think* expression. I would have wine? she said.

Yeah, that sounds good.

She went to fetch the bottle. Through an archway to our left, someone was stirring in what I guessed was the family room or the den. It was dark in there, save for a computer monitor, which emitted enough blue light to make a leather sofa and a recliner discernible. Alma's father, Eldin, emerged from the dark and stood in the threshold, followed shortly by a ginger Pomeranian at his heels, her little nails clicking on the hardwood. He was tall and bearish, with a good-sized paunch and a butcher's forearms. Though his wispy hair and beard were gray, his eyebrows were black and thick. He wore a white undershirt and had his hands buried deeply in the pockets of his corduroy trousers, worrying the change in them, as if he might be fishing around for a quarter.

Hey Daddy, Alma said, stepping forward to hug him. They embraced for a long time, her father with his eyes closed, saying nothing. When they pulled apart, she told him who I was, and he extended his hand. Wonderful to meet you, he said, very softly, as we shook. He returned his hands to his pockets and went back to jingling the change, smiling in an abashed way.

And hello to you, Daphne, Alma said, crouching to scratch behind the dog's ears. I bent and ran my fingers through her fluffy fur. Daphne seemed positively elated by this development in her life, rolling over to expose her belly, panting and kicking her paws in the air.

They've been traveling all day, Ajla said, taking down two wineglasses from a cabinet.

I see, her father said. You must be tired.

Not too bad, I said.

He gestured to the kitchen table and we all sat. Her mother brought over the glasses, poured a healthy amount of white wine into each, and joined us. Paul Simon was in the middle of "You Can Call Me Al," though it was hard to hear over the low roar of the fan hood above the stove. Somehow, it was exactly the music I would've expected a girlfriend's upper-middle-class mother to be playing as she fixed dinner.

The ziti is baking, Ajla said. She'd pulled back her hair into a ponytail, and I noticed now, in the kitchen's clear light, that she was wearing chandelier earrings made of turquoise like her necklace and faint eye shadow that was roughly the same color.

It smells good, I said.

It's a Hadzic staple, her father said, smiling at me. His eyes had the quality of looking both bright and weary at once somehow. It was as if he were a good-natured person who couldn't help but look that way even though he was very tired.

Her mother inhaled sharply, like she'd suddenly remembered something. Have you given him the tour, Alma?

Nope, Alma said. It's all you.

Ajla scraped back her chair. Come, come, she said excitedly.

We followed her from room to room, Eldin trailing behind, hands in his pockets. The "den," from which Eldin had emerged, seemed to be where they spent most of their time. MSNBC played, muted, on the television. A messy computer desk and a swivel chair were nestled in the corner. On the monitor, a digital chess game was paused, and a dozen or so Post-it notes were stuck around the edges. Ajla took down a framed photograph from one of the shelves and showed it to me. It was her and Alma as a little girl, wearing what looked like flight suits and floating against the backdrop of a spiral galaxy, as if in zero gravity. She smiled expectantly. Space Camp, she said finally, as if this explained everything.

Oh, I said. Okay. What's Space Camp?

You've never heard of *Space Camp*?

I couldn't help but laugh. No, I haven't.

Not everyone went to Space Camp, Mom, Alma said.

Ajla seemed briefly troubled by this revelation but went on to explain the photo. They used a *green screen,* you know this?

Yeah, I know what you mean.

We lay on these green pillars and raised our arms and heads up. They had fans to blow our hair back.

Cool, I said.

Alma wanted to be like Einstein. She wrote a story when she was little about building a time machine and going back to meet Einstein. She told you this already?

No, I said.

He doesn't need to hear any more about Space Camp, Alma said, splotches of color rising to her cheeks.

It *was* a good story, Eldin said, as if he had to admit it, begrudgingly.

Ajla led us through the rest of the house—the bedrooms and pink-tiled bathrooms upstairs, the dining room. When she flipped on the light in the living room, it was, as I expected, one of those preserved, museum-like living rooms. There were china cabinets and polished end tables with mint dishes and an antique sofa with tufted, floral-print upholstery. The bookshelf housed the Great Works of the Western Canon, a set that ran from Plato's *Republic* to Hemingway's *The Old Man and the Sea,* the compilers deciding, apparently, that this was as good a place to stop as any. It looked like a living room straight out of a Cheever story, which is to say it looked thoroughly WASPish and American. I don't know what I expected. I should've taken Alma at her word, that they were more or less totally assimilated. Still, some part of me had anticipated . . . what? Eastern folk music? Prayer rugs? One of the exotic Bosnian foods I'd Googled instead of baked ziti? There were a few clues, if one looked closely—a coffee set of engraved copper, the decanter tarnished blue-green; a small charcoal drawing of a mosque with two thin minarets. There were pieces of pottery, with arabesque patterns of tulips and cypress fronds and the tail feathers of peacocks. A sideboard, between two windows, held an ornately carved book rest, upon which lay an open Quran with a tasseled bookmark. These few things, as far as I could tell, were the only pieces of evidence in the house that they were in fact Muslims.

While the ziti cooked, we drank our wine and ate from a platter of cheese at the kitchen table. There was camembert, goat cheese, smoked Gouda, served with a sleeve of Ritz crackers. Maybe I looked a little disappointed. At one point, Alma asked her mother, Do we have any Vlašić cheese, Mama?

We do, Ajla said. Why? Do you *want* Vlašić cheese?

Well, I think Owen was excited to try some Bosnian food.

This is fine, I said. Don't worry about it.

Ajla spread her hand between her clavicles and gave her daughter a look of mortal alarm. Why didn't you *tell* me?

It's not a big deal, Alma said. I was just wondering.

I'm so sorry, she said, turning to me, sincerely grief-stricken.

It's okay, really. This is great.

I'll get it right now, she said, rising from the table.

Don't worry about it, I said, but she was already drawing a wedge from the refrigerator and unwrapping it.

It's made from sheep's milk, Alma explained. It's sort of like feta.

Better than feta, Eldin said.

Okay, well, whatever. She patted my hand on the table. You'll like it.

Ajla returned with the Vlašić cheese and set it on the platter. This came from EuroMart, she said.

Ah yes, Alma said. Good ol EuroMart.

This is a Bosnian grocery? I asked.

The guy who owns it is Croatian, right, Daddy?

Yeah, Bogdan. His son has testicular cancer.

Oh God, Alma said, grimacing. Peter?

Eldin nodded slowly.

Since when?

Since three weeks ago. Your mother diagnosed it.

Not formally, Ajla said. I just checked it and referred him to a colleague. We've known his family a long, long time.

He's your age, Alma said to me.

Wow, I said.

Ajla sighed and gestured at the cheese. Anyway, she said. Please, eat some.

I tried the cheese, smearing it onto a cracker, and we sat in uncomfortable silence for a moment while I chewed and thought about Ajla informally checking poor Peter's testicles. The Vlašić cheese did taste like feta, only much brinier. It's good, I said.

Good, Ajla said. I wish you'd told me, Alma, I would've made burek.

You don't have to do anything special on my account, I said.

No, no, she said. You want Bosnian food, I'll make you burek, you'll love it.

The ziti was okay. Eldin and Alma got right down to business, eating eagerly and silently. Ajla ate like a bird and asked me about my life, which required me to eat slowly as well, so as not to speak while chewing. Her questions were standard and polite, though I got the sense she already knew the answers from Alma and was merely going through the motions. Where was I from? Did I have siblings? Where did I go to college? There was a certain standoffishness to her questions, as if she were afraid I'd think she was prying, or did not want, really, to bring up touchy subjects. But my life was full of touchy subjects. When she asked about my parents, and I mentioned they were evangelical Christians, she grew conspicuously silent and asked no follow-up questions.

Once the plates had been cleared, Ajla poured us fresh wine. She'd offered Eldin wine three times throughout dinner, and three times he'd declined with an upturned palm. A little wine won't kill you, Eldin, she said this time. We have guests. This is celebratory.

Celebrating what? he said.

Alma's new friend.

He sighed and said, Right. Okay, but just a little.

She poured him a glass as full as the others. As we drank and talked, her parents' accent, which was more noticeable than Alma had let on, grew even more overt. Most often, it was that they dropped articles—"the" usually. They said, for example, "United States" rather than "the United States." They, like my parents, corrected themselves sometimes, repeating a sentence fragment and reinserting the omitted article. They talked about their work for a while, their minor health concerns, the recent weather. They talked about Alma's older sister, Adna, who was in her fourth year of medical school at the University of Pennsylvania and had recently matched for a residency program at Georgetown. We're so pleased, of course, that she'll be here, Ajla explained. We even offered for her to stay in her old room, but she wants an apartment for some reason. I told her, I said, "Adna, every time you pay rent, you flush that money down the toilet."

She's twenty-nine, Mama, Alma said. Can you really blame her for not wanting to stay with her parents?

Yes! Ajla said. I can! What's so wrong with living with your parents? Eldin and I, we lived with my parents for two years after we first got married.

So you've told me, Alma said.

They asked Alma about the progress of her novel and what it was like at Ashby. She did not mention the position she'd been offered, but she said she liked it there. She called it "pastoral."

What sort of thing do you write, Owen? Eldin said. The wine seemed to have emboldened him.

I gave him my stock answer—that I wrote about the town where I grew up and the people I knew there and the changing South, et cetera, et cetera. I thought about mentioning the Harry Crews Cottage but something about it seemed pathetic.

Tell him what you told me the other day about colonialism, Alma said.

She was referring to an offhand comment I'd made about rural America as a kind of colony. It was the sort of half-baked opinion you share with your significant other but would be embarrassed to repeat. It wasn't very interesting, I said.

It *was* interesting, she said. Go ahead.

Eldin looked at me, waiting, his eyebrows arched.

Just that rural America has been colonized by urban America, I said. And that rural texts could be looked at through a postcolonial lens.

Eldin made a sound in his throat and nodded subtly. Well, that's one way to see it, he said finally. But, you know, we live in a city—the suburb of a city. Does that make us colonizers?

He'd meant this as a joke, I guess, but it came off slightly hostile. Ajla laughed a breathy, nervous laugh.

I wouldn't say that, I said.

He just means there's exploitation, Alma said.

There's exploitation in cities, too, Eldin said. But still we voted the right way.

It's complicated, Alma said.

It is, Eldin said, smiling vaguely, picking at the corner of his frayed napkin.

My ears and throat grew warm. I spoke before I could think through what I was saying. It's not actually worse in cities, I said.

Okay, Alma said, squeezing my hand on the table. Didn't mean to open a can of worms. It's bad everywhere, let's just say that.

That's the truth, Ajla said. I don't know where this country is going.

Naturally, from here, our conversation turned to Donald Trump. Eldin and Ajla went through the expected liberal talking points and platitudes. I agreed, of course, with all of them, the thrust of which was that Trump was a bigot and a con man, but it left a bad taste in my mouth nonetheless, knowing that if MSNBC were unmuted in the den, I'd be hearing more or less the same talking points and platitudes, delivered in nearly the same rote fashion. It was aesthetically displeasing, like a canned phrase or a stale image.

When the subject of Bosnia arose, however, I perked up. The prospect of a Muslim registry was beginning to seem unlikely, but Eldin said he wouldn't be surprised at all if it happened. When people start making lists, you know things are bad, he said. The Serbs did that. They had informants go with them, house to house. They'd point and say, "Muslimani, Muslimani, et cetera." He mimed pointing out the houses. People think it's not possible, but that was only thirty years ago, he said.

I thought about what my mother had said about Trump's "filter." His supporters act like he's just giving voice to what everyone's thinking, I said. But not everyone's full of anger and suspicion.

Eldin rapped the table with his knuckle. *Yes*, he said emphatically. Not everyone. But he gives the people who *do* think that way permission. He sanctions them. That leads to bad behavior.

What do you mean? Alma said. She was looking at him intently, as if he were not usually given to this kind of talk.

He took a swallow of wine and clanked the glass down a little too hard. He twisted the glass by its stem, staring at it, formulating his answer. I just mean that people are looking for any excuse, he said. In the war, for instance. These people who called themselves soldiers were not really soldiers. They were just men with guns. Half-assed paramilitary goons. Suddenly, if you were a Serb, and you had fatigues and a rifle, you could play soldier, and that gave you license to go and rape and pillage and murder people. That's what is most disturbing, you see—that regular people have this barely hidden animosity. It's tenuous. All it takes is a little chaos, and they see their excuse to act out.

I knew a man, for instance—a Serb, who lived in the neighborhood. He was a policeman, this man. Always polite to me, always waving, saying, "Good morning, Eldin," and so on. Well, when war breaks out, this man, the policeman, joins a militia. He comes to our neighborhood one night, very late, he and his brother, and they rouse a Muslim family from their beds down the street. The policeman and his brother rape the mother. They slit her throat. Then they have the father and the two young boys carry her to the field nearby and dig her grave and their own graves. Then they slit their throats as well and bury them. Now, you tell me, where are these men—the policeman and his brother? Where are they now?

He seemed to be asking me. I told him I didn't know.

Why, they're in their village! he said. They're playing soccer with their children, drinking at the pub and smiling politely at their neighbors when they pass them in the street. He chuckled grimly, rubbed his jaw. Ajla had averted her face, embarrassed. Eldin poured back the rest of his wine and wiped his lips with the neckband of his T-shirt. People are waiting for their opportunity to behave like animals, he said. Remember that. It's happening now with this Trump business.

After this, nobody spoke for a long time. It got so deathly quiet I could hear the thermostat click on and the furnace igniting in the basement. We all just stared into our wineglasses, as if whatever we were supposed to say next could be found there.

We sat in the den for an hour. Alma and I, so sleepy we could hardly hold our eyes open, said good night and left her parents to watch MSNBC. Her father had returned to his chess game on the computer. Her mother had opened another bottle of wine and was drinking a glass and flipping through a *New Yorker*. Rachel Maddow seemed, mostly, to provide background noise—a congenial voice in the room that you could listen to only when you wanted.

We tramped upstairs and collapsed facedown onto her bed. How are you feeling? she said, her voice muffled by the quilt.

I turned and raised up on my elbows. Exhausted, I said.

Not because of my parents, I hope? she said, her face still pressed into the bed.

Roll over, I said. She rolled over and looked up at me, tangled hair across her face. They're great, I said. Very friendly.

My dad's a little socially awkward.

I didn't notice, I said, though I had.

He doesn't ordinarily talk about that kind of stuff.

Really?

She nodded and used the corner of her mouth to blow a strand of hair from her eye.

I guess it's not exactly an ordinary time.

She sighed, turned over my hand, and traced the creases in my palm with her finger. She often did this, as if she were reading it, only I never got to hear my fortune. She ran her fingers past my palm to the tendons of my wrist and further, to the green veins forking beneath the skin of my forearm. There were little pale scars there, places where I'd been scraped by twigs or torn the skin lugging a big limb to the chipper bed. Her hands were small and delicate, their bones fragile.

I wanna go to EuroMart, I said.

She smiled. Prepare to be underwhelmed. It's in a strip mall, next to a tanning salon.

Perfect, I said. Summer's coming up. We can get a base for beach season.

That would be very eastern European of us.

Did your mom really check that kid's testicles?

Alma buried her face in the blanket and laughed. Oh my God, I forgot about that, she said. That was weird.

Right?

People are always asking her to check stuff like that though, she said, looking back up at me. Moles and rashes and lumps. And my dad, of course, gets all the tooth-related questions. There aren't a lot of Bosnians in DC, but my parents know all of them basically. Plus just a lot of other families from the mosque.

Poor Peter, I said.

She frowned and drew her brows together. I know, she said. I shouldn't be laughing, it's really not funny.

We undressed, climbed into bed. Alma drifted off quickly when we'd switched off the light. I lay there for a long time, staring up at the green glow-in-the-dark stars stuck to her ceiling. I could hear the downstairs television faintly, playing well into the night, and though I was very tired, I couldn't seem to close my eyes. My heart was pumping fast. I could hear the blood beating in my head. It was a familiar anxiety, but difficult, still, to put my finger on. It was like déjà vu, in a way. The shocking recognition that I was really *here,* in this girl's house, with her parents—this family whose troubles I could never really understand. At some point in the past, I'd wanted to be with her, and now here I was. But had I known, really, what I wanted? Had I understood the responsibility of attaining it?

I reached for Alma. She murmured a little in her sleep and nestled against me. I felt for her heart beneath her breast and found the pulse, steady and insistent. The tempo of my own heart slowed, and at some point, miraculously, I slipped into my dreams.

WE SPENT THE NEXT DAY IN THE CITY. ELDIN DROVE US IN their Audi, with Ajla in the passenger seat and Alma and I in the back. We listened to Bruce Springsteen on the twenty-minute drive from Alexandria, including "Born in the U.S.A." as the Capitol building and the gleaming obelisk of the Washington Monument came into view. Eldin had the volume loud and smacked the steering wheel in time to the snare shots. Alma nudged my arm and gave me a *what-did-I-tell-you* look.

You like the Boss? Eldin shouted, glancing at me in the rearview.

Of course, I said. Who doesn't?

That's good, he said, as if the question had been a test.

I wanted to bring Pop back a picture of the World War II Memorial, so we stopped there first. I snapped a picture of the Kentucky pillar, then we stopped at the Lincoln Memorial briefly. I'd been to DC on an eighth-grade school trip and seen most of the standard sights. So, for the afternoon, we decided on the National Gallery, since I'd never been, and Alma hadn't been since she was a kid.

Ajla was one of those museumgoers who liked to listen to the guided audio tour and spent more time reading the placards than actually looking at the art. Eldin, on the other hand, seemed to know the names of the artists, if not the titles of the paintings themselves, without reading the placards, and would mumble the names just loud enough that those around him could hear, but not so loud that it would seem implausible that he was talking to himself. I liked to be close, but not right beside, a museum companion. Alma was the same way. Now and then, if we saw a painting we really admired, we'd call one another's attention to it, but mostly we kept to ourselves. I caught Ajla glancing at us worriedly a few times, as if we were missing the really important information being piped through her headphones.

He painted this during a period of bankruptcy and failure, she said, appearing behind me as I looked up at a Rembrandt self-portrait. I nearly jumped out of my skin.

Is that right? I said.

She nodded soberly. He was very sad, that Rembrandt. You can see it in his eyes. She pointed to her own eyes, rather than his.

Thanks for letting me know, I said.

I spent a long time standing with my arms folded in front of Modigliani's *Gypsy Woman with Baby*. It reminded me of Alma, of course—the cut and color of her hair, her small mouth, her long, slender neck. It was an affinity I'd thought of before, being an admirer of Modigliani's portraits, but it was particularly striking in this painting.

Alma came up beside me and took hold of my upper arm. I could tell she was smirking without having to turn. She looks awfully familiar, she said.

She is my type.

Verrrry interesting. Who would you say is your type? Like, if you had to name one representative person who isn't me?

I thought about this a moment. Emily Dickinson, I said.

Alma threw her head back and laughed, loud enough that it echoed in the high-ceilinged room and a few patrons glanced over their shoulders. Of course, she said. The Reclusive, Slightly Anemic Art Girl.

We strolled on into the next gallery, where a crowd of high school students were gathered around a woman giving a guided tour. They were all snickering and whispering and did not seem interested at all in the paintings.

What do you like about her? Alma said. As a person, I mean. Not her poems.

Are they separable?

You know what I mean.

Well, I sighed, I guess that she seems quiet and modest and formidable. She's sort of mousy.

I should be taking notes. *Buttoned-up, modest, keeps her mouth shut.*

Ha ha. You left out "formidable."

You know "mousy" isn't usually a compliment.

I'm only half-serious.

Very, very interesting, she said, nodding slowly, as if filing away the information for later use.

Ajla bought a Titian postcard in the gift shop on our way out. I buy a postcard in every museum gift shop I visit, she explained.

What do you do with them?

She looked at me blankly, as if the question did not compute. I keep them, she said.

They fill up storage space in the upstairs closet, that's what she does with them, Eldin said.

Ajla ignored this remark and recited the factoids she'd learned as we walked out to the parking lot. Van Gogh painted the self-portrait we'd seen in a sanitarium. Constable switched to watercolors after an illness crippled his right hand. Only thirty-five authentic Vermeer paintings survive.

We're stopping by EuroMart to get stuff for dinner, Ajla announced on the road.

Great, I said.

Is that absolutely necessary? said Eldin. This traffic is terrible. It was nearing rush hour and the interstate was stop-and-go.

I'm making burek, Ajla said, definitively.

All right, okay, Eldin said. Onward to EuroMart.

He eased up the volume on the stereo. I looked back at the low-slung city behind us as we crossed the Fenwick Bridge—the glittering Potomac, the white dome of the Jefferson Memorial. Alma scrolled on her phone and nibbled her thumbnail, reading the news. Bruce was singing about engines and highways and breaking free from traps.

Who is Wendy? Alma said, without looking up from her phone.

What? said Eldin.

Wendy. He's always talking about Wendy in the songs.

She's his muse, Eldin said, as if it should be obvious.

Burek turned out to be a flaky pastry, similar to baklava, only filled with a mixture of ground lamb and beef. Ajla took nearly two hours making it when we'd returned from EuroMart. I spent this time reading about Modigliani on my phone, whose life I knew little about, while Eldin played computer chess and Alma read *Sense and Sensibility.* Periodically, one of us would offer to help in the kitchen, but Ajla steadfastly refused.

It seemed that Modigliani had sex with most of the women he painted. Painting them and falling in love with them were the same act. He was an alcoholic and a drug addict. He had tuberculosis. His last lover, Jeanne Hébuterne, was a frequent subject of his portraits, and an artist in her own right, though she never got the chance to make a career of it. She was disowned by her strictly religious family, who believed that Modigliani was good for nothing—which was kind of true, in a sense, if you set aside his paintings. When Modigliani succumbed to tuberculosis, Jeanne, eight months pregnant, threw herself from a fifth-story window and died at the age of twenty-one. The inscription on her tombstone read DEVOTED COMPANION TO THE EXTREME SACRIFICE. In photographs, she looked so distinct from Modigliani's portrayals of her, even taking for granted his style. But then, her portrait of him was not much of a likeness either. That was the saddest thing about the whole story to me. They never seemed to have seen each other clearly. Or worse, they did, and chose willfully to live in a fantasy, with all its pleasant distortions. That was the thrill, I supposed, for all those avant-garde bohemians at the turn of the century—life was whatever you wanted it to be, however you made it in your art, until suddenly it wasn't and you found yourself standing on a windowsill, looking down.

He sounds like an asshole, Alma said, when I told her the story. We could smell the burek baking now, the pastry bread and the gamey lamb. Glasses and silverware clinked in the kitchen. Ajla was setting the table.

His paintings are good though, I said.

I never much cared for them, she said. He's sort of one-note. It's like, I get it, Amedeo, you discovered African masks and now you think you're doing something really novel, when actually it's just appropriative. And who knows? Maybe Jeanne's paintings would've been better.

His life was sad though, you have to admit, I said. He endured a lot of suffering.

Alma shrugged and turned over *Sense and Sensibility,* which had been splayed facedown on her lap. At least he got to do what he wanted, she said.

I had no response to this. Eldin seemed to be losing his chess game. Every time his opponent put him in check, a tinny trumpet sound emitted from the computer speakers. The trumpet had sounded three times in the last ten minutes. Unbelievable, he muttered, his face a few inches from the screen. He sat back in the swivel chair, arms folded, jaw clenched. His pupils scanned rapidly, considering moves and sequences. He noticed me staring and I looked away quickly to the television, where pundits were discussing the travel ban.

After the burek, which was rich and delicious, we sat around the kitchen table, talking and drinking wine. Even Eldin had a glass, which surprised Alma. Two nights in a row, eh? she said.

He took a sip and shrugged. Special occasion, he said.

Ajla brought out a few picture albums and Alma's "baby book," which she had compiled in the States after learning it was something other Americans did.

Is this really necessary? Alma said.

Why not? said Ajla. You were a beautiful baby.

I flipped through the baby book, with Alma and her mother leaning over the table to see what I was seeing. Eldin did not seem interested. She was a striking newborn, with curious eyes and a head of black hair. One page listed her exact dimensions at birth. Another had milestones and their dates—first word, first time crawling and walking. There were photos with her parents, before they immigrated. Eldin looked much thinner and livelier. He had a dark mustache to match his woolly eyebrows and his hair was shaggy. Ajla, though she wore a lot of makeup and had her hair permed and crimped, was very beautiful, and looked so much like Alma that it made my heart flutter. I got the sense that she'd brought out these albums not just so that I could see Alma, but so that I could see her—that she was once twenty-six, as well.

In one photo, Eldin held his daughter beside a white Mercedes van, and a downward-sloped street could be seen behind them, lined with houses. The houses were stucco with terra-cotta tiled roofs, laundry draped over the rails of balconies. Cloud-wreathed mountains stood in the distance, stubbled with coniferous trees. They looked like Kentucky's mountains, like the Appalachian foothills. One of the stucco walls was marred with graffiti, the word "Hope" in English. The *o* had been turned into a frowning face.

This is Bosnia, Ajla said, tapping the photo. The street where we lived in Sarajevo.

I see, I said.

The next photo was of Eldin and another man, who held Alma.

I could tell, somehow, before they explained, that it was Eldin's brother. They had the same tired, good-natured eyes.

Damir looks good there, Eldin said, touching his brother's face.

My uncle, Alma said to me.

He was always blinking in photographs, Eldin said. It was like he did it on purpose. But his eyes are open here.

Does he live in the States? I said.

Eldin didn't seem to have heard me, and Ajla kept flipping pages, as though the subject hadn't come up at all. Alma touched her fingers to my kneecap—a subtle signal that I should shut up. It looks like a nice apartment, Alma said, steering us away from Damir, the brother.

Oh yes, said Eldin. I loved that place. Who knows who is living in it now.

The night you were conceived . . . headed the next page in the album. Alma covered her face with her hands. That's so embarrassing, she said. Why would I need to know that? Why would *anyone* need to know that?

What's so embarrassing? Ajla said. It's just love. You were conceived in love.

Alma gagged. I can't, she said. I can't read it.

Ajla had written an account in pencil. I read the first few lines. *We wanted June baby, since Baba and I were both born in June. But we started trying in October and nothing happen.*

We looked through the other albums, Alma and her mother narrating. When an hour had passed, Eldin yawned and the yawn spread like a contagion to the rest of us. We were flying back the next day so that I could attend class on Monday, and Ajla was lamenting the short duration of our stay. We never see you for very long, she said. She made a pouty face and reached to brush a strand of hair from Alma's eyes.

I'll be back soon, Alma said. She was wearing a maroon thrift-shop sweatshirt with a picture of a trout and a cigarette-burn hole in the left sleeve. She looked like a ragamuffin sitting next to her mother, who had on a cream-colored cashmere sweater and slacks and bangles on her wrists.

Well, I'll feel better when you get back to New York, Ajla said. It's closer, and Baba and Deda are there.

I'm not sure that I'll go back to New York, Alma said. Eldin and Ajla both turned and stared at her. In the intense silence that ensued, Alma pressed her thumb to the flakes of pastry crust on the table and ate them with an affected nonchalance.

And why not? Ajla said.

There's a job at Ashby, Alma said. A teaching job. It's tenure-track, and basically, I've been told it's mine if I want it.

In Kentucky, Ajla said flatly, without the upward inflection of a question.

Yeah, at Ashby.

And you're considering this?

Of course I am. She finally made eye contact with her mother. It would be good money, great benefits. I can't keep paying for health insurance through the exchange, it's too much.

You don't have to worry about that, Ajla said. We would help you. Money is not something I want you to worry about.

Ajla, Eldin said.

What?

He said nothing, but it was clear from his tone that he felt the topic should not be discussed in front of me. Ajla looked at the window in an unfocused way. She seemed to be holding her breath. All at once, she forced air through her nose, turned back to Alma, and smiled curtly. Okay, she said.

Okay what?

You're an adult, do what you like. She stood and took her plate and Alma's over to the sink. I rose to take mine myself, but she grabbed it from my hands and said, Please, no—almost rudely.

Our conversation thereafter was stilted. We finished our wine in the living room, and maybe it was my imagination, but I could've sworn I caught Ajla giving me accusatory looks. I guess she thought I was behind it somehow, that I'd convinced Alma to take this position, though nothing could be further from the truth. I hated that we would leave things like this. We would depart in the morning and they would have their private conversation about how my influence had led to this transformation in their daughter. I wished I could tell them I was on their side of things.

Later, in the prolonged silence of a muted MSNBC commercial break, Eldin sat up straight, as if he'd suddenly remembered the oven was on. What sort of stuff do you write, Owen? he said.

You already asked him that, Daddy, Alma said.

Eldin clenched his eyes shut. No, of course, he said. Sorry. You write about Kentucky.

It was foggy and gray at takeoff, but as we rose above the clouds, amber sunlight filled the cabin. Alma looked out the window, squinting at the glare. Neither of us speaking now, content with the sedative humming of the engine. We hadn't spoken much that morning either, absorbed in the ritual of the airport. I hated return-ing to Kentucky by plane. I had this fear that something would fail, and as the machine plummeted, I would know I was dying for a trip I didn't even want to take. I had a selective fear of flying. If I was going somewhere worthwhile, I knew, at least, that the ter-ror of careening to the earth would not be made worse by regret. The most important thing, I felt, would be to have someone next to you who would hold your hand. When I flew alone, I was always relieved to find grandmotherly types in the seats next to mine, for I knew they would hold my hand without question if the plane went down. If, however, my seatmate was a businessman with gelled hair and a Bluetooth device, my anxiety spiked. Though maybe that wasn't fair. Maybe the businessman would hold my hand just as readily. Anyhow, it didn't matter with Alma beside me. I felt no fear or regret. I could take her hand anytime I wanted, whether or not we were falling toward certain death.

What happened with your uncle? I said. Damir.

She went on looking out the window, as if she'd expected this question. Her face lit brightly, so that I could see the downy hairs on her earlobes and cheeks. The clouds were like a tundra below us.

We don't really talk about it, she said.

You don't have to tell me, I said, though I didn't sound very convincing.

She pulled the window shade halfway down, took a sip of Sprite from the little plastic cup on her tray table. My father got visas for my mother and sister and me, she said. He stayed for a while with Damir. I've never gotten the full story, but I think Dad thought he should stay and look over the apartment and our stuff. He thought we would be coming back. But things kept getting worse. My dad won't speak of it, but my mother showed me his letters. It was total chaos. This opportunity came up, a truck taking people to Croatia. I don't know exactly what the deal was, but Dad didn't have papers. It was a sketchy situation, I think. Basically, there was only one spot left on the truck, and my father went instead of Damir. Damir insisted on staying behind, and my father let him, even though he was older and should've been the one to stay. In his mind, anyway. He paid all of his savings to this guy with the truck, got to Croatia. Then, eventually, he got the visa to Germany and joined us.

And Damir is still there?

We think he died, she said. They tried to track him down after the war, but never heard anything. I've had this idea for a while to write a novel about him, where he's still alive, living under an assumed name, and just shows up in America one day. Like, surprise! I'm alive! But then, I think, maybe it's corny. Or maybe it would only work if he was a ghost, who appeared to the father, and the father thought he was real. I don't know.

She shrugged and took a sip of Sprite. She poured herself some more and watched the effervescence. He's probably in a shallow grave somewhere, she said. No papers, no ID. They're still finding people, you know. Maybe they've already found him and didn't know who he was.

I felt the urge to hold her hand suddenly, a germ of panic sprouting in my chest. I wished I hadn't asked about Damir. Now my fear of the plane plummeting was present once more. Death was real. It wasn't a metaphor, a movement from one place to another. It was simply absence. A speechless mystery.

It's the greatest regret of his life, according to my mother, Alma said. He lives with the shame. But, you know, what was he to do? He had a family. I don't blame him.

No, I said. Who could?

Soon, we descended through the mist, the fuselage vibrating. She raised her shade. Raindrops quivered on the glass and ran backwards in lines. You could see, through the fog, the flashing of beacons on the wing, but nothing beyond. Only dense gray. I took her hand and squeezed tight. I couldn't help it. I thought, as I always do, that we could just keep falling into this, that the ground might never appear below us. But it did. The green earth, the trees. It always did.

WE GOT BACK LATE. I SLEPT FOR FIVE HOURS, WENT TO work, and dragged myself into Critical Theory Monday afternoon to hear about the subject-object distinction. The subject-object distinction was the source of a lot of confusion, according to Dr. Person, who was channeling the theorist Bruno Latour. We treated the world as something outside of us, to be observed, when really, we were always part of it. Self and world formed an interdependent whole.

She read aloud from Latour's essay, which quoted Jesus in the book of Matthew: *Every kingdom divided against itself is brought to desolation.* Lincoln had quoted the same passage in his "House Divided" speech, in 1858. Lincoln who was born in Kentucky, that dark and bloody ground, the crossroads of so much trouble—not far from the birthplace of Jefferson Davis, in Fairview, Kentucky. My thoughts were scattered, unfocused. Mingled with daydreams. I imagined Kentucky as a frontier, the way it was for my kin when they passed through the Cumberland Gap. I pictured Kentucky's flag—two men shaking hands, one in a suit, the other in a coonskin cap. The Pioneer and the Statesman.

My eyes had trembled shut and snapped open when someone tapped my shoulder. It was one of the rhetoric PhDs. You're bleeding, he whispered.

What?

He pointed to my elbow where a gash had opened, smearing blood on the table. It must have happened at work. I went to the bathroom to clean up, and rather than return, I decided to go home—to Pop's. I hadn't been there in almost a week.

He was right where I expected him to be when I walked in—studying an almanac with a magnifying glass in his recliner. Well, well, he said, peering up at me as if my face were out of focus. Thought maybe you'd skipped town.

I did actually, I said. I went to Virginia.

What's in Virginia?

Alma's parents.

Pop set the almanac on the end table and placed the magnifying glass on top. I's trying to figure out if Ernest Borgnine is still alive, he said.

I'd think not, but maybe.

You'd be surprised who's still living, he said. So you met the girl's folks, huh?

Yep, I said. I swept popcorn kernels from the other recliner and sat. The house smelled like sour garbage and unwashed dishes.

What did you make of them?

I drew a deep breath and thought about it. They don't think I'm good enough for her.

They *said* that?

No. I don't know. I just got the feeling.

What does she think?

I think she believes that too, on some level. Maybe unconsciously.

Pop nodded and made a series of pensive sounds. Has it occurred to you, he said, that maybe *you* don't think you're good enough, so you imagine that she must feel that way, too?

You're saying I'm projecting?

Hell, I don't know what I'm saying. But I think a person can talk himself out of something based on what he imagines, and what he imagines about the way other people think is based on how he thinks, cause that's the only thing he has to go by. That make sense?

You're saying I'm projecting.

Well, okay, then. You're *projecting.*

I let my eyes skim over the living room, the grease-splotched paper plates on the coffee table and the dirty glasses, the carpet, printed with boot treads. My grandmother, had she been resurrected, would've keeled over again at the sight of her house in such a state. I'd spent so much time at Alma's that Pop's no longer felt like my home. My things were there, my books and clothes and other meager possessions, but it wasn't where I felt I belonged.

I'm gonna wash some dishes, I said.

You really wanna do something for me, you could trim that maple out back.

It doesn't even need it, Pop, I said. Just let it be. I stood and began to collect the plates and empty glasses.

Pard, he said.

I turned to face him. What's up?

Well. He looked down at his hands, massaging the palm of his left with his right, his brow deeply furrowed. I need to ask you something, he said. I need to ask you about my bayonet.

My heart skipped. I tried to keep my face from moving or making some outward sign of guilt, but he wasn't looking at me.

It's not where it ought to be, he said. Where I left it.

Is that right?

He looked up at me now, his eyes glassed over and shining. You wouldn't happen to have moved it or know where it could've gotten to, do you?

I sure don't, I said.

No, I guess you wouldn't. He looked so disappointed. He lowered his gaze to his hands once more, which were creased and scabbed with age spots. There was a frayed hole in the elbow of his flannel. His trousers, which he'd worn, I'm sure, for more than a week, were wrinkled and spattered with mustard stains. No one was around to do the laundry.

I went on gathering dishes and brought them to the sink. I turned on the tap, waited for the water to heat. An itchy sweat had broken out on my back and in my armpits. As I began to soap and rinse the plates, I heard Pop turn on the television. It was the Duke, naturally—though I couldn't make out the dialogue over the sound of the faucet.

When the drying rack filled up, I went back to the living room, sat on the edge of the other recliner, and began lacing my boots. The film was *El Dorado*. Wayne and a young James Caan, who wore a fringed leather jacket and was named Mississippi, ran around shooting people and throwing stools through windows. When they shot people, they shot them in their gun hands. They were the good guys.

Going somewhere? he said, without looking from the screen.

Alma's, I said.

He turned to me. His face flickered with blue light, shadows in the sockets of his eyes. Why don't you stay a minute? he said. Watch this with me.

I finished tying my left boot and left the other undone. I wanted to say no, to get out as quickly as I could, but there was something dire about the look he was giving me, like a lot depended on me staying. All right, I said. But I can't stay for all of it.

He smiled, reached across, and patted my hand on the armrest. We eased back in our chairs and watched the movie. He'd started it earlier, so I was a little lost, but they all followed a similar enough formula. There was always someone innocent—a homesteader, a family man—and there was always a gang, usually involving Mexicans, who wanted something from him, something unfair. The local sheriff, debilitated by alcoholism, was unable to settle the dispute, so the Duke was called in to restore justice. It was almost identical to *Rio Bravo*. The drunkard sheriff was played by Robert Mitchum, rather than Dean Martin, and James Caan played the young greenhorn rather than Ricky Nelson, but the roles and the moving parts of the plot were the same. At the center of it all, of course, was the Duke, reluctant at first to enter the fray, but relenting finally for the sake of justice. And it was always a sense of justice that moved him, however warped. There was a tenuous harmony to things, even in the West where laws were provisional, and when someone misbehaved, the harmony was disrupted, and common folk, meek and disillusioned, turned to the strongman, whose methods, perhaps, were not always savory, but who could still, nonetheless, get things done and right the wrongs and take them back to better days et cetera, et cetera, et cetera . . .

I stayed till the end. The Good Guys triumphed. Wayne got the girl. Justice was restored. When I looked over as the credits began to roll, Pop's eyes were closed. I bent to lace my other shoe and rose quietly, looking for my jacket. I could hear Cort coughing in his bedroom, a thin bright light at the doorsill.

You know you could tell me anything, Pop said. I froze with one arm in the sleeve of my jacket. His eyes were still shut, his face still lit blue. You could tell me anything and it wouldn't change my opinion of you.

Okay, I said quietly. I wanted to tell him. I knew he would forgive me, that it wouldn't matter in the end. It was only a piece of metal and a little money. But I was ashamed and couldn't bring myself to say it. He kept his eyes closed, his fingers laced across his belly. The credits rolled on against a painted backdrop. I shrugged the jacket onto my shoulders, took up the keys to the truck—Pop's truck—and went out into the night.

IN SPITE OF IT ALL—THE DISAGREEMENTS, THE MINOR QUARRELS— when I stood above my time with Alma and appraised it, I had to say it was good. We had a routine. We had our regular places. On Sundays, we ate bagels and lox at Nancy's on Frankfort Avenue, took a long time drinking our coffee and watching people pass in the sunlight through salt-scummed windows. We talked about writing. I'd never had that, with anyone. We could talk about the books we liked and what they did so well, the rules they broke, why we could or couldn't break the same rules. We talked about what other writers got away with. We talked about blind spots, how your greatest weakness could become your greatest strength. I didn't know if I believed half of it. We made it up as we went along, but it was easy to get caught up in the fantasy. I liked getting caught up with her.

We went on walks, as the spring came on, as the days distended. We had our favorite streets. St. James Court, with its Victorian mansions, its turrets and arabesques and flickering gas lanterns. The narrow brick streets of Butchertown, the market on the corner that sold pit barbecue. The haze of hickory smoke, links of bratwurst hanging in the window. Cherokee Park, with its limestone cliffs, its shallow creeks gurgling. Just sitting on the bank. The smell of cold mud. The rippled, alluvial sand. Dappled blue Saturdays passing with nothing to do and no one to talk with except each other. Bored hypotheticals. Would you still like me if I looked like this?

From the guesthouse, we could walk to a row of strip malls and gas stations. We ate dim sum at Song's. There was no sign until you got to the door. It was housed between a Mexican grocery and a Dollar Tree. I don't remember how we found it, but it felt like a secret. We were always the only ones eating. A woman and her husband owned the place. They spoke little English; she ran the register and waited tables, he manned the wok in the back, singing along to Chinese pop music on the radio. We could sit for as long as we wanted, a fragrant pot of jasmine tea on the table, sipping from our little cups. The tea got stronger and darker as we sat, bitter to drink, a sediment of leaves in the cups, and it was good to be there on cold nights, when we couldn't stand to be cooped up in the guesthouse.

We went to thrift shops. Antique stores. There was Crazy Daisy's on Mellwood, where you could spend all day at the stalls, flipping through milk crates of records, digging through racks of clothes from estate sales that stank of mothballs. We tried on blazers and leather jackets. We wondered if anyone had died in them. We fantasized about living in a house with all the broken radios and casserole dishes and hanging macramé. Every room would be a time capsule from a different decade. We'd begun to talk about this fantasy house as if it would belong to both of us, though occasionally, we slipped up and used words like "mine" and "yours," which always broke the spell.

There was Fat Rabbit, the vintage shop in Germantown. Alma would take an armful of clothes into the fitting room and I'd browse the record bins nearby. Every few minutes, she'd step out and show me the outfit. A heavy tweed skirt and pale yellow sweater. Very Sylvia Plath, I'd say.

In a good way or a bad way?

Good way.

She'd look at herself in the mirror, turning side to side, smoothing the wrinkles, her brow drawn up with concentration. I loved that. I loved seeing her ankles under the curtain. Hearing her unzip her jeans and sighing to herself, as though she were alone, as though there was more than just a curtain between her and this room, all the detritus of the twentieth century arranged around us, made fresh and attractive. She would open the curtain and appear as someone new—a beatnik this time, or a flower child in a crocheted top and embroidered blue jeans. It made my heart race, the suspense of not knowing what would be next. I could do this all day, I'd think, just watching her become these different people, knowing all the while that in the end she would be herself again and we would walk out together, in this town that was only temporary, a station along the way before we got to better things—something permanent, the people we would be forever. All the complications and unspoken tensions—our differing backgrounds, our families, the job at Ashby—all of that would sort itself out in time, I was sure. I stood above our life together in these moments and I knew it was good. I wrote it down, so that later, I could not convince myself otherwise.

WE'D HAD SEX THAT MORNING. WE WERE ON OUR SIDES, AS if spooning. I had one hand on her shoulder, the other pulling her hips back against me. She asked me to tell her how I found her. This was the latest fantasy. She liked the idea of me being a stranger who wandered into the guesthouse and found her in bed, naked and playing with herself. I wasn't very good at coming up with these scenarios, but I was getting better. I could hear you moaning all the way down in the street, I said.

She laughed at this.

What?

Nothing, she said. Sorry. How could you tell what I needed?

I thought about this question for a beat longer than I should have. What would I be thinking if I were a stranger, strolling past this fancy stone house, and I heard a woman moaning from an open window?

I just knew, I said. I knew you were waiting for me.

This was a passable answer, which was often the best I could hope for. I tried to buy in to the fantasy, to pretend that she was a stranger, a person I didn't know, who didn't love me and for whom my value was only instrumental, but it wasn't sexy to me. And anyhow, I couldn't suspend disbelief. The pattern of moles on the left shoulder blade were Alma's. The wisps of hair at the nape of the neck were unmistakably hers, the knuckles of her spine as she arched her pale back. Her mouth was Alma's mouth, sucking my thumb, and it was her voice telling me what she wanted. A breeze drifted through the open window, freshening the muggy air. Birds were twittering. I wondered if there was someone down below who could hear us.

We pulled on our jeans and ate bowls of oatmeal shirtless on the couch. I had the pages printed. A month had passed, and it was finally the day when she would read what I'd written—sketches and scene fragments and exchanges of dialogue. About eighty pages' worth.

I was nauseous with anticipation. Light from the window shone brilliantly on the red pine planks. I paced as she read, the wood warm on the soles of my feet. She'd gone through three pages when she looked up and said, Maybe go get a coffee or something? You're making me a little nervous.

Right, I said. Of course. I told her I'd be back in a couple hours. I stepped into my boots, threw on a shirt, and cut across campus to the art school building, where there was a pleasant café run by students. It was a sunny room, with beat-up recliners and leather couches. Art students stared at MacBooks or sat cross-legged on bean bags, sketching, a vague undersmell of paint and plaster discernible beneath the aroma of coffee. I sat by a window overlooking the lawn and a sidewalk lined with flowering pear trees. It was like a colonnade, white petals drifting, only instead of a Greek temple, it led to the John Schnatter School of Business, named after the founder of Papa John's Pizza. We'd trimmed all of them for clearance back in the early fall and cut out the dead, and I saw now that we'd done good work. They were shapely and so impossibly white that they looked artificial.

Two hours passed. When I'd finished my coffee and read the same paragraph of an Isaac Bashevis Singer story about four times, the print growing blurrier with each successive attempt, I started back for the guesthouses at a trot. She was fully dressed when I came in, sitting primly on the edge of the cushion. The pages were upside down on the coffee table. Did you finish? I said, out of breath.

She nodded slowly. Yes, she said.

Okay . . .

Sit down, let's talk about it. She stared at me, unsmiling.

Just tell me, I said. I'm gonna have a heart attack.

I'm not sure what you want me to say, she said. Obviously, the writing is good, but you already know that. And obviously, you felt very comfortable using private, personal details from our life—from my life. You felt comfortable making me look like a stuck-up, spoiled rich girl with no class awareness. So yeah, I'm not sure if you're expecting me to be happy about that or sanction it or what. I don't know what you want to hear.

I just told the truth. I didn't make anything up.

If you think this is the truth, you're delusional.

Are you pissed?

She huffed a bitter laugh and looked up at the ceiling, blinking rapidly. If I told you that I was, that would be unfair, right? I mean, I'd be pissed if you told me that you were off-limits, but I'm not sure I'd put you in this position. So, yeah. Whatever. I guess I'm pissed. She shook her head and peeled back a hangnail on her thumb. Her cuticle was raw and bleeding. I mean, what did you expect my reaction to be? Seriously?

I chewed on the inside of my cheek and thought about this. I was shivering slightly and hoped she couldn't see.

Because it's not just me, you know. You put my parents in this. You wrote about my uncle and Bosnia, how my dad let him stay behind. My father would be crushed if that got out. He would be so hurt and embarrassed. You didn't even change their names.

I can, I said. I would, obviously, before I sent it out.

That's not the point! she said, nearly shouting. That's *so* not the point! You've written this thing where you get to be the hero. You used your real name. It doesn't matter whether you change the other names, people will read it as the truth, instead of as what it is, which is—I don't know, a fucking fantasy. I mean, is this really how you see me? This rich girl that you got to defile? Is that what gets you off?

Defile? No.

My parents would still recognize themselves, even if you changed the names. And they're *my* family. You can write about your fucked-up family all you want, because that's *yours.* I've been trying to write about my parents and their experiences and that house where I grew up for *years.* For *years,* I've tried to get that right. And so how do you think it would feel seeing someone use it as window dressing in their project? And not just *someone.* My *boyfriend.* How would that make you feel?

I kept my head bowed like a scorned child, but my mind was a swarm of objections. It's my life, too, I said finally. When I went to your parents' house, I was experiencing it from my vantage point, and that's all I was trying to write about. I think I have a right to use my own experience.

It's *my* material, she said, pointing to her chest. You don't own the objects of your experience. You share them with other people, people who have greater claims than you. It's a form of plagiarism to use something from someone's life when that person is a writer and they've already written about it.

What if you weren't a writer?

I am though. That's the point.

I looked around the room grimly and held my breath, stoppering the ill-advised and petulant things I would've liked to say. I exhaled finally and wiped my clammy palms on my pant legs. I just don't think you get to call dibs on situations we're both involved in, I said lamely.

You're right, she said. Maybe I don't get to tell you what to do. I also don't have to be with you. We can split up and you can write about me all you want, and I won't be able to say shit.

I felt very cold suddenly, and my shivering grew more blatant. I don't know why you'd say that, I said. You know I don't want that.

She looked at me, her eyes softening a bit. How would you feel if you were the object of someone's art, and you had no control over that? she said. If you had no control over how they saw you or shaped the story? Like, even now, I'm looking at you and I can see the wheels turning. I don't know if you're taking mental notes or memorizing what I say to use later. Being with someone means cul-

tivating a shared privacy with that person. In other words, a *trust.*
Don't you see that?

I'm letting you read it, I said. I'm giving you control. And anyhow, shouldn't it tell you something about how I feel, that *you're* the object? That the book is about you?

The book is about *you,* she said. It's not about me. I'm only a representation in this. She thumped the pages with her knuckle. My family, my life—it's all just your representation. We could get into how *fair* it is—and I don't think it is, especially to your parents, who you made look like idiots—but that's sort of beside the point. It's the fact that I'm represented *at all.* That you took a family secret and used it to your own advantage.

So you're pissed that I wrote about your family.

I'm pissed that you beat me to the punch! she said. Okay? She was leaning forward, her neck strained. It's not just what you wrote—that you used my life, or my family. It's that you got to write it first, before me. And it's good, so congratulations, I guess, if that's what you wanna hear.

You wanted it to be bad.

She folded her arms, staring at the floor.

You expected and hoped that it would be bad, so that you could go on feeling superior to me.

I'm not worried about that. Believe it or not, the Terry Crews Fellowship in Tallahassee does not threaten me.

Fuck you. It's the Harry Crews Cottage. You're getting it wrong on purpose.

She glanced at me quickly, her facade of righteous anger slipping a bit. Don't go thinking you're a genius or something, she said. The writing is fine, okay? It's fine.

Great, I said. Thanks for the valuable feedback.

I didn't know what she wanted me to say. I'd come to believe that so much of life was fiction and artifice that you never really got past representation. It was all material, and so, to do something "for the material" was merely to do something because it was valuable, and worthy of attention. That's what made it art. But another part of me wondered if this was only sophistry. I'd gotten so used to looking for narratives in the world—for signs and wonders—that maybe I'd deluded myself into believing they were really there. Noticing every little thing, writing them down and believing them significant, was only a step away from the schizophrenic who memorizes license plate numbers, believing they contain coded messages from the CIA.

Maybe the sin in this was simply that I wasn't present. I wasn't wholly in the moment with her. A background process was always at work, making meaning. If it was all grist for the mill, you couldn't make exceptions. And wasn't this just the artist's lot in life? How did this narration differ, really, from the inner monologue—the story that everyone narrates to themselves whether or not they're writers? The answer came to me as soon as I'd posed the question: the difference is that an inner monologue is private. Unlike a book or a poem or a painting, it wasn't a thing out in the world.

I'll throw it out, I said finally, when we'd been sitting in silence a few minutes.

That's not what I'm asking you to do.

You kind of are. But it's fine.

She felt guilty then, and went on to tell me that there was a lot of good in it. She said I should use portions in whatever I wrote next, and that she wasn't opposed to a character being *based* on her, though the exact bounds of what this meant were a little fuzzy and I didn't exactly feel encouraged to give it a try.

The conversation ended and we went on with our day, as though it had never happened. We cooked supper later, listened to a few records and her ongoing playlist. It was like any of our other ordinary evenings, except everything was slightly off-kilter. I caught her watching me as she chopped an onion, and when I turned, she averted her face, like someone you passed on a street at night, alone. Someone you didn't know.

KELLY ANNOUNCED THAT JAMES WOULD BE GETTING THE JOB as supervisor. This came as a surprise to all of us, including James, I think. Everyone clapped his back and shook his hand. Even Rando offered his begrudging congratulations. James smiled sheepishly and said it was no big deal, but you could tell he was delighted. I was happy for him.

At the arboretum, we started on a dead ash that was leaning slightly over a clearing. A great beard of ivy and dead vines clung to the trunk, and we had to clear them first, so the tree would fall where we wanted it to fall and not be pulled one way or another. Rando gathered the vines as they fell and pushed them in big tangled knots into the roaring chipper. In the surrounding trees, young leaves were unfurling from the tips of branches, light in color, and the smell in the woods was no longer the desiccated smell of winter, but rather of new green life, of dried soil and the compost of leaves re-saturated with rain. A vegetal, green onion smell that blurred my eyes a little. The clearing was thickly carpeted with clover and dandelion, and at the edges, in cool shadowy places, bloodroot was blooming, its white flowers lambent even in the shade. Naturally, I was disappointed about the job. I wasn't sure whether I would've taken it, but it would've been nice to receive an offer. Regardless, it was hard to be grumpy in such surroundings, sunlight warming my shoulders.

When we'd cleared the vines, I found a small placard nailed to the diamond-patterned bark. Many of the trees were like this—they'd been donated or were meant to memorialize a departed loved one. THE TRUE MEANING OF LIFE IS TO PLANT TREES UNDER WHOSE SHADE YOU DO NOT EXPECT TO SIT, read the placard. IN MEMORY OF TROY CARTER. I pried it loose with a screwdriver and slipped it into my pocket. I cut a notch from the trunk, kicked the chunk of wood loose. My phone buzzed, and when I glanced at the screen, I saw it was my mother calling. This was odd, since she knew I'd be working, but I ignored it.

I started the felling cut, then locked the chain brake and placed the orange wedges, tapping one into the cut with the other. James and Rando watched from either side of the chipper, hands in cuffed gloves at their sides, wood dust hanging like smoke, shot through with rays of light. I gave them a thumbs-up. They returned the gesture. I triggered the throttle once more, grinding through to within a couple inches of the notch on the other side. I slipped the bar out quickly and jogged to the chipper, but I could already hear the great creaking whale song of the tree as it began to fall. It was always like this—slow at first, with the dumb heave of inertia, then as the falling quickened, you heard the wood fracture and split, cracking like a rifle. The moment after, when the trunk had broken from the hinge and the crown had not yet crashed into the earth, was a moment of almost reverent silence. There was a kind of sadness in this moment, for me, even when the tree was dead, because you knew it had grown for decades or centuries even, attaining its prominence, and it took so little effort to topple. I'd mentioned this to Rando once, that I sometimes felt bad about felling a tree, and he told me I was being emotional. There were loggers—*real* timber cutters—who felled a hundred trees a day without thinking twice about it. What we were doing was really very small, and was for the sake of beautification and clearance, he claimed—keeping things up to code. For these reasons, I should not feel guilty. We're like surgeons, he'd said, grinning slyly at his own poetic license. We cut out the parts that make the body sick, and when there's nothing to save, we dispose of the remains.

This had seemed, at the time, like a good enough metaphor. But as we finished our lunch, the tree lying across the clearing, ready to be limbed and ground to bits, I couldn't shake the feeling that it was a sin, somehow. It was such a strange way to make a living, and it was not an occupation I ever thought I'd have. So why did I feel wistful that I hadn't gotten the job? James was sitting next to me on the edge of the chipper bed, our boots dangling. The bed was burnished silver, yellow paint scratched and scuffed away by thousands of limbs, and I had my palms pressed flat behind me against the sun-heated steel. We were in no hurry to start the limbing.

Rando sat on the tailgate of the pickup, using a twig to scrape the caked mud from his boot treads. He was giving James a hard time. Oh you'll be on easy street dude, he said. You'll be eating organic steak and eggs for breakfast every day and watching all the premium channels.

James laughed and took a bite of string cheese. Is that what you think rich people do, Rando?

You'll be a different man, he said. You'll pretend not to recognize us when you see us on the street. Oh there's Rando, you'll think. A peasant I used to know. And you'll just keep on walking. We'll be like those untouchables over in India. The top-class Indians would rather juggle dogshit than lay a hand on those untouchables. That'll be you dude. I give it six months.

It's not like I'll be rich, James said. But it will be nice. I'm tired of living in shitty apartments, driving a shitty car that breaks down all the time. I'm tired of not having a *dishwasher*, man. That's my number one priority. Live someplace with a fuckin dishwasher.

It *starts* with a dishwasher, Rando said. Next thing you know, you've got servants clipping your toenails and regulating your body temperature with palm fronds.

Before we limbed the tree, James had to move the chipper to the other side of the clearing. As he circled around, tires sinking into the soft earth, Rando and I stood watching. Rando had a smoke and a Pepsi. I asked if I could bum one and he fished the pack from his breast pocket. You seem a little glum there, General, he said, when I'd gotten the Pall Mall lit. I took a drag and blew out a thin stream of smoke.

I applied for the job, I said.

Rando pondered this. He shook the can of Pepsi to see how much was left and took a swig. Maybe Kelly didn't think you'd stick around, he said. Did you really want it?

I wanted it, I said. Why wouldn't I want it?

James had thrown the chipper truck into reverse, beeping loudly across the clearing. Rando dropped his cigarette filter into the Pepsi can, where it hissed, and turned to look at me. It was an expression I'd never seen on him—an expression of great concern. He worked his lips like he was trying to say something but couldn't form the right words.

You'd never be happy here, you know that, right? he said. You're too ambitious.

I dropped my eyes to my boots, embarrassed. What could I say?

James finished parking the truck and stepped down from the cab. He cupped his hands around his mouth and shouted, This okay? I gave him a thumbs-up. Thanks for the cigarette, I said to Rando.

Hey, I've let you two smoke up all my cigarettes for seven months, he said. I'm running a Pall Mall charity. No reason to stop now. He smiled, to let me know he wasn't serious, and clapped my back brusquely.

What about you? I said. You gonna stay on here?

Shit, I'll make them fire me before I quit.

I wouldn't be surprised if that's how it shakes out, I said.

I know that, he said. He crushed the Pepsi can, tossed it clanking into the bed of the pickup with all his other empties. If it happens, I'll live on unemployment, take it easy for a few months. Then I'll find something else. I've done it before. You don't have to worry about me.

I wanted to believe this, but as Rando hitched his pants and waddled out across the clearing, each inhalation wheezing in his throat, I knew he would not find something else, or that if he did, it wouldn't matter. What lay ahead of him was not easy street, that much was certain. It struck me only later that when he'd said I was too ambitious, he wasn't only saying something about me. He was saying something about himself and the way his life had gone.

The three of us went to Schadenfreude after work. I'd never been there during the day. The patrons were not hip. They were whiskered and shabby and drinking alone, and they had the red-ringed, drooping eyes of alcoholics. In the unforgiving light of day, you could see how dirty the bar was—the smudged brass rail, the sour-smelling rags in buckets of gray water.

Rando slid over a bowl of salted peanuts and ordered coffee. We don't really have a pot brewed right now, said the bartender, the only hip-looking person around. She must've drawn the short straw when it came to shift assignment. She wore high-waisted jeans and a Dale Earnhardt T-shirt she'd turned into a crop top and had metal studs in her eyebrows.

You have the ability to brew one though, I'll bet, Rando said.

She stared at him vacantly, then turned and took down the coffee filters from a shelf with theatrical annoyance. While it was percolating and the tender was pouring beers for James and me, my mother called again. I ignored it and set my phone to Do Not Disturb.

We talked for a couple hours. James said he planned to continue his history degree, maybe try for a PhD after. The market's tough, he kept saying, by which he meant, I guess, the history professor market. You can't do shit with a master's, he said. They sell it like it's this versatile degree, that you'll be able to do so much with it, but it's a racket really. It's how they get cheap labor. Get your TAs to teach intro courses as part of their quote unquote *funding package,* and you can avoid actually paying them a living wage.

So why'd you do it? I said.

He shrugged. He was on his third glass of strong beer, and you could tell it from the languid way his mouth was moving. The love of knowledge, I guess, he said. That's how I'm treating it anyway. It's a good thing to know about history whether or not it leads to anything. The degree, I mean. Although history doesn't lead to anything either, necessarily. Except the present moment. But you know what I mean—there's not anything like fate. Whatever. I'm drunk.

How do we keep history from repeating itself? Rando said. That's what I'd like to know.

James rolled his eyes and ignored this. Point is, he said, don't get a master's degree, unless you're already in the middle of one, in which case go ahead and finish it because you might as well.

What if you're only one semester into a master's degree? I said.

That's a tough one, he said. I don't know how it is for English. What are the job prospects for a master's?

Even more dismal than for history, I'd imagine.

He grunted and took a slug of beer. Yeah, I don't know, man.

How do we keep history from repeating itself? Rando said.

How do I keep you from repeating that question? James said. I heard you the first time and made a conscious decision not to answer because it's not very interesting.

Jesus, Rando said, never mind. Just thought I'd consult an expert in the field on an important question—maybe the most important question of our time. But, never mind.

Maybe for starters, don't vote to elect a fascist, James said. How's that?

Oookaaay, said Rando, raising his palms in surrender. Forget I asked.

James turned to me. He studied my face a moment, suppressed a belch with his fist to his breastbone. I'm sorry I broke your nose, he said. I really didn't mean to.

I probably deserved it, I said. I'm sorry you got mixed up in it.

It's in the past, he said. He swiveled back to his beer and drained the dregs of it. This has gotta be the last one for me, he said.

Me too, said Rando, raising his coffee mug. It's past my bedtime.

The sun hasn't even set, Rando, I said.

I go to sleep early so I can wake up in the middle of the night and listen to *Coast to Coast*. You know about *Coast to Coast*, right?

Yes, Rando, James said. You've only told us about a million times.

Outside, Rando repeated his congratulations and left James and me alone on the sidewalk, Budweiser signs glowing in the fogged window behind us. He waved as he drove off in his old Saturn, and we waved back. The streetlamps had just ticked on. To the west, behind the office towers and hotels of the city, the sky was smoldering. We floated a cigarette for the road—the last in his pack.

You should take that fellowship or whatever it is, James said. The Florida thing. He passed me the cigarette and hugged his bare arms against the breeze.

Why? I said.

Because why not? You wanna get out of Kentucky, then get out of Kentucky.

I'm not sure Florida will be much better.

Florida is world renowned for its enlightenment values, he said.

I smiled and took a drag. We stood there silently for a little while, just looking at the city over the black treetops. The crickets were tuning up, and I could hear the faraway whooshing of traffic on the interstate. People were going places. Meanwhile, all the little shotgun houses of Germantown were glowing from within, as the young people inside—the students and musicians, the line cooks and waitresses and baristas—cooked their stir-fry suppers and played their records and scribbled notes in the margins of their novels.

I don't want to leave Alma, I said. I hadn't been sure that it was true until I said it, but there it was.

James motioned for the cigarette and I gave it back. That'll work itself out, he said. Do what you need to do. If it's meant to be, it's meant to be.

That's a cliché if I ever heard one. I thought there was no such thing as fate?

There's fate, and then there's just the way things pan out, he said.

But if it's meant to be, then that means that it couldn't have been otherwise. That's fate, or it might as well be, as far as I'm concerned.

All I'm saying is that you have to do what's right for yourself and your career, James said.

Everybody keeps telling me that. Since when did a career become the most important thing? What about my *life*?

So stay, he said. But she'll do what's best for her, you better believe that. She'll go back to New York, or she'll take that job here. Either way, you'll be stuck someplace you don't want to be. And that's bad news, man. That's how you turn bitter.

I couldn't decide whether this was true—that she would act in her own self-interest regardless of what I wanted—but it was discomfiting, and I took this as a sign that maybe he was right. The hip crowd was beginning to show up at Schadenfreude, dudes in black denim with Texaco trucker hats, girls with violet lipstick and stonewashed mom jeans, showing off their tattoos. We were wearing our work clothes still, our steel-toes, our salt-stained Husqvarna hats. They didn't seem to notice us as they mounted the steps and went inside.

You don't have to take that job, you know, I said. You could do whatever you wanted. You could go anywhere.

I *want* the job, he said. And I love it here. I grew up here. My mom's here. He took one last quick draw from the cig, pulling with his cheeks, then dropped the filter and ground it with the toe of his boot. Not everyone wants to leave, he said.

We shook hands and I congratulated him again before we set off in opposite directions. I was halfway to the Ranger parked at the end of the block when I checked my phone and saw that I had fourteen missed calls from my mother. I called her back and she answered on the first ring. I could tell she'd been crying just from her hello.

What's going on? I said.

Where are you? she said, her voice shaky. I've been trying to call you for hours.

Germantown. I went out after work. What's up?

The line was silent for a long time as she sniffled and breathed into the receiver. I knew Pop was gone before she said it. Who else could it be? I felt for my heart, and though it was beating fast, pushing against my ribs, I did not feel panicked. Instead, a feeling of serene exhaustion came over me—so strong I thought my knees would buckle. I sat on the curb. People passed by, chatting casually, walking their dogs. What happened? I said.

She couldn't just tell me that he was dead. She had to explain first the chain of cause and effect. There'd been an accident. Cort had called an ambulance. They managed to get a pulse, but his heart had been stopped for a long time and it quit again en route to the hospital. They couldn't bring him back a second time. That was it. End of story. He died at 2:37 p.m. She repeated this three times, as though it were an important detail.

What kind of accident? I said.

We don't know, exactly, but it was a head injury. He lost a lot of blood. It was Cort that found him.

How did it happen? I said. She wouldn't answer. I could not imagine, offhand, how bumping his head could result in sudden death. I'm coming to the hospital, I said.

We're not at the hospital anymore. We're at the Ramada off Preston Highway.

Where's Pop?

At the funeral home by now, she said. Cort's with us. He's all torn up.

Now that I had all the basic information, I drew a long, deep breath and let it go. It was dark now. The curb where I was sitting was in front of a house, and when I glanced over my shoulder, I saw the plastic blinds parted in one of the windows and a pair of eyes searching out.

Are you okay? my mother said.

I think so.

Come to the hotel. We've got pizza.

Are *you* okay?

I'm very sad, she said, her voice breaking, but I can't say it's a surprise, really.

I thought through what it would be like to spend the rest of the evening in a room at the Ramada and decided I couldn't go through with it. I told her this. Maybe it was selfish on my part, but I just couldn't do it.

Where will you go? You have nowhere to go. That girl's house?

Maybe, I said.

She clucked her tongue. You should be with your family.

I just need time, I said. To process.

Do *not* go to your grandfather's house.

What, I'm not welcome there now? All my stuff is there still.

That's not why.

Why then?

Because I said so.

You mean because Cort said so.

Cort can barely speak, he's so torn up, she said. I'm telling you not to go there, and you just have to trust me.

I'm getting off the phone.

Owen.

I love you.

I sat on the curb for a while after I'd hung up, elbows on my knees, hands dangling limp between them, just watching the passersby and hearing snippets of conversation. Two women walked past, one of whom was extolling the benefits of kimchi. A couple with a stroller were in the middle of a mild argument, in which the man kept saying, That does *not* count as a lie.

I felt so powerfully tired that the fifteen paces between the curb and the Ranger at the end of the block seemed insurmountable. But I managed, somehow, to get there. I rose, took one step and then another, then I was sitting at the wheel, turning the ignition, driving away. I merged onto the interstate, southbound, and in twenty minutes, I'd arrived at Pop's house. It looked no different from the outside. You wouldn't know someone had just died there, but then, I don't know what I was expecting, really. Police tape? A skull and crossbones painted on the door?

I let myself in with my key. The living room was dark, but the light in the kitchen was on and the back door was wide open. I went to shut it, and when I pushed through the saloon doors, I found the kitchen linoleum smeared with blood. There were big droplets and red boot prints. It was dark blood, the color of wine, in various states of drying. I had the feeling of weightlessness in my stomach one gets while topping a hill on a country road—a sudden, brief cancellation of gravity.

I stepped out onto the back porch. There was blood there, too. I used my cell phone light to follow the droplets, down the flagstone path to the grass, where it disappeared. I gazed across the lawn, letting my eyes adjust. At the foot of the hill, where the old dying maple stood, I caught a glint of orange. I started that way, drawing closer. It was Pop's Polaris chainsaw. A ladder was propped against the tree. There were a few sawn branches scattered about, nothing that couldn't be clipped with a pruner. I crouched and swept the blue light over the grass to the trash barrel, and the cinder blocks surrounding it. One of the blocks had blood on its corner. Best I could tell, he'd fallen from the ladder and hit his head on the block.

I stood, a little dizzy. I got my bearings and went back to the house, following the trail from the kitchen to the hallway. So much had soaked there that the carpet squelched under my boots. I flipped on the bathroom light and stood in the doorway. There was blood everywhere—pooled on the tile, spattered on the shower curtain and the fuzzy seafoam cover of the toilet lid. There were red handprints on the edge of the vanity and the faucet, dried rivulets running to the drain in the basin—as if he'd pulled himself up here, tried to wash his hands. I stared at the mess a moment longer, the fluorescent bulb strobing subtly above the sink. I switched off the light.

For a few minutes, I paced in the hallway. I didn't know what to do. What do I do? I said aloud. The house was silent. There was nothing to do. Everything had been decided already. Everything in his life had led him to that moment, in the backyard, cutting branches he'd asked me to cut a half-dozen times. His hobo days, the Great Depression, the war in the Pacific—all of it had led to that.

I trudged down into the basement for some reason. I don't know why. I was a small entity riding around inside my head, watching my legs move, observing the carriage of my shoulders and arms. I turned on the light and looked at my things—my clothes and books and records. Nothing I couldn't leave behind.

I avoided looking at the blood upstairs. I kept my eyes on the front door and moved in that direction. Outside, I dropped the keyring twice, trying to lock up. My hands were shaking bad. I made it to the truck—the truck that was never mine, that now belonged to a dead man—and sat there with the keys in the ignition, catching my breath. It was a clear, beautiful night, a gibbous moon lighting the lawns of the neighborhood. I opened the glovebox, looking for a napkin or something to wipe the sweat from my face. There was a receipt in there with something scrawled in Pop's handwriting. *Podiatrist 3 o'clock Monday,* it said. Then I was crying. Tears were dripping and rolling down my cheeks. I hid my face in the crook of my arm and leaned against the steering wheel. When some time had passed—half an hour, an hour, I don't know—I started the truck and drove to the Ramada.

HE'D WANTED TO BE CREMATED. HE'D MENTIONED THIS several times, to me and to others. He'd hated the idea of an open casket. I don't want all them people coming by and saying how good I look, he'd said. "He looks like himself," they say, when really, the guy just looks *dead.*

My great-aunt, however, believed that cremation was a sin. In the end times, she said, when Christ returns, our physical bodies will be resurrected, and how can a body be resurrected when it's been turned to ashes? It took a lot of willpower on my part to resist calling this asinine. But then, what difference did it make, really? Funerals were for the living. They did at least honor his request for a closed casket. A man in uniform played "Taps" on a silver trumpet, and two other men in dress uniforms and white gloves folded the American flag. As they were about to hand the tucked, tricornered flag to my mother, my cousin's cellphone went off, and he scrambled to silence it. His ringtone was "Bad to the Bone."

After the service, I stood outside the funeral home eating Skittles. I'd bought the blazer I was wearing at a Goodwill and there had been a bag of Skittles in the inside pocket for some reason. I'd torn it open and started eating them just for something to do, so I wouldn't start crying. Alma had been drawn into a conversation with three of my male cousins, who were explaining the horsepower and towing capacities of their vehicles while their wives rocked babies and glanced about with bored expressions. My father was out there, as was Bonnie, who looked somehow even worse than the last time I'd seen her at the Rebel Smokehouse. We embraced briefly in the parking lot. You could see the shape of her skull behind her face, the sockets of her eyes so deep that they welled with shadow. She asked how "my studies" were going, of all things.

All right, I said.

Good, she said, her voice very faint. She nodded feebly, then turned and scuffled to the car.

My dad lingered behind, patting the pockets of his slacks for his car keys, though he was already holding them. They're in your hand, I said.

Right, he said. He was pale, sweat beaded on his forehead. She's decided to stop treatment, Dad said. She doesn't necessarily want a lot of people to know, but I thought I'd tell you, so you could be prepared for another funeral.

How long?

You know how the doctors are, he said. Could be weeks, could be months. They say it's not an exact science. I'm like, "What are we paying you for then? Isn't medicine an exact science?"

Maybe they mean dying isn't an exact science.

Yeah, well. He wiped the sweat from his upper lip. Damp splotches were spreading out from his armpits underneath his jacket.

I'm sorry, Dad, I said.

My mother walked up then and hugged my father, which was so strange to see. They turned to face me, my mother dabbing tears from her eyes with her knuckle, my father smoothing his paisley tie, looking slightly dazed. There they were: the two people who'd made me. Their talents and flaws, their fears and joys. My mother screened her eyes from the sun's glare. The asphalt lot was stifling, stinking of hot tar. Cousins and distant relatives streamed out cradling bouquets and wreaths, leaving trails of perfume.

Pop would be proud of you, my mother said. He was proud of you.

Thanks, I said, though I wasn't sure who I was thanking. I poured a handful of Skittles into my palm, tossed them back. I didn't want them to see me cry. I thought if I could just focus on chewing the Skittles, I couldn't start crying.

We're proud of you, too, Mom said. Aren't we?

My father didn't seem to hear her at first, then looked up, startled. Sorry, what was that?

I said we're proud of him.

Yes, I am. We are, I mean. I know I don't always say as much, but I am.

Tell him what you were doing when I met you.

I was working in a liquor store, he said. Before I started with the fire department. I had no prospects.

Uh-huh, I said. I was trying to swallow the saccharine bolus of Skittles, my hands sweaty and smeared red with the dye. I blinked and the tears spilled out. I'm sorry, I said. I tried to hide my face.

It's all right, my mother said. She put her arms around me. My father stepped forward, hesitantly, and did the same. We all stood there in this uneasy embrace, huddled and sniffling. For a moment, with my eyes closed and their arms around me, I could almost imagine that I was a child and that nothing had gone wrong, that I knew nothing of the world beyond our little family and the little town where we lived in Kentucky, and that this is where I belonged and always would belong, whether I liked it or not.

Then I opened my eyes to the gleaming day and the sunbaked parking lot, and I remembered why I was there and why I could never go back to that safety. I remembered Pop, who was completely and irrevocably gone. I missed him. There was no poetic way to put it. No way to pretty it up. I wished I'd been there to help him. I wished I'd seen him before he died. *The things you think are dull become the things you long for,* he'd told me, and I was beginning to understand. I longed to sit with him and watch a Western. I longed to eat a bucket of KFC at his kitchen table. I longed to give him back the bayonet, to have him see me the way he saw me before—not as a thief, but as someone lost, someone who needed a place to live. His own blood.

TWO WEEKS AFTER THE SERVICE, ALMA AND I WENT FOR A long drive in the country, winding up near Bardstown and the Abbey of Gethsemani, where Thomas Merton was buried. Our argument from the week before had not come up again, but its residue remained. A bitter aftertaste.

Neither of us had read Thomas Merton's books, but his name always came up as a Kentucky writer, and the abbey where he'd lived as a Trappist monk was close enough that we figured we might as well visit. Alma read his Wikipedia entry while I drove. It was horse country around Bardstown—rolling pastures of Technicolor green, bordered by stacked fieldstones and white slat fences. Breezes swept across the bluegrass in ripples. Horses grazed on the slopes, tails swishing, and the shadows of clouds passed swiftly over the land's contours. This was the idyllic image, what people thought of when they thought of Kentucky—if they thought of it charitably. There were big houses of red brick set off from the road—some of them old Georgian mansions, others reproductions, constructed in the same style. I pointed out the fences of stacked stones to Alma. There's no mortar, I said. They were dug up tilling the fields. I always heard them called "slave fences."

Why? she said.

Why do you think?

Closer to the abbey, the land rose into wooded hills, though along the road it was still farmland—plowed fields and cover crops. As we climbed a rise, a steeple came into view, then the abbey's grounds, enclosed by a stone wall. I turned at the entrance and paused before driving on. A statue sat atop a grassy hill in the distance. Wind blustered against the car, rocking it slightly. Wow, Alma said, still looking at her phone. He died by electrocution. Something involving an electrical fan.

Not the way I'd wanna go, I said.

We parked and strolled through the grounds. There were chapels and dormitory-style buildings where the monks lived, and gardens wound through with paths. We perused the gift shop briefly, where fruitcakes and cheeses and bars of fudge were sold. I'd been hoping for Trappist beer, but I was out of luck. They only make that in Europe, the woman at the counter told me. I settled for smoked Gouda instead. Alma bought a wedge of peanut butter fudge and a copy of *The Seven Storey Mountain.*

In the small cemetery, we found Merton's gravestone. Alma peeled back the plastic wrapping on her fudge and pinched off little nibbles. With the wind blowing, I noticed how much longer her hair had gotten since we first met. She'd collect the strands across her eyes and cheeks and tuck them back, and the wind would fling them across her face again. Near the dormitory in the distance, I saw a monk—an old man with a scraggly beard and a black-and-white robe. He lifted his skirts to mount the steps leading to the door. He was wearing Crocs underneath.

Alma was watching him, too, chewing her fudge. You think you could take a vow of silence? she said.

I don't think I'd want to.

Obviously not, but I mean hypothetically.

I think I'd have to be pretty tired of talking. Like, existentially tired. But maybe it would make life easier. Or less complicated.

See, I'm not sure I'd want that. Complication makes life interesting.

Yeah, well. Maybe that gets old. Maybe you get sick of it.

They still communicate, she said. They have sign language. I read about it.

That seems like cheating.

They write too, obviously. She nodded at Merton's grave, then rewrapped the fudge and slipped it into the hip pocket of her jeans. With a sigh, she turned to face me, squinching her nose, ribbons of hair flinging out wildly. She raised her hand to the light, so that its shadow covered her eyes. What's up with us? she said.

How do you mean?

I mean things are weird.

I'm still upset.

Between you and me, she said. You know what I mean.

I looked out over the graves and the stone wall and the berm of grass beyond the road. It was strange that this place existed, in Kentucky no less. Aside from the gift shop and the monks' choice of footwear, it hadn't changed much since its founding in the mid-1800s. Outside, the whole shitty slow-motion apocalypse of late capitalism was unfolding, but here, within the stone walls, there was peace and quiet—this weird little place on earth where everyone agreed to simply shut up and let the world be what it is. You could hear the birds trilling. You could hear the shushing of wind in the shaggy oaks. But then, how did one account for Merton, who betrayed this silence by writing about it?

I'm going to Florida, I said.

When I met her eyes, she seemed confused. What's in Florida?

The residency, I said. The writing thing.

Oh, she said.

I think I'm gonna go.

Well, good, she said. That's good. That isn't what I asked about though.

I might leave early, I said. I surprised myself with this. It hadn't actually occurred to me before, but as soon as I'd said it, I knew it was what I wanted to do. The program started in August. I could go down in May or June, work for the summer.

And you're telling me this because—what, you're breaking up with me? Is that what's happening? You're breaking up with me in a Trappist cemetery? Or is this about to turn into a marriage proposal?

I laughed, then felt like I might cry, and lowered my head. It had been like this since Pop's death—my heart twisting suddenly, emotions like cloudbursts, passing as quickly as they'd arrived. I'm not breaking up with you, I said. I'm just saying—I'm leaving, and I can't come back here. If you stay, I can't come back.

I see, she said. You mean if I take the job at Ashby.

Right.

I see. She turned away from the sun's glare and inhaled deeply through her nostrils. Well, she said finally. All right, I guess.

You're supposed to say, "Please don't go."

You know I can't say that. And is that really what you want me to say?

No, I said. I blinked to keep the tears from falling and pressed the heels of my palms to my eyes. She put her arms around me.

Let's just see, she said, her voice muffled against my shoulder.
Let's just see what happens.

IN THE MONTH THAT PASSED AFTER THAT DAY AT MERTON'S
grave, many things happened in my life. I inherited the bayonet
from Pop, along with $5,000, which I was not expecting. He'd
added the bayonet to his will sometime in the weeks after I'd stolen
it, as a way, I liked to imagine, of absolving me, though I did not
feel absolved. I even went back to the pawnshop to see if I could buy
it back, which would've been poetic, but of course it wasn't there.
The owner of the shop remembered me, said he'd sold it to a collector in Lexington. I'd give you his number, the owner said, but you
know how these Civil War guys are. It's already in a glass case by
now, I'd wager. His tone was almost apologetic, as if I was far from
the first person who'd come back looking for something valuable
they'd given up.

I quit my job with campus groundskeeping, which is to say I
called in sick three days in a row, and then simply stopped showing up. James texted to ask if I was still alive, and I told him I was.
My attendance in Critical Theory and Victorian Gothic had already
been sparse, but I left off altogether when the $5,000 came through,
and consequently failed them both. I told the man in Florida I'd be
accepting the fellowship for sure, and that I planned to come down
early and work for the summer. I lived with Alma in the meantime.
I moved my handful of boxes from Pop's basement into her attic.
There was some discussion about whether to mix my books with
hers on the shelf, but I decided, ultimately, to leave them in their
boxes.

I bought a plane ticket, made my living arrangements. Then,
suddenly, my departure was no longer abstract. I was really leaving.
Somehow, it still seemed impossible. Events would conspire against
me to prevent it, I was sure. But day by day, hour by hour, the
appointed date grew nearer and took on its own center of gravity. I'd
left Kentucky before, of course, but I'd had no reason to go to Colorado, beyond my own whims—nothing to recommend my presence

there. Things were different now. Someone was asking me to leave for official reasons. They wanted me. I was wanted somewhere else.

Then there was Alma, who put on a good face, who encouraged my decision and told me it was a good opportunity. She'd finished a draft of her novel finally, had given it to her editor, and was in better spirits as a result. In the end, she told the director of the English Department that she'd take the tenure-track job, and that was that. You're a Kentuckian now, I said. How does it feel?

I reckon it feels perty good, she said.

But underneath all this optimism, I had doubts. We both did, I think. As we read on the couch or cooked or walked on campus after supper, I'd catch her looking at me sadly, and when I asked what was wrong, she'd force a smile and say nothing. In these moments, I'd ask myself, What are you doing? Everything could be canceled. The ticket, the lease, the fellowship. All of it could be erased and you could stay with her. You're free to do as you please. Nothing is inevitable.

But the days kept arriving. News cycles repeated, the stories so eerily similar you could've sworn you'd just heard them. A litany of mass murder and bad weather, of war and betrayal and vanity, and we hardly noticed. I'd wanted us to have a story, to be like those lovers in novels, who meet in a time of conflict, who fight to be together and are carried away by the sweep of history. But there was nothing grand about us. We were just two little people who'd tried to love each other in the middle of a mess. Now that was ending. No fanfare. No big to-do. I marveled sometimes at how much she had changed since I met her. Or was it only the way I saw her that had changed? Surely, I had changed, too. I was someone other than the man she'd met. And it was always like this, wasn't it? No one was ever exactly who you wanted them to be. They became themselves the more time you spent with them, which is to say they became what you could never have predicted.

When she dropped me at the airport, I still expected, on some level, a cinematic moment. But there was a cop in a yellow vest, shouting and waving people on. She hugged me tight around the neck and kissed me. Maybe I'll visit soon, she said. We can eat key lime pie. That's a Florida thing, right? She dabbed a tear from her eye with her knuckle and smiled at me.

Let's go, let's go, the cop shouted.

I kissed her again. I made a mental note to remember what she smelled and tasted like, but her gums had been bleeding recently— a mild case of gingivitis—and so her mouth had a metallic taste, like pennies, and this was not exactly what I wanted to remember. I'll call you when I land, I said.

If I don't answer, I'm taking a nap, she said.

Okay.

Okay.

We hugged once more, then I took up my bags and started for the automatic doors. I could see her reflection in the glass, standing there a moment, wiping her eyes with her sleeve, then ducking back into her car, driving away.

I was held up in security due to a jar of sorghum in my carry-on bag. Alma had bought it for me, and it was exactly three ounces, and even said so on the label. But whatever machines they have that detect liquids had flagged it for some reason, and two security guards launched into a ten-minute debate about whether I should be allowed to carry it through while I stood by, glancing periodically at my watch. It really doesn't matter that much to me, I said finally. You can throw it away.

You don't want the sorghum? said the woman arguing on my behalf.

I do want it, but I don't want to miss my flight.

It looks like good sorghum.

I'm sure it is, I said.

It's got a good color. She held it up to the light and peered through it admiringly.

They decided to let me keep it. I jogged to the gate, the duffel strap cutting into my shoulder, and found, once I arrived, that the flight had been delayed half an hour. I sat down on the hard plastic seat, panting, and picked my T-shirt away from my armpits. I had time to buy a snack, so when I'd caught my breath, I went and got a candy bar and a magazine. I scarfed the candy bar, then paged through the magazine cursorily, not really reading. I felt jittery. My knee was jumping. I took out my phone and tried to think of something to text Alma. *About to board,* I typed. I added a heart emoji, then deleted it, then added it again. I stared at the text a long time, then turned off the display and returned the phone to my pocket.

The woman at the desk announced the first boarding group. People stood from their seats and began to line up. They coughed into their fists, scrolled on their phones. They rocked fussy babies on their hips and held sedated cats in mesh carriers. My heart was beating wildly. The attendant announced the next boarding group, and then mine less than a minute later. Everyone was standing now, shuffling over to the line—everyone but me. I was the only person still seated at the gate. *I'll get up as soon as my heart slows down,* I told myself. *As soon as I can breathe normally.* But my heart only picked up, and my legs were locked in place. The attendant announced all boarding groups. The line filed through, the scanner beeping as she took the tickets. Any moment now, I thought. Any moment now, I'll get up. I'll walk through the gate and leave. But the end of the line went through, and still I was sitting there, unable to move. Last call to board was announced, and there I was, still sitting. If this were a book, I thought, I'd get up and run. I'd leave my bags and run to her and I would never regret it. But the gate was closing, and this was not a book. It was my life.

Acknowledgments

I have to thank to the City of Aurora's Forestry division for giving me a job dragging brush when I had few prospects. Without that job, the book would not exist.

My agent, Peter Straus, believed in the book and guided me every step of the way. For that, I'm truly grateful.

I feel unendingly lucky to have Jordan Pavlin as my editor. Her insight and care brought out the best in the novel.

I'm indebted to Andrew Ridker, Bobby Lamirande, and Sanjena Sathian for their invaluable advice, steadfast support, and, most of all, for their friendship.

Thank you to Annie Bishai for all her hard work throughout the process. Angus Cargill's incisive, thoughtful notes were so helpful. Many thanks to Eliza Plowden, Sam Coates, Tristan Kendrick, and Matthew Turner for the vital parts they played.

Thank you to all the wonderful people at the Iowa Writers' Workshop: Sam Chang, Charlie D'Ambrosio, Ayana Mathis, Tom Drury, Connie Brothers, Sasha Khmelnik, Jan Zenisek, and Deb West. Thank you to Chris Adrian, who helped me find my voice.

A number of other people went out of their way to support and encourage me—too many to name, but here are a few: Kiki Petrosino, Paul Griner, Ryan Ridge, Brian Weinberg, Sarah Thankam Mathews, Dale Billingsley, Aaron Williams, Zia Choudhury, Brick Green, Tim Cook,

John Golightly, Madelyn Cole, Chrystal Cole, Vickie Cole, Sherry Hixon, and Rick Orr.

I owe a lot to Ian Stansel, from whom I probably learned the most about writing, and who told me I should keep going.

Ariel Katz played such an important part in the writing of this book. Her wisdom, love, and support have made me a better person and a better writer.

I'm so thankful for my parents, Hal Anthony Cole and Amanda Orr, and my grandparents, Martha Shelton, Mildred Cole, and Hal Cole, who gave me more than I could ever repay.

Lastly, my grandfather, Creston Shelton, to whom the book is dedicated. He lived a true life of adventure, in a world that is long gone now. If I know how to tell a good story, it's because of him.

A NOTE ABOUT THE AUTHOR

Lee Cole was born and grew up in rural Kentucky. A graduate
of the Iowa Writers' Workshop, he lives in New York.

A NOTE ON THE TYPE

The text of this book was set in Garamond No. 3. It is not a
true copy of any of the designs of Claude Garamond (ca. 1480–
1561), but an adaptation that probably owes as much to the
designs of Jean Jannon, a Protestant printer in Sedan in the
early seventeenth century, who had worked with Garamond's
romans earlier in Paris. This particular version is based on an
adaptation by Morris Fuller Benton.

TYPESET BY SCRIBE, PHILADELPHIA, PENNSYLVANIA

PRINTED AND BOUND BY FRIESENS, ALTONA, MANITOBA

DESIGNED BY ANNA B. KNIGHTON